APRIL'S RAIN

BOOKS IN THE TUCKER SERIES

Tucker's Way
An Unexpected Frost
April's Rain
March On

APRIL'S RAIN

David Johnson

LAKE UNION
PUBLISHING

April's Rain is a new release of a previously published edition. This new edition has been updated and edited.

Published by Lake Union Publishing, Seattle

www.apub.com

Amazon, the Amazon logo, and Lake Union Publishing are trademarks of Amazon.com, Inc., or its affiliates.

ISBN-13: 9781477827048
ISBN-10: 1477827048

Cover design by Jason Blackburn

Library of Congress Control Number: 2014943976

Printed in the United States of America

This book is dedicated to the memory of my parents, Willie and Martin Johnson. They instilled in me a belief that I could do anything, if I worked hard enough. I watched them devote their lives to helping others, most often those who were less fortunate. Having grown up in the Great Depression, surviving on what their families could grow on a farm, my parents never forgot that most people are not poor by choice. From them I learned to never judge a book by its cover.

CHAPTER ONE

The homely house that harbors quiet rest;
The cottage that affords no pride nor care;
The mean that 'grees with country music best;
The sweet consort of mirth and music's fare;
Obscured life sets down a type of bliss:
A mind content both crown and king is.
—*Robert Greene*

TUCKER:

I reach out an' put m' hand on top o' th' headstone and slowly kneel on one knee. With m' index finger I trace the letters an' then th' numbers.

"Eight years. I can't believe it's been eight years since y' left me, Ella. Why is it that this here ache in m' chest won't completely go away? After all that I been through in m' life an' picked up an' moved on from, why is this so hard fer me?"

I pause like I might actually hear Ella answer. But th' only sounds are th' mockin'bird on top o' th' church steeple nearby imitating every other bird's song. After every trill he flies straight up 'bout three feet an' then right back down on his perch, kinda like a jack-in-th'-box.

I always wondered what a mockin'bird's real song was. Does he really have one o' his own? 'R does he only know how t' imitate? It'd be sad if he didn't have one o' his own.

Grabbin' a handful o' sage grass, I pull it out o' th' ground 'round th' edge o' Ella's headstone an' toss it t' th' side. I do th' same with a few other clumps that've showed up over winter, their amber-colored blades in sharp contrast t' th' colorless Febr'ary surroundings.

Puttin' up a headstone in a cemetery was Judge Jack's idea. I thought it was stupid 'cause Ella wasn't there. I plowed 'er into my garden jes' like she asked me to. That way she's givin' back t' th' earth. Ella was all 'bout givin'.

But I'll have t' admit that I like comin' here and talkin' to and touchin' this stone. That was probably th' only good idea Judge Jack ever had.

After Ella died an' I was give all that money, I decided t' let Shady Green tear m' house down an' keep what he wanted. Then I went an' bought me one o' them double-wide mobile homes. If I'd a known how much I'd like havin' an indoor toilet, I'd a done had one put in m' old house. Two things I don't miss is goin' t' th' outhouse in July and goin' t' th' outhouse in January.

I thought th' trailer might make April happy, but it didn't seem t' make any dent in 'er. She crawled into herself an' closed th' door behind 'er, jes' like a hibernating bear. It was like she was there, but she wasn't there.

"It's time fer me t' update you on how things is goin'. T' tell y' th' truth I don't know what t' make o' our sweet April. She's seventeen goin' on twenty-five. She stays holed up in 'er bedroom all th' time, talkin' on th' phone and playin' that loud, stinkin' music. Sounds worse than a combine with a bearing gone bad.

"And that boy I told you 'bout last time is still hangin' 'round. I caught the two of 'em in 'er bedroom one Saturday last month. It didn't look like they was doin' nothin' but that didn't matter t' me. I picked th' boy up by the back o' his belt an' walked 'im on his tiptoes t' th' front door. He was squealin' like a little schoolgirl by th' time I throwed 'im off th' porch.

"April didn't talk t' me fer two days after that. It was then that I started noticin' she's got some o' her mama in 'er, much t' my misery. She can have a 'to hell with everybody' attitude an' then want t' sit in my lap an' hug my neck like she did when she was little. I feel 'er gittin' further an' further away from me. I didn't do no good raisin' Maisy and I ain't done such a good job with April neither, don't look like.

"I sure do wish you was here. You'd know what t' do with 'er, wouldn't you, Ella?" I pat 'er rock and, grunting, stand up. "If you can find a way t' send me a message on what t' do with our girl, I sure would appreciate it.

"I still think 'bout little March sometimes. Wonder if he's dead 'r alive. Guess if he is alive, he ain't little no more. Don't guess we'll ever know what happened t' him.

"I still see Smiley Carter on occasion. Age is catchin' up with him. Seems especially since August went off t' college, Carter is feelin' extra lonely.

"That's sort o' the blessin' and the curse o' havin' known you, Ella. You taught us all how t' love, but with that love come all that hurt when you left us.

"You know I still love y', Ella. Always will. I'll be back again t' visit."

Lookin' at my watch I see it's time t' go pick up April from school.

I make my way t' my truck and, grippin' th' steerin' wheel, pull myself inside. The door squeaks as I close it. April hates this truck, tells me I should buy a new one since I can afford it. But when I seen this 1976 Chevy sittin' on the back o' Ted Spence's car lot I knew it was jes' what I needed. Ted said it had been in a wreck an' he replaced th' driver's side door, which is why it was a different color than th' rest o' th' truck. Th' engine uses a little oil, which makes 'er smoke some, but she runs fine. Besides, I wasn't 'bout t' pay th' kind o' money they charge fer a new truck.

When I turn the ignition key, th' engine roars t' life. Lookin' in th' rearview mirror, I see a small cloud o' white smoke rise behind th' tailgate. Shifting into drive, I head toward the school.

CHAPTER TWO

My prime of youth is but a frost of cares,
My feast of joy is but a dish of pain
—Chidiock Tichborne

APRIL:

Sitting up, I look in the rearview mirror of Mark's truck and tighten the ponytail on the side of my head and put the scrunchie back in place. "The bell must have rung. Everybody's coming out to the parking lot. Roll your window down and get rid of all this smoke."

Grinning, my boyfriend, Mark, rolls down his window and begins fanning. "That was some good shit. Where'd you get it?"

For the last hour Mark and I have been sitting in his truck in the school parking lot making out and sharing a joint. It's a lot better than sitting through my boring sixth period class. I'm failing in there anyway, so what's the point?

"What difference does it make where I got it?!" I snap.

"Geez, what's your problem? I just asked a simple question."

"I should have already been at the front of the school waiting on Tucker. If I'm not there when she pulls up, she'll give me the third degree." Tugging on my leg warmers, I open the passenger door.

Classmates are beginning to stroll by.

"Hey, April," comes the sing-song voice of Marcie, "missed you in algebra last hour."

"Hey, Mark," her boyfriend, Caleb, calls out, "was it good for you?"

Mark's only response is a stupid grin that mirrors Caleb's.

I ignore Marcie.

Sneaking my hand underneath my oversized sweater, I get my boobs back in place inside my bra. I sometimes wonder if Mark would still be interested in me if I didn't let him manhandle them all the time. He's crazy about them. I don't get it.

Before closing the door, I lean down and say, "Call me tonight."

As I turn toward the school I see a cloud of white smoke rising in the back of the line of vehicles in front of the building. I grit my teeth. I'm so sick of her and that pile of junk she calls a truck!

"April Tucker!"

I jump at the voice of Mr. Hardin, the vice principal. He's striding toward me like one of those German soldiers he drones on about in history class.

"Yes sir, Mr. Hardin."

"I got a report that you skipped your sixth period class again. Is that true?"

"Ms. Collins asked me to help her with a project in the library," I lie. "I'll bring you a note on Monday."

Mr. Hardin puts his hands on his hips and fixes me with a stare. "Bad choice of an excuse, Miss Tucker. Ms. Collins left at noon today."

"You're just bluffing, trying to get me to admit I broke a rule."

"I'm bluffing. I'm bluffing!" He laughs out loud. "That is the best line I've heard all week. You know what's going to finally happen, don't you?"

I dispense with my charade. "Do you really think I care? Go ahead and threaten to kick me out of school. As a matter of fact I wish you would. I'm sick of this place, this town, and everybody in it. I'm ready to leave here and start living, 'cause what you people around here do sure ain't living."

Mr. Hardin's face softens a bit. "Look, April, I know you have not had an easy life—"

Without thinking, I draw back my fist. "Shut up! Don't even start! You don't know anything about me or my life. I don't want your pity and I sure as hell don't need it! Why don't you go find somebody who wants saving. I'm doing just fine."

I'm suddenly aware of students gathering around us. I'm practically panting I'm so out of breath. My fist hangs in the air as if on a string. I slowly lower it.

In a voice that only Mr. Hardin can hear, I say, "Please, just leave me alone. Please." I walk away without waiting for a rebuttal.

Shoving my way through the other students I walk purposefully toward Tucker and her truck. She's stopped and gotten out, standing with her door open. Her face is without expression as I approach. We both get in at the same time.

The squeak in her door feels like an ice pick being shoved in my ears. I clap my hands over them. "When are you going to get that thing fixed? Don't you get tired of it?"

Ignoring my questions, Tucker looks straight ahead and drives slowly forward. "What was all th' commotion in th' parkin' lot? You in trouble again?"

"Hi, April. How was your day at school, April?" I say in a sarcastic tone. "Why do you always think I'm in trouble, Tucker? Don't you think I ever do anything right?"

"Was you with that boy again? I'm tellin' y' April, that boy's no good. All he'll do is git you in trouble. Boys is what got yore mama in trouble and what eventually got 'er killed. I jes' don't want you t' follow in 'er path."

"I am not my mother!" I scream at the top of my lungs. "I am not my father! And I am not you! I am me, and if that's not good enough for everybody, then they'll just have to get over it."

Tucker's face reddens and her knuckles turn white as she grips the steering wheel. My arrows have found their mark. I feel a sadistic sense of pleasure in seeing her wounded.

The rest of the drive home not a word passes between us. As soon as the truck rolls to a stop in front of our trailer I get out and slam the door behind me. Opening the front door to the trailer, I hear the squeaking truck door as Tucker closes it.

I quickly make my way to my bedroom, close the door behind me, and lock it. My stereo bursts to life as I push the button. Bon Jovi screams, mimicking the screams in my head.

Then I go into my bathroom. Opening my jewelry box, I lift the velvet cloth in the bottom and take out a folded piece of paper. Holding it in one hand, I unbutton my pants as I walk toward the toilet. I pull my pants down below my knees and sit on the lid. Unfolding the paper, I remove a razor blade.

Turning my head to the side, I peer down at the outside of my left upper thigh. Surrounded by a sea of white skin are rows of the letter *M* in various stages of healing. Some are already thick with scar tissue. The most recent ones are scabbed over but have angry red outlining them. I count fourteen *M*s.

Shifting positions, I look at my right thigh. It's a perfect match, except that I only count thirteen *M*s. "I guess it's your turn, then," I say quietly.

My heart begins racing and my breathing accelerates. I slide a washcloth under my thigh. Gripping the razor between the thumb and forefinger of my left hand, I push the point of the razor into my thigh until it breaks the skin. A drop of blood springs up. With my teeth clenched I pull the razor through my skin to make the first leg of the *M*. A streak of red is left in its wake.

I watch in fascination as the droplets of blood find each other and their combined weight gives way to gravity and slowly runs down the side of my thigh onto the washcloth. A bead of sweat appears on my upper lip. Warmth spreads through my body. I feel nothing as I carve the other three lines to complete *M* number fourteen.

CHAPTER THREE

The day is past, and yet I saw no sun,
And now I live, and now my life is done.
—Chidiock Tichborne

MARCH:

I feel the sensation of movement.

Everything is dark.

Unfamiliar voices from above me—"What's his name?" "There was no ID on him." "How long had he been lying there?" "My guess is forty-eight hours."

Then nothing.

Sounds—rhythmic beeping, but not in time with each other. A click. A whoosh.

Suddenly I feel as if I am choking. Something is in my throat! I reach to pull it out but my hands won't move.

Voices—"Quick, he's waking up again. Go ahead and give him some."

Then nothing.

A dream, or is it a memory? A black boy throwing dirt clods at me. Laughing.

Then nothing.

I am awakened by someone gently shaking my shoulder. It is so dark in the room I can't tell if my eyes are opened or closed.

"You need to try and wake up," a woman's voice says. "You're in Blount Memorial Hospital in Maryville, Tennessee. Can you hear me?"

Why won't someone turn the lights on so I can see? I try to answer her but nothing comes out.

"Your throat is probably dry and irritated from the ventilator tubing."

I feel something being placed between my lips.

"Suck on this straw. This juice might help."

I pull a swallow through the straw and taste apple juice. Its cool sweetness moves slowly through my throat and I feel it go down my esophagus to my apparently empty stomach.

"Does that taste good?" the woman asks.

In a voice that sounds more like a wood rasp filing a sticking door than anything human, I manage a yes.

I hear someone snapping their fingers, followed by loud whispering. I try to string thoughts together so that I can form questions but everything seems scattered like the seeds of dandelions blown by a spring breeze. I can neither grab one nor make sense of the whole.

"Well good morning." A man's voice. "I'm Doctor Niedenhaur. I was beginning to wonder if you were going to ever join us or not. How do you feel?"

"Spring false how bacon." I hope what they hear makes more sense to them than it does to me.

"Mmm. Well, yes, I see," the doctor says. "Things are still quite fuzzy for you, as is expected. But that will improve. We've had you heavily sedated for quite some time while you made up your mind whether to stay or leave. But we'll continue reducing that to help you wake up. I'll be by again later to check on you."

After a moment the woman's voice speaks again. "Don't mind him. He's got the personality of cardboard, but he's a very smart doctor. Is there anything I can get you?"

I pick through the pile of disconnected words that are dumped on the floor of my brain. I choose one that makes the most sense. "Sun."

"You have a son?" she asks. "What's his name? Where does he live? What's his mother's name? Do you have a phone number?"

I shake my head. Searing pain!

Then nothing.

Consciousness comes slowly, from far away. The voices sound as if they are coming from the other side of a lake. Standing on the opposite bank, I only catch every other word or so. And again it is pitch dark. Don't these people ever turn the lights on?

Most of the words are medical terms. Their meanings are unknown to me.

"Turn on the lights." The sentence forms in my brain and I think I speak it, but the voice isn't mine.

"Good morning."

That pleasant, familiar woman's voice.

"My name is Naomi. I am a nurse and I've been caring for you since you first arrived. I realize it is hard for you to speak because of the damage done to your throat. Let me encourage you to be careful about moving your head suddenly like you did the last time you were awake. You've experienced tremendous head trauma and your brain is quite bruised."

I try to take in everything she is saying but I can't connect it to anything. How does her description apply to me? Damage? Head trauma?

"Lights," I say. "Turn on the lights."

"Can you tell me your name?" Naomi asks. "We don't know your name or anything about you. There were no identifying papers or billfold with you."

I don't like having my question ignored, but I shift to answer her question. "My name is . . ." I have nothing to put in the blank. Why can't I tell her my name? More importantly, what is my name? I frantically flip through the pages of my memory, but all the pages are blank.

"I . . . I can't . . . remember . . ."

"I see."

A tone of concern has crept into Naomi's voice.

"Well, we've been calling you Levi because that was the only name we found anywhere on you. You know, your Levi's jeans. Is that okay with you?"

I feel irritated that I can't remember my own name but accept Naomi's offer. "Sure. Okay."

"Good," she says. "Now open wide and let me take your temperature."

She places the thermometer under my tongue. As we both wait for it to finish its job, a new voice comes from further away.

"How is he this mornin'?"

Sounds like a black man. An older black man.

"Hey, Willie," Naomi answers. "He's awake and talking this morning. What about that?"

In a louder voice, Willie says, "That's the way t' show 'em. Be tough, young man. Be a fighter! You's in good hands with Naomi—good hands."

"You're just saying that because it's true," Naomi says.

The thermometer beeps and she slides it out of my mouth.

"See you 'round," Willie says.

"Yes," Naomi replies. "You stay out of trouble, okay?"

Willie's voice is even farther away as he calls out, "I ain't makin' no promises."

I start to ask again about the lights but I'm interrupted by the voice of Dr. Niedenhaur.

"So, I hear our patient is awake this morning."

"Meet Levi," Naomi says. "He's decided he likes that name."

"Oh?" Dr. Niedenhaur sounds surprised.

Whispers pass between him and Naomi.

"Oh, I see," the doctor says. "Seems you've lost some memory, Levi. That's not uncommon. But that may—"

"Turn on the damn lights!" I finally blurt it out.

"The lights? You mean no one's told you?"

"Told me what?"

"Levi," for the first time Dr. Niedenhaur's voice takes on a human quality, "I'm very regretful to inform you that you are permanently blind."

CHAPTER FOUR

Falsehood is worse than hate.
—*John Donne*

APRIL:

Aapriiilll!"

I wake with a jerk. Only Tucker's train whistle of a voice can reach decibels higher than my stereo. It's practically not even a human sound. Thank god she only uses it when we're alone and not around my friends.

Feeling moisture on the side of my face, I sit up and realize that I've been drooling while taking a nap. The mirror reveals sleep lines creasing the side of my face. I think I see an *M* in the design and wonder if I unconsciously created it.

I don't remember when the letter *M* started being such a central part of my life. Anytime I see billboards or magazines or advertisements, if there is an *M*, it jumps out from all the other letters.

"April!"

"What!" I yell back through my closed bedroom door. "What is wrong?!"

"Ain't nothin' wrong. I's jes' lettin' y' know that supper's 'bout ready. Better git washed up."

"Yeah, whatever," I mutter quietly. Ain't? Jes'? Git? Is there anyone else in the world that has English as bad as Tucker's? It is so embarrassing, especially if she answers the phone when one of my friends calls, which is why I try not to ever let that happen.

Just then the phone rings. I snatch it up before it finishes the first ring. "I got it!" I yell out to Tucker.

Holding my breath, I listen for any clicking sound that will indicate Tucker has picked up. When there is nothing but silence, I say, "Is that you?"

"Sure it is. You gonna be able to sneak out tonight?"

"It's *going*, stupid, not *gonna*. How many times do I have to tell you?"

"Oh yeah, that's right. Going. Are you going to be able to sneak out tonight?"

I don't like the patronizing tone in Mark's voice. "Look, don't get smart with me," I hiss. "You just show up at the usual place. I'll be there if I can."

"Sure thing."

I hear a click on the phone line. "Yes, Martha, that algebra test is tomorrow. Good luck. Talk to you later." I hang up the phone.

When I walk out of my bedroom I see Tucker walking away from the phone.

"Listening in on my conversations again?" I ask.

"If I trusted y', t'wouldn't be no need to."

"I don't know why you don't trust me."

Tucker stops and turns toward me. Folding her arms across her chest, she says, "Y' want me t' make y' a list?"

Arms across her chest. Now that's a sure sign to tread carefully. Looking down at the floor, I say, "I'm sorry. I don't blame you for not trusting me. You're so good to me and I'm always disappointing you."

Tucker's arms drop to her sides. "No, no, April Tucker. Don't say that. They's a good heart in you somewhere. It jes' got lost along th' way."

Yes, be sure and remind me of my last name. It wasn't so bad in elementary school but once I hit junior high, "Tucker" was morphed into vulgarity, especially by the boys. Boys have such corrupt, dirty minds.

"And I know you'll help me find my way back," I reply to Tucker. "That's why I love you so much."

A smile spreads across Tucker's face, softening its normally hard edges. "That's m' April. Now give me a hug."

I step into her bear hug. There is a feeling of tenderness and warmth that touches the edges of my heart. I start to return her hug, then push away. Laughing I say, "Whew, Tucker, you can sure smother a girl. What's for supper that smells so good?"

"How's fried pork chops, mashed taters, corn, an' homemade rolls sound? An' fer dessert I made y' some o' my famous nanner puddin'."

Each of those foods is my favorite and my mouth salivates in spite of how I feel emotionally. Tucker's cooking can break down most any wall of resistance.

My twitching taste buds trigger an irrepressible smile. "Don't let me knock you down getting to the table."

"That's what I like t' hear."

Cracking my bedroom door open, I see the flickering lights of the television in the dark living room. I step quietly down the hallway and see Tucker asleep in her recliner. Her snoring practically drowns out the voice of Johnny Carson coming from the TV.

I retrace my steps into my bedroom and silently shut the door. Making my way to the other side of my bed, I raise the screenless window. Zipping my jacket, I stick my legs through the window and lower myself the few feet to the ground below.

The cloudless night allows the full moon to bathe everything in soft blue hues and shadows. I look up and see a huge ring around the moon.

The first time I ever saw a ring around the moon I was six or seven years old. Tucker woke me up during the night and took me outside into the warmth of summer. Crickets and tree frogs were singing. I'd already learned about them from her. The rich smell of freshly cut hay permeated the air. It was seasoned with just a touch of aromas from the barn—manure, horses, cows, pigs, sweet feed.

Being carried by her big strong arms, I felt like a little puppy, dependent, a little afraid, but protected by her strength.

"Looky up there," she'd said. "Y' see that circle 'round the moon?"

I followed the direction of her pointing finger. I put my arm parallel to hers and traced the circle with her. "That one?" I asked.

"That's th' one. Now that right there is a sign. It's a sign that within th' next twenty-four t' forty-eight hours we's gonna have a rain. An' th' bigger the ring, the bigger th' rain'll be."

Standing now outside my bedroom window, I feel what seems like a slight tapping on my heart. I shudder, then shake myself.

I listen for any indication that Tucker has heard my exit. Confident that my escape is undetected, I start walking toward the Obion River bottom.

CHAPTER FIVE

A Death blow is a Life blow to Some
Who till they died, did not alive become—
Who had they lived, had died but when
They died, Vitality begun.
—*Emily Dickinson*

MARCH:

The day after Dr. Niedenhaur dropped the bombshell that I was permanently blind, I hear a new voice.

"Levi? Hi, my name is Kate Kapperton. Dr. Niedenhaur asked that I drop in on you. I am a psychiatrist with the University of Tennessee School of Medicine in Knoxville. How are you today?"

I'm trying to connect and remember names. Niedenhaur, Kapperton, University of Tennessee. The word *psychiatrist* is the last one to register. "Why are you here?" I ask.

"I was over here doing a consult on another patient and Dr. Niedenhaur happened to see me in the hallway. He said yours was an interesting case and he wanted my input."

"So I'm some sort of guinea pig that everyone wants to observe playing in its cage, is that it?" I think I hear someone writing. "Are you writing all this down? I'm none of your business!"

"Let's try this again." Dr. Kapperton's voice has softened. "Tony, put your pen and notebook away."

I hear a pen click. "Who's Tony? Who all is in my room? How many are in here?!"

"I'm very sorry, Levi. I should have made that clear. The only ones in the room are you, me, and my intern, Tony Esterhauser. We'll not write anything down, if you don't want us to. And the only reason I am here is to see if there is something I can do to help."

I wait a few moments for my breathing and heart rate to slow. Control is essential. Where did that thought come from?

"Are you remembering something?" Dr. Kapperton asks.

"No."

"Levi, do you mind if I ask you some questions?"

"You can ask, but I don't promise any answers."

"That's fair enough. Do you remember what caused you to end up in the hospital here?"

"I think there was some sort of accident."

"Now this is important, Levi. Do you remember the accident or do you remember that someone told you there was an accident?"

I try to ferret out the truth and feel like I'm Alice in Wonderland and have tumbled down the rabbit hole. Naomi's voice comes and goes, along with the words *broken leg, Little River, larynx, lucky, dead, tibia, contusion*. "I guess I'm not sure of the answer to your question."

"I see. I'm told you don't remember your name. Is that correct?"

"Of course it's correct! You think I'd make something like that up? Look, lady, I don't remember anything—nothing. It's a blank slate."

"Levi, I'm not accusing you of anything. I'm just searching, that's all."

"So what do you think is wrong with me? Am I crazy or something? Will I ever get my memory back?"

There is a pause. For a moment I think everyone has left the room.

"Well, you certainly deserve some answers, at least the answers we can give at the moment. Clearly we can say you have amnesia. But amnesia can occur for multiple reasons, mainly physical reasons or psychological reasons. My explanation for amnesia is summed up in one word—trauma. It is a response to some sort of trauma, whether it be physical or psychological."

"So what kind is mine?" I ask.

"No doubt you've experienced physical trauma. Your broken bones and the severe head trauma are real enough and certainly would be an explanation for your amnesia. But because you have no memory to assist us, we can't know if you've ever experienced any psychological trauma, either recently or in the past."

"Well we've got new guests, I see." Naomi's pleasant voice fills the room.

"I'm conducting an interview of this patient." Dr. Kapperton's tone has icicles hanging on it. If she has a long nose, she's probably looking down it at Naomi.

"Yes, Doctor, I'm sure that you are. You go right ahead while I check Levi's vitals. Dr. Niedenhaur is a stickler for having these done regularly. If you know him, you know how he is. Maybe you can afford to lose your job, but I can't. I've got ten children to feed and both of my parents are—"

"Let me assure you," Dr. Kapperton cuts Naomi off, "that Dr. Niedenhaur will know everything about this."

Sounding unmoved by this not-so-subtle threat, Naomi says cheerfully, "Thank you so much. Please do that and mention I got Levi's vitals right on schedule."

Two sets of feet exit my room. Naomi fiddles with my pillow. She is muttering to herself. I give her opportunity for some steam to release.

"Ten?" I ask.

"Ten? Ten what?" she replies.

"You've got ten children?"

The laughter that pours out of Naomi sounds like a spring-fed creek running over a rock-lined bed—bubbling, bouncing, splashing.

"Oh my lord, I hope not! You just looked like you had had enough of Miss I-Know-You-Better-Than-You-Know-Yourself. The woman may be good at what she does, but the way she goes about it rubs me the wrong way."

I laugh, but the sound of it seems foreign to me. "Naomi, I need answers to some questions. Will you be truthful with me?"

"I'll tell you what I know. And what I tell you will be the truth. What do you want to know?"

"First of all, what's wrong with my voice? Even though I've lost my memory, my voice doesn't sound right to me."

"Okay," Naomi says, "Let's start with that one. You suffered a blow to your larynx. Some people call it the voice box. It's where your vocal cords lie. The damage done has altered your voice. That could be the result of swelling. After the swelling goes down your voice may change. But the way it sounds now could also be permanent. Besides, there's nothing wrong with the way it sounds. It's sort of like Rod Stewart. You may have a singing career waiting on you."

"Rod Stewart . . . Rod Stewart . . . Sorry, doesn't ring a bell."

Naomi is silent.

"Another question—tell me about my injuries, head to toe."

"Hmmm . . . Okay, let's start with your toes. You broke your left pinkie toe."

"My pinkie toe?" I laugh. "Are you serious? What did you all do, x-ray me from head to toe?"

"Actually, we did," Naomi replies. "I'm telling you, you looked like you had been wadded up, stuffed in a small trash can, then taken out and thrown in the river."

"Wow, that sounds bad."

"Trust me, you have no idea. I've been working in the ICU for fifteen years and you looked worse than anyone I've seen."

It's my turn to be silent as I consider Naomi's description.

"Next up," she says, "is your right leg. You broke, or more accurately, *shattered* your right femur. That's your thighbone. They performed surgery on it and pinned it back together."

"So that's why it feels so much heavier than my left one."

"Yeah, you've got a cast that starts at your groin and goes all the way to your foot. We're about ready to get you up on it and see how you do using crutches."

It's funny how I haven't even thought about the fact that I haven't been out of this bed. "You mean I haven't been up since I've been here?"

"Goodness no, Levi. You've been tethered to your bed with IVs, your catheter, and that ventilator until recently."

I reflexively try to touch my mouth with my right hand and am reminded of the pain in my elbow. "I figured out that something is wrong with this elbow. I've felt the heavy bandage on it, but I'm not sure what's wrong with it."

"You're right," Naomi agrees. "But you're getting ahead of me. It's toe to head, remember? So next, after your right femur, is your pelvis, which was fractured. Your spleen had to be removed because it ruptured. Ribs were broken on both sides. Then your right elbow

23

was dislocated. It's wrapped up pretty tightly right now so that it's immobilized."

"Good grief," I moan.

"I know," Naomi sympathizes. "Like I said, you were a rag doll when you showed up at our doorstep. Now, I've already told you about your throat. You've got some fractures to your facial bones that a plastic surgeon had to come in and try to reconstruct."

"What do you mean, reconstruct?"

"Well, he didn't have anything to go by, like a photo on your driver's license or anyone with you who could give him some idea of what you looked like. So he just used his best guess."

"Good lord! I'm beginning to think I must look like Frankenstein." Frankenstein—where did that come from?

"Hey," Naomi says excitedly, "that's your first memory. Do you remember what Frankenstein's monster—actually it was *Dr. Frankenstein's* creature that looked like a monster—looked like?"

I think. I feel like I'm putting my arms elbow-deep into a box of confetti. All I see are disconnected letters and words. There is no order to be made of any of it.

"Nothing?" Naomi asks.

"Nothing," I reply.

"That's okay. I'm told it sort of goes like that. Sometimes people regain their memory a tiny piece at a time and others have it all come crashing back at once. But this does make me ask you a question. Do you want your face shaved or do you want to let your beard regrow?"

"I had a beard?"

"Yeah. You looked sort of like a bear. As big as you are, plus that brushy, full-face beard, I thought Sasquatch had come to East Tennessee."

Suddenly I am astounded by what I do not know about myself. "Just how big am I?"

"Oh my gosh, I hadn't even thought about that. You really don't remember anything, do you?"

"I'm telling you, Naomi, I feel like my memory is there but it's been put through a paper shredder."

"Well, my guess is that you are about six feet, four inches tall. Our scales weighed you at two hundred and forty-eight pounds."

The picture that Naomi paints of me is incongruent with my own perception. I feel like a small child in a large bed—tiny and fragile, lost and alone.

Exhausted, I say, "If I'm going to look like a monster anyway, let the beard grow back. Is there anything else wrong with me?"

Naomi touches my hand. Hers is warm and soft. I feel my throat squeezing and pressure building in my chest.

"No, no, I'm not saying you look like a monster at all. That was your expression, not mine. I cannot imagine how hard this must be for you. But since we've gone this far, I'm going to tell you everything.

"Besides the broken facial bones and damage done to your optic nerve, you also suffered a closed-head injury. That can be fatal, so you are lucky in that sense. But the internal pressure on the brain from that type of injury can cause problems. It might make it difficult for a person to walk or speak or do other things. It's very unpredictable. Our best guess is that, even if you hadn't broken your leg, you are going to have difficulty in keeping your balance and walking."

I sigh. "Lucky. I'm lucky, huh?"

"You're lucky in the sense that you get a chance to put your life back together again."

I let that thought sink deeper. "Or maybe a chance to start life brand new."

CHAPTER SIX

Better late than never: yea, mate,
But as good never as too late.
—John Heywood

APRIL:

Walking in the moonlight makes me feel like I am walking in a dream-like trance. The pale blue light makes it look like there are ghosts floating everywhere.

After I've walked about a mile I see the rising fog from the backwater of the Obion. It looks like a wall of white up ahead. Two dim, red lights let me know Mark is waiting.

I open the passenger door of his truck. The interior light makes me squint, but I can still see and smell that he's already been drinking. "Gee, Mark, could you not wait? How many have you had?"

Looking at me with bleary eyes, he slurs, "I haven't even finished one yet." Then he grins.

"Oh sure," I say. "Haven't finished one, have you? So why do you talk like you have a mouth full of marbles?"

Fumbling with his jacket, he reaches inside and brings out a rectangular jar.

Grabbing it out of his hand, I say, "What's that?" I remove the cap and sniff. My head snaps back as if I've been slapped.

"Just a little whiskey," Mark says as he reaches for the bottle.

His reflexes are slow and I easily jerk the bottle out of his grasp. "You're insane, you know it? You've already gotten pulled over once when you were drunk. The cops gave you a break by not charging you with a DUI and underage drinking. Now you come out here and you're stinking drunk. I can't believe how stupid you are!"

He leans toward me and reaches for my breast.

"Oh, come on," he says. "Don't be mad. Let's have some fun."

I knock his hand away with my left elbow. At the same time I drop the whiskey bottle and slap him with my right hand. "No!" I yell.

Mark shows no sign of being stung by the force of my slapping him. He slides to the middle of the seat, crowding me into the door. "So are we going to play rough tonight? That'd be a new twist for us. But I'm game if you are."

This time he reaches for my chest with both hands and grabs my jacket.

"Mark, stop!" I try pushing him back but can't get any leverage.

I hear my zipper being undone and feel my jacket opening. Suddenly his hands are everywhere. He shoves me against the door. My head bangs against the window. I see stars. "Mark, you're hurting me. I said to stop. I mean it! Stop!"

All of a sudden he pulls me down onto the seat on my back and straddles me. Grabbing the waist of my jeans, he fumbles with the button. "Tonight's the night, baby. You've been promising me more and tonight I'm collecting on your promise."

Panic grips my throat like the talons of an eagle. "Not like this, Mark. Please, not like this. We need to go to a motel or something."

He pauses in his clumsy attempt to unfasten my jeans. His alcohol-bathed brain tries to process what I am saying.

In that moment, my right hand goes to the floor and finds the whiskey bottle. As a twisted grin forms on his face, I strike the side of his head with all my might. The glass crushes between my hand and his head. Mark's grin is interrupted and morphs into a questioning look, then his eyes unfocus and he collapses on top of me.

Not realizing what has happened, I kick and scream and slap as hard as I can. I pull his hair and bite his ear. Realization dawns that Mark is not moving.

I lay panting, trying to get my breath. But his weight is making it impossible. I shove him onto the floorboard, where he lies in awkward angles.

Jerking open the passenger door, I fall onto the road, get up, and begin running toward my trailer. After sprinting for fifty yards, I stop and lean over to catch my breath. Suddenly I begin vomiting.

Once the retching is over, I straighten up and look over my shoulder at the taillights of Mark's truck. The amber glow of the interior light spills into the ditch from the open passenger door.

I turn and face the truck. I keep waiting to see Mark's silhouette in the interior of the cab and then him driving away. Several minutes pass with nothing happening.

Slowly, I begin walking toward the truck. When I arrive at the tailgate, I pause, listening. When I am sure there are no sounds or movements, I ease carefully down the side of the truck to its yawning door. When I peek inside, the truck appears empty, then I remember that I had shoved Mark onto the floorboard.

A couple more steps and I have a complete view of the interior. Mark is lying on his side. One leg is still half on the seat, his foot wedged between the seat and the armrest.

Easing my head inside, I softly say, "Mark?" It's then that I see a dark circle surrounding his head on the floorboard. I touch it with my index finger and slowly bring it under the interior light. For a moment I can find no reason to explain its red color.

Then, with the force of a train striking a vehicle at a crossing, realization crashes in. Blood! "Oh my god, Mark! Mark, can you hear me?! Wake up. You've got to wake up. I'm sorry. I didn't mean to—"

A hand grabs my arm from behind, lifts me off the ground, and pulls my body through the air in an arc until I land with a thud on my back on the grassy side of the road bank. Looking up, I see the face of Tucker.

CHAPTER SEVEN

Forget not yet, forget not this,
How long ago hath been, and is,
The mind that never meant amiss,—
Forget not yet.
— *Sir Thomas Wyatt*

TUCKER:

I wake up t' th' sound of Ed McMahon laughin'. Lookin' at m' clock on th' wall, I see it is almost eleven thirty. I lean forward so that th' foot o' my recliner will go t' th' floor. Carefully, I stand up, makin' sure I've got m' balance before goin' t' th' bathroom.

There ain't been one time that I've sat down on m' toilet that I haven't thanked th' good Lord above fer m' indoor plumbin'. What a sweet blessin' it is!

As I start toward m' bedroom, I pause, turn around, and go t' April's bedroom. I put m' ear against 'er door. After a moment, I silently open it. All th' lights is out.

When m' eyes git adjusted t' th' light, I see she is under 'er covers, sound asleep. I start backin' out o' th' room when I stop.

Somethin' caught m' eye, but I ain't sure what it is. I scan th' room again. Then I see it. Her window is open.

I walk 'round 'er bed t' close th' window an' discover th' screen is missin'. Th' hairs on th' back o' my neck twitch. I feel a twistin' sensation in m' gut.

In two quick strides I reach th' light switch an' flip it on. I grab April's covers an' fling 'em off the bed. Her pillows are lined up lengthwise underneath. But no April.

My heart begins racin' but no faster than m' mind. I'm stopped by a memory from nine years ago when I walked in March's room an' found him gone. The note he left was the last I ever heard from him.

I spin slowly 'round th' room lookin' fer a note sittin' out that April might've left. Seein' nothin', I go into 'er bathroom an' look on 'er makeup table. No note there, but stickin' out from under a towel on th' floor is a stained washcloth. I bend over an' pick it up. As I hold it under th' bright lights of 'er makeup mirror, th' red looks jes' like blood.

Stuffin' th' washcloth in th' pocket o' m' overalls, I head t' m' bedroom. Once there, I reach under m' pillow an' pull out m' pistol and put it in m' other pocket. From behind m' bedroom door I grab m' axe handle. Pausin' in the kitchen, I grab a flashlight an' m' truck keys. Then I head out th' door.

I walk 'round t' th' side o' th' trailer where April's window is. There I find th' screen propped against th' trailer. Kneelin' down, I switch on th' flashlight an' scan th' ground. I spy what I'm lookin' fer—April's footprints. I follow 'em from behind th' trailer t' th' road an' get a general sense o' th' direction she took out fer. Damn, it looks like she's headed fer th' river.

Th' moon's so bright I leave m' headlights off. Driving slowly, m' truck barely above idling speed, I peer into th' distance. After a few moments I see th' fog from th' river bottom. Squinting, I see what looks like two red lights inside th' fog bank. I shut off m' truck an' let 'er coast.

I roll m' window down an' listen. All I hear are th' rocks crunching under m' tires on the tar and gravel road surface. When I'm fifty feet from th' other vehicle m' truck rolls to a stop. I can see that th' passenger door is open. Suddenly I hear April scream.

Grabbin' the axe handle beside me on th' seat, I head fer th' sound of 'er voice. I recognize it is Mark's truck as I jog t' th' passenger side. April is standin' in the open door and screamin' Mark's name.

I grab 'er an' fling 'er t' th' ground. A quick scan lets me know there ain't no obvious wounds. Turning t' Mark's truck, I step toward th' open door. "I'm gonna kill you, you sorry son of a bitch. I promised you that if'n you ever tried t' hurt m' April that I'd kill you."

When I look in, all I see is his foot twisted against the opposite door. Then I notice him lyin' on th' floorboard. "Ain't no use in you tryin' t' hide from me. Git out here an' take what's comin' t' you."

I grab him by th' collar.

"Tucker, no!" April screams from behind me.

I notice th' limp way Mark's head hangs and feel April tuggin' at m' arm.

"He's hurt, Tucker. Let him go and get back out of the way."

Giving in t' her persistent tugs, I let go o' his collar. His head lands on th' floorboard with a splat.

April squeezes in front o' me.

"Is he okay?" her voice pleads. She looks down at his still form. "Is he dead, Tucker?"

"We'll check that out in a bit. First of all, you better tell me what happened. An' jes' skip all th' part 'bout what ya'll was doin' out here an' how long y' been meetin' up like this. I'll git that from y' later. Right now you need t' tell me why he's lyin' on th' floor-board in a pool o' blood."

I grab th' sleeve of 'er jacket an' spin 'er around t' face me. Her eyes are wide with fear. "An' if there was ever a time you told me th' truth, this needs t' be it."

"It was crazy, Tucker. I've never seen him like he was tonight. He was more like an animal than the boy I know. First of all, he'd been drinking whiskey, something I've never known him to do. And as soon as I got in the truck he started coming at me."

"Whadda y' mean, comin' at y'?"

"Unzipping my jacket and grabbing at my breasts. I blocked most of his moves until he slammed my head against the window and then threw me onto the seat, under him. That was when he—"

Her whole body is shakin' an' 'er voice breaks off.

Grittin' m' teeth, I say, "That was when he did what?" I guess I didn't do such a good job o' hidin' th' sound o' my risin' anger. April stops cryin' an' looks at me calmly.

"He started trying to get my pants off me so he could rape me."

All I see is red. I step back an' move t' th' other side o' th' open door. Gripping my axe handle with both hands, I swing it like a baseball bat an' strike th' windshield. Spider cracks run from one side t' th' other and top t' bottom. Moving t' th' front o' th' truck, I bust out both headlights.

With each blow o' my axe handle, April lets out a terrified scream.

I approach th' driver's door an' strike th' windshield again. This time it falls out o' its frame into th' cab. I smash th' window on th' driver's door.

Out o' breath, I bend over t' try an' get some air. Once I finally get a good breath, I stand up an' scream at th' top o' my lungs, "Not my April!"

Suddenly I realize that April is in front o' me. She has gripped th' bib o' m' overalls and is shakin' me.

"Tucker, stop! You're scaring me! Stop it!"

Without warnin' my knees buckle and I fall t' th' ground. I use th' axe handle t' keep from falling flat an' find myself sittin' on th' blacktop.

In a flash April is on 'er knees beside me.

"Tucker! Are you okay? What do I need to do? What are we going to do about Mark?"

"I'm okay, child. Jes' help me t' git up."

Once I'm standing, I lean back against th' bed o' th' truck. "Did he rape you?"

"No, he never got my pants down."

"Then what happened?"

"I think I went sort of crazy. All I could think about was getting away from him. My hand was on the floor and I felt the whiskey bottle. I grabbed it and hit the side of his head with it. Then he just went limp."

I think fer a minute. "Well let's see if he's dead 'r alive."

Walkin' t' th' other side o' th' truck, I reach inside an' put m' hand on the boy's chest. I don't feel nothin'. Then I put m' finger on 'is throat. Nothin'. "He's sure 'nuf dead, April."

The sound that comes outta her is more like th' mewing of a kitten than it is somethin' human. "What are we going to do? I've killed Mark. They'll send me to prison!"

Grabbing both 'er arms, I give 'er a shake. Her head snaps back an' forth like a puppet's. "First thing you is goin' t' do is calm down. Git hold o' yoreself. Now ain't th' time t' be panickin'."

Her eyes lock onto mine and she takes a slow breath.

"Tell me what to do."

"You's fixin' t' walk back home, shower, an' go t' bed. I'll take care o' everything here."

A crease appears between her eyes.

"What do you mean?" She shakes her head. "We've got to call the sheriff's department and an ambulance."

"Ain't nobody callin' nobody. Y' hear? You do what I said."

"But—"

"Git home, now! I got things t' do an' not a lot o' time t' do 'em."

CHAPTER EIGHT

My youth is spent and yet I am not old,
I saw the world and yet I was not seen;
—*Chidiock Tichborne*

MARCH:

Standing on the rock ledge, I scan the world below. It is flat and uninhabited, all the way to the horizon. The wind is so strong and gusty that I have to grip whatever small crevices I find between the rocks to keep from being blown off my perch. I have no sense of fear. On the contrary, I feel peaceful and excited.

The voice of a little girl beside me startles me.

"Are you ready?"

I thought I was alone. I turn my head toward her voice. She, too, stands with her back against the rock cliff. Her blond hair swirls around her face, blurring her features.

"Ready for what?" I ask.

"To jump."

I realize that she is right, that is why we are here. "Sure, if you are."

"I've been ready. Let's do it."

She lets go of her grip on the rocks and leans slightly forward. When she turns her head toward me, the wind suddenly blows her hair back from her face. Recognition flickers.

I pull my fingers free from the crevices I've been gripping. Smiling, I lean forward. "On three. One . . ."

She puts her hand on mine and squeezes. "Levi?"

"Two . . ."

She squeezes harder and says more insistently, "Levi."

"Three." Gripping her hand, I jump, and in that moment realize that the voice calling my name is not hers. Terror seizes me. What am I doing?

A hand shakes my shoulder. "Levi, wake up. You're dreaming."

I awaken with a jerk and tumble from my dream into the present. It is Naomi. I turn my head toward her voice.

"Goodness," she says, "that must have been some dream. Your whole body was trembling."

"I think I knew her."

"Knew her? Knew who?"

I quiet my mind and try to drift back into my dream. Every thread that I pick up leads me to emptiness. Shaking my head, I say, "In my dream, there was someone I thought I recognized. But all that remains is a sense of recognition. Trying to recapture the pieces of the dream is as difficult as catching a baby pig."

Naomi slips the blood pressure cuff around my arm and begins rhythmically pumping it tight. Her cold stethoscope slips under the edge of the cuff. The *sssss* of the air escaping is the only sound in the room. Then she undoes the Velcro fasteners and pulls the cuff off. It is a familiar routine. She will next place her fingers on my wrist.

I wait patiently.

"Okay," she finally says, "so you had a dream and there was someone in there who you thought you remembered, right?"

"I think so. It was so real just moments ago but now I'm not so sure."

"Did you ever raise pigs?"

Until her question, the significance of my comment about catching a baby pig didn't even register. "I don't know. Do you think that means something?"

"It's just not a common expression, unless someone has ever tried to do that. I grew up on a farm as a kid and we raised pigs. Let me tell you, pigs don't have to be greased to be difficult to catch."

I hear footsteps enter my room. When the person doesn't speak, I say, "Who's there?"

"Oh, hi, Willie." Naomi says. "You've got to speak up when you come into Levi's room. He likes everyone to be announced."

"Willie has entered the room!" A black man's booming, bass voice echoes off the walls of my room.

"Fifty-eight," I say.

"Huh?" Willie replies.

"Oh it's this silly game Levi plays with everyone he meets," Naomi explains. "He tries to guess their age."

"Well then," Willie says, "if nothing else works out for you, Levi, you can always get a job with a carnival 'cause you guessed my age right on the barrelhead—fifty-eight. That's amazing."

"How old am I?" I ask.

"Lord, boy, I ain't no good at that kind of stuff," Willie replies.

"Don't even try to get out of it, Willie," Naomi says. "He'll pester you to death until you give him a guess."

"Well," Willie begins, "if I had t' make me a guess, I'd say somewhere around oh let's say twenty-six or -seven. How close am I?"

"Nobody knows," I answer. Tapping the front of my head with my index finger, I add, "It's all empty up here. Or else what is up there is so scrambled that I can't make any sense of it."

"Sure enough?"

"It's true," Naomi confirms. "But enough with this circus act. We've got work to do. Today's a big day for you, Levi. We're going to get you up out of that bed and see how you do."

Excitement and fear race each other to the center of my chest. "How come nobody warned me?"

"Because all you would have done is lie awake all night thinking about it," Naomi explains. "It's better this way. Anyway, that's why Willie is here. He's going to help us. Come on over here, Willie."

Willie steps closer to my bed. A hand picks up my hand and shakes it.

"Nice t' meet you, Levi."

His hand is so big that his fingers nearly reach all the way around my hand. Reaching with my other hand, I feel his arm. His biceps feel as big as my thigh. From my position I cannot reach his shoulder. "Nice to meet you, too." Turning my head toward Naomi, I say, "If you thought I was Sasquatch, what do you call this giant?"

Willie laughs. "Now be nice, Naomi. Don't tell this young boy all the awful names you call me."

In a loud whisper, Naomi says, "I'll tell you later, Levi."

Willie laughs again, but this time I have the sense that I've heard it before.

"Are you ready to try this, Levi?" Willie asks.

"Yes and no. I guess I'm a little scared of not knowing what's going to happen."

"It's the not knowing that scares all of us," Willie says.

I feel my covers being pulled off my bed. The bed whines and creaks as its electric motor raises me to a sitting position. Willie's arm slides under both my legs and he turns them toward him. My left leg dangles off the bed while the cast on my right leg keeps it rigid and sticking out.

"Here's what I'm going to do," Willie says. "I'm going to straddle both your legs and put my arms around you under your arms.

You put your arms around my neck. Then on three we're going to stand you up. You just hold on to me, lean on me, whatever you need to do. All we want to do is stand still. Okay?"

I feel a bead of sweat on my upper lip. Where is my security blanket? "Naomi?" I say.

"I'm right here."

She is very close, perhaps right beside Willie.

"It's okay," she says. "Willie is good at what he does. Trust him."

Raising my arms like a baby toward its mother, I say, "Let's do it."

Willie's thick arms surround me securely. I put my arms around his neck.

"Remember, on three," he says. "One, two, three."

I lean forward and Willie straightens up, lifting me from my bed. The tile floor is cold on my bare foot. The feeling of my weight balancing on my legs causes me to wince. I draw a quick breath and blow it out audibly.

"You're doing good, Levi," Naomi says. "Just use Willie, don't try to do it all on your own. How do you feel?"

"Like the room is tilting. I feel like if Willie wasn't holding me, I'd fall down."

"Yeah," Willie says, "I can feel him leaning to the left on me."

Sweat trickles down my temples. "Let's try to take a step."

"I don't know 'bout that," Willie says. "What do you think, Naomi?"

"The doctor told me to see what he could do," Naomi answers. "If he wants to try, you lead the way."

I feel Willie moving away from me while still keeping his grip on me.

"Come to Papa," he says.

Trying to calculate the degree to which the room is tilting, plus the extra weight of the cast on my right leg, and trying to figure out which foot I should lead with, I suddenly feel like all my circuits are overloaded and a breaker is about to trip. I don't know what to do next. But the upper half of my body is already leaning in a forward direction without realizing the bottom half is engaged in a board meeting to determine how to proceed. I'm feeling out of control. Must keep in control; that now-familiar mantra appears again.

"I think I'm fixing to fall," I say.

"Go ahead and fall," Willie tells me. "I won't let you."

Without warning, all my muscles desert their posts and I collapse forward. Willie steps into me and lifts me. My feet clear the floor.

"I've got you, big boy," Willie says. "It's nothing to be concerned about. This was just a test run. We had to get an idea of what kind of work we need to do with you."

He sets me on the edge of my bed and releases his hold on me. A cool, damp washcloth rubs across my face.

"Here," Naomi says, "use this to wipe your face. You look like you've been working in the heat of summer. Looks like you two have your work cut out for you."

"What does that mean?" I ask.

"Willie is a physical therapy assistant. It's his job to whip you back into shape."

"It's true," Willie adds. "We gonna be seein' a lot of each other. Everyday, you and me, doing one step at a time. You ain't lazy, are you?"

I puzzle over his question. "You know, I don't think I am. At least I don't feel like I am."

"I don't think you are either. Young man built with a body like yours has not been a stranger to hard work. But I'll push you to your limit, 'cause that's my job."

"You do your job," I say, "and I'll do my best to keep up."

"Your best, that's all I'm asking," Willie replies.

CHAPTER NINE

Signs are my food, drink are my tears;
Clinking of fetters such music would crave;
Stink and close air, away my life wears
Innocency is all the hope I have.
—Sir *Thomas Wyatt*

TUCKER:

It's five o'clock in th' mornin' when I drive back through Dresden. Before headin' toward home I pull up t' th' well-lit but deserted car wash an' drive into one o' th' vacant bays. Gettin' outta m' truck, I reach in m' pocket an' take out a handful o' quarters. I grab th' wand and slip the quarters into th' control switch. I make sure th' setting is on "Soap." Immediately th' spray explodes from th' end o' th' wand.

Droppin' the tailgate o' th' truck, I begin washin' out th' bed. I watch as the white foam, streaked with red, rushes over th' tailgate an' into th' drain underneath. Only when I don't see no shade o' red 'r pink in th' rinse water do I finally shut the wand off and return it to its holder.

I git back in m' truck and rest m' head on th' steerin' wheel. "Lord God an' Jesus above, what I done, I done fer April. I ain't askin' forgiveness fer it, 'cause I don't deserve it. You done already give me more grace an' mercy than I know what t' do with. I'm a bad woman an' have done bad things. Hell is waitin' fer me, no doubt. But April is th' one I'm worried 'bout. She don't deserve bad things. Her life ain't been easy. Please don't hold it against 'er fer what she done. She surely didn't mean to. Besides, if that boy tried what April says he tried, then he got what he deserved. Least, that's th' way I see it. This may be th' last time I'll be talkin' t' y' 'cause I ain't got th' heart t' face y' an' feel th' disappointment y' must be havin' 'bout me. Amen."

Sittin' up, I wipe th' tears off m' face.

When I walk into my trailer I notice the kitchen clock says it's ten 'til six. After puttin' on some coffee, I go into m' bathroom an' take a shower. I stand under th' water, lettin' it chase th' chill outta m' bones. Once th' feelin' comes back t' my toes, I scrub myself clean.

With fresh clothes and clean socks on, I go back into th' kitchen an' find April sittin' at th' table. Her hair looks like a bale of wheat straw that fell off th' wagon an' burst outta th' strings holdin' it in place, no two strands is layin' in th' same direction. Black streaks run down 'er cheeks where 'er mascara got wet, an' there's dark circles under 'er eyes. This ain't th' cocky teenager that come home yesterday. This here is a scared little girl.

"Mornin', April. You's up mighty early fer a Saturday. Want a cup o' coffee?" She don't act like she heard me. She's starin' at something, but it ain't inside our trailer.

I git th' milk outta th' refrigerator an' mix it with some coffee in a cup. I set it in front o' her. "Sip on this while I fix us some breakfast."

She latches on t' my hand like a drownin' woman grabbin' a rope.

"Where have you been all night?" she asks. "I checked in your room more than once and you were never there. And the truck was gone, too."

I pat 'er hand an' pull free from 'er grasp. Turnin' t' th' stove, I switch on the eye an' set th' cast iron skillet on it. Over m' shoulder I say, "Girl, you must a had bad indigestion last night that give you nightmares, 'cause I don't know what you're talkin' 'bout." I put four bacon strips in the skillet and lower the heat.

"What did you do with Mark's truck?" she asks. "What did you do with Mark?"

"Mark?" I shake m' head. "April, you ain't makin' no sense. I ain't seen Mark since I picked you up from school yesterday afternoon." I put my hand on 'er forehead. "You ain't got no fever, do you?"

April's eyes search my face, scanning one eye an' then th' other an' then my mouth. Her chin begins t' quiver.

"Don't try to make me feel like I'm crazy. I know what happened last night. And it wasn't a dream!"

Turnin' th' bacon over with a meat fork, I say, "Well why don't you tell me what happened, 'cause I'm th' one in th' dark it appears."

"I killed Mark Allen! He tried to rape me and I killed him. And you sent me home."

"Well don't y' think if I was there, that I'd remember you killin' him?"

April puts 'er hands on th' sides of 'er face an' shakes 'er head. Suddenly she looks at th' palm o' one of 'er hands. Thrustin' it my direction, she says, "And how do you explain this?"

Deep red cuts crisscross 'er open hand.

"Don't you remember?" I say. "After supper last night you was helpin' me clean up th' dishes an' you dropped yore tea glass. You was careless 'bout cleanin' it up, got in too big a hurry, an' messed up yore hand. How does it feel this mornin'?"

She turns 'er hand t' look closer. Uncertainty shows in th' corner of 'er eyes.

"A tea glass?"

"That's right. We might shoulda taken you t' the 'mergency room at th' hospital, but you said it didn't hurt all that bad."

Shakin' 'er head, April looks at me an' says, "But Mark's truck—it was down by the river. I snuck out through my window and met him there."

I reach inside th' 'frigerator an' bring out eggs. "You want yores scrambled 'r fried?"

She has that distant look in 'er eyes again, an' she's frownin'.

I crack th' eggs in a bowl and stir them before pouring them into th' bacon grease. Silence fills th' kitchen.

When I turn back toward 'er with our plates, she is lookin' uncertain again.

"Nightmares? You think I had a nightmare about killing Mark?"

"That's th' only thing I can figure. Dreams is strange things, April. An' yore memory can play tricks with you, too. You jes' need t' ferget 'bout all them bad things. Now eat yore breakfast. We got a big day today."

"Big day?"

"You forgot, ain't y'? Smiley Carter's comin' today t' help us plant our taters."

CHAPTER TEN

Send me some Token that my hope may live,
Or that my easelesse thoughts may sleep and rest.
—*John Donne*

APRIL:

I wince when the water from the shower runs over the cuts on my hand and the most recent *M* carved on my thigh. Using my index finger, I trace the scab. Gritting my teeth, I rub harder and harder until the scab peels off and blood starts running down my leg. I feel nothing.

I turn to face the showerhead and the water hits me in the chest. I grip the handle of the faucet and begin slowly turning it toward Hot until the heat stings. As my skin adjusts to the temperature and replaces pain with numbness, I turn the faucet further to the left until it is completely hot water sluicing down my body. Steam so thick I can barely see fills the stall.

Images flash through my mind as if I'm looking through the View-Master I used to play with when I was little. A fog bank, Mark's truck, his bleary-eyed face, him grabbing my breasts, my head banging against the window, the whiskey bottle smashing against the side of his head, him lying on the floorboard. I watch the scenes dispassionately, like a commentator reporting on a murder trial.

A dream? How could such vivid images be a dream? But Tucker had been so calm about it. She couldn't have just made that up. I've got to call Mark on the phone. That will settle my mind.

The steam begins to clear as the hot water tank empties itself. Hot turns to warm, to lukewarm, to cool, to the icy temperature of well water. I begin to shiver.

"April, are you all right?"

Tucker's voice slices through the locked bathroom door. I believe her voice could penetrate a locked bank vault full of hostages. "I'm getting out," I call back.

"Okay. I'll meet y' at th' barn. Dress warm. It's kinda cool this mornin'."

"Yes, ma'am."

My body shakes uncontrollably due to the drop in my core temperature. Gripping the faucet handle with both hands, I shut the shower off. Stepping out of the shower stall, I begin toweling off, being careful not to disturb the freshly clotted wound on my thigh.

On my way to my dresser I turn on my stereo and slip an Aerosmith CD into the tray. After a couple seconds, the raucous music bursts through the speakers, making me feel prickly all over. Goose bumps run up and down my body, while at the same time my nipples flex outward. I scrub my body hard with the towel and the resulting increased blood flow smoothes out my sandpaper-textured skin.

I slip on a pair of faded jeans and an old sweatshirt. Once I put on my sweat socks, I walk to the back door and put on a pair of mud-caked rubber boots. Slipping on my cotton jersey gloves, I head out the door and walk to the barn.

As I get closer to the barn, I hear Smiley Carter's tractor approaching from down the road. We arrive at the turnoff to the barn at the same time. He slows to a stop, his bright smile beaming across his black face.

"Look who's gotten outta bed with the chickens," he says. "It's mighty early for a teenager on a Saturday."

I've loved Smiley Carter ever since the day I met him. His strength and joy for life always had a way of making me feel safe and hopeful. When I was little he would pick me up and throw me so high that it would take my breath. It was terrifying and exhilarating. Landing securely in his arms, I would find my voice and squeal with delight.

Despite my gloomy mood and scrambled mind this morning, I manage a smile. "Tell me about it. Why we have to get up so early to do this I'll never understand. Looks to me like the potatoes would go in the ground just as easy after lunch as they do first thing after the sun comes up."

Laughter bubbles out of Smiley as easily as fizz out of a shaken-up bottle of Dr Pepper.

"That's just Tucker's way," he says. "She's done it this way ever since she was a child and there ain't no sense in trying to change her. Climb up here with ol' Smiley Carter and ride with me the rest of the way."

I grip the fender with my left hand while offering my right hand to Smiley. He scoots his foot so that I can place my boot on the footrest. I bounce a couple times to get some momentum going. Sensing my timing, Smiley grips and pulls me up. I land safely on the rear axle.

"Hold on now," he says.

I grip his shoulder with one hand and the fender with the other as he takes off slowly.

Tucker watches us approach. Resting at her feet are a washtub, a two-gallon plastic pail, and a bulging burlap sack.

For an old woman, Tucker has very few deep creases on her face. That's because she shows very little expression. Nobody can read Tucker's face as good as I can and as we pull up in front of her I can tell she is pissed off. But there is something else. The tiny furrow between her eyes signals fatigue or maybe worry.

"Must be nice havin' a chauffeur t' drive you over here," Tucker says to me.

God, she has a way of making me feel like someone has rubbed me with coarse sandpaper! Nothing's ever easy or simple with her. "I didn't see how it hurt anything to ride over here. It's not like I planned it or anything like that."

Shutting off his tractor, Smiley steps off and says, "And good mornin' to you, too, Tucker. Why, yes, it is a fine mornin' and no, it wasn't no trouble to come over here and help you plant your taters."

As he's talking, he limps straight toward Tucker. Arthritis has set up in his left knee in the last year. I know what's coming. It's something he's done ever since Ella died.

When he gets in front of Tucker, he throws his arms around her in a bear hug. "I love you, Tucker. Now, you tell me you love me." He steps back expectantly.

As she always does, Tucker brushes herself off as if he has contaminated her. "Ain't no fool like an old fool an' lord knows you are old. I ain't never made no bones 'bout how I feel 'bout you an' there ain't nothin' changed 'bout that."

Grinning, Smiley looks at me and winks.

"She can't help herself. She's always had a thing for me. It's only because I have incredibly strong willpower that we ain't never got married." Peals of laughter erupt from him as he throws his head back.

"Are y' here fer a bunch o' foolishness or are y' here t' help with these taters?"

"Maybe I'm here for both," Smiley replies. He turns and looks at the garden plot. "Looks like it's dried good since I plowed it Tuesday. I'll go ahead and disk it while you two get the taters ready."

As he drives onto the turned furrows of dark earth, I squat beside Tucker and open the sack of seed potatoes. Without speaking or looking, I reach up and feel the handle of a knife placed in my palm. As I have done every year since I was six years old, I slice up the potatoes into the washtub.

Smiley finishes cutting the dirt into a fine powder at the same time I slice the last potato. He joins us at the washtub. Tucker stands quietly looking at the garden while leaning on her hoe.

I wonder if she is thinking about what I'm thinking about—the first time I saw Ella in this garden. She got on her knees and thrust her arms into the dirt up to her elbows. As I think about it now, I realize it was a very sensual experience for her. It was like she felt the energy of life coming from the earth's core. I've never met anybody like her.

I want to put my hands over my ears because, again, what's about to happen has become a ritual since Ella died.

Tucker closes her eyes and Smiley takes off his hat and bows his head.

"Ella, we's here again t' plant our taters. I know you're here an' listenin'. We still miss you ever' day . . . Ever' day."

Her voice always catches on those words. Get on with it! Let's finish this job so I can go back to bed!

"Lord God an' Jesus, bless this plantin' an' give us a good harvest when it's time. Amen."

"Amen," Smiley echoes.

I rub my thigh and make it sting.

Tucker walks toward the waiting humus as she hands the rake to Smiley. I fill the pail with potato slices and join them. In movements as practiced and precise as an orchestra's, Tucker digs a hole, I drop in a potato slice, and Smiley covers it.

We work in silence for a bit, then Tucker asks, "How's August gittin' along?"

"That boy, or that man, is about to finish up his senior year at UT, Knoxville. He's done real good. Don't see him as much this year as I used to. He says he's having to really bear down on his studies. He's trying to make grades good enough so he'll be accepted into a law school."

"I still can't believe he wants t' be a lawyer," Tucker says. "If he makes it, it'll force me t' stop talkin' bad 'bout lawyers in general."

The sound of a vehicle catches our attention and we turn to see a gray van slow in front of our trailer. A crack in the windshield runs from one side to the other. The right headlight is broken out and the right front fender is crumpled. A cloud of smoke seems to emanate from the belly of the van.

It pulls up in front of our trailer. A man wearing a red plaid shirt steps out of the passenger-side door and strides to our front door. Though we can't hear, it is obvious he is knocking. After a moment, he returns to the van.

"Who's that?" Smiley asks.

"How the hell should I know?" Tucker snaps.

Once again I feel myself tumbling down the rabbit hole. "I think it's Mark's stepdad."

CHAPTER ELEVEN

Heaviness in the heart of man maketh it stoop: but a good word maketh it glad.
—*Proverbs 12:25*

MARCH:

Sweat runs down the small of my back as pulsating music encourages me to keep synced to its beat.

"Come on, Plow Boy, just a few more feet."

Willie's voice urges me forward. Ever since that first day we met he's been calling me Plow Boy. When I asked why, he said it was because I looked like one.

"Yes, sir, drill sergeant, sir," I answer him. I place the tips of my crutches forward a couple feet. Gripping the handles, I swing my body and land my feet a little bit past the crutches. Trying to make use of my momentum, I move the crutches ahead as I am landing and swing forward.

"That's m' boy!" Willie cheers me on. "Just one more."

Panting, I say, "I can't."

"I ain't sure, but I think I heard somebody say, 'I can't.' Don't nobody tell that to Willie. Move it, Plow Boy."

Pushing through my exhaustion, I make one last desperate lunge forward. Willie steadies me by putting one hand on my chest and the other on my back.

"Did you other folks see that?" he calls out. "Give my boy a hand."

There is a smattering of applause, one whistle, and a weak "Atta boy."

In a whisper meant to be heard by all, Willie says, "Don't pay them no mind. They's all white folks. They don't know how to turn loose and let their voices be heard. But that don't matter 'cause you and I know you done good. Right?"

Still trying to catch my breath, I say, "How far did I go? And don't lie."

"Now you've done it. You've done hurt Willie to the quick. How can you accuse me of lying to you? To use a sayin' from my red-skinned cousins, I don't speak with a forked tongue."

I'm in no mood for banter, well meant or not. "Just tell me how far I walked, if you want to call it walking."

"You covered ten feet in one direction, turned around and covered ten feet in the opposite direction. That's twenty feet total."

"Help me sit down."

"'Help me sit down,' what?"

I know what he wants but I don't want to give it to him. "I'll do it myself."

Swinging one of my crutches in a wide arc, I feel it strike something to my right and hear the chair scoot. Gathering my crutches, I inch toward the sound until the cast of my leg strikes something. I turn around and begin lowering myself.

"You're gonna miss it," Willie says.

I freeze. Angry, frustrated, and afraid, I feel fresh beads of sweat burst out on my face. "Where is it? Move it for me."

"'Move it for me,' what?" Willie says calmly.

Standing up straight, I throw one of my crutches. Through clenched teeth I yell, "Please! Move it for me, please!"

"Glad to oblige," Willie says softly.

I feel the edge of the chair nudge against the back of my left leg and hear it make contact with the cast on my left leg. But with only one crutch I am helpless to seat myself. Sweat and tears sting my eyes. In a low voice I say, "I need your help, please."

I hear Willie move from behind me and I smell him in front of me. He slips his arms under my armpits.

"Just ease straight down, Levi."

Once seated, I feel my body trembling from the leftover effects of my adrenaline surge. A chair scoots across the floor until it stops in front of me.

"Listen to me, Levi," Willie says, "you cannot do this on your own. Even if you was able-bodied and could see. Nobody can do life on their own. There ain't nothing wrong with asking for help. As a matter of fact, a man told me one time that the best gift you can give someone is the opportunity to help you."

"But—." My voice chokes off. A feeling close to terror has gripped my throat. I cough to try and free up my vocal cords. "But I don't have anybody. I'm alone. It's just me and I've got to learn to do things by myself."

Willie's hand falls onto my shoulder and he grips my neck.

In a voice thick with emotion, he says, "I don't know what to say to you about that, except I'm really sorry. But I believe you are a man with a good heart and people with a good heart are not alone. Your past is going to come back to you and when it does you are going to find it filled with people who have missed you and who are eager to help you."

"But you don't know that," I counter. "What if my past is dark? What if I'm on the run? What then?"

"Then you'll come live with ol' Willie. I'll hide you out in my garage and feed you through a slot under the door."

I'm stunned by his callous reply.

Then he bursts into laughter. "Lord, I wish I'd had a picture of your face just then. You looked like the little boy whose ice cream has fallen off of his cone. I forget that you can't see my expression and tell when I'm just pulling your leg. Seriously, though, I don't have the answer to all your 'what if' questions. My grandmother used to call those questions the worryin' kind, and I try not to worry about things. Just taking care of what I have to do today is enough for me without adding the worry of what might be tomorrow. Now, let me go get you a drink of water and a cool towel to wipe your face with."

His chair scrapes the floor as he rises. I listen to his retreating footsteps. How can I not ask questions? Questions are all I have. Everyone keeps telling me that I will remember, but I sure haven't had any signs that that's going to happen.

I hear Willie speak to another patient as he walks across the room toward me. He places a cool, damp towel in my hands.

"Here, wipe your sweat off with this," he says.

Burying my face in the towel, I try to let its coolness pull all the heat out of me. I don't move for a few moments.

Willie speaks in a sympathetic tone, "Here Levi, take a drink of this."

He gently pulls the towel from my face and places a cup in my hand.

I take a big drink and hold it in my mouth before swallowing. Even though it had been warmed a bit from my mouth, I can still feel a cool sensation slide down my esophagus. The chill radiates through my chest and my breathing finally returns to normal.

After I drain the cup, I say, "Are you married, Willie? It's strange that I've known you for Hasn't it been three weeks now? And I don't know anything about you."

"Now this is a good sign," Willie replies. "You're getting curious about the world around you. Yes, it's been three weeks since we met and during that three weeks you ain't been thinking about nothing except yourself. Me and Naomi's talked about that. I know we're not the great and mighty Dr. Kate Kapperton, but we thought it was sorta odd that you ain't asked nothing about none of us."

"You're right," I say. "I don't know why I haven't. It just now struck me that I don't know anybody, or at least anything about anybody I know."

"So, let me see, you want to know about me, huh?" Willie replies. "Yes, I'm married and I have five children."

"Can I ask what their names are?"

"Sure, I don't mind. There's Calvin, Cleotus, Charles, Cincinnati, and little Matilda. We decided to use a different letter for Matilda. She pretty special because she was born premature and nearly died. So she had to be given a strong name."

"I like the way the name Matilda sounds," I say, "but it doesn't sound all that strong to me. Sounds sort of girlie."

"I agree," Willie replies. "But she's named after my great-grandmother, who was the strongest woman that ever lived. She raised all eight of her children by herself. Everybody around knew her, both black and white folks. She helped lots of women birth their babies. Everybody called her Mama. Her given name was Matilda but she was always called Mama Mattie."

CHAPTER TWELVE

Even in laughter the heart is sorrowful; and the end of that mirth is heaviness.
—Proverbs 14:13

APRIL:

I feel as if all my blood has drained into my feet and turned into concrete. The urge to run tugs frantically at my sleeve, but I find it impossible to lift my feet.

The gray van, leaning to one side because it's Mark's fat mother driving, makes its way slowly toward us. It's as if I'm a corpse waiting for the hearse to come and retrieve my cold body.

I clasp my hands behind my back and dig at the cuts in my palm.

Mark's mother cuts off the engine, or at least turns the key off. But the engine keeps coughing and sputtering like someone who has smoked for forty years. Finally, after one last hiccup, it dies.

The driver's door opens and Mark's mother disembarks from her ship. Once she lands on the shore the van rocks back, trying to correct its previously unbalanced alignment. Her shapeless, chartreuse dress glows like a lightning bug on a dark summer night. She is so obese that her arms stick out at forty-five-degree angles. In spite of the February cold she is wearing flip-flops. Like a hippo on land, she waddles toward us.

Tucker moves about ten feet in front of me and obscures Mark's mother's view of me, though I can still peek and see her.

Out of breath, his mother pants out her words.

"You must be Tucker."

Tucker folds her arms across her chest but doesn't reply.

"Well ain't you?"

"What business you got bein' here? We're busy plantin' taters an' ain't got time fer talkin'."

Flustered, Mark's mother looks expectantly to her right. Her eyebrows go up and her mouth opens. She then turns around to the van and yells, "Billy, get your ass up here! You said you'd be right behind me." Turning back toward us, she mutters, "He ain't worth the bullet it'd take to kill him."

As if suddenly remembering the reason for her trip here, she looks back at Tucker. "I'm Margaret Allen, Mark's mother."

"I know who you is an' who yore mama was an' yore grand-mama. Wasn't neither one of 'em worth killin'. Yore dad, though, was a good man."

Mark's mother's eyes pop so wide they look like they will fall out and roll across the ground. She tries to reply but can't put any words together coherently. "Who do . . . I . . . You better . . . The nerve." When she sees Billy come up beside her she turns on him. "Are you going to let this woman talk to me like that?!"

Billy looks like the country music character String Bean that Tucker showed me pictures of when I was little. Apparently over the years Mrs. Allen's tongue has filleted all the flesh off of Billy leaving him no more than a skeleton with skin stretched over it. Mark's told me stories about her going on for hours yelling and demeaning him.

Either bolstered by his wife's words or terrified of what might come next, Billy takes a half step toward Tucker and, in a high, quavering voice, says, "Now see here, Miss Tucker, there ain't no need for you to—"

"Oh shut up," Tucker cuts him off. Stepping toward the two of them, she adds, "State yore business an' then be off o' my place. We got work t' do."

Billy slinks back behind Mrs. Allen. She swats at him like she would a horsefly. No doubt from years of practice, Billy avoids the sting of her hand.

I notice Smiley Carter is moving in a circle and coming up to the side of the Allens.

"You're crazy just like everybody says," Mrs. Allen accuses Tucker. "I ain't looking for no trouble. I'm just lookin' for my boy, Mark, and wanted to know if you seen him lately."

"What business have I got with yore boy? Can't you keep up with yore own children? Sounds like a sad state of affairs t' me."

"Where's that girl of yours? I'll lay money down that she knows something. Where is April?"

Tucker's arms slowly uncross and fall to her side. I notice her fists are clenched.

Just as I'm about to step out from behind Tucker, Smiley Carter walks between the two women.

"Say your boy's missing, Mrs. Allen? Now that's a disturbing piece of news. How long since you last saw him?"

Thankful to have someone else to speak to, Mrs. Allen addresses Smiley. "He didn't come home last night. He spent the night with some of his friends Thursday and was supposed to come home yesterday."

"Well, you know how kids is," Smiley says. "He probably decided to sleep over with somebody and just forgot to call you. Hadn't he ever done something like that before? I know my boy used to do that when he was a teenager. I'd be scared to death something done happened to him and just about the time I was ready to go see the sheriff, my boy would come waltzing through the door like he was the King of Siam. I'll bet your boy's gonna do the same thing."

The thin voice of Billy comes from somewhere behind Mrs. Allen, "That's exactly what I told her."

Mrs. Allen does the best imitation that a four-hundred-pound woman can of a ballerina twirling around on one foot. However, her inertia can't be stopped and while she spies Billy and begins to whip him with her tongue again, her body continues to turn. Suddenly she loses her balance and begins tipping to one side, much like her van.

Her tiny feet shuffle amazingly fast to correct her tilting center of gravity, but the movement only succeeds in giving her more momentum. I feel like I'm in a lifeboat watching the *Titanic* sink, knowing everyone is helpless to prevent it.

I step out from behind Tucker to get a clearer view. When Mrs. Allen spies me, a look of confusion mixed with shock spreads across her face. I'm not sure if it's because she has seen me or if it's because she knows she's going down.

You'd think when someone that big falls down that it would happen quickly, but it's more like she's in slow motion. She screams.

Billy calls out, "Maggie, be careful!"

Smiley Carter takes a couple steps toward her but realizes that discretion is the better part of valor and stops short of reaching for her arm.

I start to run to help but Tucker's hand shoots out and grabs a handful of my jacket.

"Jes' stay right here," she says quietly. "Let 'er fall an' then we'll see 'bout 'er."

When she hits the ground she makes a sound like air rushing out of a deflating air mattress. Her body seems to flatten and spread, then it rebounds and finds its original rotund shape.

"Maggie!" Billy cries as he rushes to her.

I jerk free from Tucker and run to Mrs. Allen.

Smiley is the first one to her side. He kneels down to get a better assessment of any damages.

On the ground, Mrs. Allen starts waving her arms and legs. I suddenly have the image of a turtle lying helplessly on its back.

"Get me up! Somebody help get me up!"

Billy makes the mistake of getting close enough to his wife for her to grab the front of his shirt.

Jerking him off his feet, she yells, "Did you see what these people did to me?"

Unfortunately Billy lands spread-eagle on top of her. He partially disappears as he sinks into her fat. Then Mrs. Allen starts trying to buck him off, while screaming, "Get off me, you fool!"

Smiley and I look at each other and burst into laughter. I laugh so hard I can barely get my breath, while Smiley's laughter rolls like peals of thunder. When I look at Tucker, she is bent double. It isn't until she straightens that I see she is laughing, too, one of the few times I've ever seen her truly laugh with abandon.

I'm unexpectedly struck by what a serious life she has lived. What little she has revealed to me about how she grew up gives a portrait of deprivation and abuse. By the time she was my age she was on her own and raising my mother. It wasn't until Ella entered her world that much good ever came her way. Sitting on my heels, I stare at her, pleased to see her enjoying the moment.

Suddenly Mrs. Allen succeeds in bucking Billy off, and he lands broadside against me and Smiley. The three of us tumble in a pile. In spite of being surprised, this triggers a new fit of laughter from Smiley.

I manage to extricate myself from the tangle of legs and arms and stand up. Billy springs up next and the two of us extend our hands to Smiley to assist him. Still grinning from ear to ear, Smiley wipes his tears first and then grips our hands.

"I'm sorry, Mr. Carter," Billy says apologetically.

"Forget about him!" Mrs. Allen exclaims. "Somebody get over here and help me up."

She has managed to roll herself into a sitting position. Her face is crimson and there are mud stains on her dress.

Billy gives us a pleading look. He whispers, "There ain't no way in hell I can get her up by myself. I ain't even sure if all of us together can do it." He glances at Smiley's tractor. "We might have to use your tractor."

As we walk over to Mrs. Allen, Smiley says, "Come on over here, Tucker. We's gonna need all the help we can get."

"Why should I help somebody who's jes' tryin' t' cause trouble fer me?"

"'Cause you a Christian, that's why," Smiley snaps.

Smiley Carter's the only person I've ever known who can talk to Tucker like that and get away with it. She tolerates things from him that she doesn't tolerate from anyone else. I think that ever since Ella died the two of them have recognized the hole that was left in each other's life, and they've tried to step in and fill that emptiness. They would never say it, but they love each other. Not like a man and a woman but like best friends. It's a feeling I don't think I'll ever experience, which is fine with me because all it does is make you weak.

Following Smiley's directive, Tucker walks over to us.

"I'll grab one hand," Smiley says, "and you grab the other. Billy, you get behind her and push. April, you just stand back out of the way."

Once everybody is in place, Smiley says, "On three. One . . . two . . . three."

Tucker and Smiley lean back as they pull. I can hear Billy grunting somewhere behind Mrs. Allen. Nothing moves and for a moment I am afraid they are going to tear her arms from her body.

"Oww!" she squeals. "You're hurting me!"

"Push, Billy!" Smiley yells.

A muffled "I *am* pushing" drifts up as Billy buries his face into the folds of his wife's back.

"Let go!" Mrs. Allen cries. "It's hurting. Stop! Stop!"

Smiley and Tucker look at each other and, shrugging their shoulders, simultaneously let go. Mrs. Allen tilts backward and ends up on her back again in the turtle-on-its-back position, arms and legs flailing. Billy is nowhere to be seen.

Then, like a snake slithering out from under a rock, Billy's thin hand and arm slowly appear from under Mrs. Allen. He waves weakly.

"Oh my lord," Smiley exclaims. "We've got to roll her off of Billy before he smothers to death."

The three of us get on our knees beside her and, disregarding her protests, roll her onto her side.

Looking like he has been run over by a steamroller, Billy gasps, coughs, and gasps again. In a hoarse whisper he says, "Thank you." He sits up on his own and blinks slowly, like he is trying to get his bearings.

"How are you all going to get her on her feet?" I ask. I'm tiring of the circus and eager for them to be gone.

Looking at Tucker, Smiley says, "You still got that block and tackle and that old horse collar you used to have?"

"Sure," Tucker replies. "What y' got in mind?"

"Well if we can spread that horse collar wide enough so that it'll halfway fit around her, then fasten the block and tackle to my tractor, maybe we can winch her up."

"I know where it is," I say. "I'll go get it." Without waiting for an answer, I turn and jog to the barn. I'm thankful to distance myself from the intense and wide-ranging emotions that have been spilt in the last twenty minutes. Stepping into the dark hallway of the barn, I feel for the light switch and turn it on. Only then do I see the drying blood on my hand.

I look into my palm and see the wounds that I viciously reopened minutes ago. Calmness sweeps through my body and I smile. Squeezing my fist, I watch drops of blood escape and fall to the dirt floor.

I go to the tack room and retrieve the horse collar and grab the block and tackle off the barn wall as I exit.

By the time I get back to the group, Smiley has positioned his tractor in front of Mrs. Allen, who is once again sitting up.

His plan works perfectly and Mrs. Allen is slowly pulled up onto her feet. Her dress couldn't be any dirtier if she'd thrown it into a hog pen. With her pride more damaged than her body, and apparently having forgotten why she came in the first place, she doesn't say a word to anyone but jerks the horse collar off and heads to the security of her van. Jerking open the door, she gets inside amazingly fast, cranks her engine, and drives off.

Shocked, Billy stares helplessly at the retreating taillights.

CHAPTER THIRTEEN

Behold this fleeting world, how all things fade,
How everything doth pass and wear away;
Each state of life, by common course and trade,
Abides no time, but hath a passing day.
—Barnabe Googe

MARCH:

Levi, Levi."

Naomi's voice comes from the other side of a large canyon and the echoes reverberate in the distance.

"Levi. It's Naomi."

She is getting closer.

Suddenly I'm in the present. All the sounds around me mash up against me, giving me a sense of being squeezed. I know I'm not in my bed because the surface under me is as hard as concrete.

"I don't know what happened," I hear Willie say. "He must have gotten too hot during our workout or something."

"You pushed him too hard." Naomi's tone is harsh.

"Where am I?" I ask.

"Levi!" Naomi says excitedly. "Are you okay? Are you hurting anywhere? Don't try to move just yet."

My sense of smell filters in and lets me know I'm still in the workout room. I must be lying on the floor.

"What happened?" I ask.

"Levi, this is Willie. Are you hurt anywhere? We don't want to move you until we're sure you're not hurt."

I give my body a scan from head to toe and notice no new pains. "I think I'm fine. Help me to a chair." I quickly add, "Please."

I hear footsteps move to my head.

Willie says, "I'm going to sit you up, then Naomi and I will help you stand."

His strong hands slip under my armpits and he pushes me up and forward until I'm sitting.

"Still okay?" he asks.

I nod.

After Willie and Naomi help me into a chair, I ask, "Is someone going to tell me what happened? The last thing I remember is the ice water and cool towel you brought me. How in the world did I end up on the floor?"

"Based on what Willie's told me," Naomi says, "you passed out. It must have been from your workout. Maybe your blood pressure suddenly dropped on you."

"Yeah," Willie chimes in, "one moment you were sitting in the chair and the next you were out like a light and you slid right onto the floor. Scared me to death."

Something dances on the edge of my consciousness, but it is only a shadow, like a dream I can't recall the specifics of. Yet it has left the scent of a feeling on me. "There's something else," I say.

"Something else?" Naomi repeats. "Something else about what?"

"I don't know. It's like trying to catch a breeze in a jar. I can't get hold of it long enough to know what it is. Damn, it's frustrating!"

Naomi places her hand on top of mine.

"I know," she says gently. "Just give it some more time. Now, Willie, let's put him in a wheelchair and head back to his room. Dr. Niedenhaur is supposed to be coming by for a visit."

"Well lord knows we don't want to keep the pope waiting," Willie says.

I hear the sound of someone slapping skin.

"Ow!" Willie cries. "I'm reporting this to Human Resources. Abuse by a coworker."

"You better watch your tongue," Naomi says. "You've been in trouble before, you know."

As Willie rolls me through the hallways to my room, familiar voices call my name.

"I've took care of you again, Levi. Your meal is just as you like it." That's Cora with food services, who always gives me extra salt with my meals.

"How are you, Levi?"

"Good, Tina," I reply. She has only been out of nursing school for a month.

"Haven't been to see you in a while, Levi. I need to drop by."

That's Ginger, who works in the lab. "Keep your distance, vampire lady," I reply.

"Watch it, Naomi. Levi is mine." Charlotte, a nurse who prefers working nights on the weekend, is always playing up the male-female aspect of any situation.

"You guys are just going to have to fight it out over me," I retort.

The smell of whiskey and cheap aftershave drifts past. "What's up, Max?" I say. "Putting a shine on these floors today?"

"You know it, Levi," he replies.

"My gosh," Naomi says, "is there anyone who works here who you don't know?"

"Hey," I answer, "you guys are the only people I know. If you think about it, that's a pretty small number of people to get to know during the four weeks I've been here."

Willie slows and makes a sharp right-hand turn, signaling the arrival at my room. "Chair or bed?" he asks.

"I think I'll stay in the chair for a while, at least until after the pope has called on me."

Willie laughs.

"You still there, Naomi?" I ask.

"Yes, I'm here."

"So what's the good doctor coming by to talk about?"

"We'll know soon enough. He told me to find him when you got back in your room. I'll be back in a few minutes. Willie, can I see you in the hall for a second?"

"You hear that, Levi?" Willie asks. "That tone of voice does not bode well for this black man. If you don't ever hear from me again, be sure you request an investigation by the FBI, 'cause there's sure to have been foul play involved."

"I'll tell them that Naomi was the last person I saw you with." I pause for effect. "Oh wait, I don't think they would believe me, would they?"

Laughing, Willie calls out as he's leaving my room, "Remember Levi, the FBI."

The door clicks shut behind them. Initially silence fills the room. Then the tiny, familiar sounds that have become comforting to me begin filtering in: the soft whooshing sound of the heat and cooling duct in the ceiling over my bed, the slow drip of the shower-head in my bathroom, an ambulance siren whining as it pulls up to the entrance of the emergency room below my window, the muted intercom in the hallway outside my door.

I reach for and find the talking clock, something that Beth, the hospital social worker, got me from the Society for the Blind. I press a button, and it announces, "The time is ten twenty-two a.m." I press another button. The mechanical voice clarifies further, that it is "Tuesday, February the twenty-second."

There are two knocks on my door and the sounds of the hallway spill into my room as the door is swung open.

"Levi, this is Dr. Niedenhaur. Naomi tells me you had a bit of a spill this morning. How are you feeling?"

"I'm fine," I reply. "Don't worry, I'm not going to sue anyone."

"Uh, yes, well we certainly hope not."

The jerk can't even tell that I was only joking. I decide it's not worth the effort to try and explain because it'll probably fly over his head anyway. I wait on him to continue.

There is an awkward silence.

I hear Naomi clear her throat.

"Well," Niedenhaur finally continues, "the reason I've come by is to tell you that we've done for you all that we can here at this hospital. We're going to transfer you to another facility where your rehabilitation needs can better be met. You've been an excellent patient and I wish you the very best. Naomi has more of the details for you. Best of luck."

He takes my hand—his is soft and tiny—and shakes it. I listen to him exit the room and the door closing behind him.

I am stunned. Leaving here? Leaving the only world I know? Leaving Willie? Leaving Naomi? I feel tightness in my throat and a sharp stabbing pain in my chest. "Naomi? Did you know this was going to happen?"

"Everyone leaves a hospital eventually, Levi. You know that."

I think I detect a thickness in her voice. "But this is the only world I know. I guess I've sort of grown to think of this as my home."

The latch on my door clicks and someone enters the room and closes the door.

"It's me," Willie says. "You okay?"

"Okay? You want to know if I'm okay when I'm going to be torn away from all I know? How would you feel?!"

"I'd be scared," Willie says simply.

I hear Naomi sniff.

"This is the difficult side of working here or at any hospital," she says. "You get to know people, you become a part of their life, you care about them, and then they are gone. We cross paths at extremely emotional crossroads of people's lives, which only enhances the intensity of feelings. So it's normal to feel whatever you feel, whether it's fear, anger, sadness, confusion, or whatever."

Tears sting my eyes. My already-altered voice sounds even more unfamiliar when I speak. "And how do you feel?"

"I'm happy and sad, too," Willie says. "I'm happy because this means you've progressed so well that it's time for you to graduate to a better place. But I'm sad because I'll miss you, Plow Boy."

Naomi clears her throat before she speaks. "I guess I'm all over the place emotionally. But that's my right, isn't it, because I'm a woman? Like Willie, I'm happy and sad. But I'm also frustrated that I still haven't learned to keep myself distant from patients so that times like this won't hurt so badly."

"Come here, girl," Willie says.

I hear them move toward each other. I imagine Willie giving her a hug.

"But that's what makes you such a good nurse, too," he says to her. "You really do care about your patients, not like some of these people who are only here to draw a paycheck."

"So where am I being sent?" I ask. "What kind of place is there for blind, crippled people? A nursing home?"

"No, no," Naomi says. "Actually we've been able to secure you a place close by in one of the finest rehabilitation facilities in the United States. It's the Patricia Neal Rehabilitation Center in Knoxville. You have so many needs, Levi, and they can meet them all. There is nursing care, physical therapy, and counseling, too. And they have vocational rehabilitation to help you learn a skill so you can support yourself some day."

I hear her words but they are like the letters from a Scrabble game that have spilled onto the floor with no apparent connection to each other. I cannot see a pattern or make any sense of what she is saying. Tears begin to flow into my thick beard. They work their way through the coarse hair and run down my neck. My nose begins to drip.

When I reach for the box of Kleenex on the table beside my bed, my hand strikes my clock and knocks it clattering to the floor. "Shit!"

"I'll get that," Willie says. "I think I need one, too."

I listen to the tearing sound as he pulls a couple of tissues from the box then feel the box placed on my lap. Pulling out a handful of tissues, I wipe my face and blow my nose.

This is really going to happen. I am going to have to leave this place. The ache in my chest suddenly opens a door in my heart. Inside there is an old pain that is a mirror image of what I am feeling right now, but I don't know where it came from or how it got there. Old tears from deep within begin to flow. The emotional tsunami swallows me up.

CHAPTER FOURTEEN

Pleasant words are as a honeycomb, sweet to the soul, and health to the bones.
—Proverbs 16:24

TUCKER:

After I drop th' last spoonful o' wet biscuit dough on th' pan, I open th' door t' th' hot oven. The heat rises up an' warms m' face before I slide th' pan inside an' shut th' door. Turnin' around, I head t' April's bedroom.

When I put m' ear t' her door, I don't hear nothin'. I grip th' door knob, expectin' it t' be locked but it ain't. I ease open th' door an' step inside.

Th' soft gray of early mornin' gives jes' enough light fer me t' see th' usual scatterin' of 'er dirty clothes on th' floor. Holdin' m' breath so I can hear better, I listen t' April's soft breathin' comin' from 'er bed. I sit down on th' edge o' th' bed. She don't even move; sleepin' th' sleep o' th' young.

Oh, m' April, where's that little girl who used t' sit in m' lap while I drunk iced tea in th' porch swing a long time ago?

I reach out an' stroke th' tangled mat o' hair on 'er head. An image flashes in m' mind o' the Christmas she sung "Amazin' Grace" fer all of us after Ella helped 'er find 'er voice. That night she looked jes' like a china doll m' mama had when I was little, hair as shiny as a sweatin' horse an' skin as smooth as milk in a bucket.

She moans.

"April, it's Monday an' time t' get ready fer school. I gotta pan o' cat head biscuits in th' oven. They's yore favorite."

She rolls on t' her back an' rubs 'er eyes. She looks like a little raccoon with all that makeup smeared.

"Looks like somebody fergot t' wash their face last night."

She yawns an' says, "I was too tired last night. I just wanted to sleep."

Suddenly 'er eyes pop open wide.

"School! What am I going to do if Mark's not at school? What if Mrs. Allen shows up at school asking questions?"

She sits up.

"What am I supposed to do? I don't want to go to school today! Not today."

Pattin' 'er on th' cheek, I say, "T'day's jes' like any other day. Y' go t' school jest like y' always do. If'n that boy ain't there, that ain't no business of ours. Who knows, he might a run off jes' t' get away from that sow of a mother he's got."

Jes' like she did Friday night, April searches m' face t' see if she can 'cipher if I'm tellin' th' truth 'r not. Uncertainty blankets 'er face. It hurts me t' lie t' her face like this.

Standin' up, I say, "Have you still got that ol' nightmare stuck in yore head? I'm tellin' y', that must a been one bad dream y' had. Now y' get on up while I check on them biscuits. I opened a fresh jar o' homemade blackberry jelly. Y' know y' don't want t' miss that. Hurry up 'r you'll be late."

When April's legs swing out from under th' covers, I head on back t' th' kitchen confident she's gittin' outta bed.

They ain't no tellin' what's gonna happen at school t'day when Mark don't show up. My stomach's been clenched up all night jes' thinkin' 'bout it. As good as them biscuits and sausage smell I still don't believe I could eat a bite.

My hands is shakin' so bad th' coffee splashes on me when I pour a cup. I jerk m' hand back an' drop the cup. It lands with a crash and scatters across th' floor. "Damn! I'm sorry, Lord, that one slipped out."

"You okay?" April asks as she comes into th' kitchen.

Grabbin' the broom, I say, "Yeah, jes' butterfingers this mornin'. Have a seat. Them biscuits is fresh out o' th' oven. Eat 'em up."

As she sits down she pulls stragglin' strands o' hair outta her face an' slices open a biscuit.

"Who taught you how to make biscuits?" she asks.

"I guess I was makin' biscuits when I was 'bout half yore age. M' mama showed me how. That's at least one good thing I learned from 'er."

April licks th' jelly off th' side of 'er biscuit as it squeezes out.

"How come you don't ever talk about your parents and growing up? I mean, I know your daddy was mean and you all were poor, but weren't there any good things that happened?"

I look at th' locked doors on th' vault o' my childhood memories an' feel a mixture of anger and terror. I mentally squint t' see if I can find somethin' that I know April will enjoy hearin' 'bout. "Some o' my best mem'ries involve our horse, Betty. That horse could pull a plow as steady as a mule an' run as fast as th' wind, too. She hated m' daddy an' would always try t' bite him 'r kick him if she got th' chance, even though he'd beat 'er when she tried. She wasn't afraid o' nothin'. There ain't never been but one Betty. I remember thinkin' 'bout ridin' off on 'er an' never comin' back."

I notice April smilin' as she's listenin'.

"We should buy us a horse. It sounds like I would really enjoy having one."

"Well, y' know, I guess we could think 'bout doin' that. It might be good fer y' t' have some responsibility. Horses takes lots o' time an' attention. As strong as they is, they are a fragile animal when it comes t' infections an' stomach problems."

April puts both hands on th' table an' looks at me with dancin' eyes.

"Are you serious?! You mean we can get a horse?! Oh Tucker, I can't believe it. That is so cool!"

"Now all I'm sayin' is we'll look into it. I ain't priced no horses in years. Smiley Carter's got a cousin that's always swappin' and tradin' horses. I'll have him look into it."

April jumps up, comes 'round th' table an' throws 'er arms 'round my neck.

"Oh Tucker, you're the best!"

"I may be th' best, but you're gonna be th' last one t' school if'n you don't get it in gear." I slap 'er on th' butt fer emphasis.

She squeals and jumps.

Runnin' to 'er room, she calls back, "You grab the keys and be ready. I'll be out in a second."

I slip on m' jacket, get th' truck key, an' open th' front door. My heart turns t' ice. Standin' there is Sheriff Ron Harris.

CHAPTER FIFTEEN

My crop of corn is but a field of tares,
And all my good is but vain hope of gain.
—Chidiock Tichborne

APRIL:

A horse! I'm going to get a horse! I can't believe it! I must have caught Tucker in a weak moment because she hates spending money on something she doesn't think is useful.

I brush my hair quickly and slip on my boots. Grabbing my jacket, I race toward the front door, knowing that Tucker will be waiting for me in the truck.

Just as I arrive at the door I notice it isn't shut. I hear voices through the opening.

"Well they're concerned."

It's a man's voice that sounds familiar, but I can't quite place it.

Tucker says, "We don't know nothin'. I ain't seen him."

"What about April?" the man says.

Recognition strikes. It's Sheriff Harris. What's he doing here?

Suddenly Tucker closes the door. The voices become muffled and indistinct. I open the door and step onto the porch. Tucker frowns at me.

"Mornin', April," the sheriff addresses me. "How are you feeling?"

"Feeling? Uh . . . I'm feeling fine. Why?"

Tucker shifts her weight. "I told th' sheriff that you was feelin' a little under th' weather an' I wasn't sure you'd feel like talkin' t' him 'r if you was goin' t' school or not."

I wrinkle my forehead as I look at Tucker, trying to figure out what is going on. Just two seconds ago she was barking at me to hurry up and get ready for school. She knows I'm feeling just fine. I decide to say nothing. I return the sheriff's watchful gaze.

Holding my eyes with his, the sheriff says, "I'm here about Mark Allen. When's the last time you saw him?"

The blow from his question stuns me so that my heart stops beating. My mouth goes dry. I hear a roaring sound in my ears and tiny pinpricks of light dance around the edges of my vision.

Tucker's voice seems to come from far away. "Jes' tell 'im th' truth, April."

Slowly the stars disappear and the roaring subsides. Like a steam engine starting from a dead stop, my heart begins beating slowly and picking up tempo. "Why are you asking about Mark?" I ask. "Is something wrong?"

The sheriff's eyes are like lasers, unblinking. "Mrs. Allen called our office and reported him missing on Saturday. She said she last saw him on Thursday, but that he was supposed to come home on Friday. I told her we'd just wait until the weekend was over to see if he showed up before we started any investigation."

He finally releases me by blinking and turns to Tucker. "Teenagers are always changing their minds about their plans without telling their parents about it. If I went charging off investigating something every time one of them didn't come home when they said they were going to, I'd never get any work done. But Mrs. Allen called before seven this morning to say he hadn't been home and she hasn't heard a word from him since Thursday. She called some of his friends but none of them knew anything."

"That's what they said," Tucker remarks, "but who knows th' truth? They may be tryin' t' cover their own butts."

"True enough," the sheriff agrees, "but I thought I'd start asking around myself."

He turns his attention back to me.

"I know you and this boy have been seeing each other. My deputies have had to send you home more than once after they found you out by Davis Chapel church. You've been dancing on the edge of trouble for the past couple of years, April. It's time you grew up and started acting in such a way that would make both your grandmothers proud."

I grit my teeth in anger. Steel walls go up around me. "It's my life, I can live it any way I want, not that that's any business of yours. And you've got no right to bring up my grandmother Ella."

The air is so charged between the three of us that it would register on a voltage meter.

"There ain't no need t' get smart, April," Tucker says.

There's an edge in her voice and I glance at her, but she is looking at the sheriff.

"Look," the sheriff tries again, "everyone knows things haven't been easy for you."

"Shut up!" I snap. "I'm sick and tired of people saying that. I've had it just fine. Save your sympathy for someone who needs it. Unless you're going to arrest me, I've got to get to school."

I make a move toward the steps. The sheriff makes just enough of a shift in his position that I can't get by him without touching him. I'm close enough that I can smell the bacon and coffee on his breath.

"You still haven't told me when was the last time you saw Mark."

I take a step backward and pinch the *M*s on my thighs. Fixing him with a cold stare, I say, "If you must know, the last time I saw him was at school on Friday."

"And you all didn't have a date on Friday night?"

"Look, Sheriff," Tucker cuts in, "she done tol'ja that th' last time she saw th' boy was at school. You know how that boy's mama is. If I was him, I'd a run away from home a long time ago. There ain't but one thing in th' world that's bigger than she is an' that's 'er mouth. Maybe he finally decided t' make his move."

The sheriff ignores Tucker and says, "Some kids from school said you two were planning to get together Friday night."

"Who said that?! Nobody knows my business. People are just trying to make trouble for me."

"April never left home all weekend," Tucker says. "Me, her, an' Smiley Carter planted taters on Saturday an' we was lazy an' rested all day yesterday."

Giving his attention to Tucker, the sheriff says, "And so April has never snuck out of the house during the night to meet up with Mark or anyone else?"

Besides being angry, I'm scared, too. I feel like hitting and scratching the sheriff like a cat, but I also feel like jumping on that horse I hope to get and letting it run as fast as it can until no one can find me.

The sheriff takes a small step toward me, "Do you really think there's anything that goes on in this county that I don't know about? About you and your drinking? You and your marijuana smoking? And about you and Mark Allen?"

Tucker puts her hand on my chest and gently pushes me backward. Then she steps between me and the sheriff. Folding her arms across her chest, she says to the sheriff, "I believe we're done with this. You're jes' out on some kind o' witch hunt. If you already knowed somethin', you'd a done come out with it. If you're worried 'bout that Allen kid, why don't y' start by askin' questions over at his house? I wouldn't put it past her or that sliver of a man she's shacked up with t' have done somethin' to th' boy. You know, they might a had some kind o' insurance on him."

"You know, Tucker," the sheriff replies, "just about the time I think you've changed and turned over a new leaf, you show me just how big a fool I was to believe it. I'll leave, but I may be back again." Touching the brim of his Stetson, he turns and heads to his patrol car. He opens the door and pauses. "Oh, by the way, the boy's truck is missing, too. We've got an APB out on it, but you might keep an eye out for it, too." He nods toward Tucker's truck. "Your truck's looking unusually sharp for winter."

I glance at her truck and see that he is correct. I try to remember what it looked like over the past few days and figure when she may have washed it, but I never pay that much attention to how it looks so I give up the mental chase.

Tucker stands like she is carved out of stone and is just as silent.

Once he sees that she is done talking, the sheriff gets inside his car and drives off.

After he is out of sight, I step in front of Tucker and grab her arms. "It wasn't a dream. I knew it wasn't. Why are you lying? And what have you done with Mark's body?" But she is wearing the mask that is her trademark, a mask that is impossible to read.

"I done tol'ja what I tol'ja. It's jes' some sort o' coincidence that th' boy disappeared at th' same time you had yore bad dream. Now come on, you're done late fer school."

She walks past me and heads to her truck. I feel like I am losing my mind. Clenching my fists, I feel the sting in my right palm. I open my hand and look at the jagged cuts. That is real. Nothing else may be, but there is no explaining away my torn flesh. Even though I may cut myself sometimes, what I am looking at is no deliberate act. And I clearly remember when it happened. Like a clap of thunder in my head, the truth shatters the mirage that Tucker has been creating: I killed Mark Allen!

CHAPTER SIXTEEN

The things which I have seen I now can see no more.
—William Wordsworth

MARCH:

The only name I have is Levi. I'm sure you've got records some-where that tell you I have amnesia." Already I'm sick of this place and I've only just arrived. I don't like the way it smells and I sure don't like Miss whatever-her-name-is social worker who is asking questions that she already has the answers to.

"You've been through quite a lot over the past four weeks, that's for sure," she says. "And now you are being asked to adjust to another brand-new situation. I promise you that everyone here will do their best to help you. Our goal is to help you become as independent as possible, so we'll always be pushing and challenging you."

I hold up my hand. "I'm sorry, what did you say your name is?"

"Debbie Cooper."

"Well, look, Debbie, all you know about me is what you have written in my records. But I know things about you and I only met you a few minutes ago."

I detect no change in the pitch of her voice as she says, "Really? So what do you know about me?"

"You're about five feet, eight inches tall. You took a shower before coming to work this morning and washed your hair. You're wearing tennis shoes, jeans, and some kind of nylon top or jacket. You were not raised in this area but you've probably lived here for ten years or so. There is a ring on your left finger so I'm going to guess you are married. And as for your age I'd say you are twenty-five years old. Those are all the things that I know, but I'm going to guess you were athletic in high school and that you have been working here for less than two years. Oh, and one last thing. You didn't eat breakfast this morning."

Without warning, she takes my sunglasses off my face.

"Hey!" I snap. "Put those back on. You've got no business—"

"I had to find out for myself if you really are blind," Debbie says.

She begins to slide my glasses back in place.

I turn my head sharply and grab the glasses from her. "Do us both a favor and don't ever do that again. I don't like people getting in my personal space without permission."

"That's fair enough," she replies. "I apologize. I shouldn't have done that. I was just so shocked by how accurate you were with your description of me that I decided my coworkers were playing some kind of practical joke on me. You've got to help me understand how you knew all that."

"It's easy. Your height was given to me by how far above me your voice sounded when you stood by my chair. I can smell your soap and your shampoo, two different smells. One is sort of like lavender and the other more like strawberries."

"That's amazing. You're exactly right."

"I heard the squeak of one of your tennis shoes when you approached me. When you crossed your legs it sounded like denim. If you couple that with tennis shoes, jeans makes sense. And your top makes sort of a whistling sound, like nylon, when you move."

"It's a windbreaker," she explains. "So how did you get all that information just by listening to my accent?"

"Well you don't have the twang of people who were born and raised in this area but you do have some of the flat-sounding vowels. So you've lived here long enough to have started unconsciously mimicking the accents around you. I'm not sure where you grew up. I would guess that you grew up up north, maybe Chicago or somewhere in Michigan."

"Detroit," Debbie says.

"And you moved down here when you were a teenager, right?"

"This is the most amazing thing I have ever heard. Did you used to have a former life working for a carnival guessing people's ages and weights? Because if you didn't, you could sure make a fortune doing it now."

I laugh. "You're not the first person who's told me that in the last month."

"But you're wrong about one thing."

"What's that?"

"Having a ring on my left hand."

I'm puzzled. "But when you grabbed my wheelchair, I distinctly heard metal contact the metal of the left handle behind me. Didn't I?"

"Well," Debbie says, "you did. But it wasn't a ring on my left hand. You see, that's impossible because I don't have a left hand or a left forearm. I have a prosthetic instead."

Even though Debbie's voice contained no caustic tones, I feel like I've been slapped in the face. How could I be such a stupid fool!

"Look," I begin, feeling my face reddening, "I'm sorry . . . I didn't mean anything . . . I mean . . . that was stupid of me . . . I had no—"

"No you didn't," Debbie says evenly. "So you couldn't have meant anything mean by what you said. It's easy to make assumptions about people, though, isn't it?"

I tap the cast on my leg. "You see how big the bottom of this cast is with the heel on the bottom?"

"Uh, sure I do. Why?"

"Can you tell me how I was able to stick that whole thing in my big mouth and make a fool of myself?"

There is a pause before she understands my meaning, then she laughs. It's a nice laugh, sort of like tiny wind chimes.

"How do you think I felt when I took off your sunglasses?" she replies.

"Like a fool?"

"Exactly!"

"Yeah, I know the feeling."

Silence suddenly picks up the corners of our conversation and folds it up. Awkwardness takes its place. I sense her studying me like a slide under a microscope. I shift uncomfortably. "Man, I'll be glad when I get this cast off. You ever have an itch that you couldn't scratch?"

Her wind chime of laughter plays its fanciful song. "All the time. My hand and arm itch sometimes and there is no hand or arm there. It's weird. But I think I read somewhere that you'll be getting that cast off pretty soon. I'll tell you, though, you may wish you'd kept it on because when the cast comes off, the therapy will really kick in in earnest."

"You won't catch me crying uncle. And I can't imagine these physical therapists being any tougher than the one I had in the hospital. This huge black guy worked me like he was preparing me for a prize fight."

"Sounds like Willie Carter," Debbie laughs.

"Willie Carter? I don't know about his last name—funny that I never asked him—but the Willie I know is one awesome man and a no-nonsense slave driver when it comes to therapy."

Her laughter is now almost uncontrollable. She actually snorts a couple of times, she is laughing so hard. When she catches her breath, she says, "Willie does some work for us, too. You may not have escaped from his clutches like you thought you did."

"What?! Are you serious?" I feel emotions filling my chest until they reach my throat and my voice is choked off. I blink hard behind my glasses, trying to hold my tears back. After a moment I say, "Why didn't he tell me he would see me again?"

"It's hard to say for sure. Willie is a very wise man. But maybe, based on just the little bit that I know about you, he was trying to help you learn how to let go." There is a change in her tone of voice. It becomes more distant and hoarse. "I know he helped me do that one time."

CHAPTER SEVENTEEN

The heart of the prudent getteth knowledge; and the ear of the wise seeketh knowledge.
—Proverbs 18:15

TUCKER:

After I take April t' school, I come back home an' make a phone call. Then I make m'self busy takin' care o' chores 'round th' house.

Jes' as I'm finishin' eatin' m' lunch, I hear a car pull up. Walkin' t' th' door, I see Mary Beth Chandler get outta the driver's side.

Mary Beth is the onliest friend I've had since childhood. I knew she'd come when I called 'er this mornin'. I can always count on 'er.

To my surprise, th' door on th' passenger side opens. An old man gets out, but his back is t' me an' I can't tell who it is. Mary Beth walks 'round t' th' passenger side, reaches in, and hands th' old man a cane. With 'er help he gets turned around so she can close the door. He looks like he's on 'is last leg. When he lifts his face t' look at m' trailer, I'm shocked. In spite o' th' man's feeble condition an' aged face, I'd still know him anywhere. It's Judge Jack McDade!

As the two of 'em walk up t' m' porch, I step outside.

Mary Beth holds up 'er hand at me an' says, "Don't say a word. Not one. You called and asked for my help, so don't complain about how I do it. Now help me get him up the steps and inside."

Seein' Judge Jack up close like this, he reminds me of an old bull that's done been dehorned an' castrated, harmless all the way around. In spite of our past, I feel a little sorry fer him.

He looks at me but nothin' registers for a few seconds. Then he looks at Mary Beth.

"I told you," Mary Beth says to him, "that we were coming out here to see Tucker because of problems with your granddaughter, April. Remember?"

"April," the Judge says. "Yes . . . April." He looks at me. "And Tucker."

"Come on in, Judge," I say. "We'll see if I can rustle you up a cup o' coffee 'r somethin'."

Once we're inside an' Mary Beth gets the judge seated on th' couch, I say t' her, "Why don't you come help me get us some coffee?"

When we're alone, I whisper loudly, "What th' hell is he doin' here?!"

Mary Beth puts 'er hands on 'er hips an' looks up at me. "Do you want to help April, or not?"

"That's a stupid question that you know th' answer to. But what's that ol' man got t' do with it?"

"Because even though he's old and washed up, he has connections with important people who owe him favors. A phone call from him might open doors that neither you nor I could open. Let's just go sit down and talk through all this together."

Mary Beth always thinks she's right an' things have t' be done her way. She's always been like that, so I figure arguin' is a waste o' time. "Okay," I say, "we'll do it yore way."

Carryin' mugs o' black coffee, we traipse back into th' livin' room.

Mary Beth hands one o' th' mugs t' Judge Jack.

As the judge sips it, he peers over the edge an' looks at me. Setting the mug on his knee, he says, "Mary Beth says there's some trouble with our granddaughter, April. Is that so?"

'Bout th' only good advice I remember my mama tellin' me when I was little was that if y' ever tell one lie, you'll have t' tell another one t' cover it up. But I've done started down this road t' protect April, an' there ain't no turnin' back now. "Yes sir, Judge, that's right. It's like I was tellin' Mary Beth, April's not doing no good in school. Her grades is lookin' real bad an' she gets in trouble fer skippin' class all th' time. I'm afraid if somethin' ain't done, she ain't gonna graduate. I'm worried t' death 'bout 'er."

Suckin' his teeth, the Judge says, "I knew she should have come to live with me after Ella died. I could have provided her with so much more."

I feel like someone done stuck me with a cattle prod. I'm on m' feet. "Look here, ol' man—"

Mary Beth springs up outta her chair. "Hold it right there, both of you! I knew this would probably happen, but I thought maybe we might have at least a few civil words before you all took your knives out."

I look over th' top o' Mary Beth's head at th' judge as he calmly sips his coffee. Still as arrogant as ever!

He looks up at me an' says, "She's right. What's done is done and I should have kept my opinion to myself."

That's prob'ly as close to an apology as he can give, so I say, "All right then," an' take m' seat.

"One thing I thought about," Mary Beth says, "is that April is getting close to the age of eighteen. And once she makes it there, there isn't much we can force her to do. Isn't that correct, Judge?"

We both look at him, waitin' fer an answer, but he jes' sits there starin' into space. It's like all of a sudden, he ain't there.

Mary Beth looks at me, her eyebrows raised.

Maybe Mary Beth is smarter than me, but even I can see that all th' worker bees in his brain is out t' lunch. I take m' index finger an', pointin' at th' side o' my head, make circles with it.

Mary Beth scowls at me. Then she puts 'er hand on his arm an' says, "Judge? Did you hear me?"

His eyes slowly refocus on th' room an' he looks at th' two of us like he ain't never met us before. "Yes?" he says.

"It's Mary Beth and Tucker, Judge McDade, and we're talking about April, your granddaughter. Remember?"

He blinks his eyes a couple o' times an', jes' like that, I can tell he's back here with us. "You are correct. Once the girl reaches the age of eighteen, she's free to make her own choices. But if she's a minor, we can use the power of the courts to force her into situations she might otherwise resist."

Mary Beth gives me a satisfied look of "I told you so."

I shrug m' shoulders.

Still lookin' at me, she says, "So what did you have in mind for April?"

"I think she needs t' be sent off somewhere, like t' one o' them places that takes troubled kids an' helps 'em with their problems. A place where she'll have t' stay fer several months."

The judge an' Mary Beth look surprised.

"April has got lots o' problems," I continue. "She's prob'ly needed help fer a while, but I kept thinkin' she'd work 'er way outta them. Now I'm afraid I've waited too late."

Judge Jack frowns. "Why not just let her come live with me? Perhaps she needs to have a father figure in her life, someone who can give her a firm hand."

This ain't goin' th' way I was hopin' it would. I can feel some sweat poppin' up above m' upper lip. "No, I think she'd be better off gettin' plumb away from here. She's done got 'er a bad reputation at school an' tryin' t' live down a reputation is too much of an uphill climb. I should know." I turn t' Mary Beth.

She, too, is frownin'. "Hmmm," she says. "This sounds more serious than I thought. The problem is, I don't know of any such places in West Tennessee. Do you, Judge?"

He shakes his head. "No, no, nothing like that."

"Well," Mary Beth says, "before I came out here I decided to give a friend of mine a phone call to see if she would have any suggestions. Her name is Dr. Andrea Sydney. She was an intern under me when I worked at DCS, a very bright girl who decided to go on to medical school and become a psychiatrist. We've sort of kept in touch through the years. Now she works at the Patricia Neal Rehabilitation Hospital in Knoxville, but she does all kinds of consultant work. She's very much in demand."

Finally this conversation is movin' t' where I was hopin'. "So what did she say?"

"It turns out she's on the board of directors of a place just like you describe. It's called Spirit Lake, and it's right next to the Smoky Mountains National Park. She said it is a therapeutic treatment facility for teenage girls who have both behavioral problems and problems with depression or anxiety, things like that. They also make sure they keep up their school studies."

The judge says, "The name *Spirit Lake* makes it sound like some kind of religious cult sort of place."

"Dr. Sydney would not be involved in anything as extreme as that," Mary Beth says. "But she did say that one of the things that is emphasized there is the spiritual life of the girls and their need to make a connection with God."

"Well, th' good Lord above knows April needs t' get t' know him," I chime in. "I ain't been able t' get 'er t' go t' church with me fer over a year."

Things go quiet as we all mull things over. Then an important question comes t' my mind. "How long do th' girls stay there?"

"Dr. Sydney says the average stay is six months, though some are there for a year."

The judge clears his throat. "What about security issues? Is this a safe place? And what about privacy? I don't want people knowing that April is there."

"My guess," Mary Beth says, "is that it is very private because it is ten to fifteen miles from the closest town. And I'll bet that Dr. Sydney has made it clear that no information is given out to anyone who might inquire about one of the girls. You know yourself, Judge, that even if an officer of the law showed up, the girls are protected by laws of privacy and anonymity."

Mary Beth has rung th' bell that I've been listenin' fer. "That settles it. Spirit Lake is where she's goin'. How soon can we get 'er there an' how do we go 'bout doin' it? Th' sooner th' better."

Mary Beth turns t' the judge. "That's why you are here, Judge. Because I'm afraid she's a risk for running away, even jumping from a vehicle if we try to take her, we need to come up with an ironclad plan to make this happen."

He don't say nothin', an' at first I think he's checked out again. Then I see his eyes is still focused an' he's frownin' like he's thinkin'.

After a minute 'r two, he says, "The most surefire way is to contact the law enforcement from wherever Spirit Lake is closest to. Find out if they might be transporting a prisoner from there to a jail close by. Then they can put April in the back of their patrol car for their return trip home. I can take care of all that with just a couple of phone calls."

"And I'll call Dr. Sydney," Mary Beth says, "to find out how we can manage all the paperwork and forms via my fax machine at home. That way no one from here will have to make the trip to East Tennessee."

I am dumfounded. It's really goin' t' happen. April's gonna be swept away from here before trouble shows up at m' door. Unexpected tears sting m' eyes. I pull out m' red bandanna an' blow m' nose.

Jes' then the phone rings.

I walk over an' pick up th' receiver. "Hello, this here is Tucker." I listen fer several moments. Hangin' up the phone, I turn t' Mary Beth an' the judge. "Ya'll better hurry an' get t' work. That was th' school. There's been trouble with April. I gotta go see 'bout it."

CHAPTER EIGHTEEN

Hatred stirreth up strifes: but love covereth all sins.
—Proverbs 10:12

TUCKER:

As I pull into th' parkin' lot of April's school, I see at least three police cars with their blue lights flashin'. This ain't a good sign. I knowed th' principal said there was trouble, but I didn't expect t' see this.

When I git outta m' truck I can hear somebody screamin' an' cussin' like a sailor. I steel myself fer th' worst an' walk toward th' school buildin'. Jes' then an amb'lance careens off th' highway an' heads up th' drive t' the school building, barely missin' me as it speeds past.

Gittin' closer, I see Officer Warren, who I thought had retired ten years ago, openin' th' door t' a squad car. Half o' his shirttail is hangin' out, an' th' bloody handkerchief he's holdin' t' his nose tells me he prob'ly wishes he had retired. He ducks inside th' car an' grabs th' microphone t' his radio.

I'm gettin' closer t' whoever is screamin'. At first I feared it was April, but I can tell now that it ain't.

Then suddenly I see what looks like a wad o' people. Arms an' legs are at ever' angle. There's blue uniforms and flashes o' chartreuse in amongst them. The officers' faces is the color o' beets. An arm as big around as a small hog an' as flabby as a deflated inner tube shoots out from th' pile an' knocks one man's eyeglasses off his face.

Margaret Allen! Nobody told me Mark's mama was here at th' school. My chest starts hurtin'. I'm scared fer April an' what that fat cow might a done t' her. She'd better hope April's all right, cause what she don't know is that I've slaughtered hogs before an' I can do it again.

'Bout that time, a police officer comes outta th' school leadin' Mark's stepdad, Billy, whose hands is handcuffed behind him. One o' the officers wrestlin' with Margaret looks at the officer passin' by an' says, "Throw him in the back of a cruiser and get back here to help! This woman's so round there's nothing to grab hold of to move her along."

Not seein' April anywhere, I head into th' buildin', where I'm met by th' vice principal, but I don't remember his name.

"Mrs. Tucker, I'm so glad you came quickly after I called. We've had a serious—"

"Shut up an' show me where m' April is. Is she all right? 'Cause she better be 'r somebody's gonna have t' deal with me."

"Look, Mrs. Tucker, there's no need for you to—"

"Tucker!" A woman calls from down th' hallway.

Me an' the vice principal turn in 'er direction. When she gets close enough t' see 'er in th' light, I smile in spite o' th' tension I'm feelin'. She walks up t' me an' we hug. "Hi, Elizabeth. You're as pretty as ever. How Mary Beth could a had a girl as pretty an' tall as you is a mystery t' me."

"You're sweet, Tucker. But we've got serious problems here. April is in my office. Let's go."

Without another word, Elizabeth turns an' starts walkin'. I follow 'er down a couple o' hallways 'til she stops in front of a door that says Guidance Counselor on it. Takin' a key from 'round 'er neck, she opens the door an' steps back fer me t' go in first.

When I step inside, April is sittin' in a chair. She's got 'er feet pulled up in t' th' chair. Her knees hide 'er face. I can see 'er peekin' through th' crack between 'er knees.

April drops 'er feet t' th' floor an' like a snake sendin' out a warnin', she hisses, "What's she doin' here?"

Elizabeth motions fer me t' sit in a chair an' she takes one, too. "Tucker is your guardian, April. She is who I am obligated to call in emergencies."

April snorts defiantly. "I'll tell you what the emergency is. The emergency is that I murdered my boyfriend but this woman, who actually saw him, is acting like it never happened."

Th' pain in m' chest feels like a sharp knife an' I'm suddenly havin' trouble breathin'. I look at Elizabeth. "She had this really bad nightmare, y' see, an' she jes' can't get it outta her mind. She ain't hardly slept in th' past two 'r three nights 'cause of it. Don't pay 'er no mind."

Elizabeth is quiet. Her face is expressionless, but she is studyin' me closely.

"What I wanta know," I say, hopin' t' change th' subject, "is what's goin' on with the commotion out front? Did that woman show up tryin' t' make trouble fer April?"

Elizabeth seems relieved t' be able t' talk 'bout somethin' she is certain of. "This morning Mrs. Allen and her husband came to the school to see if Mark had shown up. She hasn't seen him since last Thursday. She is very distraught about it and was very emotional when she arrived here."

Elizabeth pauses t' glance at April. "Unfortunately, April was taken to the principal's office about the same time over an incident that occurred during one of her classes. And—"

"Wait a minute," I say, holdin' up m' hand. "What kind o' incident are we talkin' 'bout?"

"Why don't you tell her what happened, April?" Elizabeth asks.

April makes some sort o' gruntin' sound.

Elizabeth keeps lookin' at April like she's expectin' 'er t' talk, but I know better. Once April don't wanta talk, she ain't talkin'.

"April, I think you need to be the one to tell this. You know we've discussed this in the past, how you need to be more open with Tucker."

"Fine!"

April's explosion surprises me. When she pushes 'er hair outta her face, I see she's gotta black eye an' a swollen cheek.

"What th' hell?!" I exclaim.

Elizabeth puts 'er hand on m' arm. "Tucker, please, let's let April tell the story and then we'll discuss all the details."

April glares at us. Then she says, "When I got to school this morning I looked for Mark's truck in the parking lot. It wasn't there, so I went to my locker. He usually meets me there if we don't catch each other in the parking lot. I waited there until the bell rang for first period. It didn't surprise me that he didn't show up, but I guess I was still hoping that somehow he would and that Tucker was right about me and my nightmare.

"I started walking to class, and Jennifer, Mark's cousin, came up to me and asked if I'd seen Mark. She's been sticking her nose into my business ever since me and Mark started seeing each other. You'd think she was his mother or something the way she tries to tell him what to do and what not to do. So I tell her that it's none of her business whether I've seen Mark or not and that makes her mad, which suits me just fine.

"By then we're walking into the classroom because we have the same class first period. She says to me, 'You better not have done anything to Mark.' And I say, 'What do you mean by that?'"

"She doesn't answer me. We take a seat in our desks, which are two rows apart. Halfway through class, Michael, the boy behind me, hands me a folded piece of paper. My name is on it. When I unfold it, I see it's from Jennifer. It says, 'What did you do? Did you murder Mark and get rid of his body like your grandmother did to her father?'"

April pauses in 'er story an' looks at me. We hold each other's eyes, neither of us blinkin'. After a few moments, she drops 'er head an' says quietly, "I guess something inside me snapped. I stood up and yelled, 'You're a bitch!' Everyone in class snapped their heads in my direction. Mrs. Simmons yelled at me. And Jennifer turned to me and gave me some kind of a smart-ass smile. I felt like I was on fire and she just poured gas on me.

"I pushed my way through the row of desks between us. I lunged at Jennifer and grabbed her hair with one hand and punched her in the face with the other. What happened after that is all a blur to me. People started screaming. People were grabbing at me and at her. I swung my fists at anyone who got close."

It's quiet fer several minutes 'til Elizabeth finally speaks. "Then Mrs. Simmons took April to the principal's office, not knowing that Mark's mother and stepfather were in there asking about Mark." Elizabeth shakes her head and sighs. "You can only imagine what happened when they all saw each other. That's when we called the police."

I stand up. "So what's gonna happen now?"

Elizabeth looks startled. "Happen? Well, for now I think you need to take April home. Then we'll all need to meet with the principal in the morning because there are going to be consequences for April's behavior."

I motion at April with my head. "Come on. Let's get you in th' truck an' go home. We ain't done talkin' 'bout this yet."

April gets up an' huffs loudly as she stomps past me. The door slams like a thunderclap behind 'er.

Turnin' t' Elizabeth, I say, "You're a good woman, jes' like yore mom was. Thank you fer tryin' t' help m' April."

Elizabeth stands. "Tucker, April has so much potential that she is wasting. I really think you should consider putting her into some counseling before it's too late."

"Thank you fer th' advice. I've done been thinking' 'bout that. Now I better go an' make sure April ain't run off. We'll see y' later."

CHAPTER NINETEEN

My food shall be of care and sorrow made,
My drink nought else but tears fall'n from mine eyes;
And for my light, in such obscured shade,
The flames shall serve which from my heart arise.
—Sir Walter Raleigh

APRIL:

Slamming the door to the guidance counselor's office behind me, I head toward the front of the school. Classes are changing so the hallway is thick with students. They all stare at me. Some point and whisper to the person beside them. But none of them have the guts to actually say something to my face. They are such losers!

Someone laughs loudly—too loudly. I turn, looking for the source and spy Becky Williams. As soon as she sees me looking at her, she stops and turns her back to me.

I stomp over to her. Grabbing her shoulder and spinning her around, I lean my face into hers and yell, "What's so funny?!"

She turns as pale as milk. Her voice trembles as she says, "Someone told a joke. That's all."

"Oh yeah?! So why don't you tell me the joke so I can laugh, too?"

"Hey! Back off, April."

I whirl around and see Becky's boyfriend, Randy, coming through the crowd with his football buddies following in his wake. Suddenly everything turns red. I charge him as hard as I can, burying my shoulder in his stomach. The move catches him off guard and he falls backward into the arms of his entourage. My momentum carries me with him and we tumble to the floor.

I scramble to my feet.

Randy gets up and faces me. His face is crimson and his nostrils are flared. "You stupid little bitch. You are psycho but I don't care because I'm going to whip your ass."

I squeeze my hands into fists and brace myself. "Come ahead, you witless fool."

In my peripheral vision I see people scattering. Then, just as Randy starts coming toward me, Tucker steps through the crowd and stands between me and him.

"I b'lieve this here's gone far enough. You boys go on 'bout yore business. Me an' April's leavin'."

Before anyone can move or say anything, Tucker turns around, grabs my arm, and starts ushering me toward the door. I try to jerk away from her, but her iron grip just squeezes that much tighter.

"Ow! You're hurting me!" I cry.

Without looking at me, Tucker keeps walking and says, "Don't tempt me, child. Don't tempt me."

When we get outside I see cop cars everywhere. Four or five cops are wrestling with someone at the back door of one of the cars. As we pass by, I can see that they are trying to get Mrs. Allen into the car. I try to tear myself free from Tucker while yelling, "See what you get, you crazy woman!"

In my rage I strike Tucker and scream, "Let me go!"

In a flash, Tucker turns me around, grabs a handful of the back of my shirt with one hand and the waistband of my jeans with the other, and lifts me off the ground. Carrying me like a bale of hay, she keeps walking toward the truck. "I'll let y' go when an' if I git ready. Fer right now, we're gettin' in th' truck an' goin' home. I've got some rope, an' if I have to, I'll hog tie you an' put you in th' bed of th' truck."

Despite the adrenaline coursing through my veins, the reasoning part of my brain says Tucker would do exactly what she has threatened me with, so I stop resisting her.

During the drive home I keep waiting for a lecture from Tucker, but, thankfully, none comes. I have no idea what is going on with her in keeping up this charade about Mark. It's insane. What does she think is going to happen? That his body and truck are not going to be found? That they aren't going to tie me to his murder? What does she intend to do when the sheriff shows up at our door to arrest me? Barricade us inside and go to war with the world?

Once we get home and go inside, Tucker points at the couch and says, "Sit down."

Okay, so here it finally comes—the big lecture. I look at her and say, "Look, just save your breath. I know what you are going to say because I've heard it all before."

"I said sit down!"

As if she has punched me in the chest, the volume and force of her words strike me so hard that I'm knocked backward and land on the couch. I glare at her.

Sitting down across from me, she says, "April, y' know that you're th' most precious thing in th' world t' me and—"

"And you wish you had done a better job raising me and that my mother hadn't been a whore and that Ella hadn't died, and that March hadn't run off, blah blah blah. I think I've heard this one—oh

I don't know—maybe five hundred times. So just save your breath. Can I go to my room now?"

My words have just the effect I'm looking for. Tucker's eyes redden and a tear slips from the corner of her eye and runs down a crease in her weathered face. Clearing her throat, she says, "I've done made a decision about you, one that you ain't gonna like."

"What? You think that's something that's never happened before? You've made lots of decisions about me that I haven't liked, so just add this new one to the list. I really want to just go to my room and go back to bed, all right?"

Just then the phone rings. Tucker picks it up and after answering it, listens quietly. She puts her hand over the receiver and says, "Jes' go t' yore room like y' want to."

Thankful to whoever has called and delivered me from this speech, I go to my room, locking the door behind me. I go straight to my bathroom and find the razor. Pulling my pants down, I sit on the toilet lid. I try rubbing the last *M* that I carved, hoping I can trigger a release of both blood and relief. But it has been too long. It's impossible to coax it to help me.

With a trembling hand, I take the razor and quickly slice the first leg of a new *M*. Blood pours out. I have cut too deep! I watch with fascination as the washcloth underneath my thigh receives the flood of my torment and slowly turns crimson. The raging pain inside my chest subsides and I smile.

Holding the razor in one hand, I slowly turn my other arm until I can look at the underside of my wrist. I imagine all the blood racing through those veins that lie just below the surface of my pale skin. Carefully, I touch my wrist with the corner of the razor.

A new sound catches my attention. I look for the source and discover that blood has started dripping from the washcloth onto the tile floor of the bathroom. Looking back at my wrist resting on my knee like a sacrificial lamb, I say, "Maybe another time."

I get up and find more washcloths. I spend the next hour tending to the botched job on my thigh, cleaning the floor, and rinsing out the blood from the washcloths. I wash and rewash everything, over and over, until, exhausted, I collapse onto my bed and fall asleep.

The next morning, I get up and dress for school. The smell of bacon cooking slips under my door and fills my nostrils. My stomach growls in response.

Walking through the living room to get to the kitchen, I notice a suitcase sitting on the floor. I can't recall ever having seen a suitcase in the house. But my hunger is stronger than my curiosity, so I keep walking.

Tucker is setting breakfast on the table just as I walk in.

"'Mornin'," she says. Her tone is somber. Normally morning is her favorite time of day and she's irritatingly full of sunshine, but not this morning.

Sitting down, I ask, "Is that a suitcase in the living room?"

"Yep."

"What's it there for?"

Ignoring my question, she says, "You need t' eat yore breakfast while it's hot. Now dig in."

Eager to quiet the growling bear in my stomach, I sit down and begin eating. Tucker sits down, too, but doesn't have a plate.

"Where's your breakfast?" I ask.

"I ain't hungry this mornin'."

I talk around my mouthful of food and say, "So what's up with the suitcase in the living room? I didn't even know we had one."

"You remember yesterday when I tol'ja that I'd made a decision 'bout you that y' wadn't gonna like?"

I take a gulp of orange juice and use a piece of crust from my toast to push a bite of egg onto my fork. "Sure, I guess. But what about the suitcase?"

"I decided I needed t' send y' off t' a place that might could help y' get yore life on track before it's too late."

A sound like a line of dominos falling echoes in my brain. I stop chewing and look at Tucker.

"So I asked Mary Beth Chandler t' help me find a place an' she did. It's called Spirit Lake, an' it's over in East Tennessee."

I shove my plate away from me and stand up. "Whoa, wait just a minute. If you think I'm going to go to some kind of treatment facility or reform school, you are crazy. That is not going—"

A knock on the door interrupts me.

Tucker walks to the door and opens it. I hear a man ask if she is Tucker, then she opens the door wider and steps back inside. Two policemen step inside.

My heart hammers against my chest like someone from our school marching band beating the head of their snare drum.

One of the men points at me and asks, "Is this April?"

"Yes it is," Tucker says quietly.

I suddenly feel like a raccoon that has been treed by coon dogs. I look wildly around the room for a way to escape.

Sensing my thoughts, the officer says, "Don't try to run. We've got a long drive ahead of us and neither my partner nor I is in the mood to have a wrestling match with you. We can do this the easy way . . ." He reaches behind him and produces a pair of handcuffs. "Or we can do it the hard way."

Tucker brings the suitcase and says, "This here goes with 'er."

"Tucker! Don't let them take me! I'll change and straighten up. You won't have any more trouble out of me. I'll do better in school, too. But don't let them take me!"

"It's done been decided, April," she says. "It's in yore best interest. Y' can use it as an opportunity to get yore life t'gether."

One of the officers takes me by my arm as the other one picks up the suitcase. "Come on, let's go."

"How long am I going to be gone?"

"Maybe nine months," Tucker says.

I jerk away. "No way! I refuse and you can't make me!" I jerk open the knife drawer, looking for a butcher knife.

Before I know what's happened, the officers have me bent over the kitchen counter and handcuff my hands behind my back. Each of them holds an arm and they start moving me toward the door.

As we pass by Tucker, I yell, "I'll never forgive you for this! You hear me! This is it for you and me. You'll never see or hear from me again, just like March." I spit at her. In my last image of Tucker, my spittle is running down her face.

CHAPTER TWENTY

My tale was heard and yet it was not told,
My fruit is fall'n and yet my leaves are green.
—*Chidiock Tichborne*

MARCH:

After Debbie delivers me to my room I work on getting oriented to my new living space. I find my talking clock and listen for the time. Though inhuman, the voice is reassuring.

Several times I am interrupted by various personnel introducing themselves to me, welcoming me, and telling me their role in my life. But my senses are so overloaded I'm not able to retain any of their names or job descriptions.

I miss Naomi and Willie.

As nighttime settles into the hallways and rooms, I find sleep is as elusive as a butterfly. Finally, I decide to get into my wheelchair and get some exercise.

Slowly and cautiously I ease down the hallway, keeping close enough to the wall that I can reach out and touch it to keep oriented.

There is a sense of needing to have a string tied to my finger and the other end to the doorknob of my room, a tether of safety. But I push through my anxiety.

After several minutes I am stopped short by the sudden sound of a man's voice on my right side.

"You must be Levi."

His chair scrapes the floor as he gets up. There is the distinct sound of squeaking leather. The hair on the back of my neck tingles.

"Uh, yes, sir, that's what everyone calls me. Are you with law enforcement?"

The man chuckles. "Not really. I'm a member of the security department here. But I did spend thirty years in law enforcement. After I retired this seemed like a good place to pick up some extra money. What made you guess that's what I was?"

"Your belts and holster," I reply.

"I see. Well, my name's Ted. Actually it's Theodore," he adds in a whisper, "but don't tell anybody."

"Your secret's safe with me."

"You got any more name than Levi?"

"The truth is, that's not even my name. It's just the name they gave me at the hospital. I've got amnesia and so far I haven't been able to remember a single thing about my past."

"You don't say," Ted empathizes. "Now that's a shame. Don't think I've ever met someone who had amnesia. Of course you see it all the time on TV, but I just never run across it in real life. What do the doctors tell you about recovering your memory?"

"All they say is that they believe it'll eventually come back. It may all come back at once or it may come back a piece at a time." I shake my head. "I just know that it's getting really old. The only memory I have is of this past month when I was in the hospital. Other than that, it's a blank chalkboard up here." I tap the side of my head for emphasis.

Suddenly I get an overpowering urge. "Ted, do you mind if I hold your firearm?"

There is hesitation. "Well, I don't guess it'll hurt anything," Ted says. "You a fan of firearms?"

"I don't know for sure, but I have this urge to hold your pistol. What kind is it?"

"It's a Glock 9 millimeter."

I hear him releasing the strap holding it securely in its holster.

I hold out my hand and he places the handle in my palm.

Without thinking, I quickly press the magazine catch and pull the magazine from the handle. Pulling the slide back, I stick the tip of my finger in to see if I can feel a remaining round. After I allow the slide to spring forward, I point the pistol toward the floor beside me and pull the trigger. The metallic click lets me know the pistol is empty and safe. Then I pull the slide back about an eighth of an inch and pull the slide lock down. Pushing the slide forward, I remove it from the receiver. Using my fingertip I push the recoil spring assembly forward and up a little. I ease the barrel forward a little bit and lift up on its back end. Next I pull backward and remove the barrel from the slide. I pause for a beat, then reverse all my actions and reassemble the pistol.

All this I have done in less than thirty seconds. I am stunned.

A low whistle comes from Ted. "Man, if I hadn't just seen that, I wouldn't believe it. And to tell you the truth, I did see it, but I'm not sure I believe it. Where in the world did you learn to do that?"

"I don't have a clue." But, like the soft light on the eastern horizon just before the sun comes up, there is a hint of a memory. It is a face. I grab it and hold it as tightly as I can, lest it slip away. I hear Ted talking to me about what I've just done, but I dare not break this spell of memory, so I ignore him.

Wordlessly I hold the pistol toward him, handle first. "Later," I say and turn back toward my room.

I don't hear or feel anything as I move slowly down the hall. Every fiber of me is focusing on the face I've remembered. Initially it was blurry, but the longer I've held it the sharper the image has become.

It's a white male, about fifty years old. He has a shock of red hair that evidently either doesn't respond to a comb or hasn't ever seen a comb. His blue eyes are furtive and constantly darting left and right. Dark circles are under them. There is a tattoo of a tear-drop at the corner of one eye. A jagged, red scar runs from the corner of his left ear down to his tattoo-covered neck.

As if it were a movie that had been paused, someone hits the "Play" button on my memory, and I am sitting across the table from this man in a small, dark, grimy room. He is called Red.

Pointing at the table in front of me, Red says, "Do it again. You've got to be able to do it in your sleep. It's the only friend you can count on, so you better know it inside and out."

I look down at the Glock 9 millimeter on the table and in a burst of motion I disassemble and reassemble it just as I did a moment ago in front of Ted.

When I look back at Red, his face looks like a reflection in a pond that someone has thrown a rock into. It begins distorting, then fading away.

Suddenly I am alone in the hallway of Patricia Neal. I hold my bowed head in my hands. My face is covered in sweat and my heart is racing.

"Levi?" An unfamiliar voice calls from down the hallway. "Are you okay?"

Rubber soles squeak on the tile floor as the owner of the voice approaches.

"I'm Doreen. Do you need some help finding your room?"

"I think I may have gotten disoriented. I try to keep up with the number of turns the back wheels of my wheelchair make and use that as a way to find my way back. Guess I got mixed up."

"Well you're nearly there. Six more feet and you will find your door on the right. I usually work the night shift, so if you ever need something you call for me, okay?"

"Sure thing. Thanks, Doreen."

Once I'm in my room, more pieces of my puzzle drop out of nowhere and into place. But I don't have to wait for all the pieces to arrive. I already know what the picture looks like and why I ended up left for dead in the Little River.

CHAPTER TWENTY-ONE

My thread is cut and yet it is not spun,
And now I live, and now my life is done.
—*Chidiock Tichborne*

MARCH:

Gripping the small duffle bag in one hand, I sit at the table in the cramped, stark motel room. The only lamp that is working burns dimly on the dresser. Muffled sounds from adjoining rooms filter through the paper-thin walls.

Glancing at my watch, I see it is ten p.m. Right on cue someone taps three times on the door, pauses, and then taps once.

I slip my hand inside my jacket and feel the butt of my pistol. Opening the door, I see Red is alone, and I let him in.

"Hey, Big Country! How's my boy?" Red asks with a smile.

"Tired, but okay," I reply.

Red gives me a suspicious look. "Everything go smooth?"

"Just like always."

Nodding at the duffle bag in my hand, Red asks, "Is that the money?"

I offer the bag to him. "Yep. They wanted to haggle about the price but I told them there would be no negotiations."

Red spits on the floor and a fountain of profanity follows. "They got what they asked for! More kilos of pure hashish than they've ever seen. And if they expect to do business with me again, they better not hassle my courier. Right, Big Country?"

"Right." I'm tired and just want to get my cut and find a place to lay low for a while. But I know I've got to dance with him to keep his paranoia at bay.

"What about Roan and Buzzard?" Red asks. "How'd they do as drivers?"

"I don't like them," I say flatly.

Red squints at me, then looks around the room. He leans toward me and says, "What's wrong with them? Did they steal some of the hashish?" Clutching the duffle bag to his chest, he adds, "Or some of the money?"

Shaking my head, I say, "No, nothing like that. They're just a couple of perverts."

Red laughs. "Prison will do that to you, Big Country. Boys will be boys, you know. You've been lucky so far and never done any hard time, but that's 'cause I always took care of you. I've took care of you ever since I found you at that rest area outside Oklahoma City four years ago. Don't ever forget that."

How could I forget it when he tells me the same thing every time he sees me? I feel myself getting edgy. "Yeah, you've taken care of me," I say. "Now why don't you take your money and get out of here before the law accidently shows up. They watch Interstate Forty so close these days, I can't believe we've never been caught."

Red gets up, holding the duffle bag under his arm. "You're right, boy." He pauses, unzips the bag, and reaches inside. Pulling out three bundles of cash, he hands them to me. "Here's your cut. Pay Roan and Buzzard whatever you think is fair. Tell 'em it's from me. Be careful and lay low for a couple weeks, then give me a call." Without waiting for a reply, he walks out the door and into the parking lot.

I hear the diesel engine of his pickup truck fire up and rattle to life. After its sound trails off in the distance, I wait for five minutes, then exit the room.

Finding the outside stairs, I walk up to the second level. When I arrive at the room, I tap twice on the door, pause, and tap once. The muffled sounds of voices and footsteps come from inside.

After a moment, the door opens as much as the safety chain will allow.

"Is that you, Big Country?"

"No, you idiot," I reply. "It's room service. Of course it's me! Open the door."

The door closes and I hear the chain being slid off the catch. Grabbing the knob, I open the door and step inside.

Immediately, every hair on my body stands up. The air is charged. Roan, dressed only in his stained T-shirt and underwear, is standing to the side of the door. The way he keeps moving his feet to keep his balance is a sure sign he is drunk or high or both. He gives me a snaggle-toothed grin.

Lying on one of the twin beds is a young girl dressed in a tank top and jeans. She has long blond hair and eyes the color of a February sky. Even though she has enough makeup on to give her the appearance of being twenty years old, my guess is that she is fifteen. Her huge pupils let me know she's been drugged.

The bathroom door opens and Buzzard walks out as naked as the day he was born. When he sees me he lets out a rebel yell. "It's Big Country! Man, are we in for a party now." Pointing at the girl, he says, "What do you think? Ain't she a pretty piece?"

In spite of her altered state of awareness, the girl realizes she's in trouble. She struggles to stand up. "This is not what I agreed to. I'm not doing three guys. Let me out of here."

She starts toward the door, but Buzzard grabs her arm and throws her back on the bed. "Not so fast, you pretty thing."

Roan cackles like a warlock. "You first, Buzz," he says.

"Stop!" I yell.

All three look at me.

"Listen to me. You two are crazy. This girl is underage. You get caught doing this and you'll go to prison again, but this time you won't be getting out until you are old men."

Buzzard looks at the girl and then back at me. "She said she was nineteen."

"Sure she did. But I'll bet you any amount of money you want that she's not a day over fifteen."

Roan grabs his crotch and squeals. "Fifteen! Man I've got to have me some of that!" He stumbles toward the bed.

Buzzard laughs and pins the girl on her back. "Come and get it!"

Unzipping my camouflage jacket, I pull my pistol from its shoulder holster. I jerk the slide back so that a round enters the chamber.

The sound hooks the attention of both men and freezes them. They slowly turn to face me. "What the hell are you doing?" Buzzard asks.

"Trying to keep you two out of trouble, which means I'm trying to protect Red. Both of you move away from the bed." I wave the barrel for emphasis.

Roan is slowly sobering up, enough to be upset at this turn of events. "You've got no right, Big Country. This is our little party. Why don't you just go on to wherever you live and leave us alone?

The little girl wanted some money and we agreed to give her some. It's a simple business transaction."

His speech is getting less slurred as more synapses are connecting.

Buzzard's face reddens. "You always think you're better than everybody just because Red takes a special liking to you. Well one of these days Red ain't going to be around, and you're going to get what's coming to you."

I click on the safety and return the pistol to the holster. Staring at both men, I say, "Red's not here now. Come ahead if you've got something you want to prove." I spread my arms and motion them toward me with my hands.

Buzzard makes a half step toward me but Roan puts his hand out and stops him. "He's still got that pistol. Don't be a fool."

"Listen to your friend," I say. "He's making lots of sense."

I turn my attention to the girl. "Come on, now's a good time for you to leave."

She cautiously eases off the bed and starts toward me. However, her feet get tangled in the comforter on the floor and she loses her balance. She begins to fall and I lunge to catch her.

In that split-second Buzzard and Roan are on me in a flash, pummeling and kicking me. The girl screams but darts out the door to safety.

I try pulling my knees under me so that I can stand. I catch Roan on the side of the face with my elbow, sending him backward.

Buzzard knees me in my ribs and hits the back of my neck with his elbow. I see stars.

I try to reach for my pistol.

"Watch him!" one of them yells. "He's going for his gun!"

My arm is wrenched backward. With my free hand I punch someone in the groin and hear him howl.

I sense them getting winded and am able to finally get to my feet. Just as I do, out of the corner of my eye I see Roan swinging his ever-present companion, his blackjack. I both feel and hear it strike my head. It reminds me of a homerun hitter striking a baseball. Then everything goes black.

As I come to, my arms and legs are being jerked and pulled. I feel myself sliding and then falling about four feet and landing on a hard surface. I can only see out of one eye. The other must be swollen shut. It is dark but I figure out that I've just been pulled from the bed of a pickup truck and let fall to the road.

"Damn, he's heavy." It's the voice of Roan. "Let's shoot him and be done with it."

I hear a gun being cocked.

"No," Buzzard says. "That's too easy. I want him to suffer. Let him think he's going to live only to find out he's going to drown."

It's then that I hear a loud roaring noise in the background. But in my addled state I can't figure out what it is.

"Ain't no way he's going to be able to swim with that broke leg and arm." Buzzard laughs.

"What about Red?" Roan asks.

"I've already told you that Red will assume the buyers got greedy, followed him, knocked him off, and stole the money. Now help me lift him over the side of the bridge."

They grunt and swear as they put me on the edge of the bridge. The cold wind sweeps through my hair and beard and feels surprisingly refreshing. The thundering water below cascades over the boulders and rocks.

Roan and Buzzard shout to be heard.

"Did you get his pockets cleaned out?"

"Yeah, and his gun and holster, too."

Without another word, they roll me over the side and I plummet toward my cold, watery grave.

CHAPTER TWENTY-TWO

Stone walls do not a prison make,
Nor iron bars a cage.
—Richard Lovelace

APRIL:

Time to wake up, April. We're almost there."

Sitting up, I rub my eyes and look through the wire mesh separating the front and back seats of the police car that has been my prison for the past six hours. "You know," I say, "I've memorized both of your names and descriptions. I'm going to call the FBI and report that you two kidnapped me. Kidnapping a child is a serious offense."

The officer named Dan turns to his partner, who is driving, and says, "Travis, is that the fifth or the sixth time she's threatened us with that?"

"I believe it's the fifth," Travis replies. "And don't forget all those sexual battery charges that are going to put us away for the rest of our lives."

They both laugh.

I start to raise my feet to kick at the wire mesh until I remember that my feet are handcuffed to the floor because of my previous assault on the barrier. "Go ahead and laugh! Just know this, I don't forget easily. And I'm very patient when it comes to getting even. One of these days we'll cross paths again."

When neither of them offers a retort, I look out the window. We are traveling on a one-lane paved road. Both sides of the road are thick with some kind of pine trees, but not like the kind in West Tennessee. Some of the trunks of the trees are as big around as the police car, and the tops seem to disappear into the clouds. The resulting shade blocks out all but a few brief flickers of sunlight. There are no signs of civilization—no power lines, no traffic, no houses, no driveways, no people.

As we round a curve, I look out the left window and see a break in the trees in the distance. A hundred yards farther I can see that the opening is a large lake. The water is the same color as a bluebird. The small ripples across the water catch the bright sun and create thousands of shimmering diamonds over the surface.

The police cruiser follows another curve and the lake disappears. Suddenly I see the flash of a woman standing about twenty yards deep in the woods, or at least I think I do. I twist my head around and there she is, standing in the middle of the road behind us. Her hair is pulled back tightly in a long ponytail. The gray T-shirt she is wearing is dark around her neck and under her arms. She has on camouflage pants.

Turning back around, I exclaim, "Did you guys see that?"

"What now?"

"That woman in the woods! Look in your rearview mirror. She's standing in the middle of the road behind us now."

Travis glances up at his rearview mirror as I crane my neck to get another look behind us. But the roadway is empty.

"Yeah, sure thing, April." To his partner he says, "Sheesh, will I be glad when we get this package delivered."

"I'm telling you I know what I saw," I reiterate. "She was like some kind of Amazon or jungle woman. Maybe she's one of those survivalists I've heard about. Or maybe she's some kind of psycho on the run from the law. Are you all sure this place you're taking me is safe? It looks like it's in the middle of a wilderness."

"Well, actually," Dan answers, "it is in the middle of a wilderness of sorts and that's what makes it safe. Look April, I don't know anything about you, what you've done or anything, but I'll tell you this, Spirit Lake is a place of healing, a place where young girls like yourself can find themselves and get their lives on track, but only if they want to."

I'm just about to tell him he can take his opinion and shove it, when we pull into a clearing and slow to a stop. Three log cabins sit side by side and in the distance I see a barn. It reminds me of something from *Little House on the Prairie*.

"Here we are," Dan says.

"You have got to be kidding," I say. "This is it? There is no way I'm staying here."

I notice one of the cabin doors open and two girls step outside. They stop and one of them points when they see the police car, then they beat a hasty retreat back inside the log cabin.

The officers unbuckle themselves and get out of the car. Dan walks to the trunk to get my suitcase, while Travis opens the rear door. He unlocks the handcuffs from my ankles, grips my arm, and says, "Let's go."

My heart is hammering against my chest and I can hardly catch my breath I'm breathing so hard. I wish I could have a private moment with my razor blade so I could still the panic I'm feeling. I can't believe Tucker would send me to such a godforsaken-edge-of-the-world kind of place.

With Travis's assistance I finally stand up outside the car. I immediately notice a difference in the air here from how it is back home. It is sharp and clean-smelling, heavy with the scent of the thick evergreen forest. "Aren't you going to uncuff my hands?" I ask.

"Not until we hand you off to one of the personnel here."

As we start walking toward the middle cabin, the door of the cabin where the two girls appeared a moment ago reopens and they reappear with three more girls in tow. Walking toward us, they whisper and point. A couple of them laugh.

"Hello, girls," Dan says. "Is Mary here?"

A black girl steps forward. "Yeah, she's inside." Nodding her head toward me, she says, "Who's this here, the Bonnie half of Bonnie and Clyde?" She laughs while keeping her eyes on me.

I sense an uneasy edge about her, like there is magma boiling just below the surface, waiting for a fissure to open so she can erupt. She steps in closer.

"My name is Heather," she says. "I'm in charge around here. Ask any of the girls and they'll agree. As long as you do what I say, we'll get along just fine."

I jerk away from Travis's grip and drive my shoulder into Heather's chest. Caught off guard, she falls backward and lands on her butt. "It'll be a cold day in you-know-where when I let some Yankee tell me what to do," I say. I scan the faces of the other girls and notice their shocked expressions. "And that goes for the rest of you, too. Don't mess with me!"

Travis grabs my arm and jerks me away from Heather, who has bounced up and clearly wants to fight.

At that same moment, the door of the middle cabin opens and a woman steps out. "Heather!" Her voice has the authority of a drill sergeant. "You and the other girls get back to where you are supposed to be or you will all lose privileges."

All the girls, except Heather, quickly turn and trot back to their cabin. Heather squints at me and, through clenched teeth, says, "I won't forget this. You might be bad among the other white trash you live around, but I'm from Chicago and we know how to deal with fools like you. You best watch your back."

"Heather!" the woman barks again. "You've just lost evening privileges. If you don't want to lose more, do as I say."

Heather glances at the woman, back at me, and then she turns and walks away.

I give my full attention to the woman approaching us. She is tall, probably close to five-nine. She has dark features and when she smiles at the two police officers I notice a small gap between her front teeth. Dressed in jeans, a polo shirt, and hiking boots, she has the look of an ex-athlete.

"Well hello, Travis and Dan. This must be the package we've been waiting for. Is this April?"

Travis unlocks my handcuffs, and Dan says, "Indeed it is and good riddance to her and good luck to you on this one."

Rubbing my sore wrists, I look at the two officers and say, "Thanks for nothing."

After shaking the woman's hand, the officers return to their patrol car and drive off.

I watch the car until it disappears and then turn to face the woman.

"April, my name is Mary. I'm the treatment director here at Spirit Lake. I'd like to welcome you here. Would you like to follow me inside, or do you want to talk out here?"

After she was so direct with the other girls, I don't know what to make of her giving me a choice. Shrugging my shoulders, I say, "I don't care."

"Then let's go inside. Just follow me."

I dutifully follow her inside the cabin. In what looks like a large living room, there are two couches and four stuffed chairs, none of which match. The floor actually looks like the wooden floor of Tucker's old house, gray and worn.

"Have a seat, April," Mary says.

I choose one of the chairs and Mary sits across from me on a couch. On the coffee table between us there is a manila folder thick with papers.

Mary taps the table with the toe of her boot. "Based on all the information I've received about you in that folder, I'd say you've had a pretty complicated life. It doesn't sound like things have been very easy for you."

I'm just about to spring out of my chair and scream a protest when her next words stop me in my tracks.

"But I don't really care." After a pause, during which she watches me closely, she asks, "What do you think about that?"

"I really don't care either," I reply.

"Good, then we are on the same page and agree with each other. You see, I don't think life is easy for anyone. So our job is learning how to deal with life in a positive way." She taps the manila folder with her index finger. "And so far in your life, you haven't learned how to deal with it very well. Bottom line, that's why you are here.

"We have three sayings at Spirit Lake: It's all about choices, You have to earn your way, and You can't do life on your own. The first statement means that life is about learning how to make smart choices. While you are here you will be given lots of opportunities to make choices. For instance, whether you obey the rules or not while you are here is your choice. But just like life, you will learn that there are consequences connected to every choice you make.

"That you have to earn your way means that all privileges have to be earned. For instance, if you want a bar of soap to shower with, you have to earn it. If you want a mattress on your bed, you will have to earn it. And so on.

"And lastly, that you can't do life on your own comes from our belief that every person needs to recognize the need for God in their lives and to learn to lean on him and let him lead the way." She sits back and crosses her legs.

I don't like anything about what I have just heard Mary say. This is either some kind of concentration camp or a camp run by a religious cult!

"Any questions?" Mary asks.

"I don't think I belong here."

"Really? Well then, why don't you leave? There's the door."

I glance at the door and start to jump up and bolt through it. But I also feel paralyzed, like a bug stuck to a piece of Styrofoam with a pin through my chest. I know she's only bluffing me, trying to get me to admit I do belong here, but she is so calm about it that I don't think she would stop me if I did take her up on her dare and walk out. Folding my arms across my chest, I neither move nor speak.

After several moments, Mary says, "So I assume you're staying with us. Good. You wait here until Michelle, one of our therapists, arrives. She'll tell you what to do next." Then she gets up and walks out the cabin door.

CHAPTER TWENTY-THREE

A faithful witness will not lie: but a false witness will utter lies.
—*Proverbs 14:5*

APRIL

The silence in this cabin stuck in the middle of a wilderness presses down on me. My nerves ache for relief, either by being pounded with loud, pulsating music or by my cutting myself with my razor blade. According to the battery-operated clock on the wall, I've been sitting by myself for an hour. I decide I might as well take a nap and begin arranging the couch pillows on one end.

Just as I'm about to lay my head on the nest of pillows, the door to the cabin bursts open. I am so startled that I leap to my feet and face the door. Standing in the doorway is the Amazon woman I earlier saw standing in the middle of the road. Her entire gray T-shirt is now dark with sweat. Her face looks like someone has thrown a bucket of water on it. As she stands looking at me, drops of sweat drip off her chin.

For the second time in the last two hours, I feel the urge to run coupled with the inability to move. I hope some of the girls or Mary will miraculously appear at the door and distract this wild woman long enough for me to escape. My heart is galloping at a frightening pace and I can't get my breath. My fingers are tingling and stars are circling the periphery of my vision.

Removing her bow and quiver of arrows, the intruder smiles and says, "You must be April."

I am disconcerted by the pleasant smile and tone of voice of this killer. And how does she know my name?

"Mary told me you were here and that I need to finish the intake process with you." She covers the distance between us in a few strong strides. Sticking out her hand, she says, "My name is Michelle. Glad to have you at Spirit Lake."

Robotically I reach out and take her hand.

Michelle gives my hand a firm squeeze and shakes it once. Letting go, she says, "Wow, are your hands cold!" she says. "Are you okay? You look like you are about to pass out."

Folding my arms over my chest, I say, "I'm fine. I just thought you were some kind of jungle-woman survivalist who was going to kill me with your bow. I didn't realize you were the counselor Mary had told me would be coming."

Michelle gives an easy laugh. She walks over to one of the desks and pulls out a folded gray T-shirt. She turns her back to me, pulls the sweaty shirt off and puts the clean one on. Then she reaches toward the back of her head and takes down her ponytail. Turning back toward me she says, "You have a seat while I go get the girls. We'll start by having everyone introduce themselves."

I reluctantly resume my position on the couch. The last thing I'm interested in doing is meeting more people, especially after my initial encounter with Heather.

Michelle is gone for barely a minute when the door reopens and the girls file in. Heather laughs loudly when she walks in front of me, then whispers to the girl beside her. Everyone takes seats on the couches and Michelle sits in the chair beside me. All eyes shift to Michelle.

"What's our first saying here at Spirit Lake?" Michelle asks.

On cue, all five girls say in unison, "It's all about choices."

"And the second one?" Michelle asks.

"You have to earn your way."

"And the third?"

"You can't do life on your own."

"Well ladies," Michelle says, "we have a new guest at Spirit Lake and as we always do, we need to welcome her. You remember the format we use, so I'll ask you to follow it. Jessica, why don't you start?"

One of the girls stands up. She looks at me and says, "My name is Jessica. I'm from Montauk, New York. My father is a lawyer in Manhattan and my mother is a serious social climber, on all sorts of committees. They've been divorced for six years. I've been at Spirit Lake for ten months. I came here because of my addiction to marijuana. After I was busted for the third time, it was either come here or do some time in juvie. Welcome, April. If you follow the rules, you won't have any trouble here. It's taken me ten months to figure that out."

Jessica sits down and the girl next to her stands up. She has dark skin and eyes that are nearly black. It suddenly dawns on me that none of the girls are wearing makeup, and neither is Michelle.

"Hi, April. My name is Ashley. I'm from Colorado Springs, Colorado. My dad works for the National Park Service and my mother works her way to the bottom of a bottle every day. She is an alcoholic and she is a Native American, while my dad is white. I was sent here after I ran away from home for the fifth time. I was on the run for three weeks before they found me the last time. The only reason they found me then was because I was raped and dumped at a hospital emergency room. I've been here for seven months. Jessica is right. Obey the rules. There's not that many. Don't make it harder than it has to be."

Ashley takes a seat. The girl next to her is a blonde with eyes the dark blue of the evening sky. Even though she is seated, I can tell she is quite tall. Her attention is focused on her shoes and her hands are folded in her lap.

Michelle speaks, "Sarah, it's your turn. Come on, you can do this."

A quiet sigh slips from Sarah's lips. Slowly she stands up. She looks in my direction but not directly at me. It's like she's looking just over my head.

"Hi, April," she says softly. "Welcome to Spirit Lake. My name is Sarah. I'm from St. Augustine, Florida, the oldest city in the United States. My dad is a pastor of a really large church there and my mom is in charge of his television ministry. They sent me here after I tried to kill myself the second time." She pauses and she looks me directly in the eye. It is the look of a laser and I feel uncomfortable, like she can see inside my head. "The reason I tried to kill myself is because my parents forced me to kill the baby I was carrying. I've been here for almost six months and I now know it wasn't my fault. I'm getting stronger." In slow motion, she sits down.

The girl with flaming red hair beside Sarah springs up quickly. "I'm Megan and I'm from Cincinnati, Ohio. My father is a captain on a tugboat and my mother is a school teacher. They are both very busy people. So busy that they didn't realize I was drinking heavily when I was thirteen. I don't like trouble, it just seems to find me." Grabbing a handful of her hair, she says, "I blame it on this. I can't help it if I have a bad temper. It's something I inherited from my grandfather, who was also redheaded. It didn't help anything that he was the one who molested me from the time I was five until I was eleven. I've been at Spirit Lake for two months, and I still think all of you are crazy. My best advice to you, April, is to steer clear of me."

I feel like I've just been thrown out of the Tilt-A-Whirl at the carnival that comes through every summer. I'm trying to keep up with everyone's story, but the sharp turns keep throwing me off balance. The only girl who has yet to speak is Heather.

Heather rises slowly. "Since you and I already met earlier, I suppose we can dispense with names. I'm from Chicago where my mother is a famous TV anchorwoman. Never met my father and don't want to. When my mother found out I had been initiated into one of the gangs, which means all the guys in the gang raped me, she packed my butt up and put me on a bus to this godforsaken place. She told them not to send me back to her until I'd learned to respect her." Heather pauses and gives a short, disdainful laugh. "Respect her? I can't respect anybody who don't respect themselves. She may be at the top of her career ladder but she did it by lying on her back with her legs spread. I've been here for four weeks and it already feels like four years." Looking at me, she says, "My advice to you, country girl, is to watch your back."

"Well," Michelle says, "that was interesting, to say the least. Now it's your turn, April."

"Huh?"

Michelle nods. "To introduce yourself to us."

Oh crap! There is no way I'm going to tell them about Tucker and my mom. I dart through my mind looking for pieces of stories that I can string together in a way that will sound believable. Standing up, I say, "I'm from West Tennessee, close to Memphis, where my father is a very powerful judge, one of those who is appointed by the president. My mother is the most beautiful woman you have ever seen. She owns her own jewelry and diamond store. My parents asked me if I would be interested in coming to stay here and have an alternative education. I told them I was bored with the private school I was attending and that Spirit Lake sounded like a grand adventure."

I'm shocked at how fast all that spewed out of my mouth, and I hope it made sense. I sit back down and scan the faces of the girls. They stare at me and then, suddenly, burst into laughter.

"Man, that was the biggest line of bull I ever heard!"

"You expect us to believe all that?"

"The president knows your daddy? Sure he does!"

"You are one pitiful liar."

I feel my face burning and imagine it is getting redder by the second. I start to defend my story but decide that would only make me look more guilty, so I say, "Believe me or not, I really don't care."

CHAPTER TWENTY-FOUR

Deer April,

I done had to do lots of really hard things in my life. I used to think that losing my friend Ella was the hardest thing, but after watching them policemen put you in their car today I can now say that's the hardest thing I ever done. I seen the hate in your eyes when you looked at me for the last time. That's a look I might not ever forget but I hope I can. Hate is something I know a lot about. I spent most of my life living on hate. It was your grandmother Ella who helped teach me how bad it was for me. How it poisoned me. I hope you'll figure that out too while you're at Spirit Lake. I know I don't do no good when it comes to letting you know how I feel about you. I always had a tender spot in my heart for you. I loved your brothers, August and March, but you was my favorite. That might not have been right, but that was just how I felt. You was like this beautiful rose placed in the rusted tin can of mine and your brothers' world. There wasn't nothing I wouldn't do for you. It's just that I couldn't do much cause I didn't have nothing. If God hadn't sent Ella to us I don't know if you'd ever have started talking. I won't never forget that Christmas when you sung Amazing Grace in Ella's living room. I hope you got some good memories that you can hold on to, too. I hope all of them ain't bad when you think about me. But if you don't you can't let bad memories or a bad past chain you down. You can do anything you want to in your life. You can become somebody great. That's why I decided to send you away cause I got afraid for you. Afraid that you wasn't never going to amount to nothing if you stayed here. And once I talked to that woman at Spirit Lake, her name is Mary, I knew that was a place that could help you get a leg up on life. Mary seemed to be sort of like me because she talked real plain and didn't pull no punches. But she's a heck of a lot smarter than me and she'll know how to undo all the bad I done when raising you. I want you to remember three things—I loved you yesterday. I loved you today. And I'll love you tomorrow.

—Tucker

CHAPTER TWENTY-FIVE

Even a fool, when he holdeth his peace, is counted wise.
—Proverbs 17:28

APRIL:

Walking into the girls cabin for the first time, I'm shocked at how bare it looks. There are six twin beds lined along one wall, five of which are made up neatly. The sixth one on the end is a bare mattress. Beside each bed is a nightstand and a small chest of drawers. Except for a row of pegs that hold various-size jackets and hats, bare log walls stare back at me. A wood-burning stove sits in the middle of the large room. All of this reminds me of Tucker's house that I grew up in, gray and drab.

Pointing to the unmade bed, Heather says, "That bed is yours. Mine's right beside it. I don't like nobody messing with my stuff, so keep your hands to yourself."

"You really need to get over yourself," I reply. "If you think you are going to bluff or bully me, you've got another thing coming."

Heather spins around at me. "You want to decide this thing right here and now?! Come on, I'm ready." She crouches like a wrestler.

Jessica steps between us. "Stop it, both of you! I'm too close to leaving here for you two to mess things up for me. If there's a fight, we all get punished for it. Quit acting like ten-year-olds. Sarah, why don't you show April where the bed sheets, blankets, and pillows are so she can make her bed?"

"Sure," Sarah says softly and she heads toward the hallway. Without looking at me she says, "Follow me, April."

My eyes are still locked onto Heather's, neither of us willing to blink.

Ashley joins Jessica, blocking my line of sight to Heather. "Look," she says, "this is your first day here. Don't get started on the wrong foot. Go follow Sarah."

"Okay," I say, "but I don't let anybody push me around, understand?" Pointing over Jessica's shoulder toward Heather, I add, "She better mind her own business." I turn to go and find Sarah.

Sarah is standing in front of a pair of open doors. When I reach her, she says, "This is where all of our linens are kept. Each of us is responsible for keeping our things washed, folded, and put up."

I ignore her and say, "What's Heather's problem?"

Sarah's eyes flit toward the living area and then drop back to her shoes. "That is something you will have to discuss with her. At Spirit Lake we are encouraged to work out our own problems with each other without soliciting help from anyone."

Clearly Sarah is nothing more than a robot of some kind, parroting whatever she is told. I get the sense that she is as fragile as a pile of dried leaves in winter. I despise the weakness that I smell in her.

"Let me show you the other rooms," Sarah says.

I follow her into a room that has three deep, double sinks. On the wall over each is hung an old-fashioned washboard.

Sarah gives the room a wave of her hand. "This is where we do our laundry."

Puzzled, I say, "But where are the washers and dryers?"

Pointing at a washboard, Sarah says, "Those are the washing machines. The dryers are our clotheslines outside."

Once I absorb this shocking news, I burst out laughing. "Only Tucker would find a place like this to send me to!"

"What's so funny?" Sarah asks. "And who is Tucker?"

Sarah is looking at me as if I'm an escapee from an insane asylum, which throws me into another fit of laughter.

"Nothing," I finally say. "You wouldn't understand. And Tucker is our family lawyer who found this place for us."

From back in the living area I hear what sounds like two blows of a hammer followed by three more blows.

Sarah's head snaps in the direction of the sound. There is a light in her eyes that I haven't seen until now. With energy in her voice, she says, "That's Will. It's time to go to the barn and take care of the animals. Come on." Taking my hand, she pulls me.

Jerking my hand away from her, I say, "I'll follow you. You don't have to hold my hand. I don't like being touched."

Her head drops until her chin rests on her chest. "I'm sorry. It won't happen again."

My lord, what a weak creature she is. I push my way past her.

The front door is open and the girls are heading out. Some of them are stomping their feet into boots while others are slipping on work gloves. I hear Heather swearing under her breath as she exits the cabin.

Once outside the cabin I see an old man with a curved walking stick. He is slightly bent to one side. A full head of white hair sits atop his pleasant face. His cheeks are pink, and there is a twinkle in his eye as he calls each girl's name as they pass by him.

"You must be April," he says. Turning, he falls in step with me.

It's then that I notice him limping on his left leg and how tightly he grips his walking stick. His voice has a high raspy sound, like he may be hoarse.

"My name's Will," he says. "Welcome to Spirit Lake. My job here is to help you girls manage our animals."

"Animals? What animals?"

Will laughs. "Yeah, most girls ain't prepared for that piece of news. Well we got us seven horses, a donkey, a cow, and a hog. Oh yeah." Will whistles loudly. "And Roxie, our golden retriever."

The next moment, a huge auburn-colored dog comes bounding out of the woods and, with its ears laid back, runs at breakneck speed right toward me and Will. Just as I think she is going to slam into us like a bowling ball, Will throws up his hand and says, "Sit!"

Dutifully, the dog skids to a stop in a sitting position about three feet from us. Its tongue is hanging out, but it still manages to look like it is laughing. And its eyes, the color of a brand new penny, dance from Will to me to the other girls up ahead.

"Good girl," Will says. "Now you go on to the barn and wait on us there."

As if she was shot out of a cannon, Roxie explodes toward the barn in the distance.

I walk beside Will, letting him set the pace. I expect him to pepper me with questions and to talk about Spirit Lake, but he walks in silence, which is fine with me.

As we approach the barn I see that it is much bigger that it appeared from a distance. It has two stories, more than likely the top is the hayloft, where all the hay is stored. I follow Will inside.

CHAPTER TWENTY-SIX

A thing of beauty is a joy forever:
Its loveliness increases; it will never
Pass into nothingness; but still will keep
A bower quiet for us, and a sleep
Full of sweet dreams, and health, and quiet breathing.
—*John Keats*

APRIL:

My first whiff once inside fills my head and triggers a flood of memories. Like Aladdin on a magic carpet, I fly through time and space. I am five or six years old and holding Tucker's hand as we enter the dark hallway of the leaning barn. My brothers, August and March, are carrying blocks of hay to our horse and cow, as the hog grunts noisily outside, impatient for its daily feeding of corncobs. I look up at Tucker as she speaks. "This here is th' most important thing we do. We treat our animals right so they'll take care of us. Feedin' an' waterin' is what they need ever'day. Don't matter if'n we's sick 'r not, these animals has t' be takin' care of. You understand?"

I feel something tapping my foot and look down. It is the end of Will's walking stick. I look up at him.

"You all right, April?" he asks.

"Uh, sure. I was just remembering something I'd forgot."

"Must a been a pretty strong memory 'cause it was like you left here for a bit."

Giving my head a quick shake, I say, "Well I'm here now. What do you want me to do?"

"You ever been 'round livestock before?"

I catch myself just before answering with the truth. "Well my family owns a riding stable and I spent lots of time there."

"Really?" Will asks with raised eyebrows. "What kind of horses did you have?"

"Uh, I really didn't pay that much attention to that. We had hired hands to do all the work, so I guess I never heard them talk about what breed the horses were."

Will studies my face with his bright eyes, smiling the whole time. After a moment he says, "I see. Well let me walk you 'round the stalls so you can meet our herd."

Will stops at the first stall and I peer inside.

Jessica is brushing the most beautiful black horse I've ever seen. Its long, flowing tail and mane give it a sense of movement even when standing still. Jessica looks over her shoulder at me. "Come on inside and meet my horse, Beauty."

I look to Will for permission to enter.

"Go 'head if you want to."

Sidestepping a pile of manure, I join Jessica and Beauty.

"Isn't she beautiful?" Jessica asks. Her eyes glow with pride and admiration as she makes long, slow strokes with the coarse brush.

I rub my hand over Beauty's shimmering coat. She stops eating and turns to look at me.

"It's a new, unknown hand," Will interprets her behavior for me. "She's never met you."

"You mean she can feel the difference?" I ask.

"Girl, a horse can see, feel, and hear like no other animal. They're one of God's most attuned creatures."

I follow Jessica as she walks to the other side of Beauty. I'm shocked to see a jagged scar running from Beauty's shoulder and across her side and her hip. The flesh is thick along the length of it, creating an abrupt interruption of her otherwise smooth, fluid lines.

"What happened?" I asked.

Jessica lays her face on Beauty's neck. "Someone neglected her simply because she got hurt in an accident. They didn't call a veterinarian to sew her up. Now she'll have the scar for the rest of her life." Wrapping her arms around Beauty's neck and closing her eyes, she says, "But I love her anyway."

Will taps the door with his walking stick. "Come along, April. Let's meet the others."

At the next stall Heather is scooping up a pile of manure with a shovel. "This is the stupidest thing I've ever seen. This is nothing more than child slavery." Just as she finally corrals the last bit of manure onto the shovel, her large, muscled horse lifts its tail and dumps another load of manure to the stall floor. "What?!" Heather screams. "You stupid horse!"

I barely stifle a laugh and when I look at Will, he is grinning broadly.

"Why call a horse stupid for doin' something you do all the time?" Will asks. "I keep thinking you're gonna finally try harder to get along with the Beast, but you are sure taking your sweet time about it."

Heather glares at us. "What if I said I'm not going to clean stalls anymore?"

"That'd be your choice, but I suspect you'll have to discuss your consequences with the treatment team."

Heather rolls her eyes and huffs. "Okay, okay, I'll clean it up. But I still think it's probably against some kind of law."

I turn away with Will and find myself standing face-to-face with the long-faced and even longer-eared spectacle of a little donkey. His ears are dropped, and he has the saddest eyes I've ever seen in an animal.

"Hello, Pablo," Will says and scratches the donkey between his ears.

"How did he get loose?" I ask.

"You can't get loose if you're never put up," is Will's puzzling reply, and he limps off to the next stall.

"What does that mean?"

"It means we never put Pablo up. He's here because he chooses to be but he can leave anytime he wants."

"Who takes care of him? I mean, who feeds him and waters him?"

"Whoever thinks of doing it."

As I join him at the next open stall door, I say, "But that doesn't seem fair."

Will turns and fixes me with a somber expression. "So? What's your point?"

Not sure what to make of his callous attitude toward the beleaguered-looking burro, I shake my head and say, "Never mind."

As I look inside the stall I see Ashley pouring feed into a trough for a quiet, nondescript horse. It waits until Ashley steps away before it moves forward and begins eating. This is much different behavior than we used to see from our horse at Tucker's. That horse would knock you to the ground if you were moving slower than it wanted you to.

At the next stall Sarah is standing beside the longest-legged horse I've ever seen. I can't hear Sarah's words, but she is keeping up a constant flow of conversation.

Will sees the marvel in my eyes and says, "That there is Excelsior, a Tennessee walking horse. Remember to be careful on her blind side, Sarah."

"Yes, sir." She continues talking as she circles Excelsior to get to her other side. The horse's head comes up and her ears rotate like radar dishes. When Sarah begins brushing the other side, Excelsior returns to eating.

"Is she really blind in one eye?" I ask.

"Yep," Will says, shaking his head. "Not sure how it happened. Like the others, she had the problem when we got her."

Our next stop on the tour of the barn is Megan's horse. "Is that a mustang?" I ask.

Will nods. "Definitely has some mustang in it. Some people refer to them as paints. It's the kind of horses the Plains Indians rode. That's why we named him Tonto. They've got lots of spunk and spirit."

Right on cue, Tonto neighs loudly and steps away from Megan. Her face is as red as her hair. "Hold still! I'm just trying to brush you!"

"A calm voice and a steady hand," Will says. "That's what Tonto needs, Megan. Remember, a horse is just like a mirror. Whatever kind of energy you bring to it, it will give it right back to you. If you're frustrated, it'll act frustrated. If you're calm, it's more likely to be calm, too."

Throwing the brush on the floor, Megan says, "I don't know how to be calm! It's this red hair! It's a curse!"

Not rattled by Megan's explosion, Will says, "Then you've got a long, difficult road ahead of you, unless you want to abandon

Tonto. Is that what you want to do? I could let April take him, if she wants."

Though I didn't think it possible, Megan bristles even more. "No! Tonto is my horse!" She snatches the brush off the floor, takes a deep breath, and lets it out slowly. Facing Tonto, she says softly, "I'm sorry. I didn't mean that. I would never abandon you." She touches Tonto's flank and it twitches. He snorts loudly but stands still. "Good job," Megan says evenly. "You're a good boy."

Will gently touches my arm and motions with his head to follow him. Standing in the hallway of the barn, he says, "We have two more horses that don't belong to anyone. Sir is a good horse but he likes to push people's boundaries. If you give him an inch, he'll take a mile. So you've got to be tough to manage him. The other is Lady, a more gentle horse you'll never meet. But she's also lazy. She only wants to do the least amount of work possible, which makes some people think she is stubborn." Turning to me, he says, "So which one do you want to make yours?"

I think about all the horses I've looked at, with their varied personalities and how each of the girls relates to her animal. Then I think about what is left for me to choose from. Suddenly I feel a nudge from behind. When I turn around, I'm face-to-face with Pablo. He lifts his nose toward my face and raises his gigantic ears. I rub his soft muzzle and chin. Laughing, I say, "I think I'm the one getting chosen this time. If it's okay with you, Will, I want Pablo to be mine."

Once again, out of the corner of my eye, I see Will watching me closely. After a pause he says, "That's your choice. Pablo it is."

CHAPTER TWENTY-SEVEN

Deer April,

I hope you are doing all right. I shur do miss you. Smiley Carter says to tell you hi. He knows I'm sending you letters cause I told him so. You are a long way away from home. I wish I could see you. Those folks there better be treating you right or they is going to have to deal with me. I wonder if you's still mad at me for sending you thare. If I was you I guess it would have made me mad to be sent off like that. The thing is I was getting scared for you. It was sort of like watching your mama grow up all over again. You don't know this but when your mama gave you to me to raise I felt like I was being given a chans to do things over that I probly done wrong when I raised your mama. I was only 16 when I had her and I didn't have no mama or daddy to help me. I had to do it all by myself. Let me tell you it wasn't easy. All I knowed about raising a kid was how I was raised and how animals was raised. My raising was worse than the animals cause my daddy was a mean and evil man. So there was things that I knowed was wrong when it come to raising a kid and I made sure I didn't do none of them. But it was hard for me to know what was the right thing to do. I just had to guess my way through it. What made it bad for your mama was how mad I was at her for being born. I know that's a terrible thing for me to say and it might make you hate me for it but it's the truth. It took me a long time to figure out that my reasons for being mad wasn't her fault but by the time I did figure it out your mama was already gitting in trouble at school. I tried to be nicer to her and make up for them years I was mad at her but it was too late. She'd done closed me out of her life and wouldn't listen to anything I had to say to her. That's what I seen happening with you. You was shutting me out and you got to where you wouldn't talk to me about nothing and you wouldn't listen to anything I had to say. Then you started spending all your time wanting to be with that boy which is just what your mama started doing. She dated ever boy in the high school but wouldn't settle for none of them. It was like she was trying to see how many boys she could date. That's when her reputation started getting real bad. I know all about having a reputation cause I've had a bad reputation all my life. Everbody around here knows about me or at least they think they does. Part of me don't care what they think but now that I'm older I can see that that kind of attitude might not have been such a good idea. I hope while you're at Spirit Lake you can find out why you changed so much in these last years. Listen to what they tell you. Are you remembering them three things that I told you? Don't forget—I loved you yesterday. I love you today. And I'll love you tomorrow.

—Tucker

CHAPTER TWENTY-EIGHT

And now I see with eye serene
The very pulse of the machine;
A being breathing thoughtful breath,
A Traveller between life and death.
– William Wordsworth

MARCH:

I stop beside the closed door and, to reassure myself that I have not miscounted my steps, I feel the braille letters on the wall—Dr. Sydney, counselor.

Confident, I knock twice.

"Come in," a woman's voice calls.

I let myself in. Sniffing, I say, "That's a new candle you're burning." I sniff again. "But I don't recognize the scent."

"And hello to you, too," she says.

"Sorry, Dr. Sydney," I say apologetically. "Hello and how are you today?"

"I'm fine, Levi. Won't you have a seat?"

Using my cane, I maneuver myself to my usual nest. I fold the collapsible cane and lay it across my lap. "Are you going to tell me?" I ask.

"It's hazelnut. Do you like it?"

"Yeah, it smells like something that belongs in a kitchen."

"Does it remind you of any kitchen or anything you've smelled before?"

I pause and think. With Dr. Sydney nothing is done haphazardly or without a reason, but I can't find the scent in my memory. I shake my head. "Nothing."

I listen to her grip the rear wheels of her wheelchair and roll closer to me. She positions herself in front of me.

"What kind of week have you had?" she asks.

"About like every week since I've been here. Every day it's physical therapy, occupational therapy, recreational therapy, and school sessions for learning to improve my reading and writing of braille. By the end of the day I'm usually exhausted."

"Debbie tells me that in the six weeks you've been here you've made remarkable progress in every area. Do you agree with her assessment?"

Smiling, I ask, "What do you think?"

Dr. Sydney laughs. "Turning the tables on the therapist, eh?"

I shrug nonchalantly.

"Well I agree with Debbie. You've made remarkable strides socially, too. When you first came to group therapy you offered no feedback to the others and didn't let anyone in either. But you've become a really good listener and are insightful with your comments to the others in the group."

"Thank you."

Dr. Sydney is quiet. I can feel her studying me. It's an uncomfortable feeling to be on display like this, unable to return her gaze.

"Something's on your mind, isn't it?" she says. "Had some more memories come back to you?"

Shifting in my chair, I lean forward. "I've been doing like you suggested. I'm trying not to force anything. If something drops in, I keep my mind relaxed. It seems like I'm remembering my life backward. Ever since that first night here when I remembered how I ended up at the bottom of Little River there have been what I call snapshots that come to me. Not like a complete scene or movie, but just some still shots. Sometimes I can make sense of them, and other times I don't even know if the shots are from the same scene or time period of my life."

"I know this is frustrating for you, Levi, but don't forget what I keep telling you—you will remember what you need to remember and what you don't need to remember, you won't."

I listen as Dr. Sydney flips pages in what I presume is my file.

"So this fellow called Red found you at a rest area on Interstate Forty outside Oklahoma City, and we're guessing you were around fifteen years old. And you ended up at this rest area after you decided to run away from your pimp in Las Vegas."

An uncontrollable shiver runs through me. I shake my head slowly. "Those days in Las Vegas were hell, Dr. Sydney. I still can't believe I did some of the things I did." My voice breaks.

"Levi," she says gently, "stay here in the room with me. Don't allow yourself to go back there. You are in this room with me, right now. This is the present. Feel the arms of your chair. Ground yourself, Levi."

I do as she suggests and draw a ragged breath. Like a dog after its bath, I give my body a hard shake and blow my breath out.

"Are you with me, Levi?"

"Yes, ma'am. I'm okay."

"There is an end table to your right with a pitcher of water and a glass, if you'd like a drink."

Grateful to have a task to focus on, I slowly move my hand until it touches the table. I let my fingertips glide carefully.

"A little to your left," Dr. Sydney directs.

With that bit of navigational help I find the pitcher and the glass beside it. Surreptitiously putting my index finger against the inside of the glass, I pour until I feel the water touch my fingertip. After drinking the water, I return the glass to the table.

"Better?" she asks.

"Yes, thanks."

"So what conclusions have you come to regarding your life prior to Las Vegas?"

"I think I lived with some kind of hippie people, sort of like a commune, or maybe a cult. I've remembered a man named Alexander."

"Can you describe him to me?"

I look at the snapshot that my memory holds in front of me. "He had a long ponytail and wore sandals most of the time. His eyes were deep blue and his voice was always calm."

"I see," Dr. Sydney says. "And how did you meet Alexander? Can you remember the first time you met him?"

Breathing slowly, I tell my mind to relax. At first there is nothing but a fluid sea of colors. Then the colors begin separating, finding a stopping place on the canvas, and slowly a picture develops. "I'm at a rest stop and I'm inside the cab of an eighteen-wheeler. The driver is asleep in his bed at the rear of the large cab."

"Take your time, Levi," Dr. Sydney advises. "How does the little boy in the cab feel?"

At her question I feel panic and my heartbeat picks up speed. New, sharply defined memories are crashing in. "He's scared. He wants to get away from this man."

"So what does he do, Levi?"

"I silently open my door and crawl out of the cab. Then I race toward the bathroom. Just as I round the corner of the building I crash into this kind-looking man."

"Is it Alexander?"

"Yes. He kneels in front of me and smiles. He asks me why I'm in such a hurry and where my parents are. I tell him I've been kidnapped by a trucker and I've just escaped. He puts his arm around me and tells me not to worry, no one is going to hurt me now. Just as he does, a woman walks up and he turns to her and tells her to help me to their van. I say I've got to pee, but he says I can do it in the van."

"Levi, remember that you and I are in my office here at the Patricia Neal Rehabilitation Center. It is 1991 and you are a grown man. You are safe here in this room. Do you understand what I'm saying?"

Until she spoke, I didn't realize how small I was feeling and how anxious I was becoming. "Yes, Doctor. I know where I am. I'm okay."

"Can you tell where the rest area is located?"

I look back at the scene. As the woman is ushering me to the van, we pass a sign. "All I can tell you is there is a sign there that says 'Welcome to the Land of Enchantment.'"

"That's the motto for the state of New Mexico," Dr. Sydney says. "My sister lives there."

"Really?" I ask.

"Yes, but the thing we don't know is if you arrived there with the trucker heading east or west. We still don't know where you are from."

I sit in silence holding her last comment, then I add, "Or if I had a family or not."

"This has been a lot to take in today, Levi. Would you like to stop here and continue next time?"

I ignore her question and pick up the thread of my memory. "When I got in the van there were three boys and a girl in it, all younger than me. None of them looked alike, like they were kin. But they all looked sort of scared, just like I was. Just as the woman slid the door shut, Alexander jumped in, started the engine and drove away in a hurry.

"We drove for the rest of the day and all through the night. When we got hungry we ate peanut butter and crackers and when we needed to use the bathroom we pulled over on the side of the road. If Alexander stopped to get gas, we were told to be quiet and act like we were asleep.

"Sometime the next day the roads kept getting smaller and rougher, until finally we ended up on a small lane that twisted and turned until it stopped in front of two mobile homes. The first sensation I had was that I was being waved at in greeting, but I quickly realized that it was just multiple clotheslines that were loaded with clothes flapping in the breeze.

"The doors of the mobile homes swung open and a handful of kids poured out of each and ran toward the van. They all peered into and tapped on the windows, making faces and calling out to us. I felt like I was an animal on display at the zoo.

"Alexander got out and walked into the chorus of children, patting them on the heads and smiling. When he slid the side door open for us, we were inundated with questions from the children, so many that it was impossible to answer even one.

"As I got out I noticed three women approaching from the trailers. In turn, each of them hugged the woman who'd been with us on the trip and then did the same to Alexander, who kissed each one on the top of her head. Next he clapped his hands three times. The effect was immediate, as all the children fell silent and moved behind the four women.

"'It's time for introductions,' Alexander said. He held a hand toward the women, and the one who rode with us stepped forward. Looking at us, he said, 'This is Summer. You will call her Mother Summer.' He nodded at Summer, who smiled and stepped back. The next woman in line stepped up. 'And this is Autumn. You will call her Mother Autumn.' She, too, returned his smile and stepped back. The next woman who stepped forward didn't look as happy as the other three and wasn't as young, either. 'This is Winter. You will call her Mother Winter.' The last one to step up didn't look like she was a lot older than me, but it was obvious she was pregnant. 'And this is Spring. You will call her Mother Spring.'"

"So," Dr. Sydney chimed in, "he named each of the women after one of the seasons. How convenient he only had four. So, did he name all of you kids after the names of the months? You know, like January, February, March—"

Something like the sound of crystal breaking followed by a deadbolt being opened sounds in my head. I slowly repeat Dr. Sydney's last words, "Named after the months, like January, February, March—"

Suddenly a jolt hits me so hard that it actually knocks me to one side. As if I was below a dam whose floodgates have been opened, I feel like I am at the bottom of a cascading waterfall of memories. I turn my face up into the rushing torrent. Images sluice over, around, and through me, images of familiar people, places, and names: Tucker . . . August . . . April . . . my mother Maisy . . . the old house we lived in . . . the old barn . . . the garden . . . Smiley Carter. Tears rivaling the volume of memories that have been unleashed flow down my face. Sheer joy fills my heart. I cannot catch my breath.

I hear Dr. Sydney's voice but not her words. Her hand grips my arm and shakes me. "Levi, Levi! What has happened? What have you remembered?"

I turn my tear-soaked face toward her and declare, "I am not Levi. I am March Tucker!"

CHAPTER TWENTY-NINE

I heard a thousand blended notes,
While in a grove I sate reclined,
In that sweet mood when pleasant thoughts
Bring sad thoughts to the mind.
—William Wordsworth

TUCKER:

I hear Smiley Carter's truck comin' up th' road towards m' house. Even tho' he won't admit it, he does love that truck I bought him with some of Ella's money. He'll complain 'bout it an' say it ain't as good as drivin' his tractor, but he don't hardly drive anywhere on his tractor anymore, unless it's t' plow m' garden fer me.

Ever since Ella died he's been comin' over t' my house fer coffee once 'r twice a week. Me an' him's been knowin' each other most all our lives. He was always good t' me when I was growin' up. It's like he knowed what m' daddy was doin' t' me an' he felt sorry fer me.

But it ain't like his life's been easy 'r nothin' like that. Fer a man t' lose his wife an' then his son, too, is more than any one person should have t' bear. I think that hurt is what caused him t' turn t' drinkin' an' women.

All that changed tho' when Ella come along. Ella had that kind o' power. She changed ever'one she met. It wasn't so much what she did as it was what she was. The most powerful woman I ever knowed! Lord knows I do miss her.

I'm so deep in thought that when Smiley knocks on th' door I nearly jump outta m' skin! "Come in!" I yell.

The door opens wide and Smiley steps through. His bright, toothy smile is almost as good as sunshine fer drivin' away sadness.

"What are you yellin' at an old man for? I was just trying to be polite and knock like company's supposed to."

He tries t' look serious but he can't keep th' corners of his mouth pinned down. A burst o' laughter jumps outta his mouth like a toad tryin' to escape from a snake.

Ignorin' his laugh, I wave toward a kitchen chair an' say, "Have a seat an' I'll get us some coffee. An' before y' ask, yes I put some chicory in it jes' like y' like it."

He pulls out th' chair an' groans as he sits down. "Man, this misery in my knees and back is giving me fits today."

"Lord, you an' yore misery! You sound like an ol' man. I even think I heared yore knees squeakin'." I set our two cups o' coffee on th' table, his with a saucer underneath, an' sit down. He's gonna wonder where the pie is, 'cause I always have a piece ready fer 'im. I got a pie coolin' on th' back porch, but I'm gonna pertend like I ain't got none.

Smiley's eyebrows rise in reaction t' th' empty space beside his coffee cup. He picks up his cup an' tilts it 'til it dribbles onto th' saucer. Then he picks up th' saucer, gently blows across the steamin' coffee an' sips. It's th' way he's drunk coffee ever since I knowed him.

Drummin' my fingers on th' table, actin' like I'm perturbed, I say, "You know, a horse don't make as much noise drinking outta a trough as you do drinkin' yore coffee. Why can't y' drink coffee like normal folks do?"

He cocks his head at me. "Tucker, only you could find a way to hurt a man's feelings twice in a matter of five minutes. You know this is how I always drink my coffee. It don't seem natural any other way. And besides, where's the pie at? That's what I want to know."

I hit th' side o' my head with th' heel o' my hand. "I knew there was somethin' I was supposed t' do this mornin'—fix a pie! It clean slipped m' mind."

The corner o' Smiley's eyes and mouth slowly drift south. "Well," he says slowly as he looks at his coffee cup, "I suppose that's all right. It's just that I didn't get a chance to eat breakfast this morning and I was already thinking about a piece of your pie on the drive over. My taste buds sure are disappointed."

Fer a moment I think he actually might cry.

Slappin' th' table with m' hand, I say, "Oh my gosh, ol' man. Don't act like it's th' end o' th' world jes' 'cause you ain't got no pie." I stand up an' head t' th' back porch. "I got pie. I was jes' wantin' t' pull yore leg a bit. Let me git you some before you go into mournin'."

When I come back carryin' th' pie, Smiley's grinnin' from ear t' ear an' his eyes is dancin' like th' grandkids' used to when I gave them a piece o' candy.

Once I set a piece o' pie in front o' him, th' only sounds heard fer th' next several minutes is th' clink o' his fork on th' plate and an occasional slurp o' coffee from his saucer.

When he finishes, Smiley scoots th' plate back an' wipes the corner of his mouth with his hand, but that was a wasted motion 'cause not even a crumb escaped gettin' pushed inside his mouth.

"Now that was a mighty fine piece of pie, Tucker. You know what? I believe your pies are as good as Mama Mattie used to make, and that's high praise."

"I know what you're up to. You're jes' butterin' me up so I'll keep feedin' you pie. Besides, if I make pie as good as Mama Mattie, it's 'cause she taught me how. She used to say, 'It's all 'bout th' home-made crust.'"

There's a lull in our conversation an' we jes' sit quietly. It's one o' th' things that lets y' know you got a good friend, when y' can sit together an' not say nothin' an' both o' you is comfortable with th' silence.

Smiley's the one who finally decides t' step into th' silence. He clears his throat an' says, "What's the latest word on April?"

"Whatever word I get 'bout April don't come from her. She ain't sent one card 'r letter. There's a woman there that sends me a letter every few weeks jes' t' update me on how things is goin'."

"How long is it that she's been gone now?"

"It's been two months."

"And what does this woman tell you?"

"She says April is a hard case, hard as a tortoise. An' that the progress is really slow with 'er. Course that ain't nothin' that I didn't already know. That's how come I sent 'er there in th' first place. She kept gittin' harder an' harder. I wasn't gittin' nowhere with 'er."

Smiley sucks his teeth, which is a sure sign he's thinkin' deep. "It's a puzzle to me how such a sweet, pleasant child can suddenly turn like that. When she was little, she was just like an angel. I guess maybe it was losing her mama and then losing Ella, too, that turned her."

Images o' my beautiful, raven-haired daughter, Maisy, rise outta th' mist o' my memory. Suddenly th' evil, leering face o' my father replaces Maisy's. Every muscle in my body tenses. He reaches out an' touches my arm. I yell an' jerk away from him.

"Tucker, are you all right?!"

Th' mist clears an' I see th' concerned face o' Smiley across from me. "Huh?"

"I said, 'Are you all right?' It's like you left the room on me."

Shakin' my head, I say, "Oh I got lost in my memory fer a minute. That jes' happens sometimes. I'm fine. What were you sayin' before that happened?"

"I said it must have been losing her mama and Ella that changed April."

"I suppose you're right. She became hard after that. And o' course don't fergit 'bout losin' 'er brother March, too. All that is a lot fer anybody, much less a little girl."

"And whatever became of April's boyfriend that went missing? I don't ever hear anything about that anymore."

All th' hair on th' back o' my neck stands up an' a chill runs down m' spine. I feel m' face flush. "I don't know nothin' either. My guess is he run off t' git away from that sow of a mother he's got."

Suddenly there's a knock on th' front door that acts like an electric shock in my chair. I jump straight up, bumping th' table an' spillin' our coffee.

Smiley grabs both cups before they turn over. He looks at me like I'm a crazy woman. His eyes say, "What's got into you, woman?"

I walk t' the door an' open it. Sheriff Ron Harris is standin' there, Stetson hat squarely in place an' dark sunglasses hidin' his eyes. His mouth is a straight line.

"Tucker," he says matter-of-factly, "I think you better come with me. Someone has discovered Mark Allen's truck down the road from here in the Obion bottom."

CHAPTER THIRTY

It is not you alone who know what it is to be evil,
I am he who knew what it was to be evil.
—*Walt Whitman*

TUCKER:

Starin' at the sheriff, I feel all th' blood drain from m' face. As a matter o' fact, if feels like all th' blood in m' body has dried up. It's like th' earth has stopped turnin'.

I hear a noise behind me, followed by Smiley's voice.

"Hello, Sheriff Harris."

Th' sheriff gives th' slightest nod of his head an' says, "Smiley."

Smiley steps along side o' me. "Is there trouble?" he asks.

I can't see past his dark sunglasses, but I can feel that th' sheriff's eyes are still fixed on me, even though he's speakin' t' Smiley.

"It's the Allen kid's truck. I think it's been found."

Suckin' his teeth, Smiley says, "Is that the boy that's been missing for so long?"

"Yep, that's the one. Tucker, do you mind riding with me to watch them pull it out of the water?"

Foldin' m' arms across m' chest, I say, "What if I say I got better things t' do?"

Several beats pass before th' sheriff replies. "I'd say that's up to you. But it would make me wonder why you wouldn't want to go. After all, he was April's boyfriend. She might still be concerned, even if you're not."

My breath has come back t' me an' I'm beginnin' t' feel more like m'self. Sheriff Harris ain't no fool an' there ain't no good gonna come from me not cooperatin' with him. "You're right," I say. "I need t' go with you t' see what they've found." I turn an' look at Smiley.

"He can follow in his own truck," the sheriff says. He turns around an' walks t' the cruiser.

I follow him.

"You can ride up front with me," he tells me.

As he pulls onto th' road, I ask, "Who found th' truck?"

"It was Shady Green. He was fishing and he kept thinking he saw something under the water. Then the sun reflected off of either a mirror or one of the windows and he was sure it was a vehicle."

Shady Green! That simple-minded, tongue-tied fool! Leave it t' him t' complicate things fer me. Even though part o' me has known th' truck would eventually be found, I thought it'd be later in th' summer, when th' water was low.

Up ahead I see the Moore brothers' big wrecker sittin' crossways in th' road. Sammy, th' older brother, is standin' at th' back o' th' wrecker with a rifle restin' on his shoulder, while his younger brother, Randall, has th' hook an' cable over his shoulder an' is wadin' into th' water.

The cruiser slows to a stop. Sheriff Harris picks up th' microphone t' his police radio an' says, "I'm at the site now. Have you got hold of the TBI yet?"

Th' radio crackles back, "Yes sir, Sheriff. The agent based in Jackson is on his way. ETA is forty minutes."

"That's 10-4," the sheriff replies. Hangin' up the radio microphone, he gets outta th' car an' I follow his lead.

Just as we do, Sammy takes th' rifle off his shoulder, aims toward Randall an' fires a shot. There's a splash 'bout four feet t' Randall's left. He cries out.

"I got 'im," Sammy says with satisfaction.

"What are you trying to do?!" Randall yells.

"Killing the cottonmouths before they kill you, just like we agreed," Sammy yells back.

Randall's face has turned beet red. "But you're supposed to tell me before you shoot! You about gave me a heart attack!"

Sammy laughs. "Oh calm down, little brother, and get that cable hooked on whatever is lying under the water out there. I'll keep an eye out for more snakes. And yes, I'll let you know before I shoot." He pulls th' lever controllin' th' winch an' starts lettin' out more cable.

Smiley limps up to us. "What's the shooting all about?"

"I'm just trying to keep all those water moccasins from eating Randall alive," Sammy says with a grin.

"Well I'm telling you right now," Smiley says, "there's not enough money to get me to wade out into that swamp. I've fished down here plenty of times and sometimes I think there are more snakes than there are fish in that dark water."

Ever'one lets th' truth o' Smiley's statement stand without addin' anything t' it. Our attention turns t' Randall.

I notice the undulating wake of a snake makin' its way toward Randall. I look at Sammy t' be sure he's seen it, but th' rifle is already cradled against his shoulder an' he's takin' aim at th' slitherin' serpent. He yells, "Snake!" an' fires at th' same time.

Randall's head jerks toward th' splash. "Did you get him?"

"Of course I did," Sammy yells at his brother. "You know I don't miss."

He's tellin' th' truth. Ever'body in th' county knows that Sammy's th' best shot around.

Randall continues t' battle his way through lily pads an' th' thick muddy ooze that's at least two feet deep underneath th' quiet, murky water. All these flooded areas along th' Obion, up around Latham, between McKenzie an' Trezevant, are th' same. They're good fer duck huntin' in th' winter, fishin' in th' spring, an' snakes in th' summer.

'Bout thirty feet from th' road bed, Randall stops suddenly. "Ow! I think I've found it." He reaches down t' rub his shin.

"Try and find something heavy to put that cable around," Sammy shouts to his brother. "That quicksand-like mud has probably pulled it down deep and won't let go without a fight."

Randall leans down until his chin touches th' water as he feels his way 'round th' truck.

I suddenly realize I've stopped breathin', even though m' heart's poundin' against m' chest like a wild horse tryin' t' kick its way out of a stall. My thoughts have been hijacked by mem'ries o' Maisy's body bein' found in th' bottoms and of another time long, long ago when a girl got rid o' th' devil who'd tortured her her whole life.

"You okay, Tucker?" The sheriff's voice grabs my attention.

Drawing a deep breath, I fold m' arms across m' chest. "Sure, I'm fine. Jes' tryin' t' figure out why y' wanted me t' come see this."

He gives me another silent stare an' then turns his attention t' th' Moore brothers.

Randall stands up an' waves his arm. "Okay, let's see if this'll hold good enough to pull this thing out."

Sammy raises the rpm's on the truck an' starts takin' th' slack outta th' cable.

BAM! The sound is so loud an' unexpected we all jump, except for Sheriff Harris, whose drawn pistol is pointing toward a thick-bodied snake writhin' on th' edge o' th' blacktop. There is only a ragged, bloody wound where th' head used t' be.

"Damn!" Smiley says. "That's why you won't ever catch me down here in the summer. That water is thick with snakes."

"Good shooting," Sammy says to th' sheriff.

After he holsters his pistol, Harris points toward the submerged truck. "Let's get that thing out of there."

Randall steps outta th' water covered in mud an' vegetation as Sammy slows th' winch. Th' cable is as tight as a new clothesline. Th' motor begins t' bog down as th' irresistible force meets an unmovable object. Th' back end o' th' wrecker squats an' th' front tires lift off th' blacktop a couple o' inches.

For a moment I think th' bottom ain't gonna release th' truck from its muddy grave. Then bubbles appear where th' cable disappears into th' water.

"There she comes," Sammy says with satisfaction. "The suction's finally broken loose."

I watch th' truck comin' toward me. I feel like I did th' time I was a kid an' a man come t' our school for a program an' hypnotized some of us. It don't seem real.

After a few minutes th' truck is sittin' on th' side o' th' road. Water is seeping around the doors o' the water-filled cab. The smell o' sulphur, the result o' th' mixture o' mud, decaying vegetation, an' fertilizer runoff that has been stirred by th' exiting truck, saturates th' air.

"Shoooeee," Randall exclaims.

Sheriff Harris removes a pair o' rubber gloves from his hip pocket an' pulls them on. He looks at me an' says, "You got anything you want to say before I open the door?"

I give him one o' his silent stares.

When I don't answer him, he turns an' walks t' th' truck. Grippin' the handle he pulls open th' door. Greenish-yellow water comes pouring out onto th' road. A wad o' snakes lands at his feet an' he jumps back. It's impossible t' tell how many snakes there are, they are so tangled an' writhin'.

Two loud booms go off in quick succession an' there is nothin' left but blood an' guts sprayed over th' road an' th' side o' th' truck.

We all turn an' see th' smokin' barrels o' Sammy's double-barrel 12-gauge shotgun.

The sheriff touches th' brim of his Stetson and says, "I owe you."

Then he steps where he can see th' interior o' th' cab o' th' pickup. After a moment he pushes his hat t' th' back o' his head an' takes his sunglasses off. "It's empty," he says in a bewildered tone. Then he turns t' me an' says, "I can't believe it. It's empty."

CHAPTER THIRTY-ONE

Deer April,

I wonder if you has changed since you been gone.

Have you gained weight or got taller?

What about your pretty hair? Is it any longer?

Do you have enough clothes?

Do I need to send you anything?

What kind of food do they give you there? Is it as good as my cooking?

What kinds of trees is there way over there?

What's the weather like? Is it as hot there as it is here?

Is there any bears over there?

Do them people there let you listen to your loud music like you like to?

Are them people treating you good?

Are you learning anything?

Do you ever think about me?

Can you think about me without hating me?

Do you miss sleeping in your bed?

Why won't they let you write a letter to me?

I miss you.

I loved you yesterday. I loved you today. And I'll love you tomorrow.
—Tucker

CHAPTER THIRTY-TWO

The way of a fool is right in his own eyes:
but he that hearkeneth unto counsel is wise.
—*Proverbs 12:15*

APRIL:

Okay, ladies, let's rise and shine!"

The jarring sound of Michelle's voice scatters the pieces of the dream I'm in the middle of, leaving me to wonder just how it finally turned out. I sit up and rub my eyes. It is so dim in the cabin that the other girls look like ghosts as they stretch and try to wake up.

"Let's go take a hike before you feed the animals and eat breakfast. I'm leaving in ten minutes. Up and at 'em!"

Michelle spins around quickly and is out the door. As she exits I can see that it is barely light outside.

"Shut up and leave me alone!" Megan's angry voice echoes in the cabin.

Ever since I arrived at Spirit Lake three weeks ago, Megan's morning ritual is the same. I'm getting sick and tired of her surly attitude. She puts everyone on edge and in a foul mood. Everyone, including the horses.

One morning we were busy feeding and brushing our horses. Everything was quiet and calm. Then, as soon as Megan stepped through the barn door, late as usual, all the horses acted like a wolf had pounced into their stall. They threw their heads in the air and started snorting, neighing, and switching their tails. Even Pablo skittered away from me and went to stand in a faraway corner of the barn.

I throw off my covers and stride to Megan's bed. "Look," I say, "I'm fed up with you and your attitude. All you've got to do is get out of bed like the rest of us and fall in line with the program. You make everyone dread the morning, not because of how early we have to get up, but because you act like you slept in a bed full of cockleburs. Just shut up and get out of bed!"

Turning away, I head back to my bed to get dressed. As I pass by Sarah I can see that my behavior has terrified her. I really don't care if she's scared or not. I'm tired of her, too. Always acting like a scared sheep and never speaking her mind.

Suddenly her eyes open even wider and her hand flies to her open mouth. I hear hurried footsteps behind me, but before I can turn around Megan slams into me and jumps on my back. She grabs a handful of my hair and nearly jerks it out by its roots.

"Nobody tells me what to do, bitch!" she yells.

I try to sling her off my back by spinning sharply, but she holds on like a raccoon on a coon dog's head.

"Fight!" Heather yells excitedly as she approaches us. "Come on, give it to her, April! Hit her in the head, Megan!"

I backpedal as hard and fast as I can, finally slamming Megan against the wall. The impact makes her lose her grip on me and I hear a *whoosh* as her lungs empty. Turning around, I grab handfuls of her red hair and slam her head against the logs. Her eyes lose focus and I suddenly see the face of Mark Allen. Screaming, I let go and jump back.

Someone bear hugs me from behind and a man steps between me and Megan.

"That's enough!" the man says.

Michelle, who I've figured out is the one who has wrapped her arms around me, says, "Everyone calm down."

"So," the man says, "I'm gone for a few weeks and you all turn into a pack of wild animals?" His dark eyes snap. With his short-cropped black hair, low forehead, and camouflaged clothes, he looks like a drill sergeant. Focusing his attention on me, he says, "I don't believe we've met. My name is James." He sticks his hand out to me.

Michelle lets go of me, and I shake his hand. "My name is April."

"Nice to meet you." Looking over my shoulder at Michelle, he says, "I think it's time we give these young ladies the opportunity to learn some lessons about teamwork and cooperation."

"I think you are right," Michelle agrees.

"Not that again," Jessica and Ashley groan in unison.

"It'll be a surprise to the other girls," James says. "You two just keep the surprise to yourselves."

Michelle looks at her watch. "You all now have five minutes to meet us in front of the cabin."

She and James leave the cabin.

Not another word is spoken by any of us as we hurriedly get dressed. As we exit the cabin we immediately notice a thirty-foot piece of small chain stretched out on the ground. Every six feet there is a handcuff attached to it.

I am curious but apprehensive, too.

"As I told you earlier," Michelle says, "we are going on a hike together."

"No doubt," James chimes in, "you've been on hikes before, especially here at Spirit Lake. But except for Jessica and Ashley, you've never been on a hike quite like this one."

Michelle points at the chain. "Each of you will have a handcuff attached to your right ankle."

Heather immediately speaks up. "You're not about to treat me like some kind of nigger slave on a chain. I'm not going to do it and you can't make me."

James's voice stays even. "You are right, Heather. What do we say here at Spirit Lake all the time?"

"It's all about choices," Sarah answers for the group.

"That's right, Sarah. So Heather can refuse to make the choice to do this exercise. But for every choice you make in life there are always consequences."

"The object of this exercise," Michelle says, picking up the narrative, "is for all of you to make this hike together, as James and I have instructed you. We will not start the hike until everyone follows instructions and none of the animals will get fed until we complete the hike."

As if they've been listening for their cue, three of the horses neigh impatiently from inside the barn.

"You might as well do it, Heather," Jessica says. "They aren't kidding. They'll wait you out."

"And there's no sense in punishing your horse," Ashley adds.

Heather stands with her nostrils flared and her bottom lip sticking out. Her forehead is so furrowed I can barely see her eyes. I know how she feels—trying to take a stand for herself and giving in without losing face, both at the same time. It's a difficult balancing act.

"Do what you want to do," I say to her. "I'm not worried about Pablo. He can find something to eat on his own."

"Let's just get on with it!" Megan says, her temper still just below the boiling point. "It's stupid to just stand around like this!"

Heather lets out a breath. "I'll do it for my horse, but that's the only reason I'll agree to do it."

"Okay then," James says. "Jessica, you are first in line, then Ashley. Sarah, you'll be next, then Heather. Megan, you're behind Heather, and April, you're at the end."

Like prisoners on a work crew, we step in line and click the handcuffs on our ankles.

Michelle checks each one to make sure it's not too loose or tight. Then she walks to the front of the line as James moves behind me.

"Okay, girls," Michelle says, "let's go."

CHAPTER THIRTY-THREE

A merry hearth maketh a cheerful countenance:
but by sorrow of the heart the spirit is broken.
—*Proverbs 15:13*

APRIL:

Before I can take a step my right foot is jerked out from under me and I fall down. The pull backward on Megan spins her around and she falls to the ground, too. Like a lineup of dominos, everyone topples to the ground in succession.

We fill the forest air with a chorus of swearing. Everyone is jerking the chain behind them and yelling at each other.

"Okay, ladies," James says, "let's be careful with our language and then let's try this again."

"Look," Jessica says, "we've got to walk at the same pace and make sure our steps are synchronized."

"Quit trying to tell me what to do!" Megan exclaims. Standing up, she jerks the chain. "Come on, let's get this over with!"

Heather jumps up and jerks back on the chain. "Quit doing that! It hurts my ankle."

Ashley and Jessica are sitting on the ground, their heads resting on their knees. Ashley raises her head and pleads to Michelle, "Please make them do this right. I can't make them do anything."

Michelle leans against a tree nonchalantly. "And I can't make them do anything either. I've got all day to wait."

Finally, we all manage to stand up.

"Let's try this again," Jessica says. "On three we'll all step with our right foot first. One . . . two . . . three."

Everyone takes one step and stops. I almost lose my balance but steady myself by grabbing Megan's shoulder. Simultaneously she does the same thing by gripping Heather's arm. Soon everyone is waving their arms like we're walking on a high wire at the circus, trying to keep from falling.

Jessica counts and we take another step. We make our way across the clearing of the cabins, taking five times longer than it would usually take to step across it. When we make it to the other side, I expect the exercise to be over. But Michelle takes a turn and walks twenty feet into the woods.

With one voice we girls raise a chorus of protests.

"You know what, Michelle?" James says behind me.

"What's that, James?"

"I believe this is the whiniest bunch of babies we've ever had at Spirit Lake. My twins didn't cry this much when they were babies."

Laughing, Michelle says, "I do believe you are right. We might end up being out here all day getting this done. I sure do feel sorry for the horses."

Being baited by someone like this is nothing new to me. I've gone through school having to learn to deal with it. I grit my teeth and rub my thigh.

Oh, if I could only have a few moments alone, I could take this agitation away. So far I've been successful in keeping my habit a secret from everyone. I found a utility knife in the barn one day and, unscrewing it, I slipped one of the extra razor blades out and hid it inside the Bible they gave me my first day here.

"Anytime you're ready, ladies," James says.

We're barely ten feet into the woods before we all tumble to the forest floor.

"You all are killing me," Heather says. "Megan and April are slowing me down and you others are going too fast."

"Don't blame me," Megan fires back. "It's all this undergrowth and roots. If you all want to go faster, just say so. Me and April will keep up fine." She turns and looks at me for agreement.

"You take care of yourself and I'll take care of me," I reply. "I'll go however fast or slow I want to."

Megan's hair looks like it turns even redder. "Fine then!" she snaps.

Suddenly we notice that neither Michelle nor James is anywhere in sight.

"Where did they go?" Heather asks as she scans the area.

Sarah starts to cry. "They've abandoned us to the wild animals out here."

"No they haven't," Jessica says.

"I'll tell you who the biggest crybaby in this group is," I say. Pointing at Sarah, I say, "It's you. Don't you ever get tired of crying about everything? It makes you look and sound so weak."

Sarah bursts into tears.

"Leave her alone!" Ashley says to me. "There's nothing wrong with crying. You wouldn't know that because, according to you, you had such a perfect life. Well that's not true for everybody. Sometimes it's a demonstration of courage and honesty to let others see you cry, not a sign of weakness."

Feelings boil up inside me, almost gagging me. The pressure from inside my eyes makes it feel like they are going to burst like an oil geyser. I slap both my thighs repeatedly as hard as I can, trying to shut everything down. After several moments, the wave has passed and I stop hitting myself. My breathing eases. I notice everyone is staring at me.

"What was that all about?" Megan says.

"You looked like some kind of crow trying to fly," Heather says. She snickers.

Sarah wipes at her tears and smiles. "That was hilarious looking."

All of a sudden, they all burst into laughter. I'm so relieved that I've avoided a crisis, I ignore their comments and join in their laughter. But my laughter is the hysterical kind that comes when someone narrowly misses getting hit by a train.

Our laughter serves as a potion that takes the edge off. Everyone's face is adorned with a smile.

I look at Jessica. "So what's the story on James? How come I've never seen him here?"

"James is cool," Jessica replies. "He's fair and straightforward. You don't have to wonder where you stand with him. He tells it like it is. And he's a really good therapist, too."

"Where has he been all this time?" I ask.

"It's his wife. She's got leukemia really bad. Nobody says so, but I don't think she's going to make it. I'm guessing she's been back in the hospital, and James has been with her."

"You're probably right," Ashley agrees. "And his young twin boys, it'll be so sad for them."

"Death is just something that happens," I say flatly. "They'll just have to get over it."

Once again everyone looks at me.

"I've known some hard people," Heather says, "but I don't believe there's anybody in Chicago that's hard as you, April. Don't you feel anything for anybody?"

Looking directly at her, I say, "What's the point in that? All that will happen is you will get hurt because people are going to either let you down or leave you. It's safer just to take care of your own business and let everyone else take care of theirs. That way you never get hurt."

A sudden noise in the woods snatches everyone's attention. As the sound gets closer, we all stand up in a huddle. Some low-hanging limbs part and James and Michelle appear.

"See," James says as he points at us, "it is our group. I told you it was."

"But I thought I heard laughter coming from this direction," Michelle says. "I just knew that couldn't be our bunch of girls. Our girls either fight or they whine. They never laugh."

In spite of ourselves, we smile back at them.

"It was April," Sarah says. "You two should have seen her. She was hilarious."

Michelle looks at her watch. "Anyone getting hungry?"

"Yes!" we all answer at once.

"Then let's finish this hike," James says. "Lead away, Michelle."

Michelle turns and strides back in the direction she just came from.

"Everybody watch the person's feet in front of them," Megan says. "Try to match their movements."

For the next hour we struggle through the hike. The difference is that when someone falls down, the ones beside them help them up. There's no angry yelling or accusing. No one jerking the chain.

Just before we break into the clearing, we pass a tree with a sign on it that reads, "R & R Tree." There are small piles of rocks all around the base of it.

Pointing, I ask, "What is that?"

Jessica and Ashley look at each other.

"We're not allowed to say," Ashley says. "You'll eventually learn about it."

Megan and I share a look and shrug.

"Let's stop for a minute," James says. "Everyone sit down and let's process what's happened on our little hike."

After we all get situated comfortably on the ground, James asks, "So what did you all get from this exercise?"

Heather raises her hand.

"Heather?" James says.

"I learned that I could never have made it as a slave. My ankles were not made for shackles."

Everyone, James and Michelle included, laughs out loud.

"Well," James says, "a good therapist never argues with what someone gets out of an experience, so we'll have to let that one stand. What about someone else?"

Jessica raises her hand. After James acknowledges her with a nod, she says, "You might think you can make it through life without anyone else, but it's not true. Everyone has to learn to trust others and to lean on them for help." As she finishes, she is looking directly at me.

I notice that James and Michelle are taking mental notes of who the target of Jessica's comments is. They look at each other.

"Anybody else learn something?" Michelle asks.

Sarah raises her hand.

"Go ahead, Sarah," Michelle encourages her.

"In life everyone falls down and needs someone to help them up."

"And sometimes," Megan adds, "the person you need to help you might be someone you've been unkind to in the past, so you wonder, 'Will they be there for me?'"

"I think it's interesting," Ashley says, "how much better we all felt and got along after we had a good laugh together. There must be something therapeutic about that."

The sound of cicadas high in the trees begins to fill the air as the temperature rises. I swat at a pesky tassel fly.

"No one else has anything to say?" James asks. I can feel him looking at me but I keep my eyes on a trail of ants carrying leaves to their underground home.

"Fair enough, then," he says. "Michelle, unlock the handcuffs and let our prisoners go feed their horses."

CHAPTER THIRTY-FOUR

Deer April,

Have I done the wrong thing in sending you to Spirit Lake? I just had me a dream. It was about when I made you go live with Ella to see if she could help you start talking. When I woke up from that dream I was fraid that you felt like I sent you to Ella's cause I didn't love you or I just wanted to get rid of you. That must have been real hard for you cause you didn't know Ella very much then. Was you scared? Did it make you mad at me? The more I thought about it the more guilty I got. I had to write this letter quick so I could get it off my heart before it broke in two. It's akchally hard to write cause I'm crying so much. That's what them smudges are that's on the paper. April I didn't mean to hurt you when I sent you to Ella's. You ain't got no idea how much it hurt me to let you go. My chest hurt nearly ever day for a couple of weeks after you went down there. Did I tell you why I sent you to Ella's? It wasn't just so you'd start talking. It was cause the state was going to take you from me if you didn't start talking. That's right. They was going to take you away from me. I don't rightly know what would have happened if they had really come to take you but I'll bet some folks would have wished they hadn't tried. Don't nothing make me bristle like somebody messing with my kids. So that's why I asked Ella to help me. I didn't want to ask her cause I don't like asking for help and I especially don't like having to trust people. But them right there is two things I learned from Ella—that asking for help is okay and some people can be trusted. In her own sweet way Ella saved all of us. But after my dream I also thought about how me sending you to Spirit Lake may have reminded you of that time I sent you to Ella's and that you think I'm wanting to get rid of you all over again. Nothing could be further from the truth. I'm hoping that Spirit Lake can do the same thing for you that Ella done. You ain't forgot have you? I loved you yesterday. I loved you today. And I'll love you tomorrow.

—Tucker

CHAPTER THIRTY-FIVE

Farewell, love, and all they laws for ever,
Thy baited hooks shall tangle me no more.
—Sir Thomas Wyatt

MARCH:

Sitting outside on the bench, I lift my face into the warm sunshine. A mockingbird incessantly repeats every sound it has ever heard, never making the same sound twice. I imagine it sitting on top of a power pole or the peak of a rooftop, giving its wings a quick flap after each burst of song and flying straight up about three feet and landing back in the same place, over and over again.

The soft spring breeze brings a familiar scent my way. Turning my head to the left, I smile and say, "Hi, Debbie," just as the sound of her footsteps enters range.

She sits beside me.

"Lord help the person who tries to sneak up on you," she says. "Who needs to see when they have radar like yours? I think I'm going to quit washing my hair and taking showers. Then we'll see if I can slip up on you."

I laugh. "Trust me, if you do that, you'll be giving off a scent that everyone will be able to detect. But you'll probably have a lot more room at your cafeteria table."

Her pleasant laughter bubbles out of her throat.

"You know that I've told you how much I love your laugh. I remember it was one of the first things I liked about you. It's musical." Pointing, I add, "Almost as musical as that mockingbird over there."

She shifts on the bench. Her knee touches mine and she keeps it there. "I see it now," she says. "How can you be sure it is a mockingbird?"

"Just listen. That was the song of a black-capped chickadee. That one is of a cardinal. And that one is of a tufted titmouse. They are all different. The only bird that can do that is a mockingbird. It's the Tennessee state bird, you know."

"I probably should know that, but I guess I forgot. You certainly seem to know a lot about them." She shifts back to her original position and our knees lose contact.

I miss the warmth of her touch. "The first time I learned about mockingbirds was when August, my brother, and I were helping my grandmother, Tucker, in the garden. There was this large oak tree that we kept our water jars underneath in its shade. Tucker pointed to the top of it and, in her high-pitched voice, said, 'That thar's a mockin'bird. It's th' onliest bird I know that ain't got its own song. Seems sorta sad, dontcha think?'" I chuckle at the memory.

Placing her hand on top of mine, Debbie says, "I think it is a miracle how your memory has come back to you in such a flood, after remembering nothing for so long. Ever since you had that breakthrough in Dr. Sydney's office two weeks ago it's like a different you is evolving right in front of us."

I hear her words but I'm focused on how wonderful the feeling of her hand is, and I wonder what she feels. Probably nothing. I'm just another patient to her.

"Levi? It is still Levi, isn't it?"

"Yes. I've decided to keep that name. It's part of my new life."

"Well then, Levi, are you listening to me or to your friend the mockingbird?"

"Oh, I'm sorry. I guess my mind was drifting. What did you say?"

"I was talking about how much you've changed since your memories have been coming back." She withdraws her hand.

"Other people have said the same thing. I guess I don't notice it. But it's been sort of like finding a long-lost family photo album and enjoying the stories connected to all the pictures. Like things August and I used to do. You won't believe one of the games we played."

"Oh really?" Debbie replies. "Please tell me. I'm interested."

"I've told you that we were very poor, country people. So toys were practically unheard of. But we used to get out in the plowed fields around the house and throw dirt clods at each other."

Debbie is silent for a moment. "That's it? That was your game?" There is a tone of disbelief in her voice.

Laughing, I say, "I told you you wouldn't believe it. Yes, we had more fun doing that than just about anything."

"And you actually tried to hit each other with these dirt clods? You were allowed to play this game?"

I cock my head. "You know what's frustrating for me?" I ask.

"No, what?"

"That I can't see the expression on your face. I don't know if you're smiling, frowning, sad, or happy. All I have are your words and the tone of your voice. But there is so much expressed by a person's face."

"Then why don't you read my expression?"

"And how do you suggest I do that?"

She takes my hand and puts it on the side of her face. "By feeling it."

This is something we've practiced in some of my group work sponsored by the American Society for the Blind. But I've never done it with someone outside of that setting. My heart beats faster as I let my fingertips explore Debbie's face. "You've got a cute nose," I say.

"Think so? Looks more like a pug nose when I look in a mirror."

"Oh my goodness, you've got dimples! You never told me you had dimples. I love dimples in a girl." The depression of her dimples deepens as her smile spreads. Though I'm fearful she'll stop me, I touch her lips with my thumb and she allows me to run it along their length. They are soft and full. "Wow, that's a nice mouth, too."

Having no reason to keep my hands on her face, I remove them. "You are very pretty, Debbie."

"Thank you, Levi. I don't think I've ever had someone look that closely at my face."

Silence works its way between us and pushes us back. I take a deep breath and let it out slowly.

After a few moments I say, "Where were you headed when you saw me sitting out here?"

"Actually I was looking for you."

"What for?"

"I wanted to ask you about something, if that's okay."

There is some hesitancy in how she says this. For reasons unknown, I begin to feel uneasy and wary. "What's wrong?!" I ask, and realize too late that my tone sounds harsh. "Wait, I'm sorry. I didn't mean to sound like that. It's just that I noticed a shift in your tone of voice and it got me on edge."

"Whew," Debbie replies, "you are beyond a shadow of a doubt the most perceptive man I've ever known. Nothing slips by you. Anyway, I wanted to ask you why you remain so adamant about not telling us where you are from or letting us get in contact with your family. I can't imagine what it's been like for them all these years not knowing what happened to you. I know if it were me—"

I cut her off. "Well it's not you. And it's none of your business or anyone else's business where I'm from. That was then and this is now. There's no going back for me. This is my life now and that's all that matters."

She touches my hand and I jerk it away.

"Levi, please don't be upset with me. I'm only trying to be helpful. You tell such amazing stories about your life there. I'm fascinated by Tucker, and you speak in such admiring tones about your brother, August. Though I do wonder why you talk so little about your sister, April."

I stand up and start walking away while I'm unfolding my cane.

"Levi, wait!" Debbie is beside me, her hand on my arm. "What did I say? Why are you so upset? Is it about April?"

Wheeling around to face her, I lean forward. "You say I have a good sense of smell. Well I can smell what's going on here. Good ol' Dr. Sydney sent you here on a mission. She keeps after me about the same thing. That's what this is all about, isn't it?" Tears are stinging my eyes.

"Well, she did—"

"Exactly! And here I was stupid enough to think that you actually wanted to have a conversation with me just to be having a conversation. But who would want to have a conversation with a blind man?! Well you and Dr. Sydney can take your game and shove it. What happened between me and April is none of your business. I am dead to my family. I can never go home again!"

Jerking my sleeve from Debbie's grip, I walk away from her. I feel like I'm pushing my way through a blackberry patch as overwhelming sadness tears at my heart, leaving it shredded.

I can hear the tears in Debbie's voice as she calls after me, "Levi, please don't. I've messed this all up. Please turn around and come back to me."

Her words stab my heart like a hook catching a fish on a snag line. I jerk to a stop, torn between running away and running toward. Like the long shadows cast by the setting sun, a feeling of abandonment wraps itself around me like a sad, familiar friend. Draped in its shroud, I walk away, leaving Debbie alone with her tears.

CHAPTER THIRTY-SIX

I sought my death and found it in my womb,
I looked for life and saw it was a shade,
I trod the earth and knew it was my tomb,
And now I die, and now I was but made;
My glass is full, and now my glass is run,
And now I live, and now my life is done.
—*Chidiock Tichborne*

APRIL:

Surrounded by fog so thick I can only see a few feet in front of me, I reach out and touch the glowing red taillight that has arrested my attention. Running my hand across the top of the tailgate, I recognize the vehicle as Mark's pickup truck. I look up and notice that the interior light of the cab is on, and the passenger's door is yawning open.

Strains of Shania Twain singing "You're Still the One" drift out of the cab, but the sound is distorted as if a cassette player is eating the tape. She is a siren on the rocky shoals, drawing me forward.

My heart slams one time against my rib cage like the bass drum of a marching band, and then it stops beating. I have been here before. It is a recurring dream, but, just like before, I can't wake myself up. I don't want to move because I know what's coming, yet I am drawn to the open tomb of the truck cab.

With a touch as soft as a fluttering butterfly's wings, tiny droplets of water in the fog kiss my face as I slowly step forward. Blood is streaming out the door, running across the blacktop and down the embankment, disappearing into the murky backwater of the Obion. Even in the darkness I can hear alligator gar roiling in the mixture.

In a new twist to this terrifying dream, quarter notes and half notes from Shania's song float like tiny boats on the crimson river. I wonder if someone has slipped me a hallucinogenic drug.

Standing in the spotlight created by the interior light, I look inside and see a body lying facedown on the floorboard. My heart suddenly jumps to life and beats like a frightened rabbit's. At the same time the music changes to Janet Jackson's "Together Again." It is so loud I can barely hear my own thoughts, but again the sound is filled with distortion.

My eyes are riveted on the body lying in the seemingly unending stream of its life source.

"Mark?" I say tentatively.

The head slowly comes up and turns its face toward me. "Hello, April." It is Ella! I scream and want to run away but my feet are nailed to the ground.

"Ella," I say tenderly. "Oh, Ella . . ."

Without another word, she lowers her face back into the crimson pool.

"Don't leave me," I plead with her.

"April?" A small voice beside me speaks my name.

Turning, I see my youngest brother, March, just as he looked the day before he disappeared years ago. I try to scream again, but this time vomit wins the race and I heave onto the blacktop.

When I finish, I look up and find Mark still standing there. "Oh my god, Mark, where have you been?!" I reach out to take him in my arms but they pass through him like the ghost he is.

The twin demons of guilt and regret rip through me with the force of a tornado. I am overwhelmed.

I have to find relief or this is going to kill me. I look down and see a pistol in my hand. Its hammer is cocked. Relief begins to push back the tide that is trying to swallow me up.

Smiling, I raise the pistol to the side of my head and squeeze the trigger.

I sit up in my bed, gasping for breath. It is dark in the cabin and none of the other girls are awake. I feel like electricity is running through my veins instead of blood. My hands and arms are trembling.

Like the surf following a storm, wave after wave of emotion pounds me. Relief! I have to find relief or this flood of emotions is going to kill me.

Throwing back the covers, I pick up the Bible off my nightstand and tiptoe to the bathroom. Once inside I close the door and turn on the generator-powered lights. It is one of the few times electricity is actually used at Spirit Lake. Otherwise we use kerosene lamps and candles.

I walk past the four sinks and mirrors, grabbing one of the towels as I pass. I choose the last commode stall on the left, my usual throne for this procedure. Lowering the lid, I lay the towel across it and sit down.

The Bible lies on my lap and I flip through its pages looking for Psalm 51. The closer I get to the familiar passage the more my hands shake in excitement. At last I find what I am looking for. Lying in the crease of the opening, my friend, the razor blade, smiles up at me.

The coursing emotions are so strong now that even my legs are jerking and bouncing.

I lift up the bottom edge of my T-shirt so I can see which thigh to carve on. The rows of *M*'s seem to wink at me in mocking fashion. Holding the razor in my right hand, I go to the end of the row on my right thigh. I stick the corner of the razor into my soft flesh and pull it through my skin, forming the first leg of the M. Instead of the usual small line of blood that beads up in the wake of the razor blade, blood begins streaming out in every direction. My fingers are covered in blood and the white towel I sit on begins changing color.

It takes a couple moments before I realize that my nerves have caused me to cut too deep. And still I have no relief from the pressure of emotions I'm trying to hold back.

Ignoring the growing tide of blood, I finish the first leg of the *M* and cut another into its place. With only a slight reprieve of pressure, I continue cutting until I complete the letter. Closing my eyes, I lean back against the tank of the toilet. Relief finally begins taking hold, and a calm coldness replaces the white-hot emotions. I feel a smile lifting the corners of my mouth.

I hear the metal tinkle of my razor blade hitting the concrete floor. I don't care because I got what I wanted. I just want to sit and enjoy it.

Then another sound registers. It is the sound of a dripping faucet. But it sounds as if it is in my stall. With my eyes still closed, I frown in confusion.

Sitting up, I slowly open my eyes to try and find the source of the drip. I look down and am horrified to see blood on the floor of my stall. The blood-soaked towel has reached its capacity and is only working as a conduit for the continuing flow of blood to make its way to the floor.

Trying to force the gash on my thigh to clot, I rip off a double handful of toilet tissue and press it on the wound. I glance frantically around the stall to see if someone might have left their towel hanging. Nothing.

The toilet paper has now turned bright red and is sagging with its liquid weight. I empty the rest of the paper off the roll and drop it on the floor to start soaking up the pool of blood there.

Suddenly the door to my stall opens. It is Sarah. Initially squinting in the bright lights of the bathroom, when she takes in the contents of the stall, terror grabs her eyelids and jerks them open wide. She screams. Before I can grab her and make her shut up, her eyelids flutter like a window shade and she collapses on the floor.

As if they were firemen responding to their station-house alarm, the rest of the girls respond to Sarah's scream by running into the bathroom. They stutter-step to a stop as they try to process the scene in my stall. Hands fly to cover open mouths.

There is nothing for me to hide anymore, so I stand up and step over Sarah to look for another towel. "Sarah's fine," I say. "She just fainted." The girls part for me to pass through them as if I had the plague.

Jessica speaks up, "Someone go to the other cabin to see who's there tonight, Mary or Michelle, and bring them back here quick. And make sure they bring a first-aid kit."

"I'll go," Ashley replies.

Wheeling around, I say, "No you don't! Everybody freeze! Nobody talks about this to anyone, you hear? This is my business. What happens in this cabin is just between us. We're supposed to stick together, aren't we?"

"But you're hurt," Heather speaks up. "What in the world happened?"

Thankful that at least for the moment everyone is focused on what happened and not on reporting it, I say, "I was shaving and somehow the razor slipped and sliced sideways, opening a nasty cut. While I was trying to tend to the wound Sarah walked in and did what she does best—she freaked out."

As if she's been waiting on my cue, Sarah stirs and moans.

While everyone's attention turns to her, I find a towel and washcloth and begin washing up my leg. A clot has finally formed, stanching the blood flow.

Megan joins me at the sink, her red hair seemingly alive like Medusa's. Pointing at my exposed thigh, she says loudly, "You're a cutter. You weren't shaving. You all come look!"

If it would do any good, I'd shove this washcloth in her mouth. But her efforts to incite a riot have done the job she intended. Everyone, including a woozy Sarah, gathers around me at the sink. They stare silently and point at the rows of *M*'s.

I would not feel more exposed if I were stripped naked and left standing on the court square in Dresden. For a long time this ritual has been my secret. No one could take it from me. It never failed me, never failed to give me the relief I was seeking.

But now that my secret has been exposed, I can almost feel its power ebbing. Fear and concern nibble at the corners of my heart. What will I do now when I'm feeling overwhelmed and need relief? What will save me?

From the doorway of the bathroom, Mary's voice suddenly echoes against the walls, "Ladies, do we have a problem?"

CHAPTER THIRTY-SEVEN

*And whoever walks a furlong without sympathy walks to his own
funeral dressed in his shroud.*
—*Walt Whitman*

APRIL:

James looks at me silently. I figured I would have to be here in
his office today after the drama last night and my trip to the ER.
If he's waiting for me to talk first, he's got a long wait coming
because I can sit here forever. I return his steady look.

"Do you know what the word *enigma* means, April?" he asks.

I have heard it before in English class. How stupid does he
think I am? But I will not play along. Instead, I shrug my shoulders
and say nothing.

"Well, an enigma is what you are," James says. "I wasn't here
when you first arrived, and I missed your first weeks, but based on
what Michelle, Mary, and Will tell me, you've done nothing but
spin lies and yarns about who you are, where you come from, and
the reason you are here. Then last night we learn even more disturbing information about you. I'm sure the hospital doctor told you

how lucky you are. First of all, that you haven't gotten any serious infections from all your cutting is a miracle. And then the wicked cut you made on yourself last night didn't kill you only because it was in an area where there are no major arteries. But you know what? I'm not going to tell you to quit cutting. If that's what you want to do, that's your choice."

This does catch me by surprise. I was braced for an all-out tug-of-war over the issue. I wonder if he's just trying to fake me out, so I ask, "Do I get to keep my razor blade? I mean, if I'm going to be allowed to cut myself, I should be allowed to have the proper tools."

James stands up and reaches over to the top of his desk. Picking something up, he sits back down and lays the object on the coffee table between us. The print on the small box identifies its contents as ten single-edged razor blades. "Would these make it easier for you?" James asks calmly.

I'm beginning to feel less secure of my footing with James. I can't tell if he's bluffing or not. His offer doesn't make sense, but I feel like if I don't take the razors, he's somehow won, though I'm not sure what the game is. I lean forward and start to pick up the box.

"Wait a minute," James says.

I freeze in my outstretched position. Looking at him, I say, "But you told me I could have them."

"And you can, but only after we've had a conversation about why you cut yourself."

Slowly, I ease back in my chair. So here's the catch. He wants to crack me open like an egg and see what's inside. "Is this where I'm supposed to break down crying and spill my guts?" I ask.

James smiles warmly and then laughs. "That would certainly be nice, but I don't expect that's what's going to happen with you. However, it introduces an interesting question in my mind."

"What's that?"

James doodles on his pad, and, keeping his eyes on his pad, asks, "When is the last time you cried?"

If I felt like I was losing my footing with James a moment ago, I now feel like I am tumbling head over heels down a steep hillside. Though I'm in a dizzied state, a memory pops into my mind of me, March, and August doing somersaults together down the hill behind our barn and landing in thick, soft clover at the bottom. The memory, coupled with James's question, threatens to crack the foundation of the ice castle I've constructed and lived in for so long. Unconsciously I pinch my thigh, looking for relief from the pressure I feel.

I know James has seen my move, but he ignores it.

"To tell you the truth, April," he says, "we know very little about you. You were allowed to come here as a special favor to Dr. Sydney, who asked that you be given space here. Someone who knows you knows her, or something like that. Even though you were brought here by law enforcement officers, we know you are not in trouble with the law because we checked on that.

"Mary, Michelle, and Will all say you are a liar. None of them believes the story you've told the girls about having rich and powerful parents. The elaborate stories you tell about living in your three-story house ring hollow with them. Will says you've been around animals but that you wouldn't know a thoroughbred from a nag. Sorry, but I'm just being honest with you. If we can't be honest with each other, we're never going to make any progress."

Each of James's accusations slaps me harder than even Tucker could have. I feel sick to my stomach. Gritting my teeth, I squeeze my eyes shut, hoping the wave of nausea will pass.

When I finally open my eyes, James is sitting calmly with his legs crossed. I despise his coolness. I've never seen him rattled.

Squinting at him, I say, "I hear your wife is dying. You know, if we can't be honest, we're never going to make any progress."

Without a pause, James says, "You're right, she is. But the way I figure it, we all are. As soon as we enter this world, we're all marching toward the same end." His eyes never waver, no pooling of tears.

But I'm not done yet. Returning his gaze, I say, "It's going to be pretty sad for your little boys, losing their mom and all, isn't it? And you'll have to raise them all by yourself. But that's just how the cookie crumbles."

"What do you think I should tell my boys, April? I mean, about their mom. How would you put it to them if it was you?"

"How should I know?" I answer harshly. "I've never had kids. How would I know what to say?"

"I wonder," James says slowly, "if you've ever had anyone you loved die before you were ready to let them go?"

Up to this point I've been the assistant to the knife-throwing act in the circus. Strapped to a spinning wheel, I see James's comments and questions come at me like so many knives, narrowly missing me. But this last knife was not thrown with the intent to miss. It stabs me directly in my heart and is buried to its hilt. An involuntary cry of pain escapes from me and I double over in my chair.

I look up at James and hiss, "I hate you!"

"I'm okay with that," James replies, "even though I don't think that's exactly how you feel. But you have a right to feel toward me any way you wish. Would you mind telling me what was so painful to you about my last question?"

Folding my legs into the chair Indian style, I spit my words at him, "Don't worry, I'm fine. Nothing hurts me."

"You misunderstand," James says, "I don't mind if my question hurt you or disturbed you. I'm not apologizing for it. I just want to understand why you reacted the way you did. Was it your mother or your father who died? Or maybe a sibling?"

I feel the color rising in my face. Getting out of my chair, I start pacing. Pounding my fist into the palm of my other hand, I say, "Oh well, let's see now, where would you like me to start? What about my mother, who abandoned me, leaving me to be raised by my grandmother? Or maybe you'd like to hear about the fact that I never knew my father. That is, until he murdered my mother. How about me telling you about how I was taken in by my other grandmother and I ended up killing her? Oh yeah, and I made my brother run away from home and we never heard from him again." Wheeling around to face James directly, I conclude, "Which story do you want to hear? You tell me."

There is a subtle change in James's expression. The corners of his eyes have drooped slightly and there is a crease between his eyes. His easy-going smile has disappeared, his lips having been pulled into a tight line. "So," he says softly, "you do know what it is like to lose someone you love. I appreciate your being open and honest with me and I regret that you've had to endure so much pain."

"Don't feel sorry for me!" I scream. "I am sick of people saying to me, 'I know you've had a difficult life, April' or 'I know things haven't been easy for you, April.' Just shut up! You know what? I don't feel sorry for you that your wife is going to die, and I don't feel sorry for your kids either. You want to know what I would say to your kids about their mother dying? I'd say, 'Life sucks, get used to it!'" I race to his office door, fling it open, and run to the cabin door. Jerking it open, I run toward the darkness of the forest as the heavy door slams shut behind me.

CHAPTER THIRTY-EIGHT

A merry heart doeth good like a medicine:
but a broken spirit drieth the bones.
—*Proverbs 17:22*

APRIL:

The leaves of rhododendrons and cane slap at my face as I run deeper and deeper into the woods. Occasionally I stumble as tree roots try to slow me down by grabbing the toe of my shoe. I start up a steep hill, using small trees to pull myself up the incline, until finally, exhausted and out of breath, I collapse onto the soft carpet of needles created by the towering hemlock trees that are the canopy of the forest here in the mountains.

I lie on my side until my breathing slows, and then I roll onto my back. In the distance I hear a woodpecker's *rat-a-tat-tat* as he searches inside the timber for nourishing insects. Suddenly I remember a story Tucker used to tell when I was little. There was a farmer she knew who raised his hogs in the woods. Whenever it was time for him to feed them he would take his walking stick and hit on the side of their wooden trough. The hogs soon learned his system and would come running at the sound of his stick striking their "plate." But one day a flock of woodpeckers invaded the woods. Their continual pecking on the trees had the hogs in a constant frenzy, running from one side of the woods to the other until they eventually ran themselves to death. Though I asked her repeatedly, Tucker would never come right out and say if her story was a true one or just one of her tall tales.

Looking up into the trees, it seems they are as tall as the skyscrapers I've seen on TV and in movies. They gently sway back and forth, letting speckles of sunlight slip through their branches. It is hypnotic. In a few minutes I fall asleep.

I awake with a start and am completely disoriented. The light is dim and nothing looks familiar to me. Then I remember running out of James's office and into the woods.

One thing I've learned since being at Spirit Lake is that the days end much more quickly here than back home in the flatlands of West Tennessee. When the sun dips behind the mountains, cool night air settles on everything.

I don't have a watch but I figure it is already evening. Standing up, I turn slowly in a complete circle, hoping I will see something that I recognize. But all 360 degrees look the same. A chill runs down the back of my neck as I realize that I am lost.

I breathe as quietly as I can so I can hear if anyone is searching for me and calling my name. Even though I strain to listen, the woods offers me no hope, only silence.

Ever since my arrival here, at least three times a week we girls have been reminded that we are free to walk in the woods during free time. It's one of our "choices." But we are cautioned that if we ever get lost, to stay put in one place and not wander around trying to find our own way out.

My racing heart begs my feet to get moving. It seems foolish to sit still and do nothing. As if to emphasize the folly of not trying to find my way out, a lone wolf howls from the opposite hillside. He is quickly answered by another wolf from another part of the forest. I put my hands over my ears when their duet increases to a chorus of howls.

The leftovers of daylight are quickly being gobbled up when I hear a noise. Someone, or something, is coming toward me. It stops moving. I hold my breath. Then it moves closer, perhaps forty yards away.

It's then that I realize the wolves have stopped howling. Is that what they do when they are closing in for a kill? A twig snaps loudly.

It is so dark and the undergrowth is so thick that it is impossible to see. Getting on my knees, I search blindly for a stick I can use as a weapon. My hand finds a fallen tree limb. Gripping it, I stand up to face whatever has come for me.

"April, is that you?"

It is Michelle's voice that comes out of the gloom! "Oh my god, Michelle! Yes, it's me!" I cry.

Her footsteps get closer but I still can't see her shape. Suddenly she switches on her flashlight. It sweeps back the darkness that was enveloping me. I rush to Michelle and throw my arms around her. I feel a large pack on her back. "I thought you were the wolves and they were going to attack me. Thank you, thank you, thank you for finding me!"

"No problem," Michelle says as she slips the backpack off and lays it on the ground. "Are you okay?"

"Yes, I'm fine. I just got lost and I remembered that you all always told us to sit tight if that happened."

"You did the right thing. It was easy to follow your trail. Are you thirsty or hungry?"

My stomach growls loudly in reply.

Michelle laughs. "I guess that's a yes. Well here's what you and I are going to do. We're going to spend the night right here and then hike out in the morning. First though, I need to fire this blank pistol in the air so that everyone knows we're both okay." A flash of fire from the end of the barrel and its sharp report echoes loudly after each of Michelle's three shots.

Bending over, she unzips her backpack. Pitching something on the ground at my feet, she says, "That's your sleeping bag. I'm going to build us a small fire and fix us something to eat."

Thirty minutes later I am cupping my hands around a mug of hot chocolate prepared by Michelle. The first sip has the magical effect of warming my hands and feet, which terror had frozen earlier. Looking up, I watch the yellow light from the small fire's flames dance across Michelle's face. The interplay of light and shadows creates an ever-changing mask on her features.

She is calm and purposeful in her movements. Clearly she has spent many nights in the woods. She hands me a plastic Ziploc bag. "Here's some of my homemade trail mix. It's certainly not hot food, but I'd rather not cook anything, since it could attract hungry visitors. This will give your stomach something to do besides growl, plus it'll replace all the carbohydrates and protein you've burned up."

I take the bag from her and say, "I'm so hungry I believe I could dip pinecones in this hot chocolate and eat them."

Michelle laughs again and her eyes burn brightly. Smile lines are accentuated by the firelight. She opens her own bag of trail mix and pitches a handful into her mouth. Then she lies down on her side on top of her sleeping bag.

We both enjoy our meal and hot chocolate, serenaded by the singing tree frogs. Occasionally an owl provides an alto note of harmony, while the crackling fire supplies the percussion.

"You know," I say as I lie staring at the fire, "this reminds me of when I would lie down beside a wood-burning stove during winter. The floor would feel cold, but the stove was so hot that I had to keep turning myself like I was on a rotisserie." A split-second after the last word leaves my mouth, I feel like slapping myself in the face. How in the world could I have let out so much information to Michelle?! My only hope is that she wasn't really listening closely.

Michelle's prolonged silence gives me hope that my slip hasn't done any damage. But that hope quickly evaporates.

"That's really interesting, April," Michelle says. "Maybe you can tell me about that some day. But what I really want to do is ask you about your conversation with James today."

The sound of wooden shutters being slammed shut echoes in my mind as I brace myself for her prying comments and questions. No more slips of the tongue by me! "I thought what I talk with James about is private. *Confidentiality*, isn't that the word?"

Michelle chews on another mouthful of trail mix. Once her mouth is cleared, she says, "As members of a treatment team on your behalf we share information that can prove helpful to each other. So there is sharing among your treatment team, but the sharing goes no further than that."

"So," I reply, "are you going to tell them what we talk about tonight?"

"If I think it can help them help you, absolutely I will."

Michelle is silent again. It seems like this is something counselors do, as James, Michelle, and Mary have all done it with me. Either it means they are trying to get you to start talking or it means they don't know what to do next. Whatever the reason, I've learned to wait them out.

After a few minutes, Michelle rolls onto her back and looks up into the darkness overhead. The shadow of her profile projects onto the trees beyond her, making her appear to be a giant. "Do you mind explaining to me how you killed your grandmother?"

My mind races, looking for a way to deflect Michelle's attention without my talking about Ella. But she already knows the truth that I revealed to James, so denial or pleading ignorance are not available tactics for me.

I like Michelle, though I first thought she was just trying to be some kind of a show-off. She is a good listener and she really cares about all of us. So I decide to tell her the truth. "Ella was her name. She was my father's mother. But neither of us even knew we were related when we first met. She was simply a neighbor that'd moved in next door to me and my brothers and my grandmother Tucker.

"Tucker is the one who raised us because our mother was a whore. I'm sorry for using that word but it's the truth and everybody in our town knew it.

"I had lots of problems when I was growing up, but the biggest one was that I didn't talk—ever. I don't even know why. When I got to school they said I was retarded and threatened to take me away from Tucker unless I started talking. That's when Tucker told me she was going to make me start living with Ella so she could help me learn to talk.

"The difference between Tucker's house and Ella's was like the difference between eating shredded wheat cereal with no sugar or milk and eating homemade ice cream. It was like I had found my fairy godmother.

"Ella was everything Tucker was not. She was patient, loving, tender, and soft. Don't get me wrong, no one will ever take the place of Tucker. There's no one like her on this earth. She's a self-made woman. But she didn't know how to be like Ella was. And I guess I needed someone like Ella to draw me out. And she did it. She helped me talk by using music and singing.

"I loved Ella like nobody else. And like I said, we didn't even know we were related. It wasn't until my mother was murdered by Ella's son, my father, that the truth came out. And that just drew me and her closer to each other. Even though the reason I'd gone to live with her had been fixed, I kept living with her and I'd visit with Tucker every so often."

As my explanation to Michelle makes its final turn and heads toward the conclusion, I feel the elephant of my guilty conscience place its gigantic foot on my chest. Regret begins tightening its noose around my neck until I feel like I am choking. I grab the sides of my thighs and squeeze as hard as I can.

"April." Michelle's voice floats to me through the thermals of the fire. "It's okay. Take your time. This is your story to tell in whatever way you want to tell it. Open the door and let it out."

I scream in my head as loudly as I can, "I will not cry!" I haven't cried since Ella got sick and I'll never cry again. It's the punishment I deserve for what I did to her. "What happened next," I finally say to Michelle, "is that Ella got cancer and died soon after that. And you know why she got cancer?"

Michelle rolls onto her side, facing me. Her forehead is creased with concern. "No I don't, April. Why?"

"Because I went to live with her. She was fine before I went to live with her. I think I have a curse on me. I destroy everything that I touch. The only things that I deserve are pain and death. And death can't get here soon enough for me."

CHAPTER THIRTY-NINE

Deer April,

Smiley Carter and Shady Green come over tonight and played music and sang. They both told me to tell you they said hi. We sure did have a good time. But we all missed your singing and your dancing. Don't nobody sing a country song like you do. Even though it seems like in the last couple of years it's got harder and harder to get you to sing, when you do sing it comes from deeper and deeper inside you. Maybe you have gotten harder and harder on the outside but there's still a feeling place in there somewhere and singing is what turns it loose. Maybe someday you'll want me to come see you and I'll bring Smiley and Shady with me and we'll have us one of them old-fashioned hoedowns. I bet some of them folks ain't never heard real country singing. All they heard is that junk that's played on the radios. I turn it on ever once in a while hoping I might hear an old song I know, but it just sounds like a bunch of noise to me. I'll take old Hank Williams or the Carter Family any day over that man everybody's crazy about nowadays, Gerth Brooks I think is what he's called, or something like that. I hope you're getting to sing over there at Spirit Lake. I'll bet they'd be impressed. That's why I put Ella's Autoharp in your suitcase. I thought it would be something you might want to do in your spare time. When you play it I hope you think about Ella and it makes you smile even if it does make you a little sad too. She was one sweet, special lady. I know I miss her so I'll bet you do too. I sure do wish they would let you write me a letter. I don't know why they won't but I'm going to call and talk to that Mary woman and ask her why. If they is being mean to you they'll have to answer to me. I guess that's all I got to write for now. Just remember them three things is still true.

—Tucker

CHAPTER FORTY

The reason firm, the temperate will,
Endurance, foresight, strength, and skill,
A perfect Woman, nobly planned,
To warn, to comfort, and command;
And yet a Spirit still, and bright
With something of angelic light.
—William Wordsworth, 1804

MARCH:

After rubbing my fingers across the nameplate on the door and confirming that it is Dr. Sydney's, I knock twice.

"Come in," her muffled voice beckons me from the other side.

Opening the door, I step inside.

"Hello, Levi."

"Hi, Doctor Sydney. Is your furniture arranged the way it usually is?"

"Yes. Nothing's been moved."

With her reassurance, I take four steps and stop. Reaching forward with the back of my hand, I find the back of the loveseat. I turn right and take two steps, then left and take three.

"Very good, Levi."

Dr. Sydney's voice is directly to my left, about six feet away. Turning to face her, I back up a bit until my calves make contact with the armchair, and then I sit down. The familiar chair creaks a bit as it welcomes me.

"How have things been?" she asks.

"No problems," I reply quickly. "All my therapies are going okay. I keep getting challenged by the therapists to push myself further and so I keep trying harder."

She flips pages in what I assume is a steno pad. "Yes, I've seen those reports. What you don't realize is how much you are pushing the therapists, too."

"Huh? What do you mean by that?"

"I mean you are the kind of patient everyone dreams about. You are highly motivated, internally, not externally. Because of that, you always give a hundred percent. You continually meet your goals, which requires the therapists to find new ways to stretch you. It's good work for them."

I can think of nothing to say to that, so I sit quietly.

"Levi, can I ask you a question?"

This is a favorite tactic of Dr. Sydney's, asking permission to use her scalpel as she probes deeper into my heart. I've often wondered what she would do if I said no. No doubt she has ways to get around any roadblock a patient might put in front of her.

However, each time she engages in exploratory surgery with me, it opens doors that have long been locked and sealed tight. I hesitate in replying to her question, and in her calm way Dr. Sydney waits quietly.

Taking a deep breath, I say, "Sure. Okay."

"How do you feel about Debbie Cooper?"

Her question catches me off guard and I feel like I've been jerked at right angles, off balance in every way. My heart pounds in my chest. Do I tell her the truth? Do I even know what the truth is? I've lain awake many nights chasing this very question around in my head, running in endless circles in my search for answers.

I try to stall. "Have you talked to Debbie?"

"You know I have," Dr. Sydney replies. "She is on the staff here and I talk with her frequently, just as I do with all the staff. Why are you hesitant to answer my question?"

Wiping my sweating palms on my jeans, I say, "Maybe it's because I don't know how I feel."

"Could it be that you're trying to find one word to describe your feelings when, in truth, you have many feelings about Debbie?"

This reframing of her question releases some of the pressure on my chest. "Maybe that is it. But . . ."

"But what?"

"Are you going to talk to Debbie about what I tell you?"

"Would you care if I did?"

"Sure I would . . . I mean no, I guess not . . . I mean yes, of course I would!" Flustered, I run my hand through my hair.

Dr. Sydney keeps both her voice and the intensity of the moment steady. "And why would you care? Have you not talked to her about how you feel?"

I cough nervously and twist in my chair.

"Levi, can you tell me how you feel at this very moment?"

"Nervous."

"Nervous in what way?"

"Like I used to feel when Tucker would confront me about whether I'd fed the chickens or not. I never liked feeding chickens. Their beady eyes and the way their heads were always jerking around made me nervous. So sometimes I would pretend I was going to feed them but would go play in the barn instead. But Tucker always knew. I believed for a long time that the chickens were tattling on me and that she could understand the chickens' language. When she would ask me if I fed them, I knew that she already knew the answer but was just testing me to see if I would tell her the truth. That's how I feel right now, like I'm seven years old."

"I see," Dr. Sydney says thoughtfully as she writes something in her pad. "So you think I already know the answer to my question and I'm playing some kind of game with you to see if you are going to be truthful with me?"

"Yes," I reply.

"Well then, let's get something straight. I don't play games. Lawyers might ask questions that they know the answers to, but not me. I ask questions to increase my knowledge and understanding and to make you think. I might guess or speculate how you feel about Debbie, but why waste my energy doing that when I have you right here to answer the question accurately?"

I feel the urge to jump up and run out of her office. But first of all I haven't mastered running and secondly I have no place to run to. In spite of my blindness my head turns reflexively, looking for an escape route.

"Let's do something first." Dr. Sydney inserts herself into my scattered thoughts. "Let's help you grow up."

Suddenly my focus zeroes in on her, even though what she said makes no sense. "Grow up?"

"Yeah. You said you felt like you were seven years old. So let's get you back to your correct age. Can you tell me where you are?"

"What do you mean?"

"It's a simple question, Levi. Quit looking for hidden meaning. Just tell me where you are right now at this very moment."

"I'm here in your office?"

"Are you asking me if that is where you are?"

"Okay, I am sitting here in your office right at this very moment."

"Excellent! And who is in the room with you?"

There is a part of me that feels like she is making fun of me or mocking me. But there is nothing in my dealings with her since I arrived here that would support that conclusion, so I decide to follow her lead. "Dr. Sydney is in the room with me."

"Now take a couple of slow, deep breaths," she urges me.

The fresh air filling my lungs and the following exhalation of air that feels old and stale lift my mood. I smile.

"How old are you, Levi?"

Giving a short laugh, I say, "Actually we're not sure about that one, so that is a trick question. But I'm in my early twenties probably."

"Yes you are," Dr. Sydney agrees, and I can hear the smile in her voice. "So you are not seven years old, are you?"

I feel my body relax. "No, I'm not."

"Why don't we just sit for a few moments and listen to and feel the silence. Let's relax our bodies and minds."

The first time Dr. Sydney said that to me in a session I thought she was crazy. But over time I've learned to enjoy the experience of sitting with nothing.

I sit quietly and try to clear my mind.

After a few minutes, Dr. Sydney says, "Now, without trying to filter your answer, I want you to tell me all the different feelings you have about Debbie."

Without my thinking about them, the words flow, "Warm, soft, tender, understanding, beautiful, a good listener, strong, funny—that's how I feel."

"Actually, you've described her to me, Levi. You've told me how you see and experience her. Can you look deeper and find the feelings?"

Suddenly, and unexpectedly, tears begin running down my cheeks. The scalpel has opened a door and I am flooded with emotions. The harder I try to put my back against the door and push it closed, the more rapidly emotions come, as if they are disquieted spirits that have been imprisoned in an Egyptian tomb, eager to escape and find their final resting place. Their power is so great that I lose my footing and let the door fling open.

I cry uncontrollably, shoulders shaking and diaphragm convulsing. In the torrent of emotions I see my mother's face, then Tucker's, then Debbie's, and lastly I see April standing in the doorway in that same dress she wore the Christmas she surprised us by singing. At the sight of April I slide out of my chair onto my knees. Lifting my head, I wail, "Oh April, I'm so sorry! I'm so sorry."

Folding my body, I bend forward, touch my head to the floor, and continue to cry softly. I feel someone's hand on my back, gently rubbing it.

From her wheelchair Dr. Sydney says hoarsely, "It's okay, Levi, I'm right here with you. Here, use these." She pushes a wad of tissues into my hands.

I wipe my tear-soaked beard and blow my nose. After a few moments, I'm finally able to draw a ragged breath that fills my lungs. Blowing it out loudly, I shift to a sitting position on the floor.

I hear Dr. Sydney lock the wheels of her chair. She grunts with effort and suddenly is sitting beside me on the floor. She slips her arm through the crook of my elbow. "That was tough, wasn't it?"

"Whew, yes it was. I don't know where it came from. I didn't know it was even there. How did you do that?"

"Do what?"

"You know what. Turn the key that unlocked all that."

"Levi, I can't unlock anything that you don't want unlocked. That was all about you. It's something you've been wanting to turn loose for a long time. Can you describe to me what happened?"

I retrace our conversation. "It was your persistence in making me find my feelings about Debbie. I was about to tell you my feelings, when I was overwhelmed by a flooding of emotions. I saw my mother, Maisy. And I saw Tucker. Then I saw Debbie and finally I saw my sister, April." Immediately I feel a pain in my heart and tears reappear.

"Levi," Dr. Sydney says softly, "don't you think it's time you told me about April?"

CHAPTER FORTY-ONE

The tongue of the wise useth knowledge aright:
but the mouth of fools poureth out foolishness.
—Proverbs 15:2

MARCH:

Back in my chair facing Dr. Sydney, I lean forward, resting my forearms on my knees with my hands clasped between them. Ever since I arrived at Patricia Neal and found my memory I've somehow known this moment was inevitable. Part of me feels like a condemned prisoner walking up the steps of the gallows, and yet another part of me is eager to exorcise this thing from my mind and heart.

"Levi," Dr. Sydney says, "you're doing it again. You're thinking and not talking. Get it out of your head so we can look at it together."

"If I'm going to tell this, I'm going to tell it all. It's the only way I know to do it. My brother, August, my sister, April, and I are actually just half siblings. We all have different fathers. That's because our mother was a whore. She flitted in and out of our lives, making all sorts of promises she never kept. I can't tell you the number of times we sat on our grandmother Tucker's porch waiting for her to come pick us up for a visit, but she never came.

"And what can I tell you about Tucker, our mom's mom. She is the toughest, crustiest, smartest, biggest-hearted woman I've ever known. She didn't have a raising that was even fit for a dog. Her dad was an S.O.B. and abused her her whole life. Her mother ran out on her, and her dad disappeared when she was sixteen. So she was on her own and had to raise our mama all by herself. I've never known who the father of my mama was.

"Tucker didn't know anything about raising a child, and I'm sure my mama's life wasn't easy, but that isn't any excuse for how she turned out. She kept popping out babies and dumping them on Tucker, who took us all in and did the best she could.

"We grew up poor, I mean 'welfare poor.' No indoor toilet. The house was heated with a wood-burning stove. Took baths in a wash-tub. Had cardboard on our walls to keep out the cold, even though the wind around the windows would still make the curtains move. We had a small farm with a big garden and raised most everything we ate.

"Kids at school made fun of us because of how we looked or how we smelled or because of Tucker's reputation." At this memory my throat closes up and my voice is choked into silence. The taste of bile bubbles up in the back of my throat. I grit my teeth, squeeze my fists, and swallow it back to the pit it escaped from.

"Take a sip of water, Levi," Dr. Sydney says. "Take your time. There's no hurry with this."

I find the glass and pitcher in their familiar place on the table beside me. Each gulp of the cool water takes more heat out of my throat and chest. An unconscious "ahhh" escapes, followed by a barely stifled burp. "Oops, excuse me."

Dr. Sydney chuckles. "Maybe I better check the contents of that pitcher. It's supposed to be water, you know."

I smile at her joke. Setting the glass down, I gather my thoughts. "August and I did most of the chores around the place because April was so young. August was the sensitive one and was always trying to protect me and April. I was the angry one, defiant and always in trouble. I hated my life. April was fragile and she was mute. Some people called her retarded and I sometimes thought she was, too."

As I continue inching toward the truth I don't want to tell, I have to work harder at keeping my voice steady. "Because we was so poor we didn't have many toys, so we made up games. Me and August would play war and throw dirt clods at each other. Or we'd see who could pull the sow's tail without getting bit by her. Sometimes we'd play hide and seek and let April play.

"And then one time . . ." I pause and lift my face in Dr. Sydney's direction. "This is hard."

"I can tell that it is, Levi. And it's up to you whether you continue or not."

"I've got to get this out. It's like a handful of porcupine quills in my stomach. It's why I ran away from home and why I can never go back."

"Then tell me, Levi. I'm listening."

"There was one time the three of us was playing in the house. We were in April's room and I asked if they wanted to play doctor. Everybody agreed. We took turns being the patient, the doctor, and the nurse. The patient took their clothes off. And . . . and we touched each other where we shouldn't have been touching. When we were playing, it felt fun, but afterward I felt ashamed. And that shame never left me. As a matter of fact, it kept growing bigger and bigger until I couldn't stand myself. I couldn't stand to look at April. That's why I left home."

I sit back in my chair, exhausted. My sweat-soaked shirt sticks to my skin, but I'm too tired to do anything about it.

"Levi, can I ask you some things about your story?" Dr. Sydney asks.

"Sure, ask whatever you want."

"How old were you children when this happened?"

"Well, I was about seven years old, which would have made April four and August nine. Why do you ask?"

"And you just touched each other out of curiosity? And no one got hurt?"

"No, nobody got hurt. It wasn't like that. We just touched to see what it would feel like, that's all."

"Oh my goodness, Levi." I can't tell if Dr. Sydney's voice has pity in it or sadness.

"What? I know it was wrong and God's going to send me to hell for it."

"No, no, no, Levi. You've got this all twisted up." There is a clear, passionate tone in her voice. "You need to understand something very important, something that you never knew then and that you never learned. It is not unusual at all for children to go through a stage of being curious about their bodies and how they are different from other children's. They show themselves and they touch each other and that's all there is to it. It's not abuse. No one is damaged by the experience, except in your case when you assumed that in some way you contributed to all of April's behavioral problems."

Dr. Sydney's explanation is so unbelievable that I feel like I'm listening to someone speak in a foreign language. What she has said can't be true. But why would she lie to me? To protect me? To redeem me? No, not Dr. Sydney. She's always been honest with me. "But if what you've just said is true, then . . ."

"Yes, I know," Dr. Sydney says. "Then one of the foundational pieces of your life has suddenly disappeared."

Her description is apt. I feel like I'm back on the edge of that cliff that I used to dream about after my accident. I'm teetering because my equilibrium has deserted me. The wind is blowing in my face and I don't know what to do or say. "If what you've said is true," I repeat, "then there was no reason for me to run away from home, was there?"

"I don't believe so," Dr. Sydney answers.

"And . . . and . . . and God's not going to send me to hell for what happened, is he?"

"Oh, dear child, no."

Just when I thought it would have been impossible for me to produce more tears, I find myself smiling, almost laughing, and tears wash over my face again. But these tears don't sting. Rather, like caulk filling a crack, they find their way to the open gash that has cleaved my spirit for over fifteen years, filling it with understanding and forgiveness.

CHAPTER FORTY-TWO

Now thou hast loved me one whole day,
Tomorrow when thou leave'st, what wilt thou say?
—*John Donne*

MARCH:

I fumble with my shoestrings like a first grader. My nerves have the best of me and I know why. Debbie's phone call last night, though brief, kept me awake the rest of the night and has my anxiety through the roof this morning.

"Levi, this is Debbie," she'd said.

"Of course it is," I say with a smile. "I'd recognize your voice anywhere. It's one sound that I've got locked in. I always miss you during the weekend when you're gone. I was hoping we might cross paths today."

"Yeah . . . well . . . we need to talk about that. Can we get together in the morning?"

When she told me that, I felt like my heart was being torn in two like a sheet of paper. She wouldn't tell me anything more, just that she wanted to do it face-to-face.

Last night I kept having flashbacks of times that Mama would tell me and August and April she was going to come get us at Tucker's and take us to a new house to live, and we'd have us a daddy, too. My heart would soar to the stars in response to her promise. Tucker would always warn us not to "take no stock in what yore mama says," but I couldn't help it. Nothing is more resilient than hope in the heart of a child, until that hope gets doused so many times that the flame goes out and they give up.

It was probably around the time that Mama died that I gave up on anything good ever happening to me. And my life from that time forward proved I was right. That is, until I came here and met Debbie.

My last session with Dr. Sydney showed me how much Debbie has come to mean to me. It makes me feel stupid that I let it happen. I probably have looked and sounded like a fifth grader to Dr. Sydney and to Debbie, too.

I just wish she had told me over the phone last night. It would have been lots easier than doing it face-to-face.

Finally the bow on my shoestrings stays secure and I stand up. Grabbing my cane, I make my way to my apartment door. I grip the doorknob, take a deep breath, and walk out the door to go face an old, familiar feeling—disappointment.

Even though the place she's asked me to meet her is unfamiliar to me, I'm able to negotiate my way across campus to the correct building.

When I enter the front door, a woman says, "Can I help you?"

"I'm here to see Debbie."

"Debbie?"

"Yes, Debbie Cooper."

"Oh, I'm sorry," she says. "You must be Levi?"

"Yes."

"Debbie said to send you to the third floor. If you'll take my elbow, I'll help you to the elevator."

I hear her move beside me and I lift my hand to find her elbow. She places her elbow in my grip.

"Follow me," she says.

In a moment I hear the dinging bell of an elevator and it opening its doors.

My escort lets me step inside. "Remember," she says, "it's the third floor, room three twenty-six. It's down the hallway to your right when you step off the elevator."

"Yes, thank you," I reply.

The doors close and I am alone in the silent steel chamber. If only my heart had such a chamber to go to! A place of safety from the harmful blows life sends.

I find and push the button for the third floor. The trip up is too fast. I'd have preferred a much slower ride, say, one that took a week.

When the doors open, I hear the voices of others waiting to get on. Using my cane, I find my way out of the elevator and turn right. At the first door I come to I find the numbers 320 affixed to its front. I walk past the next two doors and come to a third one. Before I can reach out to see if I'm at my destination, the door opens.

"Hi, Levi," Debbie says. "Come on in."

My mind snatches up those five words and looks for every nuance imaginable, searching for her mood and intent. She doesn't sound mad. But there is nothing warm about her greeting. Do I hear tenseness in her tone? Dread? Is she bothered that she has to even deal with me and my childish feelings?

"Levi," she says.

"What?"

"Are you going to come in, or are you just going to stand there thinking?"

"Oh, sure, I'm coming in. If you'll sort of orient me to the room, that will help."

Once I step inside, Debbie closes the door behind me. "This is one of our family meeting rooms, so it's sort of like a den. There is a loveseat about twelve feet directly in front of you. At your three o'clock position there is a pair of armchairs. Then at the nine o'clock position is some sort of sofa chair, I guess it's called. Other than that, it looks pretty institutional."

"So where should I sit?" I ask.

"I'd like for us to turn the armchairs so that they are facing each other and sit there, if that's okay with you."

Oh my gosh, this is going to be bad. I hear thundering hooves in my ears and realize it's just my heart trying to beat its way out of my chest so that it can run and hide. "Sure," I say, "that sounds fine with me."

I hear the chairs scooting on the tile floor as Debbie arranges them. She takes my hand. "Let me help you."

Even though I know what's coming, I'm so thankful for her touch that I readily let her lead me to the chair of execution where, in a few moments, my life will end.

"I didn't sleep at all last night," she begins. "I've been turning this over and over in my head, trying to find the right words and questioning my motives. For the past month I've searched my heart to see what's true. What has happened is not supposed to have happened. And Dr. Sydney says I have to talk to you about it."

My mind is racing to keep up with everything she is saying and everything she is not saying. It is clear she is dancing around something difficult. "Debbie, let me make this easier for you. I, too, have had a conversation with Dr. Sydney about you. You probably already know all about it, I guess."

"Whoa, wait just a minute," she says. "You talked with Dr. Sydney about me?"

Confused, I answer, "Yes."

"Well this is the first I've heard about it."

Like two chess players whose plan of attack has been thwarted, we both fall silent trying to reassess based on new information about our opponent.

Simultaneously, we say, "But I thought—" and then stop abruptly.

I hold up my hand. "Let me say what I was going to say a moment ago. Don't make this hard on yourself. I'm a big boy who's had to deal with lots of disappointment in my life. There's nothing you can say that's going to hurt me. I just feel foolish that—"

"Wait a minute," Debbie interjects. "There's nothing I can say that can hurt you? What does that mean?"

There's more of an edge to her tone, one that I can't interpret. I feel like I'm on unstable ground and decide to try a different tack. "That probably didn't come out right," I say. "Let me try this; when I had my last session with Dr. Sydney I told her how I felt about you, or at least tried to tell her. Me and feelings don't always get along too well. It was then, though, that I realized that my feelings for you were probably very inappropriate. So if there's anything I've done or said since I've been here that's made you feel uncomfortable, I'm truly sorry. I'm just a screwed-up mess. Just say whatever it is you want to say and I'll be on my way."

"That's a really nice speech," Debbie says. "But you know what? You really didn't tell me anything, especially how you feel about me. So let's see if I can do a better job with my speech.

"I had to have a talk with Dr. Sydney because of how I felt about you. I tried to deny my feelings to myself, but it was useless. Talking with Dr. Sydney seemed like the best option. The surprise for me was that what I told her was no surprise to her. She said she'd already noticed it."

For the second time since I walked into this room I feel like I've lost my footing. What she's saying makes no sense. Had she grown weary of me as a patient? Have I been imposing on her time? Or has she simply grown to dislike me but has been too polite to say anything?

Suddenly she takes one of my hands. "Levi, I'm going to tell you exactly how I feel about you."

I stop breathing.

Squeezing my hand, Debbie says, "I've grown very fond of you. You are strong and determined. I enjoy your quick wit. In spite of your larger-than-life appearance, you have a tender heart that I find very appealing. I look forward to seeing you and talking to you. It gives me chills when we accidently touch each other. Actually, I find you a very sexy man. And I want to spend more time with you."

When she pauses, I finally take a quick breath and begin slowly shaking my head.

"What?!" she says, a hurt tone in her voice. "Why are you shaking your head?"

"If this is a dream," I reply, "I hope I never wake up because this is absolutely too good to be true. I'm serious. I can't believe this is happening. Do you know what I talked to Dr. Sydney about? I told her how much I care for you, how much I'm attracted to you, and what an incredibly special person you are." I take my free hand and find her face. Her cheeks are damp and her chin is trembling. "But what I didn't say to Dr. Sydney, what I was afraid to say to her, is that I don't want to lose you."

Debbie leans her head to one side, pinning my hand between her cheek and shoulder. "And I was so nervous about talking to you today because I was afraid you didn't share my feelings and would think I was foolish."

I laugh out loud. "You don't know what nervous is! I didn't sleep all night and could barely tie my shoes this morning I was so nervous about this meeting. I thought you were going to tell me to stop bothering you and asking you to meet me for lunch."

"Silly man," she says. "As perceptive as you are about everything, how could you not have known how I felt about you?"

"The truth, Debbie, is that I've had no experience with any healthy females my entire life. I feel completely lost in this arena. But yet, even though I was feeling something I didn't recognize, it was a feeling that I enjoyed."

She scoots forward in her chair until our knees touch. "There is one problem," she says.

In a rush, all those fearful feelings that had subsided moments ago suddenly flood me. I'm too afraid to ask what the problem is, so I keep quiet.

"Dr. Sydney says it's not ethical for an employee to have a relationship with a patient they are treating and it's against hospital policy."

"Exactly what does that mean for you and me?" I ask.

"It means I will no longer be a part of your treatment team. Any time we spend together will be either during my lunch break or when I'm off work."

"You mean like on weekends or evenings?"

"That would be a yes," she replies.

I try to imagine what it would be like to be with Debbie somewhere outside the confines of my home here. I find the prospect exciting and terrifying. "So," I begin slowly, "would that mean we would be dating each other?"

Debbie sprinkles the air with her wind-chime laugh and suddenly things don't feel so heavy. "That's what I would call it, Levi. Would you be okay dating me?"

"I would be okay feeding the hogs with you!" I reply enthusiastically and laugh with her.

CHAPTER FORTY-THREE

It is not upon you alone the dark patches fall,
The dark threw patches down upon me also.
—*Walt Whitman*

TUCKER:

Smiley Carter's Ford tractor pulls his disc through th' turned dirt in m' garden, cuttin' it into a fine powder. Th' dark soil makes th' green o' m' tater plants look that much greener. Robins an' crows fly in t' grab 'em a worm 'r a grub that's been flushed out by th' disc. It's a routine I done seen over an' over ever since I was a kid; birds get fed while I'm fixin' t' plant so I can get fed durin' th' winter.

After Smiley makes his final pass, he pulls outta th' garden an' shuts off his tractor. There was a time when he'd practically bounce off that tractor, but not no more. Grippin' th' steerin' wheel, he pulls himself up into a standin' position, then turns 'round so he can back down the small step. He uses th' rear fender t' help keep his balance. When he lands on his good knee he teeters for a minute while he tests his bad knee t' see if he can count on it. Finally, he turns 'round and walks toward me.

Holdin' up his hand, he says, "No need to tell me that that's the finest job of getting a garden ready that you ever saw. I know I'm the best." He finishes by grinnin' real big.

"You call that good?" I say. "I thought sure you'd make at least one more pass through it t' cut them clods up."

"Clods?! What clods? You can't find no clods out there. It's cut as fine as sand."

"Oh get yore feelin's off'n yore sleeve. I was jes' jokin' with you. I'll have t' admit that between this good dirt an' you an' yore tractor, I always have one o' th' best gardens around."

"And the good Lord, too, don't forget him," Smiley says.

"Fer sure," I agree, "that goes without sayin'."

Noddin' at th' small paper sack lyin' on th' ground beside m' hoe an' rake, Smiley says, "It's the first week of June so I guess that'd be purple hull pea seeds in that sack."

I reach down an' pick up the sack o' seed. "You'd be right. I always like t' plant m' purple hulls during th' first week o' June. If I plant 'em earlier, they produce all vine and no peas. An' if'n I plant 'em later, a dry spell always stunts 'em an' they don't hardly produce no peas at all."

"You going to plant them in rows or are you going to sow them this time?" Smiley asks.

"You know good and well how I'm gonna do it. It's gonna be in rows. You an' yore ideas 'bout sowin' th' seed ain't never made sense t' me."

"How can you say that? Why, just this week Pastor Willis shared with us one of Jesus's parables where he talks about a man sowing his seeds."

Smiley's words remind me of how long it's been since I been t' church. I ain't been back since th' night April killed that boy.

Grunting, Smiley bends down t' pick up th' hoe an' says, "Then let's get busy planting those peas."

He starts layin' off a row that couldn't be no straighter if'n he'd stretched a string t' go by. Then, like he had been readin' m' mind, he asks, "You still going to church, Tucker?"

I start droppin' seeds in th' furrow left by Smiley's hoe an' say, "Guess I'd have t' say I ain't."

Smiley don't look up, jes' keeps focused on his hoein'. I know he wants me t' say more but there ain't no more t' say, but I'll let him decide how far he wants t' go. After a few moments, he asks, "Wonder what Ella would have to say about you not going to church?"

His question hits me square in th' middle o' my chest an' I drop my sack o' seed. I feel like cussin' him, but it don't seem right since we's discussin' church. I retrieve m' seed an' say, "Most likely she'd mind 'er own business an' not say nothin', which is what you should do, too."

By this time Smiley's finished layin' off the first row. He takes a long stride t' measure off where th' next row goes an' starts usin' his hoe t' make another furrow.

He ain't said nothin' out loud, but I can hear 'im mutterin' under his breath. Standin' up straight an' foldin' m' arms 'cross m' chest, I say, "Look here, ol' man, if'n you got somethin' you want t' say, then say it where I can hear it."

Smiley stops his hoein' an' leans on th' handle. "Well you need to make up your mind if you want me to say what's on my mind or not. You tell me to mind my own business, so I'll mind my own business. So what if I got reason to be concerned about one of my close friends, I'll just keep my concern to myself. So what if I might be worrying about her, I'll just keep my worry to myself." He starts hoein' again an' says to the ground, "So what if holding all that stuff inside me might just give me a heart attack and kill me. It's just Smiley Carter and he doesn't really matter."

"Okay, okay," I say, "let's go sit in th' shade an' we'll talk. Though I don't know what good it's gonna do."

We make our way t' th' makeshift bench I built last year underneath th' trees on th' fencerow beside th' garden. I hand Smiley a two-quart jar with ice water in it an' take th' other jar an' get me a cool drink.

Opening th' lid, Smiley says, "You know, Tucker, they make things called thermoses that keeps things cold and hot and are unbreakable, too. You might think about turning loose a few dollars and getting you a couple of them."

After swishing my mouthful o' water around, I spit it out and say, "Plastic! Don't nothin' taste good that's been in plastic. I've had these jars for forty years an' they work jes' fine."

He ignores my comment an' gets another drink. Then he says, "So what's happened to you and God?"

Over the last few months I've pondered jes' such a question. Wondered why I quit going t' church. It ain't like I don't like th' preacher, 'cause I do. An' even tho' people there don't rightly know what t' say t' me, at least they's as friendly as they know how t' be. So "why" keeps lingerin'.

"Ahem!" Smiley clears his throat like a horse with a piece o' corncob stuck in his throat.

"All right," I say. "I'm trying t' think how t' put it into words. Let me ask you a question. Have y' ever done enough bad stuff in yore life that you didn't think you deserved t' have nothin' good ever again?"

Smiley's eyes open wide. "Do you know who you're talking to? This is Smiley Carter. I've been a hypocrite and a reprobate most of my life. I've treated folks bad, taken advantage of them, stole from them, and lied to everybody I know. Yes, Tucker, I know what that feels like." He ends by shakin' his head an' lookin' off into th' distance, probably rememberin' some bad things he done.

228

"But you ain't done horrible things like I've done," I reply.

Smiley turns t' look at me. His dark eyes search m' face, lookin' fer somethin' that might tell him what I'm talkin' 'bout. He says, "Tucker, what are you talking about? What have you done that you think is so bad?"

I ain't sure if I want t' tell him ever'thing that's botherin' me. Ella always said that gettin' stuff off yore chest is good fer you. But t' tell Smiley ever'thing seems like a scary thing t' do. His eyes ain't left m' face. It's like he's turnin' pages in a mystery book, lookin' fer clues. "Well, fer one thing," I say to him, "I've ruined people's lives."

I'd hoped that'd be enough t' satisfy him, but by th' look on his face I can tell it only deepened th' mystery fer him.

"Now you're just talking nonsense," he says. "Whose life do you think you've ruined?"

"Let's start with m' daughter, Maisy. Why do you think she turned out th' way she did, livin' th' life of a whore? I didn't know nothin' 'bout raisin' a kid when I had 'er an' I done ever'thing wrong raisin' 'er. Then when I got a second chance at raisin' kids with m' grandkids, I screwed it up again. Why do you think March—"

When I say March's name, m' throat chokes up an' his name sticks there like a pill that you can't get t' go down. My eyes sting with tears an' I try t' blink 'em back. I cough t' try an' get m' throat clear. "Why do you think March done run away like he did? I ain't heard nothin' 'bout him in nearly nine years. He runned away t' get away from me, that's what happened. I done such a sorry job that he couldn't stand t' live with me no more."

I look at Smiley's face an' see what must be a reflection o' my own. His black cheeks shine like silver from th' tears runnin' down 'em. He don't say nothin' though, givin' me time t' tell this th' way I want to. We both reach fer our bandannas at th' same time t' wipe our face an' blow our nose.

"An' that ain't all," I continue. "Look at how I ruined th' life of our precious April. She—"

If I felt like March's name stuck like a pill in m' throat, when I say April's I feel like I'm goin' t' vomit. But it ain't m' breakfast that's trying t' come up. It's all th' sadness an' regret I been feelin' fer so long. I taste its bile in th' back o' m' throat.

Swallowing hard, I say, "I know y' loved April in a special way. An' she loved you, too. But neither you nor Ella did enough t' undo all the mess that I made o' raisin' 'er. Now she's hunderds o' miles away from here. An' I suspect she likes it that way, even though she acted like she hated leavin'. I write 'er letters all th' time, but I ain't got one line back from 'er. That tells me exactly how she feels 'bout me. What a sorry excuse of a woman I am!"

When I finish, I burst out sobbin'. I lean m' head towards Smiley an' he reaches out an' pulls me into his chest. I push m' face into th' bib o' his overalls an' cry like I ain't cried in a long time.

Smiley pats me on m' back like he would a little child an' says, "Tucker, Tucker, go ahead an' cry it out. Cry it out and let it go. Let them tears wash your soul."

I don't know how long we sit in this position, but finally m' shoulders quit shudderin' an' m' tears dry up. Smiley relaxes his hold on me an' I sit back up.

"Now then," Smiley says, "now that you got that outta you, you are going to listen to me. Tucker, you've got things all mixed up in your head. You are not the one responsible for how Maisy turned out. Could you have done a better job raising her? Well of course you could have, but so could every parent I know. You raised her better than you was raised, that's for sure. So you made improvement. The reason Maisy turned out the way she did is because of Maisy. I know that to be true by looking at my life. I had what I believe was a good raising. My mama and Mama Mattie gave me all the love and tenderness a boy could want. And they made me mind, too. Taught me right from wrong. But look what I did with my life and how I turned out. And I got no one to blame for how I turned out except myself. I wasted my good raising. Once a body gets grown, they has a choice on what they do with their life."

"Yeah, but what 'bout March and April?" I protest.

Holdin' up his hand, Smiley says, "I ain't done speaking my piece yet. Don't none of us know what got into March. He was always into trouble and walked around like he had a chip on his shoulder even when he was four years old. I think we is all born with a certain nature about us, just like a litter of puppies. Some of them is born high-strung and some of them ain't. And there ain't no explaining that. Kids is the same way. There's probably lots of reasons why March took off like he did, but it don't look like we're ever gonna find it out. It's just one of them things.

"And that brings me to talk about April, sweet, angelic April. What I think happened to April is that she never got over losing Ella. With the help of God, Ella worked magic with April. Don't none of us know how good that must have felt to April and how special that made her feel. Then God called Ella home and in April's mind and heart she lost something precious. And she ain't never let go of that hurt. That's what Smiley Carter thinks about all that."

I drop my head an' look at m' clenched hands. I squeeze 'em so hard all th' knuckles turn white. Speaking low, I say, "Even if what you say is true, an' I ain't sayin' I agree with it, that still ain't th' worst o' what I done in my life. Not th' worst by a long shot." I sit back up an' look at Smiley, weighin' whether I want t' keep goin' with this conversation. Is there any reason to tell Smiley all th' truth? Is there any reason not to?

Smiley waits on me t' decide which way I'm goin'. He even takes another drink o' water.

"Sometimes," I begin, "a person is faced with a choice, an' no matter how they choose, somebody's gonna get hurt. There jes' ain't no way 'round it. So they gotta decide. And it ain't th' kind o' situation where they can go talk t' people an' get their advice. No, it's somethin' they gotta decide right there in th' moment, sometimes a split-second of a moment. An' after they choose, it's one o' them things that can't never be undone. That's th' worst part, that there's no changin' yore mind and takin' it back 'r fixin' things back like they was. What's done is done an' you jes' gotta live with it, maybe even die with it."

I pause a minute t' get me a drink, too. It seems like all o' nature has stopped t' listen t' me, 'cause I don't hear a single bird 'r grasshopper. Wipin' m' mouth on m' sleeve, I continue talkin'. "Smiley, I been in that kind o' situation two times in my life. One time I decided that somebody had t' die an' th' other time I decided I had t' do whatever it took t' keep somebody I love alive."

I spread my arms wide. "It's because of all o' this that I been tellin' you that I ain't been back t' church. There ain't no way in heaven that God would ever forgive me an' accept me after what all I've done. No sir. Ol' Tucker's headed straight fer hell jes' as sure as you an' I are sittin' here. I ain't no better off than I was before I come t' know God."

CHAPTER FORTY-FOUR

But they that sometime liked my company
Like lice away from dead bodies they crawl.
—*Sir Thomas Wyatt*

APRIL:

Standing outside the barn, I carefully scan all the open area and as far into the woods as I can see. Roxie, Spirit Lake's golden retriever, stands beside me and seems to be looking with me. After a few moments, Roxie turns her head toward me and her bright copper eyes search my face. "Yeah, I know," I say to her. "I don't see that stupid donkey anywhere."

Walking back into the barn, I call out, "Hey, Will, have you seen Pablo this morning? I can't find him anywhere."

Will turns his attention from watching Sarah groom her horse, Excelsior. Using his ever present walking stick, Will makes his way toward me. Roxie trots over to accompany him and Will pats her on the head.

"So, ol' Pablo has flown the coop, huh?" Will asks when he gets to me. "Has anything happened between the two of you?"

At first I think he is joking with me, but there is no expression of play on his face. "What do you mean 'Has anything happened?'"

Yesterday's evening feed time bubbles up from my memory. It was the day after I spent the night in the woods with Michelle. I was tired; actually I was exhausted and eager to get through feeding so I could eat supper and go to bed.

Pablo, on the other hand, wanted to play the role of a stubborn jackass. When I carried his bucket of feed to his usual corner of the barn, he suddenly grabbed the bucket with his mouth and jerked it out of my hand, spilling all his feed onto the ground. I swore under my breath at him and kneeled down to pick up the feed with my bare hands and put it back into the bucket.

Pablo shoved his long face right in the middle of what I was doing and sniffed loudly around my face. I thought he was trying to apologize and I was regretting cussing him. That's how he caught me off guard when he pushed me so hard that I was bowled over and found myself sprawled out on the barn floor.

Without thinking, I jumped up and swung the plastic feed bucket as hard as I could. It caught Pablo squarely on the side of his face. "Get away from me, you ugly idiot!" I hissed.

Pablo pinned his ridiculously long ears back and turned away from me. He gave a quick kick aimed in my direction and then bolted at a gallop through the opening of the barn. That was the last time I'd seen him.

I suddenly realize that both Will and Roxie are staring at me. Will's bright blue eyes and Roxie's shiny copper ones look like they belong in a gold-chained locket. It feels like they have been reading my mind. "Pablo and I had an argument yesterday," I finally confess.

"What happened?" Will asks.

"He wouldn't cooperate with anything I was doing. He acted like it was the first time he'd ever been around me. I don't know what had gotten into him."

"Hmmm," is Will's reply. Turning, he walks toward the opening of the barn while motioning with his head for me to follow. We stop in the opening and Will begins searching the perimeter with his eyes as I had done earlier. Without looking at me, he says, "I'm always telling you girls that these horses, and their cousin Pablo, are prey animals. There's no other animal alive that is more aware of changes in their environment than them, even the tiniest bit of change. Anytime someone tells me there's something wrong with their horse, they are actually telling me that something has changed within *them*. I learn more about you girls by watching your animals than Mary, James, or Michelle ever learns from talking with you. Looking at them is like looking into a mirror. So I don't pay as much attention to you girls as I do to your reflection because what the horses show me is the truth, while all you girls try to do is hide the truth."

While Will's eyes continue to search for Pablo, mine are riveted on him. It's the most I've ever heard him say at one time. Living with Tucker taught me to pay close attention to someone who doesn't say a lot. Just like her, when Will speaks it's because there's something worth saying.

Reaching down to scratch Roxie behind her ears, Will says, "It ain't none of my business 'cause all I'm here for is to make sure these animals are taken care of, but what's happened in you? What's different?"

I remember playing hide and seek with August and March. My favorite hiding place was in a patch of cane that Tucker grew so she'd have something to use for sticking her pole beans. It was so thick that only I was small enough to squeeze inside its cover. August and March would have to push the stalks apart one by one, going deeper and deeper into the shade of the cane, before they could find me. That's how I feel right now, like Will is getting closer and closer to me in my hiding place.

"There's nothing different about me," I say defensively, trying to disappear deeper into the cane.

"What do you think, Roxie?" Will says to the dog. "Is April today the same April who first come here over three months ago?"

I swear it looks like Roxie understands him. Her head swivels from Will to me and back to Will. Then she sneezes.

"Me either," Will says. Turning to face me, he says, "You know, April, Pablo never had anyone spend time with him like you have. No one has ever taken the time to look at him and get to know him, except you. All he ever was the butt of jokes, and he always felt like he was on the outside, like there wasn't nothing special about him. But since you started taking care of him, he's changed. He learned that not everybody is going to make fun of him and that some people are worth trusting. I think he even started being proud of himself and how he looked."

Something about Will's words strikes a distant chord inside me, one that's in a minor key. Memories are stirred by its sound. I remember when I first started riding the school bus. People made fun of everything about me: my mismatched clothes that didn't fit; the fact that I didn't talk; the way I smelled; the house that I lived in; my mother, Maisy; and, of course, Tucker.

My heart suddenly feels like it is a sheet of paper that's been torn in two, the ragged edges exposed and raw. I feel like I want to cry, not for myself, but for that little girl on the bus who still lives in my memory and for Pablo, who must have lived the same kind of life as her. The only thing that saves me from the dam bursting is Will asking me another question.

"So, what did you do to Pablo yesterday evening?"

There is almost an audible sound as my defensive walls slam into position. "I didn't do anything to him that he didn't deserve. He tried to hurt me, you know."

For the first time, Will's face shows an emotion. He smiles. "So Pablo tried to hurt you?"

"Yes he did!"

"That's interesting. So what did you then do to him?"

I see myself swinging the bucket and Pablo wincing in pain. I do not want to tell this truth to Will, though for some reason I think he already knows it. Perhaps Pablo went and told on me. "Okay," I finally admit, "I hit him in the head with his feed bucket."

Will winces as if I have struck him. He shakes his head in disappointment. Shame envelopes me in its wet blanket.

Will looks back toward the woods. "Then I guess he's run away."

Fear and regret scissor their way through my heart. "We've got to find him!" I exclaim. "He'll get lost! There are wolves and bears out there! It's not safe!"

"You should have thought about that before you hurt him," Will says in a flat tone. "Anyway, Pablo won't be found unless he wants to be. He'll manage to take care of himself, and if he chooses to, he'll come back."

I find no hope in Will's comment that I can latch onto. "But do you think he'll come back?" I ask.

"It's hard to say." Will turns away and heads back into the barn. "I've got work to do. Today's Jessica's graduation day exercise and Mary, James, and Michelle will be here shortly."

Will ambles away, leaving me alone with Roxie. I reach down to pet her, but she walks slowly away before my hand can touch her, her tail drooping behind her.

CHAPTER FORTY-FIVE

Of all the causes which conspire to blind
Man's erring judgment, and misguide the mind,
What the weak head with strongest bias rules,
Is pride, the never-failing vice of fools.
– Alexander Pope

APRIL:

In my deserted condition I notice that on the opposite side of the barn Mary, James, and Michelle are grouped together talking and motioning with their hands. Will makes his way to the group and listens as they talk animatedly with him.

The rest of the girls have finished feeding their horses and stand watching the four adults. I walk over and join them.

"Where's Pablo?" Heather asks. "I didn't see him with you this morning."

"How should I know?" I snap. "He's got a mind of his own."

"What do you expect?" Megan laughs. "He's a complete jackass!"

Everyone erupts into laughter.

I walk up to Megan and shove her. "What's that supposed to mean?! Pablo's a lot smarter than your stupid horse, Tonto. Besides, your horse is nothing but a half-breed."

Jessica steps between the two of us just as Megan starts to swing at me. "Look, you two, this is my last day at Spirit Lake. Don't screw it up by causing us all to be punished because you two can't get along. If you have to fight, at least wait until I'm gone. I'll tell you both the truth, I will not miss either of you when I'm gone. You've been here for over three months and you still don't act like you've learned anything." She pauses, and then adds, "Actually, you remind me of myself when I got here. So I guess there's still hope for you."

Before anyone can say anything else, the adults join our group. If they saw what happened between me and Megan, they don't mention it.

Mary speaks first. "Well, Jessica, this is your last day with us and your last day to be with Beauty. So we thought we'd have you do a little exercise with her." Mary steps back and nods at Will.

"Jessica," Will says, "why don't you put a halter and lead rope on Beauty and bring her out here. April and Megan, go get those two sawhorses out of the corner over there and bring them over here. Sarah, I want you to get the largest coil of rope out of the tack room. And Heather and Ashley, you two each need to bring a bale of hay out here."

Though puzzled, we go about our assignments. Once everything Will has asked for has been assembled, James picks up the coil of rope and hands one end of it to Michelle, who starts reeling it off his arm. She walks the length of the barn, leaving the trail of rope behind her. Then James walks toward her, uncoiling the rest of the rope off his arm and making a parallel line of rope approximately three feet to the side of Michelle's. Next they walk back toward us, but as they come they put gentle, elongated curves into the pathway they've created with the rope.

Will walks down the path about twenty feet, stops and says, "April and Megan, bring one of those sawhorses and set it in the middle of the path." After we set it down where Will has indicated, he pushes it with his walking stick, toppling it over on its side.

"Now go get me the other one," Will says to me and Megan. As we go to get it, he walks forward another twenty feet and stops. We set it down as before and, again, he pushes it over.

"Heather," Will calls out, "bring your bale of hay here."

Heather hefts the bale off the ground and, bouncing it off her thighs as she walks, takes it to Will. He points to a spot just outside the path and says, "Drop it there." Heather lets go of the strings on the bale, and it lands with a thud.

"Now, Ashley, you bring your bale," Will says. This time Will has her set her bale right in the middle of the path, close to the end.

With his eyebrows raised, Will looks at Mary, James, and Michelle. "Is that sort of what you had in mind?"

Smiling, Mary says, "Yes, that's perfect. So, James, why don't explain what will happen here."

James looks at Jessica and says, "Jessica, you've come a long, long way since you arrived at Spirit Lake. You are not the same person you were when you first arrived here. It's been an honor and a privilege for us to have been witnesses to your journey of discovery and to be on the sidelines and see what amazing changes God worked in your heart. Now, as you leave here, you are reentering what people call 'the real world.' That transition will not be easy for you because you've grown so accustomed to the world here. But we all believe in you and feel that you are ready to take what you've learned here and that you can live a rich and full life."

I glance around and notice that all the horses are standing with their heads sticking out of their stalls, watching and listening to what we are doing. Quickly I look at the distant barn opening, hoping to see Pablo standing there. But the opening is as vacant as a deserted house, and it feels just as lonely.

"Michelle," James says, "if you'll step up here and help me."

Michelle meets James in front of Jessica. Beauty blows loudly, feeling some tension.

"What you are going to have to do," James says to Jessica, "is lead Beauty through this pathway we've created with the rope. You must not let Beauty step outside of the path."

Looking confident, Jessica replies, "No problem. Just tell me when to start."

"Well, there's one more thing," Michelle says with a smile. "Both you and Beauty are going to be blindfolded."

All of us girls swap stunned expressions.

"You've got to be kidding," Jessica says. "That's impossible."

"So you're not even going to try?" Mary asks. "Is that because you don't believe you can do it or because you don't believe Beauty can do it?"

Jessica turns to face Beauty.

People have always told me I have pretty hair, but if I could have hair as black and shiny as Beauty's coat, I'd never complain about my hair again. She looks elegant.

Beauty looks back at Jessica. There is pride in her bearing. She seems to have understood that there is a challenge in the air and looks eager to prove herself. For her sake, I'm hoping Jessica will not disappoint Beauty.

Finally, Jessica turns back around and says, "Absolutely, we can do this. Let's get started."

Michelle places the blindfold on Jessica while James, with Will's assistance, places a blindfold on Beauty. Michelle spins Jessica in a circle three or four times, leaving Jessica a little dizzy.

"Now then," Mary says, "it is the responsibility of the rest of you girls to yell instructions at Jessica so she can navigate this exercise successfully. Everyone understand?"

We all nod.

"Then let the exercise begin."

There is a moment of silence until we all explode, shouting directions at Jessica. All of us try to be heard and to yell louder than the girl beside us. It's so loud and jumbled that not even I can understand everything being said.

Jessica's head turns in all directions, trying to pick out a clear voice and instruction, but she makes no moves. All the noise has Beauty snorting and throwing her head into the air. Suddenly Jessica holds up her free hand in a signal for everyone to stop.

Our voices fall silent and we wait for Jessica to speak.

"When all of you speak at once," she says, "I can't make any sense out of what anyone is saying. You've got to talk one at a time."

Ashley speaks up. "Turn to your left and go forward three steps, then stop and turn right and you'll be right in front of the beginning of the path."

Jessica turns to her right and starts to step.

"Your left, I said. Your left," Ashley exclaims.

Jessica stops but Beauty is still moving forward and bumps into her. This causes Beauty to throw her head into the air again and to start backing up. She almost jerks the lead out of Jessica's hand but stops at the last second. Once again, Beauty blows loudly out her nose, making a rattling noise.

It is an unbelievably tedious process for Jessica and Beauty to make it to the end of the path. It probably took twenty minutes for them to cover the short distance. I'm not sure I'd have had the patience to do it. And I'm sure I'd have gotten frustrated with all the confusing directions everyone kept throwing at Jessica.

When she and Beauty finally complete the exercise we all cheer. Jessica takes her blindfold off and removes Beauty's. They nuzzle faces in appreciation of each other.

"Whew!" Jessica exclaims as she leads Beauty back to our group, "I never thought it would be that hard or take that long."

"So what did you get out of the exercise?" James asks her.

Jessica turns around and looks at where she has just been. "That you and Mary and Michelle made something difficult out of something that should have been easy."

Everyone laughs together.

"I think you are correct," James says. "I wonder if you've ever been guilty of doing anything like that."

"That's an easy yes," Jessica replies. "Just because my parents divorced and were more interested in their lives than mine, I chose to make my life miserable by getting in trouble just to get their attention. You know, bad attention is better than no attention. But all that did was keep me miserable, and they kept ignoring me anyway. It was foolish of me to make my life harder than it had to be."

"Does that sound familiar to any of you other girls?" Michelle asks.

"I guess I never thought about it that way until just now," Sarah says. "Even though I knew it was wrong to be having sex with my boyfriend, when I got pregnant I was excited. But my parents convinced me I had to abort the baby. They said it was for my sake, but it was really for theirs. They wanted to protect their reputation. Afterwards, I decided the only thing I deserved was to die, which is why I tried to commit suicide. But that just complicated things for me. Now I'm beginning to see that what I need to do is honor my baby's memory by living a life it would be proud of. That would make my life so much simpler and more joy filled."

"Jessica," Mary says, "what was it like having everyone giving you instructions at the same time?"

"Oh my gosh, that was the craziest thing. I had no idea where I was and no idea which way to go. Everyone's voices were so jumbled up that I couldn't make sense out of what anyone was saying."

"Then what's the lesson?" Mary asks.

"Who you listen to will determine where you go," Jessica says. "There are lots of people who are eager to get your attention and tell you to follow them, but if the one true voice of God is the one you listen to, then you'll always be on the right path."

I have a knee-jerk reaction to Jessica's words and before I know it, I say, "That's a bunch of you-know-what. Listen to God and what? He'll take care of you and everything will be sunshine and roses? That's just not true." Even I am surprised at how harsh my words and tone sound. But it's too late to take them back now.

Everyone stares at me. Sarah's hand is over her open mouth.

"Girl," Heather says quietly, "even if I thought that, I don't believe I would have said it."

I feel my face reddening. But I refuse to back down. "What is the matter with all you people? Don't you know how the real world works? My—" I catch myself before I say what I was about to say, and I start again. "I knew a woman who was a really good woman, a woman who always did what God wanted her to do. She loved him. She had a pure heart, a loving heart and only did good things. And you know what happened to her? She was abused by her husband, got breast cancer and had both of them cut off, and then she got cancer again and died from it. Is that where listening to God's voice is supposed to get you?"

I scan everyone's face and stop at James's. "What about you, James? Have you been listening to God's voice? And where's it gotten you? Your wife is dying of cancer and is going to leave you with your two boys."

By the time I finish talking I am practically shouting and spit explodes from my mouth with every consonant. I am panting and feel a deep rage in my chest. What I'd like is a good fight with someone.

All eyes are now on James to see how he will react to the sting of my words. He squats down and idly doodles in the powderlike dirt on the barn floor. Keeping his eyes on the floor, he says calmly, "My idea of listening to his voice is that he will show me how to overcome the obstacles in my path, not that he will remove them from my path. And it's the end of the journey that I'm interested in, the one that comes after the final obstacle—death."

As is usual in my encounters with James, his words are delivered softly but carry with them the weight of truth. I have no rebuttal.

In the quietness that fills the barn, Will suddenly says, "I wonder how Beauty felt during that exercise."

All heads turn to look at the largest member in our assembled group. Immediately her eyes widen as this simple shift in the group has grabbed her attention. She even backs up a step. Jessica smiles and scratches Beauty's chin. "Easy, girl, everything's okay. They're just impressed with you, that's all."

"I know she's my horse," Jessica says to us, "but I think she was magnificent. I don't know how in the world she kept from stepping on me and how she could follow me when I didn't even know where I was going."

"I think she was scared," Megan says. "If these animals are prey animals, like Will is always telling us they are, then I would think not being able to see would have to be the scariest thing in the world for them."

"But," Heather counters thoughtfully, "if they are a mirror of their handler, like I've heard Will say they are, then it depended on how Jessica felt. However Jessica felt, that's how Beauty felt."

Everyone looks back at Will for his judgment on the matter.

Even I'm curious as to what he will say. "Which way is it, Will?" I ask.

Will looks uncomfortable and glances at Mary. I think he's concerned he's overstepped his role, but Mary nods at him to go ahead.

"Did any of you see anything in Beauty's behavior that would indicate to you that she was afraid during the exercise?"

I can think of nothing and apparently neither can the other girls because no one says a word.

"So I'm right," Heather says boastfully.

"I think you're both right," Will says. "Megan is right in that a horse that can't see is normally always insecure and frightened. But Heather is correct when she says that a horse is a mirror of their handler."

Suddenly I feel like a light is beginning to glow inside my mind, like when the sun first peaks over the horizon and its beams hit you in the face. I slowly turn to James and, without thinking, say, "And if the one leading you is calm and confident, then you will be, too."

James gives his head an almost imperceptible nod. He closes his eyes for a second and, opening them, gives me a little smile.

CHAPTER FORTY-SIX

This gift alone I shall her give
When death doth what he can:
Her honest fame shall ever live
Within the mouth of man.
– John Heywood

MARCH:

H ello, Levi," Dr. Sydney greets me as I enter her office.

"Hi, Dr. Sydney." I find my familiar chair and sit down. "I guess you know I'm nervous about this session."

"Of course you are. I don't blame you. You've lived in hospitals and clinics for the past six months, almost. And now to think about living out there in the real world must be pretty overwhelming."

"When you told me last session that my time here at Patricia Neal was coming to an end, I felt a mixture of excitement, pride, and fear."

Dr. Sydney chuckles. "That's a good job on your part of identifying your feelings and expressing them."

I return her laugh. "I am growing up, aren't I?"

"I believe you are indeed," she replies.

"So, you said we would talk about options today. What kinds of options do I have when I leave?"

"The most obvious option, Levi, is for you to return home to your family."

I expected this would be one of the directions Dr. Sydney would want to go today. Holding up both hands, palms toward her, I say, "You can stop right there. I've explained over and over to you and the rest of the staff, and to Debbie, that my old life is gone. I am dead to them. All I would represent to them would be pain. I've been gone so long I don't even know them anymore, and they certainly don't know me. Living my life as if it began six months ago is the only option for me."

"I figured you'd say something like that," Dr. Sydney says with a slight tone of regret in her voice. "But I had to give it one last shot."

"Then make a note somewhere in your notebook that you tried one more time but that you were unsuccessful," I tell her. "Now can we move on and discuss realistic options?"

I listen as Dr. Sydney shuffles some papers. "Here is what I was thinking," she begins. "The life that you lived before getting hurt really didn't give you any marketable skills, at least the legal kind."

Someone else might miss it, but I detect the humor in Dr. Sydney's tagged-on comment. "That's for sure," I agree. "No doubt I could get a job as the first blind hitman for a drug gang. As a matter of fact, that might be sort of interesting work."

She joins me in laughing.

"What your treatment team has noted is that you are very good working with your hands, you have experience working on small engines, you know your way around guns, and you are familiar with farm animals. So one goal would be finding you placement where you will make use of all those strengths. Agreed?"

"Sure, that sounds good. But what kind of place would that be?"

"Hold on, hold on. I'm getting to that. Another goal that you and I have talked about is you attending school somewhere to learn a marketable trade or to get a degree in something that will translate into a career. So, we need to be sure that we incorporate both goals in your discharge plan. Have you given more thought to what career you are interested in?"

I have given it lots of thought but I'm afraid that my idea will sound ridiculous and unreasonable. Squirming in my chair, I say, "What do you think I should do?"

"And what's my response to that question going to be?" Dr. Sydney says.

"That it doesn't matter what you think, what matters is what I think, right?"

"That is exactly right. I can tell you have some idea rattling around in your head. Why not just spit it out on the floor between us so both of us can take a look at it?"

"Okay," I say, "I was wondering if I might become a vocational counselor of some kind. I've had every kind of therapy imaginable and have had multiple handicaps to overcome. I think I could relate to people and could motivate them to believe they can rebuild their lives." When I finish, I hold my breath waiting for Dr. Sydney's reaction. I've learned that it's not her way to give a snap judgment about anything. She will turn it over in her mind for a few moments before replying. But now those few moments seem to be stretching into long minutes and my fear that my idea is foolish is growing.

Finally she clears her throat. Unexpectedly, her voice is thick with emotion. "Levi, I believe you would be an awesome vocational counselor. You have a lot of the innate skills that are needed in that field, plus these last six months have been a great learning experience for you. Actually, I was hoping this would be what you wanted to do."

"Great!" I exclaim, clapping my hands together. "I was afraid you'd think that would be too hard for me or that I wasn't smart enough for it. Wooooo, that's a relief!"

"And I have the perfect plan for you," she says. "There is a facility a few miles from here that's for troubled teenage girls. It's called Spirit Lake. It's about as remote a place as can be found, right next to Smoky Mountains National Park. Girls live there for six to twelve months while they work out their problems. It is small, usually six to nine girls, and there are three counselors. I know about it because I'm on the board of directors. It's a faith-based program. There are horses and other farm animals, too. They are really changing people's lives over there."

"It sounds like a fascinating place," I interject, "but what in the world would I do there?"

"They are always needing someone to work on the generator or the lawnmower and tiller. You could do that. The man who works with the animals is in his seventies. He needs some help repairing halters, bridles, and saddles, which I know you could do or at least learn how to do. And Mary, the treatment director, recently talked with me about the idea of teaching the girls in the recreational use of firearms. Can you see how this would be the perfect place for you?"

My mind is spinning, trying to take in all that Dr. Sydney is throwing at me. Shaking my head to help clear it, I say, "But what about school and my degree? Where does that fit in?"

"What if you worked at Spirit Lake from now until December and then start school at the University of Tennessee right here in Knoxville in January? That would give us plenty of time to get all of the necessary prerequisite material together for starting school. They have a great program at UT that I'm sure you'd love. What do you think?"

"Honestly, Dr. Sydney, school sounds great, but I'm not too sure about this Spirit Lake place. Me around a bunch of troubled teenage girls? That actually sounds scary to me. And what does 'faith-based' mean?"

"The idea behind faith-based programs is that they speak openly about God. It doesn't mean there's any kind of coercion to believe in God, only that the girls are exposed to the idea of God and are given the opportunity to explore their own spiritual side. And as far as you being around these girls, my thinking is that they need to be around men who are good people, who won't judge them or take advantage of them. So many of them have been abused by men, others never had a father in their life. It's understandable that they don't know how to relate to a male."

My mind chews on Dr. Sydney's words like they are a portion of tough meat. I find it impossible to break them down into smaller, more easily digestible pieces. When I try to swallow them whole, I feel like I am gagging.

"Levi, I can tell you are struggling to process all of this." Dr. Sydney's voice sounds a long way off. "Perhaps you'd like some time to think it over." She pauses, then says, "Maybe you'd like to discuss it with Debbie."

The mention of Debbie's name has the effect of the school bell ringing at the start of class. I'm suddenly completely present in the room with Dr. Sydney. Rubbing my palms on the knees of my jeans, I say, "Yes . . . Debbie . . . That's a great idea. I need to talk to Debbie about all this."

"I thought you might," Dr. Sydney says. "She's in the cafeteria, waiting on you."

"Huh?"

"I told her you might be looking for her and that I'd send you to the cafeteria after we met."

It's then that I realize that Dr. Sydney has seen all this play out before I ever arrived in her office this morning. As is usually the case, she is a step ahead of me. Smiling, I say, "You're really good at this. You know that, don't you?"

"Good at what?"

"Knowing what people are going to do or say before they do it."

"Let's just say that sometimes I guess right. Now why don't you go on over to the cafeteria? I'm going to be here in my office the rest of the afternoon. If you make up your mind what you are going to do, then come back by and we'll put wheels into motion. If you'd rather sleep on it tonight, that'll be fine. But I do need to have an answer soon so I can tell our administrator that we have a plan on how to finally get rid of you."

I laugh. "Oh, so that's how it's going to be. You bring a poor, crippled, blind man into your hospital and then all you want to do is get rid of him just because he eats as much food as three men. It's all about the money, isn't it?"

Dr. Sydney returns my laughter. "You're absolutely right. All the other patients are complaining that their portions have been cut in half since you started eating here. Now get yourself on over to the cafeteria. Your dining days at Patricia Neal are about to come to an end."

When I walk into the cafeteria, the familiar sounds of clattering plates, tinkling silverware, and indistinct conversations fill my ears. I stand still until Debbie's soft hand slips into mine.

"Hey there, big guy, I was hoping a strong, handsome man might come by and share an exotic meal with me. Do you have any plans?"

"That sounds exciting," I reply, "but we've got to be careful because I've got this jealous girlfriend who works around here. I mean she's practically psycho she's so crazy about me, not that you can blame her, of course. But she packs a mean right hook and could knock you and me both out if she catches us."

Debbie's fist slams into the side of my arm. "Is that the right hook you're talking about?"

"Owww," I howl in mock pain. "Somebody get security over here quick!" I yell.

The cafeteria goes silent.

"Yes, please do," Debbie says loudly. "This grizzly bear is impersonating a human being and needs to be escorted back into the woods where it belongs."

Recognizing the joke for what it is, everyone breaks into laughter.

Debbie puts my hand on her elbow. "Follow me, you crazy man. I've got us a table in a corner so we can talk. I didn't think you'd ever get here. I want to hear all about your conversation with Dr. Sydney."

When we get seated, Debbie says, "There's a Reuben sandwich, chips, and a pickle in front of you. And you've got a tall glass of sweet tea."

"Thanks, but I don't know if I can eat anything or not. My head and stomach are all knotted up. Let me tell you what Dr. Sydney had to say."

Once I finish giving Debbie all the details, I carefully locate my tea and take a long drink. Normally quick to reply, Debbie is quiet. Setting my glass down, I say, "Yeah, I know, it's a lot to absorb, isn't it? That was pretty much my reaction at first, too." I decide to wait and let Debbie speak when she's ready. My growling stomach reminds me I haven't eaten, so I take a bite of the sandwich.

"Don't forget," I remind her, "that I can't hear your facial expression. Everybody in the cafeteria knows how you're feeling right now, except for me."

"You're right," Debbie says, "I did forget. I apologize. Right now I'm smiling, but it's a nervous smile, maybe even a fearful smile."

"I can see that," I say. "Now tell me why."

"Well, it's a smile because I'm happy about your desire to find a career in helping others. I think you will be an incredibly effective person working in the rehab field. It's a nervous smile because I don't know how you will adjust to being at Spirit Lake."

"Do you know anything about the place?"

"Actually, I do. It's the part of my story that I've never gotten around to telling you about. You remember I told you about being in the car wreck with my parents when I was a freshman in college?"

"Yeah," I reply, "that's when both your parents were killed and you lost part of your arm."

"That's right. Then there was the lawsuit and the windfall settlement that essentially set me up for life financially. And, of course, during my recovery I spent a lot of time receiving all sorts of rehab, which is why I decided to take a job here at Patricia Neal. All of that is the story you already know. What you don't know about is my life prior to all that."

I can detect a hint of reluctance in Debbie's voice, but can't imagine why. "Well, I'm listening like only a blind man can. Tell me the rest of your story."

"Let me begin," Debbie says, "by telling you that the person I am today is nothing like the person I used to be."

Placing my hands flat on the table, I say, "If you can't do any better than that, then this isn't going to be much of a secret because, as you know, I can say the exact same thing about myself."

"I suppose that's true. I hadn't thought about it quite like that. Anyway, my father was a powerful and influential lawyer. My mother was heavily involved in politics, ran for a few offices, and won some. They were very successful people, but not such successful parents. I was basically raised by a series of nannies. It was a series because none of them could please my mother. As soon as I got attached to one, mother would fire her. So I found alternative ways to deal with absent parents."

When Debbie pauses, I say, "Alternative ways?"

"Specifically, I started abusing my body by either forcing myself to throw up or by cutting myself."

I'm truly shocked. I cannot imagine the kind, gentle person I know being that self-destructive. "I'm sorry, Debbie. You must have been in a lot of emotional pain to do that to yourself. I've heard about people doing those kinds of things, but I guess I've never known anyone personally who did it." Suddenly, the point of her telling me this story hits me. "It's Spirit Lake, isn't it? Your parents sent you to Spirit Lake, didn't they? That's how you know about it."

"Your fortune-telling skills are showing again," she says. "Yes, they found Spirit Lake and sent me there. I lived there for nearly a year. It was the hardest and at the same time the best year of my life. I found myself there. It was at Spirit Lake that I developed an understanding of who God is and what he does for us. I learned to let go and forgive."

"Sounds like it is a very special place," I say.

"It is, Levi, but it is treacherous, too, because there are some very hard-core girls that go there. They will chew you up and spit you out in a minute if you're not careful. Trust me, I know because I was one of them."

Her tone is almost ominous and I actually have a chill run down my spine. "I love you for being concerned about me," I tell her. "But you forget that I lived on the streets of Las Vegas, among the sewers of humanity. I don't think there is anything these girls will try that I haven't had to deal with before."

"Maybe you're right," Debbie says.

We sit in silence for a few minutes.

"Hey," I say, "there was something else you said. You were talking about your smile and you said you also had a fearful smile. What are you afraid of?"

She pulls her hand away.

I feel a chill in the air, though I know the temperature in the room hasn't changed. "Now you're making me afraid, Debbie. What is it? What are you afraid of?"

She sniffs and her voice breaks with emotion when she says, "I'm afraid that all these changes in your life will cause something to happen to us. Levi, I'm afraid of losing you."

It takes every ounce of self-control I have not to grab the table between us and pitch it aside like cardboard and grab Debbie and cradle her in my arms. Reaching toward her across the table, I say, "Give me your hands."

Her hand is cold and trembling when she places it in mine.

"I said give me your hands, plural."

"But, Levi, I don't—"

In a hoarse whisper, I say, "Give me your hands, Debbie Cooper!"

She then slides her prosthesis between my hands and beside her other hand.

My large hands envelope them and I squeeze firmly. "Listen to me. You are the best thing that has ever happened to me. Nothing . . ." I shake her for emphasis. "Nothing is going to come between me and you. I will not let that happen. I give you my word on that."

From across the cafeteria, someone shouts, "Go ahead and kiss him, will you? The suspense is killing us over here!"

There is an explosion of laughter throughout the cafeteria.

Suddenly Debbie is at my side and kissing me.

I barely hear the applause over the sound of my thundering heart.

CHAPTER FORTY-SEVEN

Why are we weigh'd upon with heaviness,
And utterly consumed with sharp distress,
While all things else have rest from weariness?
All things have rest; why should we toil alone?
—*Alfred, Lord Tennyson, 1832*

TUCKER:

Lookin' 'cross the dining table, I watch August fork in a big ol' bite o' mashed taters. It does me good t' see him eat like a race-horse eatin' oats. He's grown long an' lean since he's been away at college.

I notice Smiley's done pushed his own plate back an' he's lookin' at August, too.

"Smiley Carter," I say, "I don't know which is goin' t' pop first, th' fastener on yore pants 'cause you're so full 'r th' buttons on yore shirt 'cause you're so proud o' August. An' how you could eat that whole meal an' never stop smilin' is downright amazin'."

Keepin' his eyes on August, Smiley says, "When a bachelor gets a good home-cooked meal like this one you cooked, he's gotta eat like there's no tomorrow. And when his son has come home from college and he hasn't seen him in nearly three months, a man's got a right to puff his chest out. 'Specially when the boy's done as well as August has."

August acts like he ain't even listenin' t' us. He's bitin' off half of a biscuit when Smiley says his name. When he lifts his face t' look at me an' Smiley, they's biscuit crumbs on his lips an' a dime-size patch o' taters on his chin. He raises his eyebrows, an' with his mouth full o' biscuit, gives us a muffled, "What?"

Me an' Smiley laugh.

Grabbin' his glass o' tea, August washes down th' mouthful o' biscuit. "What are you two laughing at?" he asks. "Haven't you ever seen someone eat a meal before?"

"Sure we have," Smiley answers, "but you eat like the house is on fire and you may never get another meal the rest of your life."

August grins broadly an' I'll swear he looks just like Smiley, only thinner an' not as dark. "You all have no idea what life in college is like and how pitiful the cafeteria food is. That is, if you have time to go eat. I've really had to bear down the end of this year and burn the candle at both ends with my studies. It takes extra good grades to get into law school."

"I'd think they'd take you just because of your striking good looks, like your father's." Smiley closes his eyes, cocks his head back, an' strokes his white hair with one hand.

"Whatever y' do," I say, "don't let none of 'em know 'bout Smiley. His reputation is enough t' sink any chances you'd have t' get into a good school. If you really wanta impress 'em, send 'em a bowl o' my nanner puddin'. They won't even look at yore grades!"

Our laughter rings, fillin' up th' empty places in m' heart that's been left since April's been gone.

August looks 'round th' kitchen. "Speaking of banana pudding . . ."

Snappin' m' fingers, I say, "Oh my goodness, I knowed I fergot somethin'. I swear, getting old sure is an awful thing."

Excitement slides off o' August's face like meltin' ice slidin' off th' pump handle of a well. For a second I think he's gonna cry. He looks at me with soulful eyes an' says, "But when Smiley said you were preparing us a big welcome home supper, I thought for sure you'd—"

I wave m' hand at him an' stand up. "Oh calm down an' quit yore grievin'. O' course I made you a nanner puddin'. I was just pullin' yore leg."

Smiley slaps his thigh an' laughs loudly. "Did you see the look on that boy's face? You'd have thought you told him he was going to have to spend the day hauling hay tomorrow."

August laughs at himself while I'm reachin' in th' oven t' take out th' puddin'. "I've eaten lots of foods since I've been in college that we never had while I was growing up around here, but I've never had anything that comes close to comparing to the taste of Tucker's banana pudding. It is heavenly."

Settin' a bowl o' warm puddin' in front o' August, I say t' Smiley, "You hear that? August says I'm an angel."

"That's odd," Smiley says. "I was sitting right here and I never heard him say anything like that."

Thumpin' Smiley on th' top o' his head with th' back of a spoon, I say, "He said my puddin' was heavenly. In my book that's th' same thing as sayin' I'm an angel."

"Owww! Then what's the Devil's angel doing in heaven?!"

"You two stop it," August says. "Sit down here and enjoy a bowl of pudding with me."

For th' next few minutes all of us puts our energy into eatin' th' puddin'.

After August scrapes the sides an' bottom o' his bowl one last time an' licks his spoon, he says, "Enough, enough! Don't make me eat anymore. I'm going to explode."

"Well let's go in th' livin' room where there's more comf'terble chairs," I say.

When we get settled in, August says, "Okay you two, I've got some news I want to share with you about my future."

Before August can get another word out, Smiley butts in and asks, "Did you get accepted into law school?"

"Shush! Let th' boy tell us his news in his own way."

Shakin' his head, Smiley says, "You're right. I'm sorry. I'm gonna sit back and just listen." But he scoots up on th' edge o' th' couch, lookin' like a kid who's ready t' blow out th' candles on his birthday cake.

"You two haven't changed one bit," August says, smiling. "It's nice to know that some things stay the same."

"That's 'cause we's both too old t' change," I reply. Winking, I add, "'Specially that old fool sittin' beside you."

Smiley explodes, "Will you two both hush up with all this nonsense?! Get on with telling us your news or I'm gonna have a stroke."

August lays a hand on his dad's shoulder. "All right, then. You both know that once I got into college I began to have the idea that I'd like to become a lawyer. I remember that strange little lawyer that Miss Ella had that took care of all her business. She trusted him with everything. I want to be that kind of man, the kind that people can trust and who can use the law to protect them from predators, both the legal and the illegal kind.

"So I've been studying like I've never studied before in my life, which is why I've hardly come home any. I wasted lots of time in high school and I was behind in nearly everything. But I got caught up. Then I started excelling and getting noticed by the professors. They told me they believed I had what it took to be a good lawyer.

They helped me apply to law schools, which is what you have to graduate from before you actually can become a practicing attorney."

As he's talkin' I'm thinkin' 'bout him an' March doin' chores in th' barn an' throwin' dirt clods at each other. I remember August always tryin' t' protect April from gettin' picked on by th' kids at school. I feel shame when I remember th' mornin' she wet 'er pants at th' breakfast table an' I was 'bout t' tear into 'er when August come between me an' her an' shooed 'er onto th' bus with him. I hate m'self for bein' so ill-tempered with th' kids when they was growin' up.

August pauses in tellin' his story t' me an' Smiley. He leans forward, reaches into his back pocket an' pulls out a folded envelope. Wavin' it slowly back an' forth in th' air, he says, "This right here is my ticket. It is my acceptance letter to the school I most wanted to get into."

"Hot damn!" Smiley shouts, clapping his hands together. He grabs August an' hugs him. "I knowed you could do it! I just did! That is wonderful news, the best news."

August looks at me an' says, "What do you think, Tucker?"

I open m' mouth t' speak an' nothin' comes out. I try two 'r three times an' jes' can't git nothin' out. I motion fer him t' come t' my chair. He joins me an' kneels on one knee beside m' recliner, his eyes lookin' deep into mine. M' hands find his an' hold 'em. They're th' smooth hands of a city boy, but they feel strong, too.

M' voice is breakin' when I say, "When yore mama brought you t' me t' raise, I didn't have no idea what I was gonna do with you. But even from th' start I could tell there was somethin' special 'bout you, August." I tap his chest with m' index finger. "It's yore heart, that's what has always set you apart. It's a good heart an' it's meant t' do good things fer folks. Ever'thing you've done with yoreself is in spite o' th' mess I made o' raisin' you, not because of it." Tears burn m' cheeks as they run down 'em an' drip on t' mine an' his hands. "I couldn't be no prouder o' you. You've become as fine a young man as I know. Now give me hug."

Instead o' huggin' me, August keeps his eyes locked on mine. Every time he blinks a little shower o' tears escapes. Squeezin' m' hands, he says, "Listen to me, Tucker. I can't think of anyone in this world that I admire more than you. You are truly a self-made person. I don't know everything that you faced when you were growing up, but I know enough. You had every reason and excuse to grow up to be a mean, bitter, and self-destructive woman. But you grew above your raising. To me, that is a miracle. You, Tucker, are a miracle. And I love you for the miracle that you are."

When he finishes talkin', he loosens his grip on m' hands an' slips his arms 'round me. I swear th' arms of an angel couldn't feel no sweeter. I return his embrace an' it seems like time stops. An' I don't want th' clock t' start movin'.

After a while, a loud honk comes from 'cross th' room. Me an' August jump at th' sound. We let go o' each other an' look. Smiley's got his bandanna out where he's jes' blowed his nose an' now he's wipin' tears.

Me an' August both laugh. "I thought somebody was drivin' a eighteen-wheeler through th' livin' room an' honkin' his horn."

August says, "For a moment, I thought you had a Canada goose for a house pet."

Smiley looks at us with red-rimmed eyes. "Both of you just shut up. If ya'll don't have anything better to do than to make fun of an old man who just so happens to have a soft heart, then I feel sorry for you." As if he is strikin' a nail one last time to drive it in tight, he blows his nose again. From behind his bandanna he says, "I sure could use a cup of coffee."

"That's a good idea," I say, an' I get up an' walk into th' kitchen.

After I put it on t' brew, I return t' my chair. August is back sittin' beside Smiley, who's stopped his cryin' an' has put back on his broad smile.

"Oh yeah," August says, "I almost forgot the other part of the surprise. Guess where I'm going to go to law school."

The best answer me an' Smiley can come up with is a blank stare an' shruggin' our shoulders.

"I'm going to Ole Miss in Oxford, Mississippi, where Miss Ella graduated from."

I thought I was done cryin', but this piece o' news pricks m' heart like th' thorn from a blackberry vine an' th' tears start rollin' again. "Oh, August," I say, "Ella would be so happy 'bout that. It'd make 'er extra proud o' you."

Smiley looks at August in astonishment, shakin' his head. "A black man attending law school at Ole Miss. My, my, how the world has changed since I was your age."

August replies, "I'm not the first one. That barrier was broken in the sixties." He jumps up an' says, "Let me go see if the coffee's ready. I'll pour all of us a cup and bring it back in here." As he's walkin' away, he asks, "So tell me how April's doing at Spirit Lake."

"Fer as I know, she's doin' all right," I call to him. "I don't never hear nothin' from 'er, but they's a woman that's in charge, named Mary, who calls me 'bout once a month t' let me know how she's doin'. Sounds like April's bein' 'er hardheaded self an' takin' th' hard way instead o' th' easy way."

"Ask him about the truck," Smiley says. "He might know the answer."

August looks from Smiley t' me. "What truck?"

"Well," I say, "April was datin' this boy before she got sent t' Spirit Lake an' he disappeared. But a month 'r so later they found his truck sunk in th' Obion bottoms jes' down th' road from here."

"Sheriff Harris had it pulled out," Smiley adds.

"He thought th' boy's body would be in th' cab, but it wasn't. An' he's got it in his head that April had somethin' t' do with th' boy's disappearance."

"April?" August asks. "You mean, like he thinks she helped the boy run away or like he thinks she killed him?"

"He ain't never used th' words, but I think he believes she killed th' boy."

"That's crazy!" August says. "First of all, a teenage girl killing her boyfriend is a crime that is very rarely committed."

"That may be true, but he still acts awful suspicious o' her. He keeps comin' by here t' talk t' her, but I jes' tell him she ain't here right now. He's gittin' tired o' that answer an' has threatened t' put me in jail if I'm hidin' 'er out somewhere."

August shakes his head. "This is unbelievable. But listen to me, you don't have to tell him anything about April's whereabouts. She's protected by the confidentiality laws for patients receiving psychiatric help. Even if he somehow found out where she was, he couldn't touch her. Tell me why he's so suspicious of April."

Smiley speaks up, "He sent the boy's truck off somewhere to a lab of some kind, I'm guessing the TBI lab."

"And what did they find?"

"They found th' boy's blood on th' floorboard an' three different people's fingerprints," I say.

When I don't go on, August asks, "And the other two sets of fingerprints? Whose are they?"

"April's was in there."

"But that's no surprise," Smiley says, "since she and the boy were dating. Naturally her prints would be in there."

"Then who do the other set of prints belong to?" August asks.

"Sheriff Harris ain't said," I answer. "I don't think he knows for sure whose they is. But he thinks April might know."

August looks at th' floor an' lets out a low whistle. Suddenly his head snaps up. "Where did they find the boy's body?"

"That's just it," Smiley answers, "neither the boy nor his body has been found."

When August hears this, his whole body relaxes an' he sits back. Smiling, he says, "Then there is nothing to worry about. Even though April has nothing to do with it, if they don't have a body, they don't know if a crime has been committed or not. The sheriff is just on a fishing expedition, trying to find an extra clue that'll help him solve the mystery."

Now it's my turn t' relax an' sit back in m' chair.

CHAPTER FORTY-EIGHT

Buy the truth, and sell it not; also wisdom, and instruction, and understanding.
—*Proverbs 23:23*

APRIL:

As all of us girls busy ourselves cleaning up our breakfast dishes Mary walks in, followed by a girl.

"Ladies," Mary says, "this is Crystal. She's the newest member of our family here. Would you mind pausing for a minute in your chores and introducing yourselves?"

Just as they did on my first day here, everyone gives their introductory speech like a bunch of robots. When my turn comes, I say, "My name is April. I'm from Memphis, where my parents are . . ." I pause and notice the disinterested expressions on the other girls' faces. "Where my parents are serving life sentences for assassinating a federal judge. I drove the getaway car and would have gone to prison, too, but they let me come to Spirit Lake instead."

Everyone stares wide-eyed at me. I burst out laughing. "I'm kidding! Oh my gosh, you should see your all's expressions. They are hilarious!"

No one else laughs. Crystal looks around uncertainly.

"Okay," I say in exasperation, "you guys need to quit taking everything so seriously. It was just a joke." I look at Crystal. "I'm from Memphis and have been here for close to four months. I don't have any advice to offer you except that you're on your own."

"Come along, Crystal," Mary says, "and I'll show you where you will be living while you are here."

Thirty minutes later the rest of us head back to our cabin to get prepared for our first morning class session. I'm the first one through the door. I immediately spy Crystal sitting on my bed with my Autoharp on her lap. Stomping toward her, I yell, "What the hell are you doing?!"

Crystal is so startled that she jumps and the Autoharp slides off her lap and clatters onto the floor.

I slap her as hard as I can and scream, "You idiot!"

My blow is so hard that Crystal is knocked sprawling across my bed.

Ignoring her, I squat down and pick up my Autoharp. Cradling it to my chest, I unleash another verbal jab. "This belonged to my grandmother. She left it to me. It's the most important possession in the world to me. Nobody, and I mean nobody, is to touch it except me. Who do you think you are barging in and messing with other people's stuff? I swear, if you ever touch this again, you will regret it. Do you understand?"

From across the room, Ashley says, "You told us it belonged to your mother."

Her comment distracts me from my attack on Crystal. Turning toward Ashley, I say, "Huh? What are you talking about?"

Ashley's arms are folded across her chest. "You have always told us that the Autoharp was a gift from your mother, not your grandmother."

"I have not!" I respond. "I think I should know who gave it to me."

"She's right." Sarah joins in and walks to stand beside Ashley. "Anytime any of us ask you about it, you tell us it was your mother's."

I feel my face getting red and feel unsure how to reply.

Megan walks over to stand beside Sarah and Ashley. "The truth is we don't think anything you've told us about yourself since the day you got here is the truth. We think you've lied about everything."

I look at each of their faces and then turn to find Heather sitting on her bed with her head down. When she raises her head, she looks at me and says, "Look, April, if you want to lie to us, that's your business. If you're not ready to deal with your truth, then so be it. But here's what you've got to understand—none of us respect you. It's impossible to respect a liar. When you arrived here on your very first day, you were an outsider. And you know what? You're still as much an outsider today, four months later, as you were then. That's because you've chosen to keep yourself outside your walls of lies."

Though at this very moment I despise Heather, I know she has told the truth. Even I have grown weary of myself. The chip on my shoulder has become like one of the giant hemlocks in the woods. I feel the knees of my heart buckling. But my mask is so familiar to me that I fear ripping it off would be more painful than hiding behind it has become.

Turning, I look at Crystal. The clear outline of my handprint is turning bright red on the side of her face and her lip is swelling.

The tension in the room is pulled as taut as the strings on Ella's Autoharp. Just when I feel like something is going to break, there are two quick knocks on the door and Michelle comes in.

She immediately senses the tension and quickly surveys the room. "What's going on here? Is there a problem?"

Ashley, Megan, and Sarah separate and return to their beds without making eye contact with Michelle.

Crystal rises slowly off my bed and, while making an effort to keep the side of her face turned away from Michelle, makes her way toward her own bed.

Putting her full attention on me, Michelle raises her eyebrows. "April, is there a problem here?"

"No, ma'am, no problem at all. I was just showing Crystal my Autoharp, that's all." For the first time in my life, it strikes me how easy it is for me to lie. Fifteen seconds ago I was ready to open up and tell my story, and now a lie slips between my lips as easily as a spoonful of Tucker's boiled okra used to.

Michelle looks at each of us again with the same questioning expression. After she is met with silence, she says, "Fine, that's up to you girls. All I can help you with is what you give me. I just stopped by to tell you you're running late for class and you know what a stickler James is for being on time. My advice is you better get a move on."

As soon as she leaves, everyone silently busies themselves with making their bed and straightening their area.

When we exit our cabin, a car is driving up to the main cabin. It is not one that I've ever seen here, so I'm curious about who is in it. The driver's side door opens and an attractive woman dressed in a nylon jogging outfit steps out. As she walks to the other side of the car, the passenger door opens and a man emerges. It seems it takes him forever to get out, not because he is slow, but because he is so large. He's the largest man I've ever seen. No skin is visible on his face as it is covered with a thick black beard and moustache and black sunglasses. He is so broad and thick that I'm amazed he ever got inside the car to begin with. He turns slowly in a circle but never acknowledges us girls.

When the woman gets to his side, he unfolds a white stick of some kind and holds it in his right hand. Then he takes her elbow with his left hand and they begin moving forward. As they walk, the man sweeps the white stick along the ground in front of him. Just as they get to the front door, it is swung open by Mary, who welcomes them with a smile.

"Who are those people?" Heather asks as soon as the door closes behind them.

"I have no idea," Ashley says. "Maybe they're lost. They certainly looked lost to me."

"Did you notice the woman was missing a hand?" Megan asks.

"Really?" I ask. "I didn't notice."

"Yeah," Megan says, "she had one of those artificial things for a hand."

"And the guy is blind," Crystal adds. "I recognize that cane he had. My uncle is blind and he has a cane just like it."

I laugh. "Are the roads really safe with a couple of cripples like that trying to manage a trip?"

"We're all crippled in some way," Sarah says. "That's why we need the love of God to make us whole."

Sarah's repeated references to God have finally rubbed me raw. "Really, Sarah?" I snap. "How did that work out for you when you got pregnant? Or when you got an abortion? And how whole did God make those sick religious parents of yours who talked you into getting an abortion?"

Without warning, Sarah strides directly in front of me, draws back her fist, and hits me squarely on my nose.

As I'm falling to the ground, she yells, "Shut your stinking mouth!"

Stars fill my darkening field of vision, while blood streams into my open mouth. Spitting, I try to get up but everything spins around me and I topple back to the ground. Then everything goes black.

CHAPTER FORTY-NINE

What is it, then, between us?
What is the count of the scores or hundreds of years between us?
Whatever it is, it avails not—distance avails not, and place avails
not.
—Walt Whitman

MARCH:

How much further is it?" I ask.

"We're getting close, Levi," Debbie replies.

"You're getting tired of me asking that, aren't you? I know I'm acting like a little kid, but I can't help it. I'm either really nervous and scared, or I'm excited. Or maybe it's all of those. Dr. Sydney told me to just accept my feelings as they come and to remember that a feeling can't hurt you; it's just a feeling. But that's easier said than done."

"Oh my, isn't that the truth. I feel like my heart is going to explode it's beating so fast."

Reaching out with my left hand, I find her shoulder and rub it gently. "But everything's going to be all right because you and I have a plan, right?"

Debbie chuckles. "Are you trying to reassure me or reassure yourself? Because you don't sound too convincing."

I laugh, too. "I don't guess I do, do I."

"I haven't been back to Spirit Lake since I left there. I'm surprised at all the feelings that are coming up from my past. Fear and insecurity, my personal two-headed monster, has risen out of the mist again."

"Take me to the beast," I reply in a bold tone. Shaking my folded white cane, I say, "I'll slay him with my trusty cane!"

Debbie laughs aloud this time. It's her relaxed, musical laugh, not the nervous, jittery one. "I keep reminding myself that you'll only be here for five days and then I'll come pick you up for the weekend. I think it was a smart idea that you get those two days off every week, just like the rest of the staff."

"But that's another thing that I'm nervous about," I reply. "I've never even been in your apartment and now I'm going to be staying the weekends with you in it. Remember, I've only lived in two places since I lost my sight. Adjusting to Spirit Lake and to your apartment at the same time is not going to be easy. If you've got anything breakable sitting on any of your furniture, my advice is to box it up while I'm there. I will be the proverbial bull in a china shop until I get used to where everything is."

Debbie breaks the tension in the car with another one of her musical outbursts of laughter. "What you don't realize is practically all my dishes are plastic. I broke all the glass ones when I was learning to use my prosthesis. Believe me when I say I'm the queen of clumsy."

While I have my doubts that Debbie is being completely honest, I love her for trying to help me feel at ease.

Suddenly she says, "We've been off the main highway for a while now. I'm looking for the turnoff to Spirit Lake."

I feel her letting off the accelerator and braking. The blinker comes on.

"This is it," she says and we turn to the left.

Debbie is driving slowly. "Tell me what you are seeing," I prompt her.

"It is amazing, Levi. It is exactly like I remember it; like nothing has changed. There are towering hemlock trees everywhere. The largest rhododendrons I've ever seen grow here. Occasionally there is a patch of cane growing. All sorts of colorful wildflowers are scattered around."

"What colors?"

"There are yellows, purples, whites, and lavenders, plus lush green ferns everywhere. This narrow driveway goes right through the middle of the woods so that any sunlight that slips through is filtered by needles and leaves. We are engulfed in dark shade."

I detect strong emotion in Debbie's tone. She is clearly moved. "What's it feel like for you?" I ask.

Her voice breaks as she says, "This is where God lives, Levi. It's so calm and peaceful. It's a place of heart and soul, where people can become whole again. And it has just struck me that this is exactly where you belong."

"Me? Why do you say that?"

"Because you know what it's like to be lost and to be found. You know what it's like to have been blind, but to now see. Just like we talked about last night."

"Amazing Grace?"

"Yes, indeed, Levi. You are a walking demonstration of what Amazing Grace can do to a person. These girls need to get to know someone like you. It could help them change their lives."

It's my turn to laugh. "Are these the same girls that you told me were going to chew me up and spit me out?"

"Forget that I said that, please," she replies. "That was me speaking from a place of fear. I was more interested in trying to control everything than in trusting in God to manage things."

As she finishes speaking, she slows to a stop.

"We're here, aren't we?"

"Yes, Levi, we're here."

Her door opens and the key alarm dings.

I open my door and am immediately struck by a cool breeze. I take a deep breath. The air feels lighter, much less humid than back in West Tennessee. Getting out, I slowly turn around, smelling the air. I detect the thick smell of decaying humus on the floor of the forest and the sweet, sharp smell of pine needles. I also catch a faint whiff of what smells like a mixture of soaps and shampoos, but I keep all this to myself.

Debbie comes up beside me and says, "Are you ready to begin the next chapter in your life?"

"As ready as I'll ever be."

"Then take my arm and follow me."

I unfold my cane and use my left hand to take Debbie's elbow. We walk about thirty feet when I hear a door opening in front of us.

"Hello," the pleasant voice of a woman in her late forties calls to us. "You must be Levi, and you must be Debbie. Please come right in."

Like the dancers I've seen in old black-and-white movies, Fred Astaire and Ginger Rogers, I follow Debbie's lead and manage to avoid running into anything or knocking it over. When we sit down together on a couch I breathe a mental sigh of relief at having passed one of my own tests, navigating a new environment without being told where anything is.

"I'm Mary, the treatment director here," our hosts says, "and I want to welcome both of you. Tell me, how in the world is Dr. Sydney doing? I haven't seen her in a while."

"She's doing great," Debbie replies. "And she said to give you her very best."

"She is one talented and gifted lady," Mary says. "I owe a lot to her for being where I am today."

"Lots of us could say that," Debbie agrees.

There's a moment of silence and I sense they are looking at me. I know I need to say something but am unsure what to say. "I sort of feel like an actor who has forgotten his lines," I finally manage to say. "I apologize."

"Don't worry, Levi," Mary says. "Given what I know about what you've been through the last four or five months, I imagine finding the right starting place for talking is not easy."

Clearing my throat, I say, "I do want to say that I appreciate this chance to see if I can be helpful to you."

"Then let's begin there," Mary says. "One thing you will learn about me is that I'm very straightforward and honest. I have my doubts about this arrangement, but I have learned to trust Dr. Sydney's opinion. If she says it's worth a try, then I will give it my dead level best. It will be an experiment for all of us. You will find the staff here very dedicated to what they do, and they all work within their prescribed job descriptions. The most immediate person who you will look to for guidance is Will, who should be by here in a few minutes. I remind you that your interactions with the girls here will be very limited and will occur only when your job duties warrant. They will tell you what they want you to know about themselves and you are to ask no personal questions of them. Their stories are their business. Do you understand?"

Folding my arms across my chest, I say, "Mary, if someone couldn't understand that, they'd have to be blind in one eye and not seeing out of the other." I pause for two beats and add, "Oops, I guess that'd be me, wouldn't it?"

I picture Mary's face twisted in confusion over my comments and looking uncertainly at Debbie. Finally I can't contain myself any longer and burst out laughing. Debbie joins me simultaneously.

Gasping for breath, Debbie says, "Oh, Mary, I should have warned you. Levi feasts on making practical jokes that make people uncomfortable momentarily."

Mary finally joins in our laughter. It is a deep, hearty laugh. "Whew, I thought for a moment . . . Well, I don't know what I thought. And you did something few people can do; you left me at a complete loss for words. That's two points for you."

From behind me there is a knock on the door. It opens and Mary says, "Hello, Will. Your timing is perfect. Come here and meet your new personal assistant."

Will's footsteps are uneven, suggesting to me he has a problem with one leg. And there is an additional sound that takes me a second to identify: a wooden cane of some kind.

As he comes around to the front of me, I stand up.

"Good god!" he exclaims.

His voice is about chest-high on me and has the crackling sound of age. My guess is seventy years old.

"I thought I was getting a helper, not a trained black bear from out of the woods around here. I take that back. No black bears around here are this big. You must be a lost grizzly bear from Canada."

I stick out my hand and say, "Nice to meet you, Will. My name is Levi."

He quickly grips my hand and though his is smaller, his grip is extrafirm. His palms and fingers are rough and calloused. This is the hand of a man who has known hard, manual labor his whole life.

"Introductions have officially been made," Mary says. "Levi, do you or Debbie have any questions?"

"None from me," I say.

"Me either," Debbie says.

"Then let's get on with business around here. Will, you take Levi out to the barn and show him around. Debbie, it was nice to meet you, too."

Debbie speaks up, "Is it okay if we . . ."

"If you say good-bye?" Mary finishes for her.

"Yes, please."

"Me and Will will step out for a couple of minutes to give you a moment."

Once Mary and Will leave and the door closes, Debbie throws her arms around me and squeezes like a drowning person holding on to a piece of driftwood.

I place my hands on both sides of her face and tilt it up toward me. I lean over and my lips touch hers. Their soft fullness always sends a surge between my legs. At first I was ashamed of that until Dr. Sydney helped me understand that it is natural and normal. Now it's one of the natural things I look forward to the most.

Debbie returns my kiss by pressing hard against my lips. Then her mouth opens and our tongues find each other. When that happens, I swear I almost see tiny sparks of light.

Gasping for breath, Debbie unclenches her arms and mouth from me and pulls back slightly. She grabs two handfuls of my beard. "Do you know how much I'm going to miss you?"

"Half as much as I miss you?"

Jerking my beard, she says, "No, twice as much, not half as much."

"Five days," I whisper.

"Five days," she replies.

We turn and she leads me to the door.

CHAPTER FIFTY

And he speaks best that hath the skill when for to hold his peace.
—*Thomas, Lord Vaux*

MARCH:

When Debbie and I emerge from the cabin, a girl is screaming, "I'm sorry! I'm sorry! Oh God, please forgive me!"

Mary says, "Sarah, go to your cabin. We'll deal with you later. Will, get me the first-aid kit out of my office. It's on the wall behind the door. The rest of you girls go on to the barn, where James is waiting for you. I'll take care of April."

Will comes shuffling past us. I hear him say under his breath, as he goes by, "She's had it coming to her. It's about time somebody . . ."

I can't hear the rest of what he says as he moves out of earshot.

Leaning over, I whisper to Debbie, "What's going on?"

"There's a girl lying on the ground. Her face and the front of her shirt are covered with blood. My guess is there's been a fight, probably between the girl sent to her cabin and this girl on the ground."

When I factor Will's commentary into Debbie's description, I conclude that the girl on the ground has been a pain in everyone's side and somebody finally got enough of her.

Will exits the cabin but pauses beside us. "Sorry for the interruption, Levi. Just another peaceful day here at Spirit Lake." There is almost a lilt in his voice. He proceeds to take Mary the first-aid kit.

"I think Will likes the excitement," I say to Debbie. "Or he's just happy that that girl got knocked down a peg or two."

"I believe you're right. The girl is sitting up and he's actually smiling as Mary is wiping the blood off her face. I can see now that she just has a bloody nose."

"With the amount of blood you describe, her nose may have gotten broken. Man, that must have hurt!"

"Mary's helped her to her feet and they are coming our way," Debbie says. She gently tugs my arm, signaling me to scoot in her direction.

I feel one of them brush by me and detect the scent of the shampoo I'd smelled earlier.

"Okay, Levi," Will says, "I believe we're ready to head up to the barn, now that the entertainment part of the program here has concluded. Where's your suitcase?"

"It's in the back seat of the car," Debbie volunteers.

The three of us walk to the car. I locate the back door, open it, take out my army duffle bag, and sling it onto my shoulder. "I guess I'm ready."

Debbie squeezes my arm and says, "See you in five days." Then she gets in her car and drives away.

"Levi," Will says, "I've never worked around someone who is blind. I did have a horse one time that went blind, the smartest horse I ever had. Even after she went blind I could ride her in an arena and make her do everything but stand on her head. Yes sir, she was amazing. But you are going to have to tell me what to do with you because I don't have any idea."

"Why don't we head on over to the barn and I'll tell you," I say. "I just need you to tell me a little about the terrain—is it gravel, paved, hilly, smooth?"

"This little settlement, our three cabins and the barn, sits on the top of a ridge, so it's fairly level. We'll start out walking on blacktop but it'll transition to dirt."

"All right then," I say, "you start walking and I'll try to walk beside you and a little behind you. I'm going to try and just listen to your walking stick to keep oriented to where you are."

"How'd you know about my walking stick?"

"I heard it when you came in the cabin where I was talking to Mary."

"Dang, that's a pretty slick trick."

I smile. "Well here's another trick I can do. I'm going to see if I can guess your age and where you spent a lot of time growing up."

"You don't say," Will says with a hint of skepticism in his tone. "Go ahead and give it a shot."

"My guess on your age is seventy, give or take a couple of years. And I think you grew up in western Oklahoma." Will doesn't say anything, so I ask, "Was I even close?"

"Close? Son, you hit the nail on the head on both accounts! How'd you do that?"

I laugh. "Magicians never reveal their secrets."

I hear Will's walking stick and can tell he's started walking. Giving my cane a snap so that it unfolds, I tap in front of me and follow him.

"Debbie, my girlfriend, told me this place is beautiful."

"It is, indeed," Will says. "It's almost like the Garden of Eden. It's green in every direction. That's a lot different than Texas and

Oklahoma. Mary tells me you've had experience with animals and you're really good with your hands."

"Well, I grew up on a little farm, where we raised most of the food we ate. We had a horse, a cow for milk, always had a hog or two we raised to eat, some chickens for eggs and eating, too. Another place I lived we had some goats we milked and used for meat, too." Suddenly the familiar smell of hay, mixed with sweet feed and manure, slips into my nostrils. Without even thinking about it, I am transported back in time. I see myself in the barn loft throwing a bale of hay down to August. Tucker walks by below me with a hundred-pound sack of feed across her shoulder. Without raising her face to look up, she says, "Y' better watch whatchur doin', March. Y' 'bout hit me with that hay bale."

Will's voice begins to push its way back into my consciousness, sweeping my memory back into its closet. "These horses we've got are all well broke and aren't usually any trouble, though each of them has had to deal with their own set of troubles during their life. Some of them are rescue animals, others have been given to us. If anybody gets hurt, it's not the horses' fault. It's because somebody didn't know what they were doing."

"And each of the girls is responsible for her own horse while she is here, right?"

"That's right. They feed and water them twice a day and they groom them, too."

"Is it okay for me to ask about that fight a while ago? Sounds like it was a pretty vicious attack."

"Oh that?" Will laughs. "My opinion is it was about time it happened. There's this one girl here that is as cold and hard-hearted as any girl I've ever known. And she's done nothing but lie ever since she got here. The rest of the girls is getting mighty tired of it. Funniest thing, though, is that the girl that finally socked her one was the last one I ever expected would do anything like that. She's always been meek and quiet. It just goes to show you that everybody has their limit on what they can take. I've just got a feeling that there's a bigger storm brewing between all these girls."

We walk a few feet in silence.

Will asks, "Can I ask you a question, Levi?"

"Sure you can."

"You're such a large man I expected you'd have this booming voice. But your voice sounds sort of like you swallowed a bunch of broken glass. It's ragged and high pitched."

I start to tell him that it's not always been this way, but know that will lead to more questions, so I say, "I had an accident a while back and got hit in my throat. I ruined my shot at a big singing career. I was going to be the second coming of Elvis." I strike my best Elvis pose based on a picture I saw once in Vegas of an impersonator.

Will joins me in laughing.

The smell of the barn is strong now, so I figure we're very close to it.

Will stops. "The barn's about fifteen feet in front of us. One of the counselors, James, will be helping the girls do an exercise while using one or more of the horses. It's a pretty amazing way for the girls to learn while they are doing something. I think the word Mary uses to describe it is *experiential*. My job is to keep an eye on the horse so that no one accidently gets hurt. We'll go on in and I'll take you to where your bunk is and let you get sort of settled in while I go help James."

"Sounds like a plan," I reply.

CHAPTER FIFTY-ONE

Tears, idle tears, I know not what they mean,
Tears from the depth of some divine despair
Rise in the heart, and gather to the eyes.
—*Alfred, Lord Tennyson*

APRIL:

Mary gently rubs my face with the warm, soapy washcloth in an effort to get all the blood off. She has to work around the icepack I'm holding to the bridge of my nose.

There is a knock on the door. "Yes?" Mary answers.

"It's Michelle."

"Come in."

Opening the door to Mary's office, Michelle sticks her head in. "I heard there was a problem and thought I'd see if you need any help."

"First of all," Mary replies, "I need a clean T-shirt to put on April."

"Got it," Michelle says crisply and ducks out of the door. In a matter of seconds she reenters, T-shirt in hand. "This is one of mine. It should work."

"Let me get this bloody shirt off of you," Mary says to me.

I pull my arms back through the armholes as Mary lifts the shirt over my head. Then she takes Michelle's shirt and pulls it over my head. The neck of the shirt fits tightly as it passes over my nose. I cry out in pain.

"Sorry, April," Mary empathizes. Turning to Michelle, she says, "Thanks for the shirt."

"No problem. What else do you need?"

"I need you to go to the girls' cabin and check on Sarah. She's the one who made this mess."

Michelle's shocked look is probably a mirror of my expression when Sarah hit me. "Sarah did this?" she asks. "Wow, I'll go right over there."

After a few more swipes on my neck with the washcloth, Mary says, "That's good enough until you get in the shower later. Your nose has stopped bleeding, so that's good, too. I want you to lie down on my loveseat and just relax while I clean everything else up."

When I lie back, the entire front of my face throbs with each beat of my heart. I groan out loud.

Without looking at me, Mary says, "I know. It is going to be quite painful for a few days probably." She exits carrying my bloody shirt and the washcloth.

I close my eyes. When I do, all I can see is Sarah's fist hurtling toward me like a freight engine. It had happened so fast and was so unexpected that I didn't even try to duck out of the way.

Mary comes back in and sits in her armchair across from me.

Through a slit in one eyelid, I look at her. She's staring at me. I hope she thinks I've gone to sleep. Otherwise, I know she's going to want to talk about what happened.

"April," she says, "do you mind telling me who Tucker is?"

My eyes pop open and for the second time today I'm addled. If Sarah's blow was a surprise, Mary's question is a shock. How does she know Tucker? What does she know? How much does she know about me? What's she snooping for? "Am I supposed to know someone named Tucker?" I ask.

Mary's next statement is a blow to my chest. "Will told me he saw Pablo the other day."

Forgetting my nose, I bolt upright on the loveseat. "He what?!" Suddenly a wave of nausea hits me and I feel the blood draining from my face.

"Lie back down," Mary instructs. Then she puts a couple of pillows underneath my feet.

"Will saw Pablo?" I ask weakly. "I haven't seen him for nearly three weeks."

"Yes, Will said that he saw Pablo deep in the woods, watching you girls as you were leaving the barn one evening. Once you all went into your cabin, Pablo turned and went deeper into the woods."

I picture Pablo with his long ears sticking out to the side, watching us with his soulful eyes. His coat is probably rough and ragged and I imagine he's lost weight. "Where did he go? Why didn't Will go catch him? I thought he was lost somewhere."

"Will told me that Pablo never gets lost, that he's the smartest animal we have. And he said there's no point in trying to catch Pablo. Pablo will come back whenever what's bothering him is resolved."

It makes me proud to hear Pablo described as the smartest animal at Spirit Lake. But now that I don't have *lost* as a reason to explain his disappearance, I am puzzled about what has happened. "So Pablo's been staying away because that's what he chooses to do? But why would he do that when he gets treated so well here? He has everything he needs right here. The woods is a dangerous place for him to stay. There's no one there to help him if he gets in trouble."

Mary sits in silence. When our eyes meet, she says, "I'm not sure if you're talking to me about Pablo or about yourself."

"Huh? I'm talking about Pablo," I say, though I'm feeling a little unsure of myself. I sense Mary trying to open me up, just like she, James, and Michelle have repeatedly tried to do since I arrived here. I try to put up my walls like I always do, but I don't feel or hear them moving. Maybe it's the pain of Sarah's blow or the shocking news about Pablo, but I can't seem to get my feet under me or find the strength. The room seems tilted and the floor is slick.

"I was wondering," Mary says thoughtfully. "Have you ever thought about why you chose Pablo in the first place? I mean, he's been here since the beginning of Spirit Lake and no one has ever taken on the care of him."

The truth is I have thought about it, but I don't want to reveal that to Mary. Yet, in spite of my lack of intention to talk about it, I hear myself say, "Actually I have thought about it."

"And what's your conclusion?"

"I know what it's like to live on the outside like Pablo has." The moment the word *has* leaves my mouth, I feel deep inside me something like a cork exploding out of a bottle. A surge of emotion comes from the pit of my stomach and begins boiling its way up the center of my chest. When it touches the edge of my throat, I feel like I am gagging. I sit back up. My eyes sting and I cough violently. Like the talons of an eagle, fear grips my heart.

Even though it's midday, Mary's office suddenly gets dark. A rumble of thunder begins in the distance and rolls closer to us.

Mary looks out her window and says, "Sounds like a summer thunderstorm is close by. I always enjoy them. It seems like they clean the air and things look clearer and sharper afterward." Turning her attention back to me, she says, "Tell me, April, what kind of life has Pablo lived?"

Thankful that Mary has taken the laser of her focus off me for a moment and turned it to Pablo, I look at her and say, "All he ever wanted was to look like and be accepted by the horses. People and horses alike have shunned him and made fun of him. No one has looked past what they see to learn what an amazing animal he is."

Like an exclamation point to my words, a loud clap of thunder bursts just outside the cabin. Mary and I both jump.

Scooting to the edge of the love seat, I continue talking about Pablo. "He's never felt like he fits in. He has no friends. He's been lonely his whole life." These last words barely squeeze past my swollen throat. I feel something warm running down my cheek and to the corner of my mouth. Flicking my tongue out, I taste its saltiness. Mary's image swims in front of me. "It's difficult for Pablo to feel like anywhere is home. So he's lived a life cut off from everyone."

Large, isolated drops of rain begin hitting the tin roof.

Mary leans forward slowly and rests her arms on her knees. Her eyes feel like they can see all the way to my soul. "I agree that's how Pablo used to feel. That is, until you came to Spirit Lake." Tears have pooled in Mary's eyes. "He allowed you to care for him because he knew you understood him like no one before you ever had. I've heard Will say a hundred times that these animals are simply mirrors of their human handlers. Here's what I think: I think yours and Pablo's lives have been mirror images of each other."

A flash of lightning fills Mary's office with bright light, followed by a sound like a tree snapping in two and a deafening thunderclap. The lightning must have made a small slit in the bottom of the rain cloud as the raindrops become more steady and regular.

In spite of nature's best efforts to distract me, I keep my eyes locked on Mary. I blink and two more tears escape. Clasping my hands in front of me, I say, "Then why did he run away? What is wrong with me? Why did he leave me? And why won't he come back?"

Mary takes my clasped hands in hers and says, "April, who is Tucker?"

I jerk back as if she has placed a snake across my arms. "Why do you keep asking me that?! I want to understand about Pablo!"

She sits back in her chair and crosses her legs. "I believe the answers are intertwined, April. In the papers that were faxed to us giving us permission to treat you here, the signature of the parent slash guardian had the name Tucker on it. It didn't indicate whether Tucker was male or female, or whether they were your parent or a guardian. But since you've been here, I've received a phone call about every two or three weeks from someone who identifies themselves as Tucker, asking how you're doing. The conversations probably don't last sixty seconds and then they hang up."

I imagine Tucker sitting in her recliner talking to Mary, and, like she always does, hanging up without saying goodbye. It is a lonely picture and my heart aches for her.

Mary reaches over and picks something off her desk. She shows me five envelopes, each addressed to me.

I lunge for them, jerking them out of Mary's hands. "Those belong to me! They're private property! You have no right!"

Unperturbed, Mary says, "Well that's interesting. You act like they mean something to you, yet none of them have even been opened. Can you help me understand that?"

Examining the envelopes as if I don't know they haven't been opened, I search for an answer to Mary's question.

"There's only one word on the return address of each envelope," Mary points out. "*Tucker*. Another intriguing thing to me is the postmark on the envelopes. None of them are from Memphis, where you've told everyone you live."

The envelopes quiver in my shaking hands. I blink rapidly, trying to get a clearer vision of the postmarks. A tear splatters on the corner of an envelope, right on Tucker's name. The Dresden postmark and its 38225 zip code are undeniable.

The storm outside is in full swing, the heavy downpour of rain is almost deafeningly loud.

I search Mary's face, hoping I will see something that will help me find my way. But her expression is unreadable. Raising my voice above the storm, I say, "If all of you knew the truth about me, you wouldn't have anything to do with me."

Mary's eyes light up. "April, no one wants to have anything to do with you now, not even Pablo."

If Mary had just slapped me across the face, its sting couldn't have been worse than her words. I'm shocked at her bluntness and wait for her to apologize. But there's no apology in her expression. Slumping back into the loveseat, I look down at Tucker's letters lying in my lap and I realize that Mary is right. She's right about everything. Pablo and I are mirror images of each other. I have driven him away in the same way I've driven all the girls away from me—by being dishonest and hateful.

Without thinking, I organize Tucker's letters chronologically and slowly tear open the first envelope. Unfolding it, I begin reading.

By the time I finish the fifth letter, my tears flow as intensely as the falling rain outside the cabin. Everything that has been pent up in me for so long feels like it is being ripped up. I cry out, "Tucker!" My body convulses uncontrollably, I am crying so hard.

Suddenly I feel Mary beside me. She puts her arm around my shoulder and pulls me to her.

I press my face into her chest and wrap my arms around her as if she were a buoy and I a shipwrecked sailor.

"Let your tears be your rain, April," she says gently. "Let them wash the windows of your soul so you can see more clearly. Let this be April's rain."

CHAPTER FIFTY-TWO

It is time to explain myself—let us stand up.
What is known I strip away.
—Walt Whitman

APRIL:

When I open my eyes, Mary's office is still dark. Sitting up, I say, "How long is this storm cloud going to hang around?"

"That storm went on its way hours ago," Mary replies.

I look out the window. "Then why is it so dark in the middle of the day?"

"Because it's not the middle of the day, it's evening. You fell asleep in my arms and had a pretty long nap."

I'm shocked. "Really?! It feels like it was raining only moments ago." Walking over to the window, I look outside and can see that the sky is clear and the sun is setting.

Mary joins me at the window. "Beautiful, isn't it?"

"Yes, it is."

"Don't things look clearer to you after that rain?"

I turn to look at Mary, to see if I can read her face and learn if there is a double meaning in her question, but she continues looking out the window. "Yeah," I say, "things actually do look clearer."

Now Mary turns to me. "So, what do you want to do?"

"I want to quit lying. I want to tell the girls the truth, and I want you and Michelle and James to hear it. Oh, and Will, too."

"How does it make you feel to think about being that honest?"

Mary's question turns me inward and I search my heart. "Afraid."

"And yet, when you say *afraid*, you are smiling. What's that about?"

I feel my smile broaden. "Because I will be so relieved. I think I'm exhausted from living behind my walls."

Mary's face softens. "It takes a lot of work and staying constantly vigilant to live that kind of life. Many people spend their life staying hidden behind their walls." She pauses for a moment, and then says, "Why don't I go see what everyone is doing and if they can come into the meeting room now? Let's get this done while you are ready to do it. Okay?"

I take a deep breath and say, "Sure."

Pointing to her bathroom, Mary says, "Go wash your face and brush your hair. I'll be back in a few minutes."

When I look in Mary's mirror, I'm shocked. My eyes are puffy from crying and underneath each of them there is a dark, half-circle bruise. My nose is swollen and my hair looks like I stood outside during the storm and let the wind toss it up and shake it. There is still some dried blood on the outside of my nostrils and even on my neck. "My god, what a train wreck," I say out loud.

I turn on the water, letting it run until it warms. Bending over, I cup the water in my hands and wash my face, being careful to not bump my nose.

Next, I turn my attention to taming my hair. As I am brushing it, I suddenly have a memory of Tucker fixing my hair before school. Her thick, coarse fingers made doing tiny, detailed work almost impossible. "I'm gonna put this here ribbon in yore hair," she'd say, "but God only knows if I'm doin' it right an' if it'll be there when y' come home this afternoon."

I loved you yesterday. I love you today. And I'll love you tomorrow. That's how she'd closed every one of her letters to me. It suddenly dawns on me how difficult it must have been for her to let me go live with Ella. I'm ashamed that it never occurred to me to consider how hard that was on her. Fresh tears of regret run down my reddened cheeks.

I hear the main door of the cabin open, and voices begin to fill the meeting room. Apparently Mary has been able to get everyone together. Like the beating wings of a butterfly trapped inside a jar, my heart flutters against my chest. For a fleeting moment I feel like crawling out the window and running away.

Mary appears in the doorway of the bathroom. "Thinking about running away?"

Turning to face her, I say, "How'd you guess?"

"That would be a pretty natural reaction, I'd say. Everyone's here. Ready?"

I nod.

"Then you lead the way. I'll be right behind you."

As soon as I step into the group room, everyone's voices trail off. Whatever they were discussing suddenly doesn't matter.

None of the girls looks at me, except Sarah. When she sees me, she bursts into tears, covers her face with her hands and bends over. No one makes any move to respond to her emotional outburst.

James and Michelle are sitting on tall barstools behind the girls. Will is leaning back against the corner walls, his walking stick propped beside him. The three of them are watching me closely.

I settle into the chair facing everyone. My mind races to find the best opening line. I finally settle on using the truth, and say, "I am a lying, cruel bitch."

All the girls' heads, including Sarah's, snap in my direction.

"My name is April Tucker. I was raised just outside the tiny town of Dresden, Tennessee, which is a little over two hours north of Memphis and about the same distance west of Nashville. My mother was a whore—literally. She had sex with men for money and for favors, like paying her rent or her utilities. My two brothers, who are older than I am, and I all have different fathers. Fortunately for us, our mother didn't raise us. Once she gave birth to us and played with us for a few days, she took us and dumped us on her mother, Tucker.

"Tucker is the only name I've ever heard anyone use in reference to my grandmother. She dressed like a man and was made fun of by everyone in town. Her house didn't have any indoor plumbing in it. During winter the wind would make the curtains flutter because of the big cracks around the windows. The clothes me and my brothers wore were all given to us. I don't remember ever having a new pair of shoes and no more than two pairs of used shoes at any one time. Because of how we looked, we were always made fun of in school."

I pause to catch my breath from this flood of words. It's like I've been practicing this speech all my life without ever realizing it. The stunned expressions on everyone's faces let me know that I've been an awfully good liar and disguised myself well.

"Tucker, my grandmother, is probably the most amazing woman I know. She was horribly abused by her father while growing up. At age sixteen she was totally on her own, as both her parents had disappeared. She didn't know anything about raising kids, except how not to do it.

"For reasons I can't explain, I didn't talk until I was nearly six years old. The state was about to take me away from Tucker because of it. But about that time we got a new neighbor, Ella McDade. She was recovering from breast cancer and from her life with her abusive ex-husband, Judge Jack. Ella was everything that Tucker was not: educated, outgoing, and elegant. But these two women, who were opposites, became best friends. That's when Tucker came up with the idea of letting me live with Ella so that she could help teach me to talk.

"That decision changed my life. Ella was like a fairy godmother. She opened the doors for me to a whole other way of life. I did start talking. The key she used to unlock me was music and her Autoharp, which is why that Autoharp means so much to me."

The strains of Ella playing her Autoharp echo in my memory, stirring my heart. I smile at the memory and wipe tears with the sleeve of Michelle's shirt. Some of the girls sniff and wipe their own tears of empathy.

I shudder from a sudden chill as the dark clouds of the next chapters of my life appear in my script.

"But my fairy tale turned into a nightmare. My mother was murdered, and even though she was never a real mother to me, I always held on to the hope that one day she would turn her life around and become a truly loving mother. Her death doused the light of that hope. A lengthy investigation revealed that the murderer was in fact my father and that he was none other than the only son of Ella."

There is a collective, audible gasp in the room. Murmurs ripple between everyone: "What?" "Oh my gosh!" "I can't believe it!" "This is like a movie!"

Once they quiet themselves and turn back to me, I continue. "My dad was convicted of murder and sentenced to death. A year or so after that my brother closest to me in age, March, ran away from home. That was nearly nine years ago and no one has heard from him since he ran away." As it always does, thinking about March hurts me as bad as any hurt I've ever had because I know it's my fault. A fresh wave of tears is unleashed. I sit with my head bowed and watch them drop onto my jeans, turning the faded denim to a splattering of dark blue dots.

When I look back up, there are no dry eyes in the room. Even Will has pulled out a red bandanna to wipe his eyes.

I take a slow, deep breath. "There's one last chapter. My grandmother, my fairy godmother, Ella, got cancer again and died. When that happened, something snapped inside me. That's when I started cutting myself. I hated the world and everything in it. And most of all, I hated me.

"I went back to live with Tucker, but she couldn't do anything with me. I walked around like a porcupine with all his quills out, ready to inflict pain on anyone who got close to me. Sending me to Spirit Lake was her last-ditch effort to help me get my life straightened out.

"I owe everyone here an apology. I've said mean, hurtful things to all of you. I'm beginning to finally understand enough to know why I did it, but that's still not an excuse." I slowly look at everyone in the room, from face to face. When I complete the sweep, I say, "I mean this as sincerely as I know how to say it: I am sorry. I don't want to live inside my walls anymore. I'm tired of being isolated from the world and everyone in it. I know I don't deserve it, but I want your forgiveness."

At this moment I couldn't feel more vulnerable if I was standing naked in a room full of people. The distance I feel between me and the others in the room makes the emptiness in my heart feel like a vacuum, threatening to make me implode. No one moves or says a thing.

Suddenly, Sarah dashes to me and falls to her knees in front of me. "Oh, April, I forgive you! And please forgive me for striking you."

As I bend over to hug Sarah, the others come to me en masse with words of forgiveness, hugs of tenderness, and gestures of acceptance. The dry desert that has been my heart drinks deeply from their outpouring of love and feels full for the first time since before Ella got sick with cancer.

Without warning, there is a blow to the cabin door that sounds like it was delivered by a sledgehammer. Several of us scream and jump.

James and Will exchange looks of concern. Grabbing his walking stick, Will walks determinedly to the door and opens it wide, brandishing his walking stick in front of him.

The light from the cabin fills the doorway and falls on the face of Pablo. He lays his ears back, points his nose in the air, and brays loudly.

Everyone is so stunned that no one says a word.

Will turns to look at me and says, "Pablo says he forgives you, too."

My ears are filled with the chorus of laughter from everyone as I rush to see Pablo. Throwing my arms around his neck, I say, "Pablo, I love you!"

CHAPTER FIFTY-THREE

The rainbow bending in the sky,
Bedecked with sundry hues,
Is like the seat of God on high
And seems to tell thee news:
That, as thereby he promised
To drown the world no more,
So by the blood which Christ hath shed
He will our health restore.
—*George Gascoigne*

TUCKER:

Pickin' up th' bushel basket full o' green beans, I leave m' garden an' head back t' th' house. It's been a good year fer m' garden. We ain't had a dry spell yet, which is unusual. An' even tho' I still got plenty o' green beans on th' shelf that I canned last summer, I'm still gonna can this bushel o' beans.

I like lookin' in m' pantry at all th' jars o' veg'tables lined up on th' shelves. It always makes me wonder why m' folks didn't never put up food fer th' winter. There was times we wouldn't have nothin' t' eat fer supper. My mother an' father would argue back an' forth 'bout who was t' blame. If they'd put as much work into gardenin' as they did into arguin', we'd never have gone hungry.

When I get t' m' front porch, I drop th' basket in front o' my chair. Pickin' up th' two large plastic bowls outta m' chair, I sit down, keepin' one bowl in m' lap an' settin' th' other bowl in th' chair beside me. I grab a handful o' green beans outta th' basket, drop 'em in m' bowl an' start breakin' 'em. I snap off th' ends first an' pull th' strings off th' pods, then I snap them into pieces that are 'bout an inch long.

Th' bowl in th' chair beside me is 'bout half full o' broke beans when I hear a loud motor in th' distance. I keep m' eye on th' turn-off onto m' road. In a minute, a motorcycle slows an' turns off th' main road an' heads toward m' house.

Th' driver gooses th' engine of his motorcycle an' th' Harley engine barks loudly. He looks like he's goin' a hunderd miles an hour when he kills th' engine jes' as he gets t' my driveway. As he coasts up th' driveway, his momentum carries him right up t' m' porch.

Pushin' out his kickstand, he leans his motorcycle over an' unstraddles it. Once he gets his helmet off, he looks at me an' says, "Hello, Tucker."

"Hello, Preacher Sanders," I reply. A little nervousness causes a ripple in my stomach. I'm guessin' he wants t' talk t' me 'bout why I ain't been in church for so long, but I ain't sure I wanta talk t' him 'bout all that. "I knowed it was you as soon as I seen them silver-tipped cowboy boots. You know you're the only preacher I ever heard of who wears cowboy boots all th' time an' rides a Harley ever'where he goes."

He flashes me that easy smile o' his an' says, "I'm still waiting for you to let me take you for a ride. I'll bet if you ever do ride with me, you'll enjoy it so much that you'll end up buying you a Harley, too."

In spite o' m' nervousness, I return his smile. "I jes' might surprise you one o' these days an' take you up on yore offer. You can't never tell."

Preacher breaks out laughin'. His high tenor voice gives his laugh a sound that's almost like a woman's. When he catches his breath, he says, "It's too bad I'm not a betting man because when you do ride with me you could make me a very rich man. There's lots of people who've told me they'd bet me money that I'll never get you on this motorcycle."

I frown at his comment. "How come people're talkin' t' you 'bout me?"

"I guess it's really more about me talking to people about you than them bringing you up as the subject."

"What business have you got talkin' 'bout me t' people?" I snap back at him.

He props one o' his feet on th' second step o' m' porch steps. "Do you mind if I join you on your porch? I'm an old hand at breaking beans. Growing up I spent summers with my grandparents in Kentucky, a little place called Turkey Neck Bend. They always had a huge garden and they put me to work in it when I was probably seven or eight years old. Granny put up at least a hundred quarts of beans every summer."

I'd like t' tell him t' git on his motorcycle an' leave me alone, but Preacher has always treated me good. He's one o' th' few men I truly respect. "Come on up," I tell him. "I'll go git you a bowl." Standin' up, I ask, "You want a glass o' lemonade?"

His smile widens into a big grin. "I was hoping you'd ask me that. Is it your special hand-squeezed lemonade?"

I put m' hands on m' hips. "Is there any other kind? It sure ain't none o' that powdered stuff."

He climbs th' steps an' says, "Then I'll take the biggest glass you've got."

After I go an' get him his glass o' lemonade, we both commence t' breakin' beans. It's quiet except fer th' snappin' sound o' th' fresh green beans.

Keepin' his eyes focused on th' beans he's workin' on, Preacher says, "Tucker, I was wondering if there's something that I've done or said that's hurt your feelings."

Even though I know that ain't th' main question he's wantin' t' talk t' me 'bout, I appreciate him tryin' t' ease his way into it. An' even though I don't want t' go where he wants t' take me, I'm like a catfish lookin' at a worm on a hook; I can't resist biting it. "No sir, Preacher. You ain't hurt m' feelin's. As a matter o' fact, you're prob'ly th' onliest man I've ever knowed that ain't never said nothin' outta th' way t' me."

"I'm glad to hear that," he says. "You know, because I've told you many times, that I have a lot of respect for you, Tucker."

Compliments ain't somethin' I've ever been comf'terble with an' I squirm a bit in m' chair. "Maybe that's 'cause you don't know ever'thing there's is t' know 'bout me." I'm so shocked at what I jes' said that I nearly slap m' hand over m' mouth! I can't believe I cracked open a door for Preacher.

There is a slight pause in his rhythm o' breakin' beans, then he keeps goin'. "Well I suppose if you knew everything there was to know about me, it might affect your opinion of me, too. All we can use to form an opinion of someone is what we know about them, right?"

I mull that over fer a bit an' wonder what he means when he says they's things 'bout him that'd change my opinion of him. Finally I answer, "I expect you're right about that. So I guess they's things we don't know about ever'body, ain't there?"

Tossin' a handful o' broke beans into the bowl between us, Preacher says, "Oh, I'd say that is absolutely the truth. Everyone hides behind mirrors and tries to get people to see only what they want them to see. We live false lives in that way. It seems like being completely open and honest is something that's hard for people to do, don't you think?"

"Well, maybe some things ain't nobody's business t' know."

Preacher chuckles.

"What's so funny 'bout that?" I ask.

"Nothing. It just made me think of a joke I heard one time. Seems this preacher was preaching about how important it is to confess our faults. He was really getting worked up and saying to the church, 'Tell it all, brothers, tell it all!' The congregation was getting worked up with him, giving him *Amen*s right and left. Suddenly the local bank president jumps up and says, 'I'm guilty of gambling!' 'That's the spirit,' says the preacher. 'Tell it all, brother.' The banker adds, 'And I've been sleeping with my secretary at work.' Gasps ripple across the congregation and the preacher says, 'Amen! Tell it all, brother!' The banker is sweating now and looks around wide-eyed. But the spirit has gotten hold of him, so he says, 'And I've been stealing money at the bank.' And then he sits down. 'Oh yes!' the preacher cries. 'Tell it all, brother!' Then at the very back of the church building, a man slowly gets up. The preacher points at him and says, 'Another sinner has risen. Tell it all, brother.' The man looks around nervously and says, 'Last Saturday night I had sex with my neighbor's goat.' Three women immediately faint. The preacher looks both shocked and embarrassed for the man when he says, "Lord, I don't believe I would have told that, brother.""

I bust out laughin' so hard that m' bowl o' beans tumbles outta m' lap. "Oh my lordy, that's a good one!"

When Preacher catches his breath from laughin', he says, "So I guess maybe there are some things that don't need to be told. And everyone can make up their own mind about those sorts of things. But what everyone needs to remember is that God knows all of it, down to the tiniest detail."

I know he's aimin' that punch fer me, but he done it in such a way that it don't knock th' wind outta me. It actually makes me open th' door a little wider fer him t' bring up th' subject that I believe is on his mind anyway. "Maybe that's why it's so hard fer me t' go t' church. Even though you baptized me before Ella died an' I accepted Christ, I've always had doubts that I'm safe."

We both stop breakin' beans an' look each other in th' eye. He's lookin' at me thoughtfully.

"So," he says slowly, "it's like you're ashamed to be there because God knows how much is wrong with you?"

Pointing m' index finger at him, I say, "You've hit th' nail on th' head. God don't want people like me comin' t' church. I'd be nothin' but a hippercrit an' he'd know it. There ain't no way I can look God in th' eye. If'n I did, I think it'd buckle m' knees. I'd be undone. T' be in his presence an' me bein' th' most awful sinner in th' world . . ." I shake m' head when I can't finish m' thought. Unexpected tears fill m' eyes, an' I feel m' throat swellin'.

Preacher takes his eyes off me an' turns his attention back t' breakin' beans. After a moment o' silence, he says, "Let me tell you a story, Tucker. There was a boy who grew up never knowing his father. His mother was an alcoholic. Lots of times the boy had to fix his own meals because his mother was passed out drunk in bed, or she was out running around with one of her many boyfriends. The more he thought about what a sorry excuse of a mother his mom was and about his father abandoning them both, the madder he got. Hardly a week went by that he didn't get in a fight at school and end up in the principal's office. They sent him off to reform school for a year, but that only taught him how to be meaner and how to hurt people without getting caught.

"Then one day when he was eighteen, he got drunk at a party and got into another fight. Except this time the other person had a knife. They tussled together and when they fell to the ground, the knife went into the heart of the other person and he died.

"The boy was convicted and went to prison. That sounds like a bad thing, but it was the thing that helped save this boy's life because while he was there he met the most amazing man he'd ever known. He had more scars on him than you could count from all the fights he'd been in. He'd been in and out of prison most of his adult life. He'd stole, sold drugs, raped women, and killed a man. When I met him he was close to seventy years old and had no chance of parole."

When Preacher says, "I met him," I look closely at him.

"Yes," Preacher says in answer to the question in my eyes, "I was that boy."

"You killed somebody?"

He takes a deep breath and blows it out. "Yes, I did."

This story an' revelation pushes me back on m' heels. I can't take it all in 'cause it don't seem possible—not Preacher! Shakin' m' head, I say, "How in th' world did you get from there t' where you are now?"

"Because of ol' Moses, that seventy-year-old man I met in prison. He's the one who introduced me to God. I resisted it for a long time. And even when I did finally believe that what Moses told me was true, and that God sent his son to die on a cross for me, I couldn't get past the part that I was such a bad person and had done so much bad stuff that I didn't belong with God."

I close my eyes an' nod m' head. "Oh yes. Don't I know that feelin'."

When I open m' eyes, Preacher is leanin' toward me with his arms restin' on his knees. His eyes is like two lasers. "Here's the five words that ol' Moses told me that got me over that hurdle, Tucker.

I want you to listen closely to them, take them in, and hold them tightly to your chest."

Even though I know I'm fallin' down a well an' need this rope that Preacher is about t' throw m' way, I'm afraid. It's suddenly hard t' get m' breath, an' m' heart feels like it's 'bout t' jump outta m' throat. Tears begin flowin' down m' cheeks like somebody done turned on a faucet.

Preacher reaches out an' puts his long-fingered hand on top o' m' hand. "Here's what Moses said to me: 'You can't out-sin God's forgiveness.' What I believe that means, Tucker, is that God has more forgiveness than you have sins—no matter how many you have or how big you think they are."

I feel th' rope that Preacher has throwed me slowly wrappin' itself 'round m' heart. A feelin' o' bein' safe like I ain't never felt in m' life runs through me. It's like I was a ship that's been lost at sea fer a long, long time, an' suddenly somebody pulls me t' th' safety of a dock an' ties me off, safe an' sound.

In his pretty tenor voice, Preacher starts singin' softly: "Safe in the arms of Jesus, Safe on his gentle breast. There by his love o'ershaded, sweetly my soul shall rest."

CHAPTER FIFTY-FOUR

My voice goes after what my eyes cannot reach.
—Walt Whitman

MARCH:

Up and at 'em, Levi."

Will's voice slips into my dream and breaks apart all its pieces. Sitting up on the side of my bed, I yawn, and say, "What time is it?"

"Five-thirty. The girls will be here in a bit to feed their animals. I thought you might like to join us. I know it's your first day and everything, but there's nothing like jumping in and getting your feet wet."

When I stand up and stretch, my hands hit the ceiling.

"Dang, you're as big as a skinned ox," Will says. "These are sort of cramped quarters for you, aren't they?"

"That's okay. I'll adjust. Seems like adjusting is all I've been doing for the past six months, ever since my accident." I make my way to the small half bathroom and relieve myself.

When I walk back into the room, Will says, "Man, even though you've been here less than twenty-four hours, you sure do maneuver around good. I'm impressed."

"I've always had a good sense of direction and can remember directions really well." I sniff the air. "Is that coffee I smell?"

"Sure is. I always got to start my day with a cup of coffee, so I got me a coffee maker for this apartment. You want some?"

Rubbing my hands together, I say, "Do I ever! I didn't sleep that great last night, being in a new place. I got up a couple of times during the night and prowled around a bit."

"Couldn't prove that by me. I never heard a thing after I went to sleep."

"Funny thing. Last night, I thought I heard music or someone singing way after midnight. Do they have stereos in the cabins for the girls?"

"Gosh no. This is a very primitive setting. Electricity is only used sparingly."

"Hmmm," I say, thinking to myself. "What about any campgrounds in the area?"

"Negative on that, too. Nothing around here but woods and wild animals."

"Maybe I just dreamed it. But it sure sounded like an old Hank Williams song."

"Now you're talking my kind of music," Will says. "I'm surprised a young fellow like you even knows who Hank Williams was. Here's your coffee."

I reach toward Will and feel the warm mug as he presses it into my hand. After taking a sip, I say, "That's a good cup of coffee. Maybe I'll tell you the story sometime about why I know Hank Williams and his music."

"I'd like to hear about it. I always like a good story. Right now, though, let's finish getting dressed and go to the stable area."

Once we are dressed, I let Will lead the way out of our apartment and into the stable and arena areas of the barn. Just as it did when I first entered it yesterday and again last night when I was up wandering around, the smell of fresh horse manure mixed with hay and the sound of the nickering horses sends me tumbling into the past.

I remember one of my early morning chores at Tucker's was gathering eggs. We had a little red hen that was always trying to hide so she could set and hatch her eggs. Her favorite hiding place was the barn loft. I would have to carefully comb every inch of it, sometimes twice, before I would find her. Shooing her off her nest by waving my arms or yelling at her never worked. She'd just push herself lower onto her nest, flattening herself, and look at me with her beady eyes.

If I'd had my way, I'd have secretly killed the crazy hen, but for some reason she was Tucker's favorite. "You be good to that little red hen," she'd say. "If you hurt her, I'll find out."

I learned that the best thing to do was to move quickly, so I'd grab her by her neck and in the same motion fling her into the air. She'd squawk a loud protest, which threatened to alert Tucker. By the time she'd flown back down to the loft floor, I'd have her eggs in my basket and be heading down the stairs.

Suddenly, Will's voice pulls me back to the present. "I see the girls are making their way up here. When they get here I'll introduce you and then you can tell them whatever you want to about yourself. I'll warn you, though, that over time they will ask you all sorts of questions, even nosey ones, about yourself. It's up to you to tell them as much or as little as you want. Mary always told me that if they ask something that's none of their business to tell them so."

My ears pick up the sound of scattered footsteps approaching.

I pick up the two parts of my life story, the past and the present, and consider which one I should tell these girls. As if it was a test paper I'd received an F on in school, I wad up my past story and throw it back into its familiar closet and shut the door. "This is my life now," I say to myself. "That's all that matters."

"There's that blind man," I hear one of the girls say in a hushed tone.

"Shhh! He'll hear you," another one whispers harshly. "Don't you know, people who are blind have superhearing."

"Gather around here, girls," Will says, standing at my side. "I want you to meet someone."

They move to within ten feet of me and Will and then stop.

"This here is Levi," Will says. "He's going to be working here at Spirit Lake for a while."

When Will pauses, I realize that's his signal to me to say something. "Like Will said, my name is Levi. The two questions most people have on their mind when they first meet me are how long have I been blind and why do I have such a weird-sounding voice. The answer to both questions is the same. I had an accident about five months ago. Because of blows to my head I permanently lost my vision and a blow to my throat permanently damaged my vocal cords. I'm excited and nervous about being here. It's my first chance to have a job since I completed all my rehab work. One of the things I'm going to be doing with you while I'm here that you might be interested in is I'm going to teach you how to shoot a gun, specifically a shotgun. You'll learn to shoot clay pigeons."

This produces a spontaneous explosion of comments and questions from the girls.

"Okay now," Will cuts in, "there'll be plenty of time to explain about that. Right now these animals are wondering what the holdup is for their breakfast. So let's get busy."

I hold up my hand. "One more thing. People who are blind don't have superhearing. My sense of hearing is no better than yours. It's just that I've learned to pay attention to things that I was always hearing. You can learn to do the same thing."

The girls file past me. I smile when I overhear the one who made the comment about my hearing whisper, "How'd he hear me say that?"

Soon the only sounds in the barn are the scraping of manure forks and shovels cleaning up the droppings from overnight, water from a hose filling up and rinsing out buckets, horses impatiently stomping the ground, and the muted sound of them chewing their feed.

Since Will has left me to fend for myself, I decide I'll meet the girls one-on-one.

Finding the inside wall, I tentatively feel my way to a stall door. "Can I come in?" I ask.

"Oh," a surprised voice replies. "Sure, come on in. I'm Ashley."

"I met your horse last night. He's a real gentle thing. What color is he?"

"Will says he's a roan, but he looks like a dark auburn color to me. And you're right, he's probably the most gentle horse here."

"Excuse me for saying this, but your accent has the sound of the Navajos from the Four Corners area out west."

"Who told you about my mother?" Ashley snaps.

"Oops, I think I stepped in a pile of manure," I say, trying to make a joke. When Ashley doesn't say anything, I continue, "No one told me anything about any of you girls. It was just a guess. You might even call it a hobby of mine, that is, trying to identify where people are from just by listening to their accent. I apologize if I said something that hurt your feelings."

Ashley walks toward me. "I'm the one who needs to apologize. There was no reason for me to bite your head off just because your guess was right. My mother is a Navajo from the Four Corners, but I've lived all my life in Colorado Springs."

"I always thought the Springs area was beautiful," I say.

"Yeah? I guess I never noticed. I've got to get some more feed, if you'll excuse me."

"Hey, sure thing." I ease my way back through the stall door and find the next stall.

I hear a girl's voice talking low and steady.

"Hi there," I say from the open door. "Care if I ask you some things about your horse?"

"It's Levi, right?" the girl replies.

"Yes, that's right."

"Please come in, Levi, and let me introduce you to Excelsior. My name is Sarah."

Walking carefully forward, I put out my hand. When I detect the heat from the horse's body, I lay my hand on him. His skin twitches at my touch. "There's something different about your horse, but I can't figure out what it is. When I met him last night, he let me rub one side without any problem, but when I shifted to the other side, he got real skittish."

"That's because Excelsior is blind in one eye. Will says the two sides of a horse's brain don't communicate with each other. So what he sees with one eye doesn't transfer to the other side. Even though he saw you with his good eye, when you moved to the other side it was like he was completely unaware of you."

Patting the horse, I say, "Well, Excelsior, perhaps you can teach me a thing or two about being blind."

"Oh my gosh!" Sarah says. "I'm so sorry. I forgot about you being blind. Were you in a car accident? Is that how you got hurt?"

Waving my hand at her, I say, "Hey, no need to feel sorry, Sarah. I didn't think anything about it. It wasn't a car wreck. I had a bad fall." I hear Sarah moving some buckets around. "I'm going to see what's going on in the stall next door. Thanks for letting me drop in."

"You're welcome, Levi. It was nice to meet you."

As I leave the stall I'm struck by the contradictions I sense in Sarah. Even though her accent says she's from Florida, she doesn't have any of the cocky attitude most of the teenagers there have. And her politeness is not what I expect from a girl who's been sent to a place like Spirit Lake.

As I approach the next stall, I hear an angry voice. "If you step on my foot one more time, I swear I'm not going to feed you tonight! You know exactly where my feet are and don't act like you don't! How I ever got stuck with you is a mystery to me!"

"Having trouble in there?" I ask.

"If I had any money," the girl replies, "I'd give you all of it if you would take over feeding and watering this wild mustang. I don't know why in the world they brought such an untamed animal here. It's stupid!"

If this girl were an animal, I imagine she'd be a badger. And that's probably how it feels to her horse and why it stays on edge around her. "What's your name?"

"Megan," she replies.

"Indiana or Ohio?" I ask.

"Huh? What do you mean?"

"I can't figure out if you're from Indiana or Ohio."

"Cincinnati. Why?"

"Spend lots of time on the Ohio River, I guess?"

"I practically live on it in the summer," Megan says.

"Your horse sounds like it has a mind of its own, just like a river does. You can fight against it, if you want, continually trying to get it to flow in a direction that's opposite to its nature, or you can go with the flow and harness that horse's strengths. It's just a suggestion, but I think you'll enjoy your horse a lot more if you try a different approach."

"That's sort of what Will has been trying to get me to do. I never thought about it the way you explained it, but that makes sense. One thing I've learned since coming to Spirit Lake is that I have some serious control issues. Maybe my horse, Tonto, has control issues, too, and we've been in some kind of tug-of-war."

"You're a sharp girl, Megan," I say. "I believe you're about to figure out something pretty important."

"Thanks, Levi."

Turning around, I continue making my journey to each of the stalls. At the next one I hear the sound of a curry brush being run across the horse's coat. "That's one thing a horse really likes," I say.

In what is obviously a Chicago accent, a girl says, "I enjoy it, too. It relaxes me and I feel good about doing something nice for my horse. Babe is what I call her. Even though she's a girl, she's muscled up like a guy. She'd be a bodybuilder if she was a person."

I laugh. "I agree. When I came in here to meet her last night, I thought the same thing. She's really muscled up. Do you mind me asking if you've lived your whole life in Chicago?"

"I don't mind. I was born there and have never lived anywhere else. How did you know I was from Chicago? By the way, my name is Heather."

"It's your accent, Heather," I answer her. "All of us have accents that are pretty specific to a region, though with people moving around so much and listening to so much TV, those differences are gradually disappearing."

"So where are you from?" she asks.

It's a question I expected. Smiling, I give her my practiced answer, "I've lived a little bit of everywhere. So I just tell people that's where I'm from—everywhere."

"If you don't want to tell me where you're from, why don't you just say so?" Heather says in a flat tone.

This quick change in her throws me off balance. I immediately feel defensive. I'm hoping that my beard and sunglasses are hiding my reddening face. Trying to keep my voice calm, I say, "I told you the truth."

"If that's what you say," is the only reply Heather makes.

I leave her stall as a bead of sweat runs down my back. I remember Debbie's words of warning, "They'll chew you up and spit you out." I believe that's what Heather just did to me.

Approaching the next stall, I hear Will's voice giving instructions.

"But I don't know anything about horses," a frightened girl's voice says.

"Oh hi there, Levi," he says when he sees me. "This here is Crystal. She just got here yesterday so I'm giving her some basic instructions on how to manage her horse, Beauty."

"Hi, Crystal," I say. "You a little nervous?"

"I'm scared to death," Crystal replies.

"What they told me in therapy is that being scared is pretty normal."

"You've been to therapy?"

I laugh. "Crystal, I've been in every kind of therapy known to mankind in the last six months. What I had to learn to do was trust the people who were trying to help me. I just wanted to stick my head in and meet you. I'll move on so you and Will can get back to work. Nice to meet you."

"Nice to meet you, too, Levi."

If I remember correctly, I've been to all the stalls. I feel a breeze and follow it to what I believe is the open end of the barn. Standing in the opening with my hands at my side, I take several slow breaths and try to relax myself. That brief trip through the stalls meeting the girls made me a lot more nervous than I expected.

I hear the sound of several people approaching me from behind. Suddenly something cold and wet is stuck in my palm. I crouch reflexively and whirl around. "Who's there?!"

"It's just Roxie," a girl's voice says, "our golden retriever. Gee, you're jumpy."

Standing back up, I say, "I guess I didn't hear her coming up to me over the footsteps of all you people."

There is a pause and the same girl says, "That's funny. I'm the only person here. The other footsteps you heard belong to my donkey, Pablo."

Immediately I feel all my senses being overwhelmed. I'm trying to remember if I noticed a difference in the footsteps I heard a moment ago. It puzzles me that I didn't find a donkey anywhere in the barn last night. And at the same time, far away in the back corner of my mind something is stirring, something I can't make out.

I slowly get down on one knee. Knowing golden retrievers like I do, I'm now not surprised when Roxie slips her soft, silky face into my hands. Scratching her behind her ears, I say, "Sorry I jumped when you greeted me, Roxie. You're pretty light on your feet." Roxie responds to the ear scratching by moaning with pleasure. "You like that, don't you?"

"You will now be her friend forever," the girl says. "James, one of the therapists here, says she is very codependent, while Mary says she's really narcissistic. I just say she's about the sweetest dog I've ever known."

It's the girl's accent, her flat vowel sounds and the way the consonants run together, that has put me on edge for some reason. It sounds just like I remember people sounding in northwest Tennessee where I grew up. Is the world so small that I've crossed paths with someone who grew up close to where I used to live? But still, there is something else that seems familiar about this girl.

With my brain whirring like the engine of a car at a drag strip, I say, "I agree. Every golden retriever I've ever been around has been a really good pet, especially good with children." Standing up, I say, "Can you introduce me to Pablo? And how did you end up with him as your animal?"

I reach out my hand to find the donkey. The girl takes my hand firmly, pulls me toward her, and places my hand on Pablo's soft nose. At the touch of her hand I feel something like a lightning bolt pass through me.

"Pablo, this is Levi. Levi, this is Pablo. Will says that Pablo just wandered up here one day. He doesn't have a stall. He comes and goes as he pleases. Pablo and I sort of chose each other. Each of us knows what it is like to grow up being made fun of and not feeling like we fit in anywhere."

My heart couldn't be beating any faster if I was facing an attacking bear. I move to the side of Pablo and lean against him to support my weakening knees. "Do you mind if I ask you where you are from?"

"It's a tiny place you've never heard of," she replies. "It's in the northwest corner of the state of Tennessee. Dresden, Tennessee."

I grip two handfuls of Pablo's mane. "And your name? What is your name?"

"My name is April."

CHAPTER FIFTY-FIVE

What we call the beginning is often the end
And to make an end is to make a beginning.
The end is where we start from.
—*T. S. Eliot*

APRIL:

Can you tell me what happened between you and the new guy, Levi, this morning at feeding time?" James asks me.

His question pulls me away from my thoughts about how different things seem since I last sat in his office. It's the difference between being lost and being found. "I was taking care of Pablo and introducing him and myself to Levi when suddenly Pablo went crazy. I've never seen him act like that. He started kicking and whirling in a circle, while at the same time braying nonstop, like he was trying to tell me something. Levi got kicked in the chest and knocked to the ground. I don't know how he did it, but Will was right beside Levi almost as soon as he hit the ground. And just like that, Pablo stopped and stood still, looking right at Levi."

Shaking his head, James says, "That donkey is unpredictable. If Levi had been a foot shorter, Pablo's blow would have hit him square in the face and could have killed him. Michelle is supposed to call from the hospital to let us know if there are any broken bones or internal injuries."

"Will always says that horses don't do anything accidently," I counter. "If they step on your toe, it's because they mean to and if they stomp their foot and barely miss your foot, that's exactly what they intended to do. So I think Pablo did to Levi exactly what he meant to do. I just don't know why he did it."

Rubbing his chin, James says, "Maybe our resident horse whisperer will talk to Pablo and figure something out." He glances at his notepad and continues, "But that's not really what I wanted to talk to you about. We were already scheduled to have a session together before all the commotion happened this morning."

For the first time since arriving at Spirit Lake, I'm not feeling nervous about a counseling session. I've told everyone the truth about who I am, and it has felt like a load of bricks has been lifted off my shoulders. I remember a quote Tucker used to say: "The truth will set you free." Relaxed, I wait for James to bring up whatever is on his mind.

He flips a page and taps his cheek with his pen. "I want to talk to you about the night you and Michelle slept in the woods. You remember, it was after you ran out of our last session."

Vivid details of that last session and of running through the woods play on a screen in my head. Shaking my head, I say, "That was the old April, the cruel one. I guess I was lucky something really bad didn't happen to me in the woods. Thank goodness for Michelle's tracking skills."

"You and Michelle had a conversation after you bedded down. Do you remember that?"

My forehead creases as I try to find the detail James is looking for. "I'm sorry, I don't remember."

James fixes me with his steady gaze. "You told Michelle that you were responsible for the death of your grandmother, Ella. And during our session that you stormed out of, you told me you made your brother run away from home. I just want to understand why you believe all that to be true."

I suddenly have a memory of playing chess with Smiley Carter. He'd been teaching me how to play for several months and I was getting pretty good at it, even though I thought it was a stupid game to begin with. This one particular time I thought I was getting close to winning when Smiley suddenly called checkmate on me. It caught me by surprise.

That's exactly how I feel right now, like James has called checkmate on me. I thought everything that needed to be brought out into the open had already been dealt with. I didn't think I had any more issues to look at. I thought I was close to winning.

Nervously I scan the chessboard to try and figure out what my next move should be. Hoping I can distract James from pursuing the topic of March any further, I decide to talk about Ella. "It's very hard to explain how it all happened, but Ella was getting healthier and healthier, recovering from her breast cancer, until I moved in with her. At first no one knew there was anything wrong with her and everything seemed fine. Then suddenly she was diagnosed with cancer and within a few months she died. I started figuring up the time between when she was diagnosed with cancer and when I came to live with her. It's obvious that that was when the cancer first started attacking her. I think my living with her stressed her so badly that it weakened her body's defenses and the cancer rushed it."

Tears fill my eyes as I think about Ella. "She was such an amazing mixture of traits. She was gentle, but she was also strong. If only

I hadn't been selfish and wanted to live with her, she'd have never died."

"It sounds like you've been mad at yourself for a long time about that," James says.

"It's worse than that. I hate myself for it. I was the one who should have died. I deserved to die, not Ella." I've gone over this in my head and chewed on these exact words so many times that it tastes like I'm eating my own vomit. I resist the urge to jump up and run to my cabin, where I can rinse my mouth out with mouthwash. What I really want to do—badly—is cut myself.

"April," James says, "I want to try to help you see something, something that is very important, something that you've needed to understand for a long time. First of all, everyone has to make sense of things and do things in ways that make sense to them, whether they are right or wrong. Can you see the truth of that?"

"Do you mean like when Columbus thought he had discovered a western passage to the Indies because he didn't realize there was an entire continent between Europe and the Indies? When really he'd discovered North America."

"I've never thought about that example," James replies, "but it is perfect. Columbus believed what made sense to him to believe. The next thing I want to tell you is that we seem to be born with a desire to control things around us. It's related to us feeling secure. If we can manipulate and change things, then we believe we will be safe. But here's the problem with that, especially in regard to children and how they interpret their environment. Listen closely, April."

My tears have dried and James has me fully engaged with him. I don't know where he is leading me, but I no longer feel threatened he will call checkmate on me.

James leans forward in his chair and says, "When things go wrong in a child's world, children believe it is their fault. They believe there is something they should have done or perhaps something they can do that will fix it. The problem with that belief is that it is a lie."

I blink rapidly, trying to understand what James is saying. I have the same sensation of wonder as I did when I was lying in my bed at the age of five or six and looking out the window and seeing the very top edge of the sun as it began rising.

James is quietly reading my face, giving me time to turn this over in my mind.

Cocking my head to one side, I say, "You mean my mind played a trick on me and told me Ella's sickness and death was my fault?"

James nods.

I sense the sun beginning to fill my room with its soft, yellow light. "And all this time that I've blamed myself and hated myself—" My throat closes off and I can't finish. Fresh tears appear. It is a mixture of sadness and happiness that fills me. I'm sad that I've spent so much time hating myself but yet happy that with this brief conversation with James a weight that I have drug behind me for eight years has been lifted off my heart. "I wish I had known or somebody had explained it to me," I say to James.

"Yeah, me, too," James agrees. "But there's something else I need you to help me understand. What about this brother who ran away? What's the story behind that?"

I gasp and flinch at James's question. I couldn't be more afraid if I was in a "Friday the 13th" movie and James was hockey-masked Jason. My brother March is my recurring nightmare, which I've never been able to escape. I've imagined a thousand different scenarios as to what may have become of him, and they are all scary. This is the darkest corner of my guilt-lined soul.

The chessboard is back in front of me. Only my king is left, while James still has all his pieces. They've backed me into a corner from which there is no escape. James has all but yelled "Checkmate."

Rather than trying to draw a sword and fight my way out, I bow my head and begin speaking in a low voice. "I had two brothers, both older than me. The oldest one is named August and the younger was named March. March was three years older than me and August five years. We spent a lot of time together. We didn't have many toys, so we entertained ourselves by making up games."

As I am speaking I can almost feel my body shrinking in size and my voice beginning to sound more like a child's. "One time when I was maybe five years old . . ." My voice tapers off into nothingness. I'm staring at the truth but I don't want to tell it to James. My shame pushes my head lower, and regret folds my legs up underneath me on the chair. "We were in the boys' bedroom and we decided to play doctor. We took turns being the patient, doctor, and assistant."

I literally feel my heart beating in my throat and my body shaking. I want to look up at James to see if there is something he can do to help me, but I'm too afraid to look at him. "We pulled our pants down and touched each other." Tears begin to drip onto my lap. "Nothing was ever the same between us after that and very soon after it happened, March ran away. We never heard from him again." I grit my teeth and add, "If only I'd never let him touch me, he wouldn't have felt like he needed to leave."

I close my eyes and wait for James to condemn me for what happened between me and March and August.

"I don't know what color regret would be, if it were a color," James says, "but whatever it would be, that's exactly the color all the words you've just said would be. Even your breath would be a cloud of that color. And the smell . . ." James pauses.

I look up and see him making a face.

"The smell is like something rotten and spoiled," he says. "But before I give you my reaction, I want to clarify some points. You and your brothers playing doctor—was anyone forced to do anything they didn't want to do? Was anyone threatened if they didn't play?"

"Why, no," I say.

"And was anyone hurt physically? Did anyone push anything inside you?"

"My god, no! It wasn't like that at all!"

"Then what was it like?"

"We were just curious, I guess. It was just an excuse to see how we were different. We were just kids."

"Exactly!" James says excitedly. "That's exactly what it was. It was just kids being kids. Nearly all kids are curious about those kinds of things and engage in a similar behavior. It's perfectly normal."

I stare in disbelief. I open my mouth to speak but can't find any words to express myself. Finally I say, "But if what you say is true, then that means that I really shouldn't be ashamed of what we did." I start connecting imaginary dots. "And that means that I didn't make March run away. And all the regret that I've felt for eight years has been over nothing." I look directly into James's eyes. "Is that really possible?"

James smiles. "I believe that is exactly the truth."

I frown. "Then why did March run away?"

CHAPTER FIFTY-SIX

Weep yet a while –
Weep till that day shall dawn when thou shalt smile:
Watch till the day
When all save only Love shall pass away.
—*Christina Rossetti*

APRIL:

My hand is trembling as I hold the phone receiver to my ear and listen to it ringing on the other end of the line. After four rings, there is a click and the ringing stops. I hear someone breathing, but they don't say anything. "Tucker? Is that you, Tucker?" I ask.

"Who's this?" Tucker's unmistakable voice responds.

I begin to cry. Gripping the receiver with two hands, I say, "Oh, Tucker, this is April. It's so good to hear your voice!"

"Is it really you, April? Is it really?" Tucker asks.

"Yes! Yes! It's me, I promise."

"Where are you, child?"

"I'm at Spirit Lake, Tucker. I wanted to—"

"Are y' all right?" Tucker cuts in. "Is anything wrong?"

"No. I mean, yes," I stammer. "I mean, no, there's nothing wrong and yes, I'm all right. How are you?"

There is a pause. Then, in a voice choking with emotion, Tucker says, "This is really m' April?"

I don't blame her for her disbelief and shock. She hasn't heard from me in nearly six months. Bitter tears of shame escape as I squeeze my eyes shut and bite my lip. When I open them again, the lights in Mary's office sparkle through the prisms of my tears. "I'm your granddaughter, and the granddaughter of Ella McDade, the daughter of Maisy Tucker, and the sister of August and March Tucker. It is me, Tucker."

There is a series of sharp, clattering sounds that can only mean Tucker has dropped the receiver. In the distance I hear her crying and sobbing loudly.

Suddenly, the deep, rich tones of Smiley Carter's voice come over the line. "Is that you, April?"

"Yes, Carter, it's me, April. Is Tucker okay?"

"Bless your heart child, it's good to hear your voice. Tucker's just a little overwhelmed at the moment. Your call was such a shock to her. Just give her a—"

"Quit tryin' t' make 'pologies fer me," I hear Tucker say in the background. "Give me that phone." Then loudly in my ear, she says, "It's s' good t' hear yore voice. It's like th' voice of an angel t' me."

"And it's really, really good to hear your voice, too," I reply. "Mary says I had a breakthrough today. There is just so much I want to tell you, but I want to do it face-to-face. I want you to come here for a visit. Mary says it would be good for both of us. Can you come?"

"Y' want me to travel all th' way there? That's a long way from here." Apprehension colors the edges of her voice.

I try, unsuccessfully, to keep disappointment out of my tone when I say, "That's okay, I understand. I just thought—"

"Did I say I ain't gonna come?! No, you did not hear me say that. If m' April wants me t' come see 'er, then that's jes' what I'm gonna do. You jes' tell me when."

The same feelings of happiness I used to feel as a little girl when Smiley Carter would throw me up into the air and catch me fill my heart. "Oh my gosh, that's wonderful! Mary says that this weekend would be fine, if that works for you. Pack you a bag so you can spend a couple of nights. Mary will take care of all the arrangements. I'm so excited!"

"I can't wait t' hold you in m' arms."

"And I can't wait to feel your strong arms around me. I love you, Tucker. I gotta go. Good-bye."

In typical Tucker fashion, she hangs up without a reply.

CHAPTER FIFTY-SEVEN

When will you ever, Peace, wild wooddove, shy wings shut,
Your round me roaming end, and under be my boughs?
—Gerard Manley Hopkins

MARCH:

"March, is that you?" April's young voice echoes and reverberates as if we are in a cave, dark and damp. I see a candle up ahead. A little, blondeheaded girl kneels in front of it.

"April, is that you?" I call.

The girl turns to look at me. It is my little sister. I want to run to her, but my feet won't move. I look down and in the dim light see that I am standing in water up to my thighs—and I am sinking.

"March," the girl calls. "Don't leave me."

I struggle to free myself from the thick mud below the water, yet the harder I try to escape, the deeper I go into the quagmire. "April!" I cry out.

Suddenly the candle flickers out and utter darkness fills the air.

"Levi." Neither the voice nor the name sparks any recognition.

I turn my head to try and determine who is speaking. The smell of coffee unexpectedly fills my nostrils.

"Levi, it's Will. Are you okay?"

Like a rock in a catapult I am flung into the present, leaving my dream and April behind. "Hey, Will. What time is it?"

"Close to five in the morning. But you don't have to get up. Why don't you just stay in bed and rest today? After the day and night you had yesterday, I'd think rest would be what you need most. How do you feel?"

I start to sit up but am knocked back down by the sharp pain in my chest. "Whew! I feel like I've been kicked in the chest by a jackass."

There is the rattling of pills in a plastic pill bottle. "Michelle said the doctor at the hospital sent these with you. They're for pain. You were so out of it when you got back last night that you practically passed out before your head hit the pillow. You want to take one of these?"

Gingerly, I touch my chest. "Not just yet. I want to get up. I think moving around will be better for me than just lying here in this bed. Come give me a hand."

Will's firm grip grabs my hand. "Tell me when you're ready," he says.

"Don't jerk," I tell him. "Just pull steady when I say to." I take a deep breath. "Okay, pull."

When I finally stand up, I release my pent-up breath with a whoosh, then take several quick, shallow breaths. "That Pablo may be a little fella, but he sure packs a wallop!"

"Coffee?" Will asks.

"If that's the strongest thing you've got, then I'll take it," I say with a smile.

"You know," Will says, as I hear the coffee being poured into mugs, "I've thought all night about what happened yesterday with you, April, and Pablo."

So have I, but I can't tell Will about that. It seems impossible that in all the millions of places there are in the world I would end up at a place where my sister is, too. Maybe this girl here at Spirit Lake named April is just a coincidence and isn't really my sister.

"What were you and April doing when Pablo kicked you?" Will asks.

"Doing?"

"Yeah, tell me exactly what was happening just before he kicked you."

Carefully, I answer Will's question. "She was just introducing me to Pablo. I didn't even know there was a donkey here. When I was up exploring the night before, I never felt or heard him, so I was curious about him. Then the next thing I know—pow! He kicks me right in the chest."

I take a sip of the hot coffee and feel it warm the center of my body. Will seems unusually quiet, which makes me nervous. I feel like he's looking at me, examining me.

"I see," he finally says slowly. "Look here, Levi, your story is your business. I don't know nothing about you and don't really have to. The way I see it, that's up to you. But there is something about you that either scared Pablo or made him believe you were going to hurt April. He didn't kick you where he did by accident. He hit you exactly where he wanted to."

I mull over Will's comments. It feels like there is more he is not saying. I should leave it alone, but am curious to know what he's thinking. "So what do you think Pablo believes about me?"

"I think he believes you have heart trouble. That's why he kicked you in the chest."

Laughing, I say, "You mean like I've got clogged arteries or something like that?"

"Didn't say that," Will replies. "There's lots of different kinds of heart disease."

I hear him set his cup down.

"Time to get to work" he says. "Those girls will be here soon."

Will's comment, "There's lots of different kinds of heart disease," has left me feeling unsettled. The diminishing sound of his cowboy boots as he leaves our apartment is replaced by the galloping beat of my heart.

The last thing the ER doctor told me before leaving last night was that I probably have a bruised heart as a result of Pablo's blow to my chest. I started to tell her I had a bruised heart before getting kicked.

CHAPTER FIFTY-EIGHT

Flower in the crannied wall,
I pluck you out of the crannies,
I hold you here, root and all, in my hand,
Little flower—but if I could understand
What you are, root and all, and all in all,
I should know what God and man is.
—Alfred, Lord Tennyson

APRIL:

Raising her hand and pointing, Heather says, "Hey, look who's coming."

The rest of us have been plodding toward the barn, our sleepy heads down so we don't stumble. At Heather's words, our attention snaps awake, and we look toward the woods where she is pointing. Coming toward us at a fast trot is Pablo. His ears are pointed straight up and facing us.

"Oh my gosh, look at him!" Megan exclaims.

Everyone starts laughing. But when he is twenty feet away and shows no signs of slowing down, the laughter is replaced by shrieks.

"He's going to run over us!" Heather screams.

"He's gone crazy!" yells Ashley.

I separate myself from the group by taking three steps toward the charging donkey. Pablo responds by straightening his front legs and skidding to a stop just before running into me. His nostrils are flared, his eyes are wide, and his sides are heaving from heavy breathing. I put my palm inches away from one of his nostrils. He sniffs and blows loudly, stomping his feet as he does. "What in the world is the matter with you?" I ask. "Is a black bear after you or something?"

Pablo steps closer and nudges me.

"Is everybody all right?" Will calls from the barn as he quickly limps toward us.

"It's April's crazy-ass jackass," Heather answers. "He wanted to run us over."

"He did not," I interject. "If that's what he was intending to do, then that's what he would have done. He stopped before he got to us." Rubbing Pablo's soft nose, I say to him, "Didn't you, Pablo? You weren't going to hurt any of us, were you? You wouldn't hurt anyone, would you?"

"Yeah, right," Megan says. "Try telling that to Levi."

A bit out of breath, Will reaches our group. "The rest of you girls head on to the barn and start your chores. I need to speak to April."

The thought had occurred to me during the night that Will might send Pablo away because of what he did. Though I had laid that fear to rest as absurd, Will's need to talk to me privately resurrects it. Once the girls are out of earshot, I say, "I promise, Pablo wasn't trying to hurt anyone. They were just being girls and got scared. It was nothing. Don't take him away from me, please!"

Will waves his hand. "Got no intention of doing that."

Just that quickly, my anxiety falls and my breathing slows. "Good," I say.

"But here's the thing," Will goes on. "There's something wrong here. I don't know if it has to do with you, with Pablo, with Levi, or with some combination of all three of you. But you've got to get it worked out."

I'm confused. "What do you mean?"

"I mean, you've got to find out what's wrong and fix it. Or else."

Like a bottle rocket shooting into the sky, my anxiety spikes. "Or else, what?"

"Or else one of you is going to have to leave Spirit Lake." Turning toward the barn, he starts walking way. Over his shoulder, he says, "Now let's get busy with chores."

Facing Pablo, I say, "Listen to me, Pablo, you heard what Will said. You've got to help me because you're the only one who knows what's going on." One of Pablo's ears rotates and lies flat against his neck, while the other one tilts toward me. "And what is that supposed to mean? I wish you could just talk or I could just be Dr. Dolittle for a day. Come on, let's go to the barn, but behave yourself!"

When I turn and start walking toward the barn, instead of following me like he usually does, Pablo bolts past me in his stiff-legged running style and disappears into the darkness of the barn.

"Pablo!" I yell. "Wait for me!"

CHAPTER FIFTY-NINE

All truths wait in all things,
They neither hasten their own delivery nor resist it.
—*Walt Whitman*

MARCH:

By the time I finally get dressed and walk into the stable area of the barn, I can hear the girls busy with their morning routine. From my left I hear the sound of pounding hooves and in the distance someone yelling, "Pablo! Wait for me!"

I immediately turn and brace myself for what I suppose is the charging donkey. When he is about fifteen feet away, I throw my arms up in the air and yell, "Stop!"

The aftershock from my explosion evidently stops everyone in their tracks. I can't hear any sounds, other than the heavy breathing of Pablo.

After a second, I hear Pablo slowly stepping toward me, until I feel his breathing on my chest. Reaching out, I place my hand on the side of his head. He touches my chest with his nose. A couple of the horses blow loudly from their stalls, thankful that the tension in the air has been broken. Everyone resumes their work of feeding and cleaning.

The sound of someone running through the barn door and heading toward me and Pablo reminds me of the girl yelling from outside the barn. It must be April.

She arrives breathless and panting. Between gasps, she asks if I am okay.

"Yes, yes, I'm fine," I assure her.

Her voice is calmer when she says, "And your chest, how is it?"

"It's really sore but nothing was broken and no damage was done internally."

"That's great news. Will you stand here with Pablo while I go get a halter and rope?"

"Sure, I'll be glad to." As April walks away, I whisper to Pablo, "Little fella, according to Will you are some kind of a mind reader or something. It that's so, I'm needing a little help from you. I've got to find out if this girl is my sister, without just coming right out and asking her. Will says I'm not allowed to ask nosey questions, so I don't know how I'm going to do it. Besides, even if she is my sister, who knows if she even wants me to be a part of her life again. That's where you come in. You've got to help me." I feel like an idiot talking to a donkey and wonder what Debbie would say if she could see me now. Probably something cleverly smart aleck in tone. I smile.

"You've got a nice smile," April says as she approaches. "Don't take this wrong, but with all the hair and the beard and sunglasses, it's hard to tell what your expression is."

I listen as she puts Pablo's halter on. The familiar snap of the lead line being connected is a signal that she's finished. I try to find an excuse to continue our conversation but can't find one.

Then, unexpectedly, she says, "Do you want to help me with him this morning? Will says I've got to clean his hooves out."

This girl sounds confident and self-assured, so different from the sister that I remember. It still doesn't seem possible that she is my April. "Sure," I answer her, "you just tell me what to do."

"I've got the hoof pick here," she says. "If you'll just try to keep his head still so that he can't turn and nip at me or move around and step on me, that would be great."

"I'll do my best," I say and stick out my hand for the lead rope.

April's hand takes mine and places the rope across my palm. Just like last night, at her touch I feel a jolt of electricity.

"Ouch!" April says.

"What happened?"

"I don't know. It felt like static electricity when I touched your hand, like when you walk across carpet and touch a doorknob. Did you feel it?"

"No, I didn't feel a thing," I lie.

"That's weird," she says. "Do you have hold of Pablo?"

Gripping the bottom of his halter, I say, "Yes, I've got him."

I feel Pablo's weight shift as April lifts one of his feet and begins scraping the mud and debris out of the underside of his hoof. She's halfway through the second hoof when she says, "Do blind people see when they dream? I mean, like, are you blind in your dreams, or what?"

The warnings Debbie, Mary, and Will gave me were true—the girls will ask about anything. "I don't know about other blind people, but I have my sight when I dream, just like before my accident."

"I had a strange dream last night," April says, ignoring my answer to her question. "I was a little girl and I was looking for my lost brother, March. He's been gone for a long time. I barely remember him sometimes. Anyway, in this dream I was in a cave and the only light was a candle. I thought I saw him for a moment. I called out his name and he answered me, but he wouldn't come. It was like he was trapped and couldn't move."

There is a lump in my throat that feels like it's the size of a soft-ball. Gritting my teeth, I try to swallow it and relieve some pressure. My hands tremble. Pablo puts his nose on my chest and pushes gently. "Hey, Will!" I call out. "Can you come spell me?"

"What's wrong?" April asks.

"You okay?" Will asks as he walks up to me.

"I'm feeling a little sick to my stomach." I hear the tremor in my voice. If I don't get away quickly, I'm going to lose it. Without waiting for Will to agree to take over, I let go of Pablo and walk hurriedly away toward my bedroom.

CHAPTER SIXTY

As cold waters to a thirsty soul, so is good news from a far country.
—Proverbs 25:25

TUCKER:

Ain't we there yet?! I ain't never been s' tired o' sittin' in m' life. I think m' butt's done gone t' sleep."

From th' back seat o' th' car, Smiley Carter says t' me, "Now look, Tucker, asking every ten minutes 'When are we going to be at Spirit Lake?' doesn't get us there any quicker. August is driving as fast as he legally can."

August looks in th' the rearview mirror at Smiley an' says, "Thank you." He glances over at me, then looks back at th' road. "We're getting close, Tucker. It's about a mile to where we get off this main road."

I grab th' shoulder strap an' jerk on it t' give me some wiggle room. "This here strap wasn't designed for a full-figured gal like me. Maybe them flat-chested women don't mind them, but it's 'bout t' worry me t' death."

Both August an' Smiley burst out laughin'.

"Full-figured," Smiley says while he's laughin'. "So that's what shape you are."

I try t' turn 'round an' swat at him, but all I manage t' do is create a breeze. "Y' better run when we get outta this car," I say. "I don't care if'n y' are a crippled old man. I'm gonna tan yore hide!" Rubbin' m' shoulder, I add, "An' I jes' might sue y', too. I think I wrenched m' shoulder when I swung at y'."

By now August is laughin' s' hard that he's swervin' th' car all over th' place. "You two stop it," he says. "You're going to make me have a wreck. You all really need to take your act on the road, maybe on late-night TV. I'd love to see what David Letterman would do with you two."

I'm jes' 'bout t' say somethin' back t' him when he lets off th' accelerator an' slows down.

"This must be it," August says, an' he turns off th' highway on to a little one-lane road.

Fer a moment, none of us says a word as we leave th' bright sunshine o' th' main road. Th' giant hemlock trees that surround us pull their dark shade over us jes' like I used t' pull th' bedcovers up on th' children when they was little.

"You all let your windows down," August says.

Instead o' th' summer heat I was spectin', cool, moist air blows against m' face as August drives slowly. "I ain't never seen timber like this. Have you, Smiley?"

"When I was a little boy," Smiley answers, "I remember going with my daddy and some other men to a bottom that had dried out in the summer so they could harvest the timber. They said it had never been cut on before. That was the biggest timber stand I ever saw. But I believe these trees here are twice as tall as those trees were. *Majestic.* That's the word I'd use to describe these trees."

"I remember the first time some of my classmates took me to the Smoky Mountains," August says. "We went to Clingmans

Dome, the highest point in the state of Tennessee. I felt like I was on top of the world and that I could see all the way into tomorrow. Is this your first time here, Tucker?"

"Child," I answer him, "this is th' first time I've been outside o' Weakley County."

August looks at me an' smiles. "You're kidding, right?"

"No sir, I'm serious. I ain't never left home b'fore. Never had no reason to. That's why ridin' this far jes' 'bout wore me out. I ain't never done anything like this."

Suddenly there's a break in th' canopy o' trees an' three log cabins sit together in a clearin'. Off in th' distance is a barn.

"This is it, ain't it?!" I cry. "This is where m' April is! Hurry, pull up there an' stop so I can get out." I pull th' lever on m' door an' open it.

"Tucker," Smiley exclaims, "wait till the boy gets stopped. You're gonna fall out and break a leg or something."

As August slows to a stop, th' door o' th' cabin on th' far left opens an' a line o' girls step outside. At th' back o' th' line is th' golden hair of April. I get out o' th' car an' yell, "April!"

April's head jerks in my direction. A smile bursts on 'er face. She yells, "Tucker!" an' breaks into runnin' toward me.

Throwin' m' arms open wide, I move as fast as I can t' meet 'er. She runs straight into m' arms without slowin' down an' nearly knocks me down. Her arms wrap 'round m' neck an' she starts kissin' me all over m' face an' neck. Between each kiss she says m' name. It's th' sweetest, most tender thing she ever done t' me.

Squeezin' 'er in m' arms, I lift 'er off th' ground an' slowly turn in a circle, callin' her name over an' over. Both our faces are wet with our intermingled tears o' joy.

Off t' one side, I hear a loud honk an' know without lookin' that Smiley's cryin', too. "Praise God, praise God," he says.

At his voice, April lets go o' me. "Smiley!" she cries, an' tears off runnin' t' hug his neck, too.

"Girl," Smiley says, "you look healthier than I ever seen you. This mountain air must be good for you."

"Mountain air and hard work," April says, smiling. She lifts 'er arm an' flexes 'er biceps.

From his position standing beside th' car, August says, "Don't I even get a hello?"

April spins around. When she spies him, she squeals like a little girl openin' a present. She dashes toward him. "August! I didn't know you were coming, too!"

Watchin' them hug without bein' awkward like they used t' be, I see 'em fer th' young adults they've become. They ain't little kids no more. At th' same time, I feel a little prick at th' back o' my heart an' March's face appears outta the mist o' m' mem'ry. "What's past is past," I say t' myself. "All that matters is how things is t'day. An' this here is a beautiful day!"

April leads August by th' hand t' my side an' Smiley joins us. She looks at th' group o' girls watchin' us an' says, "Ya'll come here. I want you to meet my family."

The girls gather 'round us an' gawk at us like we're somethin' out of a sideshow.

Slippin' both 'er arms 'round m' arm, April says, "This is my grandmother, Tucker. She's the one who raised me." Lettin' go o' me, she takes August's hand an' says, "And this is my brother August. He is about to finish school at UT, Knoxville." They beam proudly at each other.

Next, April walks over t' Smiley an' says, "And this man is Smiley Carter. He's Tucker's best friend an' he's August's daddy, though neither one of them knew it until August was a teenager. He's got the most beautiful singing voice you ever heard and he plays a mean guitar, too."

I believe if Smiley was a white man, he'd be blushin' red right 'bout now.

Th' only black girl in th' group points at August an' says, "You mean he is your brother? You never said your brother was—"

"I know, I know, Heather," April says. "It's all pretty complicated. I'll fill in the details later tonight, if you want them."

Heather gives August a goin' over with 'er eyes an' says, "Oh I want to know all the details about him."

The other girls laugh.

"We have visitors, I see." A woman's voice comes from behind me.

When I turn 'round, there ain't no doubt in my mind that I'm lookin' at Mary. She looks jes' like I 'magined 'er. There's a younger man and an even younger woman standin' behind 'er. "You's Mary, ain'tcha?" I offer her m' hand.

Mary gives me a solid handshake an' says, "And there's no doubt that you are Tucker. How do you do? I'm so pleased to finally meet you."

"An' I'm pleased t' meet you. This here's m' friend, Smiley Carter. An' this is August, m' grandson an' our chauffeur."

Mary smiles at both of 'em an' says, "So glad you two could come, too." Turning toward the couple behind her, she says, "This is the rest of our treatment team, James and Michelle."

"Howdy," I say.

James has a young face, but his eyes is old. He says, "Welcome to Spirit Lake."

Michelle don't look much older than April an' th' other girls. "It's great to finally meet you," she says.

"April," Mary says, "why don't you show your family around some? You all will join the rest of us for our evening meal. James, Michelle, and I will spend some time getting to know all of you this evening. And then, tomorrow we'll all go to the arena in the barn for some family therapy. Is that okay with everyone?"

"Sure," April says.

"You's th' one in charge," I tell Mary. "Whatever you say is how it'll be. Ya'll been doin' somethin' right 'cause I ain't never seen April look s' healthy. And th' change in 'er attitude, well I don't know 'bout how she's been here, but she'd become impossible t' live with back home."

The redheaded girl speaks up an' says, "Oh we've got a pretty good idea. She was the same way here until she finally figured some things out."

Though I ain't got no idea what she's talkin' 'bout exactly, all th' girls must understand 'cause they all laugh an' nod their heads at each other.

CHAPTER SIXTY-ONE

Though keeper's charge in chains the captive hold,
Yet can he not the soul in bondage bind.
—*George Turbeville*

APRIL:

Walking into the barn with Tucker, Smiley Carter, and August, I try to calm my nervousness. I've watched other girls do their family therapy session with their horse, so I know that good things can happen. But there is also the unknown, like, how will Pablo behave? How will Tucker behave? What kind of exercise will the treatment team have put together for us to do? What kinds of issues may surface during the session that I'm not even aware of?

When we walk through the open end of the barn, I see that the other girls are already there and sitting in folding chairs that have been placed in a line. Mary and Michelle are also sitting in chairs, while James is standing up. Off to themselves are Will and Levi. There is a woman standing beside Levi I've never seen before.

"You mean we have to do this in front of an audience?" August asks me.

"Yeah, it's just the way they always do this part of the therapy. It's because you can learn as much by watching someone do the therapy as you can by doing it yourself."

"Who's that big ol' wooly-lookin' fella with th' sunglasses?" Tucker asks.

"That's Levi," I answer her. "He just came here this week. He helps Will and does odd jobs, too."

"What kind o' person wears their sunglasses when they're inside?"

"He's blind, Tucker."

"Oh," she replies.

It's then that I realize that part of my anxiousness is because I've yet to figure out the connection between me, Pablo, and Levi. Will's made it clear that if I don't get the pieces put together, there's a chance he will ship Pablo away. Every time I've tried to be around Levi the past couple of days, he's made an excuse to go do something else. It's almost like he's nervous or afraid of me.

"You all come on over here," James calls to us.

When we get there, he says, "Smiley, even though you are definitely connected to this family, because you all didn't grow up together in the same house, we've decided to let you sit and watch this exercise." James motions toward an empty chair, and Smiley walks to it and sits down.

"We also have an additional guest," James continues. Pointing toward Levi and the woman beside him, he says, "Debbie Cooper, Levi's girlfriend, came to pick him up last night for his weekend away. But Will wanted Levi to be here today to help him, so Debbie agreed to spend the night and observe today's session."

Debbie smiles a nervous smile and takes hold of Levi's hand.

James addresses me, August, and Tucker. "One of the things that healthy families do is work together to accomplish common tasks. They recognize the need to cooperate, to listen to each other, and to be open to each other's opinions. That's why we've designed this particular exercise for you all." He turns and says, "Will, if you'll bring Pablo here."

Will turns and goes into what has always been an empty stall. My curiosity is heightened because I know Pablo isn't in there. He's never gone into a stall. I think it's because he's claustrophobic.

In a moment, Will steps out with one end of a lead rope in his hand, while the other end of the rope remains in the darkness of the stall. The rope pulls tight and Will tugs twice on it. Suddenly Pablo's head appears in the doorway.

Pablo's terror-filled eyes trigger an immediate response in me. I have to force myself to be still and not run to him to see what is wrong. In the next second, my question is answered as he moves forward through the doorway.

One of his front feet has a rope tied to it. The rope is pulled tight and fastened to the horn of a saddle on his back. The result is that his front foot is pulled completely off the ground and tucked underneath him. Pablo's been reduced to walking on three feet!

"Lord have mercy," Tucker mutters.

I've never seen Will do this to any other animal here. I'm furious! "What are you doing to him?!" I demand. "Stop that!" I start walking toward Will.

"April," James says calmly, "Will has assured us that this in no way harms the animal. Uncomfortable? Yes, but it is not cruel."

Pablo brays loudly and fights to free his tethered foot. My heart breaks to see him in such a helpless state. Tears sting my eyes. Anger begins to boil up inside me. "So what do you want us to do?" I ask angrily.

"Simple," James says as he hands each of us a rope. "Each of these ropes is of a different length. You all are to attach the end of your rope to Pablo's halter and then step as far away from him as your rope will let you. Then, the three of you are to lead him from where he is to where Levi and Debbie are standing."

"But that's nearly fifty feet!" I exclaim. I look imploringly to James, then to Michelle, and then to Mary, but find no expressions of sympathy.

"Mr. Will," Tucker suddenly says, "are y' sure this don't hurt this animal?"

Will's face has an extragrim look about it. "Yes, ma'am. Now is it possible he could hurt himself? Well sure, anything's possible. But working a horse on three legs is an exercise every cowboy has done at one time or another when he's breaking a horse. It just ain't my favorite thing to do to an animal."

Tucker folds her arms across her chest and says, "April, y' been livin' with these here folks fer nearly six months. Has any of 'em ever lied t' y'?"

"No, ma'am."

"Do you trust 'em?"

I nod.

"Do y' believe they want t' help us?"

"Yes, but—"

Holding up her hand, Tucker says, "They ain't no but 'bout it. Let's go fasten on t' this donkey an' move 'im like they want us to." Without waiting to see if I have a reply, she lumbers off toward Pablo.

"Come on," August says as he walks past me. "We can do this."

Though my heart is not in it, I follow them.

We all three snap our ropes onto the ring underneath Pablo's halter. Will unsnaps his rope and steps back out of the way.

"Now each of you walk to the end of your rope," James says.

When we do so, we discover that Tucker's rope is about six feet long, August's is about twelve feet long, and mine is nearly twenty feet long.

Pablo shakes his head at the noise of all the snaps striking each other under his chin and nearly loses his balance.

"Begin," James says.

The three of us stand there looking at Pablo and at each other.

"What are we supposed to do?" August asks.

"Lead him over to Levi," I answer. "But I don't know how I'm supposed to help do that when I'm so far away from you all."

"You're closest to him," August says to Tucker. "Why don't you see if you can get him to move?"

Tucker grips the rope and pulls. Pablo immediately pulls against her, throwing his head wildly into the air. He again loses his balance, only this time he falls onto the knee of his free front leg. One of the girls screams in fright.

Quickly, Pablo jerks his head upward to give his body some momentum and springs back up onto his front foot. He's breathing heavily.

"If you try to force him like that," I say, "he'll fight you every time. You've got to get him to follow you. You can't pull him."

"Y' sayin' y' know more 'bout animals than I do?" Tucker snaps at me.

The bite of her harsh tone makes me flinch. With hurt in my eyes, I look at her.

She drops her rope and walks toward me. "Oh, April, I'm sorry. I didn't mean—"

"I'm sorry," James says firmly. "You cannot interrupt the exercise. You have to keep hold of the rope and you must stand at the end of the rope."

James doesn't know it, but no one talks to Tucker like that. I want to hide in a hole from the explosion that is about to happen. "Oh, God, please help her to control herself," I pray silently.

Tucker stops in her tracks. She opens her mouth and then closes it two or three times. Her eyes blink rapidly. Finally, she says, "You're right. I'm sorry." She returns to pick up her rope.

I stare in amazement at her and give August a questioning look. He simply shrugs his shoulders, as mystified as I am at her retreat.

Back in our original positions, I say, "Let's all try pulling gently together and see what happens."

The instant Pablo feels extra tension on his halter, he tries to back up and all four of us stumble.

"Why is he making this so hard?" August asks.

"How do you think he feels?" I say. "If you had to move around on one leg, how do you think you'd adjust to that?"

"I think he's confused," Tucker says. "He don't know who he's supposed t' follow outta th' three of us. An' he's afraid he's gonna fall down, too. April, you got th' longest rope. Why don't you try standin' behind him an' drivin' him while me an' August walk in front o' him?"

"I'm willing to try anything," I reply.

When we get in our new positions, I gently pop the top of Pablo's hip with the slack in my rope. His reaction couldn't be any more dramatic if I'd shocked him with a shocking stick. He starts bucking and braying, spinning in every direction. Dust kicked up from the ground fills the air, along with the girls' screams. His spin move jerks the ropes out of our hands.

All of a sudden, Levi walks to the middle of the barn, holds up his hands and yells, "Stop!"

Everyone is so stunned that no one moves or says a word.

Levi finds his way to the now still and panting Pablo. He runs his hand down Pablo's neck and finds the rope that has him trussed up uncomfortably. Reaching in his pocket, he takes out a pocket-knife and cuts the rope free.

Levi reaches up and removes his sunglasses. His unseeing eyes are wet with tears. His voice is breaking as he says, "You can't make him do it because this is a family exercise. And your family is not complete." His whole body is trembling now. "One member of your family is missing and has been for eight years." He sobs loudly and I'm afraid he's going to pass out.

Taking a deep breath, he says, "But your family is no longer incomplete." He strikes himself on the chest and says loudly, "Because I am March! I am your lost brother! I am your lost grandson!"

Of all the moments in my life that I felt stunned—learning my mother was murdered, finding out that Ella was dying, learning the truth about who my father was, killing Mark when he tried to rape me—none of them compare to this moment. It's as if a moon from another planet suddenly created a shift in the tides of my heart and the returning ocean filled the lingering pit of loss.

Tucker, standing closest to March, grabs him and in soundless tones, mouths his name over and over.

Though blind, March knows his grandmother's hands. He grips them tightly and exclaims, "Oh, Tucker! I'm so sorry I ran away!"

August is the next to reach him. "Oh, my little brother!" he exclaims, and he reaches his long arms around March and Tucker both.

I move in slow motion toward my reunited family, taking in every detail of the scene and locking it away in a treasure chest in my heart.

As I join my family, everyone in the arena gathers around us in a tight circle, their own tears and sobs giving evidence to the power of this moment. Then softly, Smiley Carter begins singing,

Amazing Grace, how sweet the sound
That saved a wretch like me!
I once was lost, but now I'm found!
Was blind, but now I see!

ACKNOWLEDGMENTS

I was blessed to have some great teachers who, in their own ways, helped me to become the writer I am today. I'm indebted to them all!

Mrs. Julia Rich, my high school 11th grade English teacher. She taught me how to conjugate verbs and to think for myself.

Mrs. V.J. Shanklin, my high school 12th grade English teacher. She taught me the importance of good punctuation.

Dr. Porter King, who taught my English Literature classes in my Freshmen and Sophomore college years. He helped me understand form and simplicity in writing.

Author Sylvie Kurtz, who was my instructor a few years ago when I took a course in writing from the Long Ridge Writing School. She showed me how to make my stories feel more immediate and how to make the reader feel they are in the story.

ABOUT THE AUTHOR

David Johnson has worked in the helping professions for over thirty-five years. He is a licensed marriage and family therapist with a master's degree in social work and over a decade of experience as a minister. In addition to the four novels comprising the Tucker series, he has authored several nonfiction books, including *Navigating the Passages of Marriage* and *Real People, Real Problems*, and has published numerous articles in national and local media. David also maintains an active blog at www.thefrontwindow.wordpress.com. When he's not writing, he is likely making music as the conductor of the David Johnson Chorus.